SKANDAR
AND THE
UNICORN
THIEF

BOOKS BY A.F. STEADMAN
Skandar and the Unicorn Thief
Skandar and the Phantom Rider

A.F. STEADMAN

grew up in the Kent countryside, getting lost in fantasy
worlds and scribbling stories in notebooks. Before focusing
on writing, she worked in law, until she realised that there
wasn't nearly enough magic involved.

Skandar and the Unicorn Thief is her debut novel, and
an international bestseller. Don't miss the sensational
follow up, *Skandar and the Phantom Rider*.

SKANDAR

AND THE
UNICORN
THIEF

A.F. STEADMAN

SIMON & SCHUSTER

First published in Great Britain in 2022 by Simon & Schuster UK Ltd
This paperback edition first published in 2023

Text copyright © De Ore Leonis 2022
Illustrations copyright © Two Dots 2022

This book is copyright under the Berne Convention.
No reproduction without permission.
All rights reserved.

The rights of A.F. Steadman and Two Dots to be identified as the author and
illustrator of this work respectively has been asserted by them in accordance
with sections 77 and 78 of the Copyright, Designs and Patents Act, 1988.

1 3 5 7 9 10 8 6 4 2

Simon & Schuster UK Ltd
1st Floor, 222 Gray's Inn Road
London
WC1X 8HB

www.simonandschuster.co.uk
www.simonandschuster.com.au
www.simonandschuster.co.in

Simon & Schuster Australia, Sydney
Simon & Schuster India, New Delhi

A CIP catalogue record for this book is available from the British Library.

PB ISBN 978-1-3985-0273-4
eBook ISBN 978-1-3985-0272-7
eAudio ISBN 978-1-3985-0274-1

This book is a work of fiction. Names, characters, places and incidents are
either the product of the author's imagination or are used fictitiously. Any
resemblance to actual people living or dead, events or locales is entirely
coincidental.

Typeset in the UK by Sorrel Packham
Printed and Bound in the UK
using 100% Renewable Electricity at CPI Group (UK) Ltd

For Joseph
– whose selflessness,
love and infinite kindness
gave these unicorns wings

THE ISLAND

WILDERNESS

FIRE ZONE

THE ARENA

THE EYRIE

THE PRISON

FOURPOINT

AIR ZONE

CONTENTS

PROLOGUE

The cameraman heard the unicorns before he saw them.

High-pitched screeching, murderous growls, the gnashing of bloody teeth.

The cameraman smelled the unicorns before he saw them.

Rancid breath, rotting flesh, the stench of immortal death.

The cameraman felt the unicorns before he saw them too.

Somewhere deep in his bones their putrid hooves thundered, and the panic began to rise — until every nerve, every cell, told him to run. But he had a job to do.

The cameraman watched the unicorns emerge over the brow of the hill.

Eight of them. Malevolent ghouls galloping across the grassland, skeletal wings unfurling, taking flight.

Like the eye of a shadowy storm, black smoke swirled around them, thunder rumbled in their wake and bolts of lightning hit the earth far below their fearsome feet.

Eight ghostly horns sliced through the air, as the monsters howled their war cry.

The villagers began to scream; some tried to run. But it was far, far too late for that.

The cameraman was standing in the village square when the first unicorn landed.

It snorted sparks and pawed the ground, havoc and mayhem in every rattling breath.

The cameraman kept filming, despite his shaking hands. He had a job to do.

The unicorn lowered its giant head, the razor-sharp horn pointing directly at the lens.

Its bloodshot eyes met the cameraman's and he saw in them only destruction.

There was no hope for this village now. No hope for him.

But then he'd always known he wouldn't survive a wild unicorn stampede.

He just hoped the camera footage would make it to the Mainland.

Because once you see a wild unicorn, you're already dead.

The man lowered his camera, hoping that his job was done.

Because unicorns don't belong in fairy tales; they belong in nightmares.

CHAPTER ONE

THE THIEF

Skandar Smith stared at the unicorn poster opposite his bed. It was light enough outside now to see the unicorn's wings outstretched mid-flight: shining silver armour covering most of his body, exposing only his wild red eyes, an enormous jaw and a sharp grey horn. New-Age Frost had been Skandar's favourite unicorn ever since his rider, Aspen McGrath, had qualified for the Chaos Cup three years ago. And Skandar thought that today – in this year's race – they just might have a chance of winning.

Skandar had received the poster for his thirteenth birthday three months before. He'd gazed at it through the bookshop window, imagining that he was New-Age Frost's rider, standing just outside the poster frame ready to race. Skandar had felt really bad asking his dad for it. For as long as he could remember they'd never had much money – he didn't usually ask for anything. But Skandar had wanted the poster so badly and—

A crash came from the kitchen. On any other day Skandar would have jumped out of bed, terrified there was a stranger in the flat. Usually he, or his sister, Kenna, asleep in the bed opposite, was in charge of making breakfast. Skandar's dad wasn't lazy – it wasn't that – he just found it hard to get up most days, especially when he didn't have a job to go to. And he hadn't had one of those in a while.

But today was no ordinary day. Today was race day. And for Dad, the Chaos Cup was better than birthdays, better even than Christmas.

'Are you ever going to stop staring at that stupid poster?' Kenna groaned.

'Dad's making breakfast,' Skandar said, hoping this would cheer his sister up.

'I'm not hungry.' She turned and faced the wall, her brown hair poking out from underneath the duvet. 'There's no way Aspen and New-Age Frost will win today, by the way.'

'I thought you weren't interested.'

'I'm not, but . . .' Kenna rolled back again, squinting at Skandar through the morning light. 'You've got to look at the stats, Skar. Frost's wingbeats per minute are only about average for the twenty-five competing. Then there's the problem of their allied element being water.'

'What problem?' Skandar's heart was singing, even though Kenna was insisting Aspen and Frost wouldn't win. She hadn't talked about unicorns for so long he'd almost forgotten what it was like. When they were younger, they'd argued constantly about what their elements would be if they became unicorn

– 2 –

riders. Kenna always said she'd be a fire wielder, but Skandar could never decide.

'Have you forgotten your Hatchery classes? Aspen and New-Age Frost are water-allied, right? And there are two air wielders among the favourites: Ema Templeton and Tom Nazari. We both know air has advantages over water!'

Skandar's sister was leaning on one elbow now, her thin pale face alight with excitement, her hazel hair and eyes wild. Kenna was a year older than Skandar, but they looked so similar that they'd often been mistaken for twins.

'You'll see,' Skandar said, grinning. 'Aspen's learned from her other Chaos Cups. She won't just use water; she's smarter than that. Last year she combined the elements. If I was riding New-Age Frost, I'd go for lightning bolts and whirlpool attacks . . .'

Kenna's face changed at once. Her eyes dulled; the smile dropped from the corners of her mouth. Her elbow collapsed, and she turned to the wall again, gathering her coral duvet round her shoulders.

'Kenn, I'm sorry, I didn't mean . . .'

The smell of bacon and burnt toast wafted under the door. Skandar's stomach rumbled into the silence.

'Kenna?'

'Leave me alone, Skar.'

'Aren't you going to watch the Cup with me and Dad?'

No answer again. Skandar dressed in the half-light of the morning, disappointment and guilt tightening his throat. He shouldn't have said it: *if I was riding*. They'd been talking like they used to, before Kenna took the Hatchery exam, before all her dreams came crashing down.

Skandar entered the kitchen to the sound of sizzling eggs and blaring early Cup coverage. Dad was humming, leaning over the pan. When he saw Skandar, he gave him an enormous grin. Skandar couldn't remember the last time he'd seen him smile.

Dad's face fell a little. 'No Kenna yet?'

'Still sleeping,' Skandar lied, not wanting to spoil his good mood.

'She'll find this year hard, I expect. The first race since . . .'

Skandar didn't need him to finish the sentence. This was the first Chaos Cup since Kenna had failed the Hatchery exam last year and lost all chance of becoming a unicorn rider.

The trouble was, Dad had never acted like it was rare to pass the Hatchery exam. He loved unicorns so much, he was desperate for one of his children to become a rider. He said it would fix everything – their money problems, their future, their happiness, even the days he couldn't get out of bed. Unicorns were magic, after all.

So for Kenna's whole life he'd insisted that she'd pass the exam and go on to open the Hatchery door on the Island. That she was destined for a unicorn egg locked inside. That she'd make their mum proud. And it hadn't helped that Kenna had always been top of her Hatchery class at Christchurch Secondary. If anyone was going to get to the Island, her teachers said, it was Kenna Smith. Then she'd failed.

And for months now Skandar's dad had been telling him the same. That it was possible, probable, even inevitable that he'd become a rider. And despite knowing how unusual it was – despite seeing Kenna so disappointed last year – Skandar wanted more than *anything* for it to be true.

'Your turn this year, though, eh?' Dad ruffled Skandar's hair with a greasy hand. 'Now, the best way to make fried bread . . .' As Dad gave him instructions, Skandar nodded in all the right places, pretending he didn't already know how. Other children might have found this annoying, but Skandar was just pleased when Dad gave him a high-five for getting the bread the perfect amount of crispy.

Kenna didn't come out for breakfast, though Dad didn't seem to mind too much as he and Skandar munched on sausages, bacon, eggs, beans and fried bread. Skandar stopped himself asking where the money for this extra food had come from. It was race day. Dad clearly wanted to forget about all that, and Skandar did too. Just for today. So he grabbed the brand-new bottle of mayonnaise and squeezed it over everything, grinning as it made a satisfying squelch.

'Aspen McGrath and New-Age Frost still favourites for you, then?' Dad asked through a mouthful. 'I forgot to say, if you want to invite any friends over for the race that's fine with me. Lots of kids do that, don't they? Don't want you to miss out.'

Skandar stared down at his plate. How could he even begin to explain that he didn't have any friends to invite? And, worse, that it was sort of Dad's fault?

The trouble was that looking after Dad when he wasn't well – not so happy – meant that Skandar missed out on a lot of the 'normal' stuff you were supposed to do to make friends. He could never stay after school to mess about in the park; he didn't have pocket money to go to the amusement arcade or sneak off for fish and chips on Margate beach. Skandar hadn't realised to begin with, but those were the times people actually made friends, not in English class or over a stale custard cream at morning break. And looking after Dad meant that Skandar sometimes didn't have clean clothes or hadn't had time to brush his teeth. And people noticed. They always noticed – and remembered.

Somehow for Kenna it hadn't been as bad. Skandar thought it helped that she was more confident than him. Whenever Skandar tried to think of something clever or funny to say, his brain jammed. It'd come to him a few minutes later, but face to face with a classmate, there'd just be a weird buzzing in his head, a blankness. Kenna didn't have that problem; he'd once heard her confront a group of girls whispering about how weird Dad was. 'My dad, my business,' she'd said very calmly. 'Stay out of it or you'll be sorry.'

'They're busy with their own families, Dad,' Skandar mumbled eventually, feeling himself blush, which always happened when he didn't tell the whole truth. Dad didn't notice, though – he'd started stacking the plates, which was such a rare sight that Skandar blinked twice to make sure it was real.

'What about Owen? He's a good mate of yours, isn't he?'

Owen was the worst. Dad thought he was a friend because he'd once seen hundreds of notifications from him on Skandar's phone. Skandar hadn't mentioned that the messages were far from friendly.

'Oh yeah, he loves the Chaos Cup.' Skandar got up to help. 'He's watching it with his grandparents, though, and they live miles away.' Skandar wasn't even making this up; he'd overheard Owen complaining to his crew about it. Right before he'd torn three pages out of Skandar's maths textbook, screwed them up and thrown them in his face.

'KENNA!' Dad shouted suddenly. 'It's starting any minute!' When there was no answer, he disappeared into their bedroom and Skandar sat down on the sofa, the TV coverage in full swing.

A reporter was interviewing a past Chaos Cup rider in the main arena, just in front of the starting bar. Skandar turned up the volume.

'—and do you think we'll see some fierce elemental battles today?' The reporter's face was flushed with excitement.

'For sure,' the rider replied, nodding confidently. 'There's a real mix of abilities among the competitors, Tim. People are fixating on the fire strength of Federico Jones and Sunset's Blood, but what about Ema Templeton and Mountain's Fear? They might be air-allied, but they're multi-talented. People forget that the best Chaos Cup riders excel in all four elements – not just the one they're allied to.'

The four elements. They were the core of the Hatchery exam. Skandar had spent hours learning which famous unicorns and riders were allied to fire, water, earth or air; which attacks and defences they would favour in sky battles. Nerves swooped into Skandar's stomach; he couldn't believe the exam was the day after tomorrow.

Dad returned, a troubled look on his face. 'She'll be out in a bit,' he said, sitting next to Skandar on the battered old sofa.

'It's hard for you kids to understand really.' He sighed, staring at the screen. 'Thirteen years ago, when my generation first watched the Chaos Cup, it was enough just knowing the Island existed. I was far too old to be a rider. But the race, the unicorns, the elements . . . it was magic for us – for me, for your mum.'

Skandar stayed very still, not daring to turn his head away from the screen as the unicorns entered the arena. Dad only talked about Skandar and Kenna's mum on Chaos Cup day. By his seventh birthday, Skandar had given up asking about her at any other time – he'd learned that it made Dad angry and upset, learned it made him disappear into his room for days.

'Never seen your mum so full of emotion as she was on the day of the first Chaos Cup,' Dad continued. 'She sat right where you are now, smiling and crying, and holding you in her arms. Only a couple of months old, you were.'

Skandar had heard this before, but he didn't mind one bit. He and Kenna were always desperate to hear about their mum. Grandma – Dad's mum – used to tell them about her, but they liked it best when the stories came from Dad, who'd loved her most. And sometimes, when he repeated them, there were new details, like how Rosemary Smith always called him Bertie, never Robert. Or the way she had liked to sing in the bath, or her favourite type of flower – pansies – or the element she'd liked watching best – water – in the first and last Chaos Cup she'd ever seen.

'I'll always remember,' Dad continued, looking straight at Skandar, 'when that first Chaos Cup finished, your mum took your tiny hand, traced a pattern on your palm and whispered, quiet as a prayer, "I promise you a unicorn, little one."'

Skandar swallowed hard. Dad had never told him that story before. Maybe he'd saved it until the year of his Hatchery exam. Maybe it wasn't even true. Skandar would never know whether Rosemary Smith had really promised him a unicorn, because – without warning, three days after the Mainland had watched unicorns race for the first time – Skandar's mum had died.

Skandar would never have said it to Dad, or even Kenna, but part of the reason he liked the Chaos Cup so much was because it made him feel close to his mum. He imagined her watching the unicorns, the excitement building in her chest – just like it was in his – and it was as though she was there with him.

Kenna stomped into the room with a bowl of cereal balanced on her palm.

'Really, Skar? Mayonnaise at breakfast?' She pointed at Skandar's smeared plate on top of the stack. 'I keep telling you: it's not an acceptable favourite food, little bro.'

Skandar shrugged, and Kenna laughed as she squeezed on to the sofa next to him.

'Look at you both taking up so much room. I'll be on the floor next year!' Dad said, laughing.

Skandar's heart clenched. If his exam went well, he wouldn't be here next year. He'd be watching the Chaos Cup in person, on the Island, and he'd have his very own unicorn.

'Kenna, cards on the table! Favourite?' Dad asked her, leaning round Skandar.

She stared at the television, munching moodily.

'Earlier she said Aspen and New-Age Frost *won't* win,' Skandar piped up, looking for a reaction.

It worked. 'Maybe another year Aspen will do it, but this isn't a good race for a water wielder.' Kenna tucked a stray strand of hair behind her ear, a gesture so familiar to Skandar that it made him feel safe. Like Kenna was going to be okay, even if Skandar did leave her alone with Dad on the sofa next year.

Skandar shook his head. 'I told you, Aspen isn't just going to rely on the water element. She's cleverer than that – she'll use air, fire and earth attacks too, for sure.'

'A rider is always best at their allied element, though, Skar. That's why it's called *allied* – duh! Say Aspen did use a fire attack, it's not going to compare with anything an *actual* fire wielder can do, is it?'

'All right, then, who do *you* think's going to win?' Skandar sat up as Dad turned the volume higher, the commentary reaching fever pitch as the armoured competitors jostled for positions behind the starting bar.

'Ema Templeton and Mountain's Fear,' Kenna said very quietly. 'Tenth last year, air wielder, high stamina, brave, intelligent. She's the kind of rider I would've been.'

It was the first time Skandar had heard Kenna acknowledge that she wouldn't ever be a rider. He wanted to say something, but he didn't know what, and then it was too late. So he listened to the commentator trying to fill the seconds before the race began.

'For any first-timers just joining us, we're live from Fourpoint, the Island's capital. And in a few moments these unicorns will fly out of this famous arena and begin the aerial racecourse – a gruelling sixteen-kilometre test of stamina and sky battle ability. Riders must stay outside the floating markers on their way round or risk being eliminated – not easy when twenty-four other competitors are trying to hit you with elemental magic and slow you down at every turn— Oh, that's the countdown. Five, four, three, two . . .

'And they're off!'

Skandar watched twenty-five unicorns, each twice the size of a horse, explode forward as the starting bar rose above their horns. The riders' armoured legs banged against the competitors on either side as they urged their unicorns on, to get an early lead, crouching low in their saddles, gathering speed. And then it was Skandar's favourite part. The unicorns began to stretch out their great feathered wings and take off, leaving the sand of the arena far below. The microphones picked up the riders as they whooped through their helmets. And it also picked up something else – a sound that still sent shivers down Skandar's spine, though he'd heard it on race day every year of his life. Guttural bellows from deep within the unicorns' chests – more terrifying than a lion's roar, more ancient and primal than anything he'd heard on the Mainland. The sort of sound that made you want to run.

The unicorns barged each other in mid-air to get the best positions, metal armour clanking and scraping. The tips of their horns glinted in the sunlight as they tried to gore their rivals. Foam built up around their gnashing teeth, and their nostrils flared red. Now they were airborne, the elemental magic lit up the sky: fireballs, dust storms, flashes of lightning, walls of water. The sky battles raged against a backdrop of fluffy white clouds. Riders' right palms glowed with elemental power as they desperately tried to fight their way along the racecourse.

And it wasn't pretty. The unicorns kicked out at each other, tore flesh from each other's flanks with their teeth, and blasted their competitors at close range. Three minutes in, the camera caught a unicorn and rider – hair on fire, one arm hanging uselessly – spiralling towards the ground and crash-landing, smoke billowing from the unicorn's wing and the rider's blonde head.

The commentator groaned. 'That's Hilary Winters and Sharp-Edged Lily *out* of the Chaos Cup this year. Looks like a broken arm, some nasty burns and an injury to Lily's wing.'

The camera moved back to the leading group. Federico Jones and Sunset's Blood were locked in a sky battle with Aspen McGrath and New-Age Frost. Aspen had summoned a bow of ice and was firing arrow after arrow at Federico's armoured back, trying to slow him. Federico had a flaming shield to melt the arrows, but Aspen's aim was good and New-Age Frost was catching up. Federico wasn't done, though. As Aspen flew Frost closer, flames exploded into the sky above Aspen's head.

'That's a wildfire attack from Federico.' The commentator sounded impressed. 'Tricky at that height and speed. But— Oh! Would you look at that!'

Ice crystals were knitting in a web round New-Age Frost, round Aspen, until they were sealed in a frozen cocoon so thick the wildfire couldn't touch them; Skandar saw Federico shouting in disappointment as he and Sunset's Blood fell back with the effort of their fire attack, and Aspen burst through her ice shell to overtake.

'It's Tom Nazari on Devil's Own Tears in the lead, followed by Ema Templeton on Mountain's Fear. Third is Alodie Birch on River-Reed Prince, and after that incredible air-and-water combo, New-Age Frost and Aspen McGrath are now in fourth with— But it looks like Aspen is making another move.' The commentator interrupted himself, his voice rising. 'She's picking up speed.'

Aspen's red hair flew out behind her, New-Age Frost putting on an unbelievable burst of speed, wings blurring, barging past River-Reed Prince, swerving as a lightning bolt missed Aspen by inches. Then Frost's great grey wings soared past Kenna's favourite, Mountain's Fear, then Tom Nazari's black unicorn, Devil's Own Tears. And Aspen took the lead.

'Yeah!' Skandar punched the air. It was a very un-Skandar thing to do, but this was incredible – unbelievable.

'I've never seen anything like it,' the commentator shouted. 'Look how far ahead she is!'

Kenna gasped, her eyes fixed on the unicorns as they approached the finish. 'I don't believe it!'

'She's going to win by a hundred metres,' another commentator squealed.

Skandar watched, mouth open, as New-Age Frost's hooves touched down in the arena's sand. Aspen pushed him forward, fierce determination in her eyes as she passed under the finishing arch.

Skandar jumped up, shouting with excitement. 'They won! They won! See, Kenna, I told you! I called it, I called it!'

Kenna was laughing, eyes shining, and that made the victory

even better. 'All right, Skar. They were really something, I'll give you that. Those ice crystals, what a move! I've never seen—'

'Wait.' Dad was standing close to the screen. 'Something's wrong.'

Skandar approached him on one side, Kenna on the other. Skandar could hear the crowd screaming, but it wasn't excitement any more; it was fear. Unicorns were no longer coming through the arch to finish the race. The commentators were silent, the footage still – there was just a single shot of the arena, as though the camera operators had abandoned their posts.

A unicorn landed in the centre of the arena. It didn't look like any of the others – not Sunset's Blood or New-Age Frost or Mountain's Fear – whose victory parade it had interrupted. This unicorn's wings were almost featherless – bat-like – and it was skeletal, half starved. Its eyes were red haunted slits. Blood was caked around its jaws, its teeth bared at the racers, as though daring them to attack.

It wasn't until Skandar noticed the unicorn's transparent horn that he realised.

'That's a wild unicorn,' he breathed. 'Like the ones in that old video the Island showed the Mainland. The one that convinced the Mainland that unicorns were real all those years ago. The one where they attacked the village—'

'Something's wrong,' Dad said again.

'It can't be a wild unicorn,' Kenna whispered. 'It has a rider.'

Skandar hadn't noticed the person – at least he thought it was a person – on its back. The rider wore a billowing black shroud that flapped in the breeze, the bottom tattered and torn.

A wide white-painted stripe obscured the rider's face from the base of the throat to the very top of the head, leading into short dark hair.

The unicorn reared up – pawing the air with its hooves, belching thick black smoke. Its phantom rider let out a triumphant howl, the unicorn screeched, and smoke filled the arena. Skandar watched the unicorn advance towards the Chaos Cup competitors, sparks dancing around its hooves, a jet of white from the rider's palm lighting up the screen. In the moment before the picture disappeared completely in black smoke, the rider turned and – slowly and deliberately – raised one long bony finger to point directly into the camera.

Then there was only sound. Explosions of elemental magic; unicorns screeching. More screaming from the crowd, and the unmistakable thundering of feet as Islanders attempted to escape from their seats. As Islanders crashed past the camera, their panicked voices jumbling together, Skandar noticed two words repeated over and over.

The Weaver.

Skandar had never heard of the Weaver, but the more the name was whispered, shouted, screamed by the crowd, the more it began to scare him.

He turned to Dad, who was still staring in disbelief at the swirling black smoke on the TV screen. Kenna beat Skandar to the question. 'Dad,' she said quietly, 'who's the Weaver?'

'Shhh.' He waved a hand. 'Something's happening.'

The view became clearer, the smoke lifting. Half sobbing, half shouting was coming from a figure on her knees in the sand. She was still in her armour, *McGrath* painted in blue across her back, surrounded by the other riders.

'Please,' Aspen wailed across the arena, 'please, bring him back!'

Federico Jones – the fierceness of the race forgotten – managed to get Aspen to her feet, but she was still howling. 'The Weaver took him. He's gone. We won and the Weaver—' Aspen choked on the last word, tears running down her dirt-streaked face.

A stern voice cracked like a whip. 'Get these cameras off! Now! The Mainland can't see this. Get them off, now!'

The unicorns began to screech and bellow, the sound deafening. Their riders jumped into their saddles, trying to calm them as they reared and frothed at the mouth, looking more monstrous than Skandar had ever seen them.

Only one of the twenty-five riders was left standing on the sand – the winning water wielder, Aspen McGrath. But her unicorn, New-Age Frost, was nowhere to be seen.

'Who's the Weaver?' Kenna asked again, her voice insistent.

But nobody answered her.

CHAPTER TWO

LOCKED OUT

'Miss Buntress, can you tell us who the Weaver is?'

'Why did the Weaver take New-Age Frost?'

'How was the Weaver riding a wild unicorn?'

'Can the Weaver get to the Mainland?'

'SILENCE!' Miss Buntress yelled, her hand kneading her forehead.

The class quietened; Skandar hadn't heard Miss Buntress shout before.

'You're my fourth Hatchery class of the day,' she said, leaning on her elbow against the whiteboard. 'And I'll tell you what I told the others. I do *not* know who the Weaver is. I do *not* know how the Weaver was riding a wild unicorn. And, unsurprisingly, I have *no* idea where New-Age Frost is.'

The Chaos Cup had been all anyone could talk about all day. That wasn't unusual – it was the biggest event of the year. But this year was different: people were worried, especially children

Skandar's age all across the country, who had their Hatchery exams the next day.

'Miss Buntress –' Maria put up her hand – 'my parents don't want me to take the exam. They're worried the Island's not safe.'

A few others nodded.

Miss Buntress straightened up and peered at them from under her sandy fringe. 'Apart from the fact that it's the law to take the exam, who can tell me what would happen if Maria was destined for a unicorn in the Hatchery and she didn't answer the call?'

Every single one of them could have answered, but Sami got there first. 'Without Maria to hatch it, her unicorn wouldn't bond with its destined rider. It would hatch wild.'

'Exactly,' said Miss Buntress. 'And it would resemble that dreadful creature you saw at the Chaos Cup.'

'I didn't say I agreed with my mum and dad!' Maria protested. 'I'm still going to—'

Miss Buntress ignored her. 'Fifteen years ago, the Island asked for our help with their rider shortage. I understand that you're all upset about what happened – so am I. But I'm not having any students of mine shirking their responsibilities. And now, with this – this *Weaver* – on the loose, it's more important than ever that if you have a destined unicorn, you hatch it. You only get one chance. And this is your year.'

'Well, *I* think the whole thing's a big hoax,' Owen drawled from the back of the class. 'If you ask me, that wasn't a wild unicorn at all – just someone pretending. That's what I read online, and—'

'Yes, thank you, Owen.' Miss Buntress cut him off. 'That's a possibility. Let's all get on with some revision questions now, shall we?'

Skandar frowned and looked down at his Hatchery textbook. That couldn't be true. If it'd been someone playing a joke, why had all the Islanders been so scared? How had the black-shrouded rider taken on an entire race-load of the most powerful unicorns on the Island and stolen New-Age Frost? And who – or what – was the Weaver?

Skandar wished he had a friend he could whisper with at the back of lessons. Then he could've asked them what they thought. Instead, he sketched the mysterious wild unicorn in the margin of his exercise book. Drawing was the only thing Skandar really enjoyed other than unicorns. It was a way to imagine himself on the Island. His sketchbook was full of drawings of battling unicorns or hatching eggs. Though sometimes he drew seascapes or silly cartoons of Kenna or – very occasionally – his mum, copied from an old photograph.

Not for the first time, he wondered what she'd make of all this.

***

At the end of the day Skandar waited for Kenna at the school gates alone – like always – flicking through his Hatchery revision notes. Then he heard a sound he'd recognise anywhere: Owen's laugh. He always made it really low-pitched, trying to sound older – more like a man. Though Skandar thought it made him sound more like a constipated cow with a bad cough.

'I only just got them!' a higher-pitched voice cried. 'And I'm supposed to be sharing them with my little brother. Please don't take—'

'Grab 'em, Roy,' Owen barked.

Roy was one of Owen's usual cronies.

Owen and Roy had cornered a small Year Seven boy by a low wall in the playground. He had pale freckled skin and bright red hair that reminded Skandar of Aspen McGrath.

'Oi!' Skandar jogged over. He already knew he was going to regret this – possibly even pay for it with a punch in the face – but he couldn't just leave the boy to deal with Owen on his own. Besides, Owen had hit Skandar a bunch of times in the past. He was sort of used to it.

As he reached them, Skandar realised that Roy had taken a fistful of Chaos Cards from the boy.

'WHAT did you say to me?' Owen stepped towards Skandar.

Skandar motioned quickly to the red-haired boy to hide. The boy's head disappeared behind the wall.

'I was, er, just wondering whether you wanted to borrow my notes?' Skandar said, the bravery quickly leaving him. You didn't say 'Oi' to Owen and get away with it. What had he been thinking?

Owen scoffed and grabbed the Hatchery notes from Skandar's clutches, passing them to Roy. With his hands free, Owen bashed Skandar's shoulder with his fist for good measure.

'Hatchery stuff,' Roy mumbled, leafing through.

'Brilliant. I'll just be going, then.' Skandar moved sideways, but Owen grabbed a fistful of his white shirt. Skandar could smell the hair gel Owen used to make his dark hair look messier.

'You don't actually think you're going to pass the Hatchery exam, do you?' Owen said in mock surprise. 'Oh, you do! Oh, that's adorable!'

Roy nodded stupidly. 'He does. These are revision notes.'

'How many times have I told you?' Owen was right up in Skandar's face. 'People like *you* don't become riders. You're too weak, too puny, too pathetic. You couldn't control something as dangerous as a unicorn; you're more suited to a poodle. Yes, Skandar, get yourself a *poodle* and ride around on that. That'd give us all a laugh!'

Owen was just swinging his fist back for a parting punch, when someone grabbed it from behind and yanked hard.

Gravity obviously liked Owen even less than Skandar did. He was falling, falling – *WHAM* – right on to the tarmac.

Kenna stood over Owen. 'Get out of my sight, or you'll have more than a sore bum to cry about.' Her brown eyes flashed dangerously, and Skandar felt a swell of pride. His sister was the absolute best.

Owen scrambled to his feet, turned and ran. Roy was close on his heels, still clutching the revision notes. Kenna noticed – 'Hey! Is that Skandar's writing? Come here!' – and chased after them towards the school gates.

Skandar peered over the wall, heart beating fast. 'You can come out now.'

The red-haired boy came to sit next to Skandar, looking fearful.

'What's your name?' Skandar asked gently.

'George Norris,' the boy said with a sniff, wiping away a tear.

'I wish he hadn't taken my cards.' He swung his feet so they hit the wall in two disappointed bumps.

'Well, George Norris, today is your lucky day, because –' Skandar reached into his rucksack and pulled out his own set of unicorn and rider trading cards – 'I'm willing to let you choose *five* for the astonishing bargain price of . . . nothing.'

George's face lit up.

Skandar fanned out the cards in front of him. 'Come on, take your pick.' The shiny edge of a unicorn wing flashed in the sunlight.

George took a long time choosing. Skandar tried not to wince as some of his prized collection disappeared into the younger boy's pocket.

'Oh, and next time Owen threatens you –' Skandar stood up – 'tell him that you know my sister, Kenna Smith.'

'Was that who pulled him over?' George asked, wide-eyed. 'She was pretty scary.'

'Terrifying!' Kenna roared, coming up behind Skandar on the wall.

'Arghwhywouldyoudothat?!' Skandar clutched at his chest.

George waved happily. 'Bye, Skandar!'

Kenna handed Skandar his revision notes. 'Is Owen coming after you again? You have to tell me if things are getting bad. Is he making you do his homework? Is that why he had your notes?'

Unlike Dad, Kenna knew that Owen had bullied Skandar for years. But he tried not to bother her too much with it nowadays. It upset her and she was already sad a lot.

'I'm not doing anyone else's homework, don't worry.'

'It's just, well, there's a lot to do at home. You know Dad's been really off since the Chaos Cup. He keeps saying the Weaver stole his one happy day of the year. He's always bad after it anyway, but this time it's—'

'Worse,' Skandar finished for her. 'Yeah, I know, Kenn.' Dad had been watching the footage of the Chaos Cup over and over, rewinding and pausing and obsessing. Then he'd go up to bed without food or a word to either of them.

'And I know you have your –' she took a breath before she said it – 'Hatchery exam tomorrow, but everything can't stop because of that, you know? Because—'

'I know.' Skandar sighed. He couldn't deal with Kenna telling him how unlikely it was he'd actually make it on to the Island. He just couldn't, not after Owen and Roy. The hope of things changing, of a life away from here, was what made it all bearable. Unicorns were everything. Kenna had lost them, but Skandar didn't want to let go of the dream, not yet. Not until—

'You okay, Skar?' Kenna was looking at him. He'd stopped in the middle of the pavement and a little boy with a unicorn T-shirt had to toddle round him.

Skandar started to walk but Kenna didn't let up. 'Is it because people are saying the Island's not safe right now?'

'That's not going to stop me trying the Hatchery door,' Skandar said stubbornly.

Kenna poked him. 'Ooh, look who's getting all warrior-like now. Weren't so brave when you found that daddy-long-legs in your bed.'

'If I hatch a unicorn, I'll make sure it snacks on all the creepy-crawlies I hate,' Skandar joked.

But Kenna's face fell like it always did when they got too far into unicorn territory.

He still couldn't believe she hadn't passed. They'd planned to do it all together; Kenna first, and then he'd have joined her on the Island a year later. Dad would have received the money all Mainlander families got as compensation for their child going to live on the Island, and they'd have made Dad proud. They'd have made Dad *better*.

'I'll do the dinner tonight, if you want?' Skandar said, feeling guilty as Kenna punched in the code for their building. They climbed the stairs. The lift had been broken for months but no one had come to fix it, even though Kenna had complained at least twelve times.

The tenth floor smelled like stale smoke and vinegar, like always, and one of the strip lights was buzzing outside number 207. Kenna put her key in the door, but it wouldn't open. 'Dad's bolted it again!'

Kenna called Dad's mobile. And again. Nothing.

She knocked – and knocked some more. Skandar shouted for Dad through the crack under the door, the side of his cheek scraping the corridor's puddle-grey carpet. No answer.

'It's no use.' Kenna slid her back down against the door until she reached the floor. 'We'll have to wait until he wakes up and realises we're not home. He'll work it out. It's not like this hasn't happened before.'

Skandar propped himself up against the door next to her.

'Revision?' Kenna suggested. 'I'll test you.'

Skandar frowned. 'Are you sure you want . . . ?'

Kenna tucked a stray strand of hair behind her ear, repeating the movement to make sure it was truly fixed, and turned to face Skandar. She let out a sigh. 'Look, I know I've been rubbish since I didn't get called to the Island.'

'You haven't b—' Skandar started.

'I have,' Kenna insisted. 'I've been a stinking rubbish bin, a pile of dung, worse than the steamiest poo in the sewage pipe.'

Skandar started to laugh.

Kenna was grinning now. 'And it's not fair; it really isn't. Because if it was the other way round, I know you would have helped me with my homework, kept talking to me about unicorns. Dad said once that Mum had a big heart – and if that's true you're much more like her than I am. You're a better person than me, Skar.'

'That's not true!'

'Mine's made of poo. Hey! That rhymes! Now do you want my help or not?' She snatched his bag and rummaged for his Hatchery textbook with its four elemental symbols on the cover. She flicked to a random page. 'Let's start with some quick-fire easy ones. Why did the Island reveal to the Mainland that unicorns were real?'

'Kenn . . . come on! Be serious!'

'I *am* serious, Skar. You think you know everything, but it'll be an easy question you get wrong, I bet you.' The strip light above them buzzed loudly. Skandar wasn't used to Kenna being in such a good mood, especially about the Island, so he played along.

'Okay, okay. Not enough thirteen-year-old Islanders were destined to hatch unicorns, meaning they weren't able to open the Hatchery door. Which meant unicorns were hatching wild – unbonded – and the Island was at risk of being overrun. They needed Mainlander children to try the door too.'

'What was the main obstacle the Island faced when telling the Mainland?' Kenna asked, skimming through more pages.

'The prime minister and his advisers thought it was a joke because the Mainland had this idea that unicorns were mythical, harmless, fluffy—'

'And?' Kenna prompted.

'And they had rainbow-coloured poo.' Skandar and Kenna grinned at each other.

They, like all Mainlander children, had heard the stories of the days when unicorns were believed to be mythical. Miss Buntress had told them they'd have been laughed out of the door if they'd gone around saying unicorns were real. She'd passed around examples of unicorn artefacts in their first Hatchery class: a pink unicorn soft toy with curly eyelashes and a smiley face, a sparkly headband with a silver horn, and a glittery birthday card that said ALWAYS BE YOURSELF – UNLESS YOU CAN BE A UNICORN, THEN ALWAYS BE A UNICORN.

Then, fifteen years ago, everything had changed. As soon as the footage of bloodthirsty wild unicorns had rolled across the Mainlanders' screens, everything unicorn-related had disappeared from the shops. Dad said they'd all been terrified by the idea that the wild beasts might fly in a shadowy swarm to the Mainland and kill anything in their path – with teeth or hooves or horn. In their fear, people had purged their homes of unicorns – picture books, soft toys, key rings, party decorations – and piled them on to towering bonfires that raged in public parks.

Unsurprisingly parents hadn't been too happy about the idea of sending their children to a place where these creatures were roaming free. Skandar had seen old newspaper articles about protests in London and debates in Parliament. But the answer to all the complaints had been the same: if we don't help, more wild unicorns will be born and kill us all. People demanded that the Mainland go to war with the Island and kill all the unicorns, but the prime minister replied that no unicorn – bonded or wild – could be killed with a gun.

He'd been keen to emphasise that if the Mainland agreed to help, it was a win-win situation for everyone. 'Bonded unicorns are different,' he'd tried to reassure the doubters. 'Think of the glory. Don't you want your children to be heroes?'

Dad had said that people calmed down about the whole thing after a while. Mainlander families missed each other, but children weren't dying, and nobody was attacked by wild unicorns. Parents of Mainlander riders visited the Island once a year to spend a day with their children; no rider ever asked to come home. Riders ranked in the Chaos Cup were worshipped by people old and young; they were more famous than royalty. Becoming a rider was what most children wished for when they blew out their birthday candles. Slowly but surely unicorns became part of daily life, and hardly anyone mentioned *wild* unicorns at all.

Until now. Until the Weaver.

'Do you think there'll be anything about the Weaver in the exam?' Skandar asked Kenna, who was now pacing back and forth. 'Do you think the Weaver was actually bonded to that wild unicorn? That's impossible, right? I mean, the whole definition of a wild unicorn is that it missed its chance to bond with its destined rider and hatched alone . . .'

Kenna stopped pacing, so he was staring at her grey socks. 'Stop worrying. You're going to be fine.'

'You really think I could be a rider?' Skandar asked, his voice barely above a whisper. Kenna didn't have control over whether he passed, let alone whether he could open the Hatchery door once he got to the Island, but it still mattered to him that she believed he could do it.

'Of course!' She smiled at him, but he felt tears burning behind his eyes, threatening to fall. He didn't believe her.

Skandar looked down at his lap. 'I get it. I'm not special. I don't even *look* like any of the riders on TV. They're all glossy and interesting-looking. But I'm, well— My hair isn't even a particular colour!'

'Don't be ridiculous – it's brown, like mine.'

'Is it?' Skandar sighed hopelessly. 'Or is it just sort of mud-coloured? And my eyes, they're murky; they can't even decide if they're blue or green or brown. And I *am* scared of daddy-long-legs, and wasps and also sometimes the dark – only the kind when you can't see your own hand, but still. What unicorn would ever want to bond with me?'

'Skandar.' Kenna kneeled down beside him, like she used to

do when they were little and he was upset. They were only a year apart, but Kenna had always seemed much older, right up until last year when she'd failed the exam. He'd had to be strong then, as she'd shrunk and cried herself to sleep for months. He could still hear her some nights. It was a sound scarier to him than the bellows of a thousand bloodthirsty unicorns.

'Skandar,' she said again, 'anyone could become a rider! That's what's so incredible about hatching a unicorn. It doesn't matter where you're from or how rubbish your parents are, or how many friends you have or what you're scared of. If the Island calls, you get to answer. You hatch a new chance. A new life.'

'You sound like Miss Buntress,' Skandar murmured, smiling back at her.

But as they watched the sun go down together through the window at the end of the corridor, Skandar couldn't help thinking that by this time tomorrow his Hatchery exam would be over, his future decided.

CHAPTER THREE

THE HATCHERY EXAM

Skandar was awoken by the sound of rummaging. He opened one eye and saw Kenna cross-legged on her bed, balancing an old shoebox on her knees. It was no ordinary box; it was filled with objects that had belonged to their mum: a brown hair clip, a miniature unicorn, a photograph of their parents dressed up to watch the Chaos Cup, a birthday card addressed to Kenna, a mother-of-pearl bracelet with a missing clasp, a black scarf with white stripes at each end, a garden-centre key ring and a bookmark from the local bookshop. Kenna liked looking through the box much more than Skandar did – especially when she was worried about something. She said the objects helped her feel like she could remember their mum – her smile, her smell, her laugh.

But Skandar didn't have any memories of their mum. He tried not to show that it made him sad. The thing was, most of the time Dad's sadness was so big that it seemed to take up all the space in the flat, in the town, in the whole world. And sometimes Kenna was upset too, and there wasn't any room for Skandar to miss his mum at all. Sometimes it was easier to leave his feelings in the box with her things and try to forget. But occasionally, when Kenna was sleeping, he'd take the objects out, just like Kenna was doing now. And he'd make a little space for himself to be sad. To miss her. And to wish that his mum could be here to give him a hug before the most important day of his life.

'Kenn?' Skandar whispered, trying not to make her jump.

Kenna's cheeks flamed as she rushed to put the lid back on the box, and hide it under her bed. 'What?'

'It's today, isn't it?'

Kenna laughed, though her eyes seemed a little sad. 'Yes, Skar.' She cupped her hands over her mouth to make a trumpet sound. 'Hatchery exam day for Skandar Smith!'

'KENNA! Help me make a surprise breakfast for Skandar!' Dad's voice thundered through the walls of the flat.

Kenna grinned. 'I can't believe he's remembered!'

'I can't believe he's up.' Dad had eventually let them in last night, but he'd barely been able to focus on their faces.

Kenna dressed at top speed. 'Act surprised, okay?' Her eyes were alight with the kind of fire that came with Dad having an unexpectedly good day.

Skandar smiled, feeling a little more like the Hatchery exam might actually go his way. 'You know I will.'

An hour later, after some hard-boiled eggs and burnt soldiers that Skandar insisted were the most delicious he'd ever tasted,

Dad walked them from the tenth floor all the way to the bottom of the stairs. Skandar couldn't remember another time Dad had done this – not even on the morning of Kenna's exam. But then Dad had been acting oddly all morning. Happy, excited . . . but sort of agitated too. He'd dropped three eggs on the floor and spilt half a pint of milk across the kitchen table. On the way downstairs Dad had tripped over the last step and almost ended up flat on his face.

'Are you all right, Dad?' Kenna put a hand on his arm.

'A bit clumsy this morning, aren't I?' Dad attempted a chuckle, wiping sweat from his forehead. He pulled Skandar into a hug. 'You can do this, Skandar,' Dad murmured into the hair above his ear. 'And if anyone tries to stop you taking the exam—'

Skandar jerked his head back. 'Why would anyone try to stop me?'

'Just – just in case they do. You've got to sit the exam, Skandar. For your mum, that's what she'd want, no matter what. It was her dream for you to become a rider.' Skandar could feel Dad's hand shaking against his shoulder.

'I know.' Skandar stared at Dad's face, looking for a clue. 'Of course I'll sit the exam, Dad. Where's this coming from? You're so jittery – you're making me even more nervous!'

'Good luck, son.' His dad sounded unlike himself as he waved them off. 'I know we'll have a Rider Liaison Officer knocking at midnight.'

Spooked, Skandar looked back over his shoulder as Dad gave him a final thumbs up. He tried to focus on Dad's words. Midnight tonight was when potential riders would be collected, so they could get to the Hatchery door for sunrise on the summer solstice.

In the late-June sunshine they walked towards the school entrance together. Kenna began to wish Skandar good luck, but he suddenly felt panicked. He hadn't yet asked her the one question he'd been wanting to for days.

'Kenna –' Skandar grabbed her arm – 'you won't hate me, will you? You won't hate me if I become a rider?'

Before he could even look into his sister's face, she pulled him into a one-armed hug, her bag swinging and almost overbalancing her. 'I could never hate you, Skar. You're my brother.' She ruffled his hair. 'I had my chance, and it didn't work out. I want it all for you, little bro. Plus –' she let him go – 'if you're famous, *I'll* be famous and I'll get to meet your unicorn. It's a win-win. Right?'

Smiling back at her, Skandar joined the queue forming outside the gym, where the Hatchery exam would take place. People were clutching revision cards, muttering to themselves about past Chaos Cup winners or fire attacks. Others were chattering nervously while they waited for Miss Buntress to open the big metal door.

'I can't believe we're going to see an actual rider,' Mike called out excitedly to his friend Farah a couple of heads behind Skandar. 'In *real life.*'

'I bet Christchurch Secondary doesn't get one of the decent riders.' Farah sighed. 'There are so many schools that, knowing our luck, we'll get some rubbish retired rider or one that never even made it through training.'

Retired rider or not, the visitor from the Island caused a stir at Christchurch Secondary every year. It seemed unbelievable that a person who rode a unicorn, who could perform elemental magic, had – just moments ago – walked down this corridor, with Year Seven's terrible paintings of the Van Gogh *Sunflowers* on one side and a list for trumpet lessons on the other.

'Good luck, Skandar!' George, the red-haired boy, called as he scuttled into his classroom. Skandar smiled weakly at him, trying to ignore the churning in his stomach.

Excited whispers buzzed down the line as they edged forward. Miss Buntress was letting one student into the gym at a time, ticking names off her list. But when Skandar reached her, she looked shocked, maybe even faintly horrified.

'What are you doing here, Skandar?' she hissed, her glasses slipping to the end of her nose.

Skandar just stared back at her.

'You're not supposed to be here today.'

'But it's the Hatchery exam.' He half laughed. He knew Miss Buntress liked him; she always gave him good marks and she'd written in her last report that he had an excellent chance of getting to the Island. This had to be a joke.

'Go home, Skandar,' she urged. 'You're not supposed to be here.'

'I am,' Skandar insisted. 'It says so in the Treaty.' In case this was a test to enter the exam hall, he recited: '*The Mainland agrees to submit all thirteen-year-olds for testing, overseen by a rider, and to hand over successful candidates to the Island on the summer solstice.*'

But Miss Buntress shook her head.

Dad's words came back to Skandar. *And if anyone tries to stop you taking the exam* . . . He felt an odd sensation in his chest, like something inside him was snatching the ends of each breath. Skandar lurched towards the gym; the rider sent to invigilate the exam must be in there. If Miss Buntress refused to let him in, she would be breaking the law. He could try to tell—

But Miss Buntress moved faster than he did. She stood tall and placed her palms on either side of the doorway. Skandar could hear people behind him getting impatient.

'I can't let you take the exam, Skandar.' He thought she looked sorry, though she didn't meet his eyes.

'Why?' It was all he could think to say. His mind was blank, empty, confused.

'It's come from the Rider Liaison Office. High up. I don't know why – they didn't say – but I can't let you in, it's more than my job's worth. They called your dad; I called your dad. He was supposed to keep you at home.'

The impatient voices of Skandar's classmates were getting louder: 'It's almost half nine, Miss Buntress!'

'Don't we all have to start together?'

'What's going on?'

'Why's that loser holding up the line?'

'*Please,*' Skandar and Miss Buntress said together.

Then she seemed to remember that she was the teacher. 'Get out of the way, Skandar, or I'll have to send someone for the head teacher. I suggest you go home, talk to your dad and come back tomorrow.'

She must have seen him trying to look past her into the gym with its desks set out in rows, the Hatchery exam papers gleaming in the sunlight. 'That rider won't tell you anything different. So don't even think about it.' Miss Buntress called Mike forward. He shoved Skandar to the side. More students pushed towards the door, realising that the hold-up was over.

When the last thirteen-year-old had been signed in, Miss Buntress stepped into the gym and turned to shut the door.

'Please go home, Skandar. It'll be easier for you if you do.' Then she slammed the metal door behind her. Skandar looked desperately up at the clock in the corridor, heart hammering. It was exactly half past nine. Thirteen-year-olds all around the country were opening their papers for the most life-changing exam they'd ever take. And Skandar wasn't with them. He was standing alone in a stupid school corridor, his chance to be a unicorn rider gone for ever.

Tears burned behind Skandar's eyes, ready to fall, but he didn't want to move. What if Miss Buntress realised she'd made a terrible mistake? What if the rider came looking for the missing student and Skandar had gone home? He couldn't risk it. And, anyway, as a last resort he'd beg the rider for a chance and demand to take the exam. Skandar wasn't the kind of boy who'd usually demand things – he'd ask politely, probably under his breath. But if he was going to make a fuss about anything, it was this. He had nothing to lose now. This was his dream, his whole future.

Every thirty-five minutes, the corridor filled with pupils changing lessons: Maths to Biology; English to Spanish; Art to History. Then, at last, the door of the gym opened and people started to file out, clutching pens and chattering excitedly. Not one of them noticed Skandar as he stood waiting. And waiting. Until Miss Buntress appeared – alone.

'Where's the rider?' Skandar asked, much more rudely than he'd ever spoken to a teacher before. He could feel his throat closing up with panic, his breathing getting faster and faster. The rider definitely hadn't left, he would have seen—

'What are you still doing here?' All the stress seemed to have gone out of Miss Buntress now the Hatchery exam was over. She smiled sadly at Skandar. 'Were you waiting to talk to the rider?'

He nodded quickly, peering round her.

'I'm afraid she left by the back door. To the car park. She had to get back to the Island quickly.' Miss Buntress obviously sensed Skandar's disbelief. 'You can check the gym if you want. Then I expect you to go home, like I asked.'

Skandar sprinted into the empty gym, the desks set out in rows, a big clock balancing precariously on top of a basketball hoop. It was completely empty. He sank down at one of the wooden desks and burst into tears.

Skandar didn't know how long he sat there with his head in his hands. But after a while someone hugged him round the shoulders from behind. A strand of brown hair stuck to his wet cheek.

'Come on, Skar,' Kenna said gently. 'Let's get you home.'

Hours later, Skandar awoke in the dark of his and Kenna's bedroom. For a moment he couldn't understand why his eyes felt so dry and sore, why he was still fully clothed. Then he remembered the crying. He remembered he hadn't taken the

Hatchery exam. And he remembered that even if he *had* been destined for a unicorn, now he would never hatch it. It would hatch alone – wild, without a bond – and turn into a pure monster. That was the worst thing of all.

He switched on the lamp, then immediately wished he hadn't. His poster of New-Age Frost shone in the bright light: armour gleaming, muscles rippling, menace in his eyes. Skandar would never find out what had really happened at the Chaos Cup now. And unless the Island decided to tell the Mainland, he'd never know anything about the Weaver either. Or whether New-Age Frost was safe.

Kenna and Dad were talking in low voices. It was odd to hear them speaking so gently to each other. He guessed they were talking about him, about what had happened. It hadn't exactly been good when Kenna had pulled Skandar out of that gym, but it had all seemed so much worse when they'd got home. Kenna and Skandar had asked – demanded – to know why Dad hadn't told Skandar he'd been banned from taking the exam, hadn't even warned him what would be waiting for him at school.

Dad had looked at his feet and told them he hadn't known what to say, that he'd tried to tell Skandar that morning, that the Rider Liaison Office hadn't given a real reason, that it didn't sound like there was any choice, that he was sorry he hadn't been brave enough to share the truth. Then Dad had burst into tears, and so had Kenna, and Skandar hadn't ever stopped crying, so they'd all just stood there in the hallway and sobbed.

Skandar looked at the clock; it was eleven. He thought he heard Kenna moving down the hallway, so he quickly switched off the light again. He didn't want to talk. He didn't want anything any more. Apart from his mum. Somehow, though he couldn't even remember her, he needed her now more than ever. Maybe if she'd been alive, she could've told him what he was supposed to do now that his future didn't include unicorns. But she wasn't coming. She was never coming. All he'd had was a dream of being a unicorn rider and now it was gone. So he let his eyes close because there was nothing else to be done.

Skandar was awoken by five sharp knocks. He sat up in bed and saw the shape of Kenna do the same in the bed opposite.

'Was that the door?' he whispered. It was unusual for anyone to knock; they had a buzzer downstairs at the main entrance.

'Maybe someone's locked out?' Kenna whispered back.

Five sharp knocks again, just as before.

'I'll go.' Kenna climbed out of bed, pulling a hoodie over her pyjamas.

'What time is it?' Skandar groaned.

'Almost twelve,' Kenna whispered, padding out into the corridor.

Almost midnight? The midnight after the Hatchery exam? The same midnight that families everywhere were waiting up for across the country? Waiting to see if their child had done enough to be called to the Island, to try the famous Hatchery door.

'Kenna! Wait!' Skandar could hear her pulling back the bolts, humming to herself like she did whenever she was nervous or a little bit afraid. He jumped out of bed, still in his school uniform, and rushed to join his sister.

She wasn't alone.

A woman stood in the doorway, illuminated by the fluorescent lights of the corridor. The first thing Skandar noticed were the white burns across her cheeks. There was so little skin left that he could almost see the cheekbones and muscles underneath. The second thing Skandar noticed was how tall and terrifying she looked silhouetted there, her eyes darting everywhere at once, her greying hair pulled up into a high scraggy bun that made her look even taller. Skandar's immediate thought was that she looked like a fearsome pirate. He was almost surprised there wasn't a cutlass in her hand.

'Can we help you?' Kenna asked bravely, her voice barely shaking.

But the woman wasn't looking at Kenna. Her eyes were locked on Skandar.

When she spoke, her voice was gravelly and strained, like she hadn't spoken to anyone in a long time. 'Skandar Smith?'

Skandar nodded. 'What do you want?' he asked. 'Are you in trouble? It's the middle of the night.' His nerves were making him speak quickly.

The woman shook her head. 'It's not just the middle of the night. It's *mid*night.' And she did the most unexpected thing: she winked.

Then she said those words, the words Skandar had given up wishing for. 'The Island is calling you, Skandar Smith.'

Skandar hardly dared to breathe. Was he dreaming?

Kenna broke the silence. 'That's impossible. Skandar didn't take the Hatchery exam so he can't have passed it. The Island can't be calling him. There must be a mistake.' She crossed her arms, any trace of fear gone. Skandar wished she'd be quiet. If this *was* a mistake, he didn't mind one bit. If it got him to the Island, what did it matter? For once in his life he wasn't interested in fairness or honesty. He wanted a chance at the Hatchery door, and he didn't care how he got there.

The woman spoke again, her voice low as though she was worried she'd be overheard. 'The Rider Liaison Office is aware that Skandar didn't take the exam this morning. And apologises for the confusion. You see, we've been watching Skandar for months, requesting samples of his work – we do this with strong candidates sometimes – and there was no need for him to take the exam.'

Skandar could practically feel Kenna's disbelief vibrating in the small space between them. 'But I . . . I had better grades than Skandar last year *and* I took the exam. I didn't even pass. This doesn't make any sense.'

'I'm sorry,' said the woman, and Skandar thought she seemed genuine. 'But Skandar's special. He's been selected.'

'I don't believe you,' Kenna said, very quietly. Skandar knew his sister well enough to realise she was fighting off tears.

'What's he been selected for?' came a voice from behind them, hoarse with sleep.

The stranger reached out a hand to Dad. 'Good to meet you in person. Robert, isn't it?'

He grunted, rubbing one eye. 'Can I help you?'

'We spoke on the phone,' the woman prompted, drawing her hand back. And as she did, Skandar noticed something that made his heart jolt. The woman had a rider tattoo on her right palm! He'd seen drawings of them before, and glimpsed them on TV when riders waved at the crowd. A dark circle in the centre of the palm, with five lines attached, snaking up to the tips of each of the woman's fingers. But riders didn't work for the Liaison Offices.

'So you're the one who told me Skandar couldn't take the Hatchery exam? Yeah, I remember your voice.' Skandar thought Dad sounded angry.

The stranger didn't seem to notice Dad's frown or his pursed lips. Or, if she did, she didn't care. 'I'd like to come in for a minute. Skandar and I will need to be going soon.'

'Oh, you'd like to come in, would you?' Skandar's dad crossed his arms. 'I bet you would. Skandar won't be going anywhere with the likes of you.'

'Dad, please,' Skandar murmured. 'She said I've been called to the Island.'

'I'll explain everything inside.' Wisps of hair flew across the stranger's cheeks as she looked over her shoulder. 'I can't explain out here – it's highly confidential.'

This seemed to convince Dad that the woman should at least be allowed over the threshold. 'Absolute shambles,' he mumbled, leading her into the kitchen. 'First you phone to tell me Skandar can't take the exam, and now he can go to the Island after all? That office of yours needs to sort itself out.' Dad helped himself to a glass of milk without offering the woman anything. It was only Kenna who actually remembered to turn the light on.

'We're sorry it wasn't all made clearer.' The woman spoke

quickly, not sitting down but gripping the back of one of the kitchen chairs, her gnarled knuckles white against the brown wood. 'Skandar never needed to take the exam because he'd already proved himself. As I said, he's a special case.'

The woman's eyes darted around the kitchen, like she was in a rush to leave – like she was identifying the nearest exit.

'I knew it had to be a mistake.' Dad was suddenly grinning. 'Always said he was rider material –' he turned to Skandar – 'didn't I, son?'

Skandar tried to catch his sister's eye, but Kenna was biting her nails furiously and not looking at any of them.

'Are you packed?' the woman said fiercely in Skandar's direction.

'Uh, no,' Skandar croaked. 'I didn't think there was any chance—'

'We haven't got long,' the woman snapped. Skandar could hear a note of panic in her voice. 'You'd better get some things together. No phone, no computer, remember? You know the rules.'

'Right,' Skandar said, nodding, and rushed from the room, heart hammering. Mainlanders weren't allowed to take any technology to the Island. Communication home had to be through letters, via the two Rider Liaison Offices – one on the Mainland and one on the Island. Skandar was completely fine with that. His phone was a way for the loneliness of school to follow him home, and he certainly didn't want it coming to the Island. He threw it happily into a drawer.

Skandar could hear Kenna's feet on the lino behind him as

Dad chattered away in the kitchen. 'So you'll be off to Uffington, then? That chalk unicorn cut into the hill always gave me the creeps. Ghostly, you know? Though I suppose you've got to land the helicopters somewhere. You parked round the corner?'

'Something like that,' Skandar heard the woman reply.

'You know, you look familiar. Are you local? I feel like I've seen y—'

Kenna closed the bedroom door, shutting out their voices, and watched as Skandar pulled random clothes out of a drawer and stuffed them into his school rucksack.

'Skar, I don't think you should go with her,' Kenna whispered, as he scooped up his sketchbook and a pile of books about the Island. 'None of this makes any sense! All thirteen-year-olds have to take the exam to get called to the Island – that's what the Treaty says! I don't think she's a Rider Liaison Officer. Have you seen the burns on her cheeks, the scratches across her knuckles? She looks like she's just been in a fight!'

Skandar finished zipping up his rucksack. 'Stop worrying, okay? This is the real thing! I've been called; I've got a chance to try the Hatchery door—'

'Loads of people get sent back. You probably won't be able to open the door, especially as you haven't even taken the exam. This'll all mean nothing.'

The hurtful words hit Skandar hard in the chest and his temper flared. 'Can't you just be happy for me, Kenn? Can't you? I've always wanted this—'

'*I've* always wanted this!' she practically screamed back at him. 'It's not fair! I get stuck here and—'

'Like you said, I probably won't even be able to open the door. I'll come back here and you can say I told you so.' Skandar felt on the verge of tears himself now. He pulled angrily at his clothes, finally changing out of his school uniform into jeans and a black hoodie.

'Skar, I didn't mean—'

'You did.' Skandar sighed, shouldering his bag. 'But it's okay, I get it.'

Kenna ran at him. She threw her arms round him – rucksack and all – and sobbed. 'I *am* happy for you, Skar. I am. I just wish I could come too. And I don't want you to go; I don't want to be here without you.'

Skandar didn't know what to say to that. He wished she could come too; he didn't know who he was without Kenna, not really. He swallowed back tears. 'If I open the door, I'll write as soon as I get there. I've got my sketchbook; I'll draw you pictures of everything. I promise. I know it's not the same, but—'

Suddenly she pulled away and rummaged in their mum's shoebox.

'Kenn, I've got to go!' Skandar croaked. 'There's no time.'

'You should have this.' Kenna held out the black scarf.

'You don't have to.' Skandar knew that Kenna secretly wore the scarf to bed, especially when she was sad. She'd even sewn a name tape into it – PROPERTY OF KENNA E. SMITH – in case the scarf ever went missing.

When Skandar didn't reach out to take it, she placed it round his neck.

'Mum would have wanted you to take it to the Island.' Kenna

smiled, even though tears still streamed down her face. 'Imagine how happy she'd be if she knew you were wearing it while riding a unicorn. You're going to make her so proud.' The last word was mostly a sob, so Skandar just hugged Kenna tight and said 'thank you' into her hair.

Moments later, Skandar hugged Dad goodbye. 'Be better,' Skandar whispered in his ear. 'Be better for Kenna, okay?' He felt Dad nod against his cheek.

The stranger stared as Kenna kept adjusting the black scarf round Skandar's neck as though she didn't want to let either of them go. Kenna was still crying when Skandar waved and turned, and he felt so guilty and sad – and so happy and excited at the same time – that he wanted to stand there and work out whether he was doing the right thing. But the stranger was disappearing down the endless flights of stairs, and Skandar didn't want to lose her, so he turned away from Flat 207 and followed.

'You're not who you say you are, are you?' Skandar said, once they were outside.

'Aren't I?' The woman turned, the light of a blinking street lamp making the scars on her cheeks shine.

'No,' Skandar persisted, as he followed the woman round the corner of the tower block. 'You're a rider.'

'Am I?' The woman chortled, as they reached the entrance to the communal garden. It was the first time Skandar had seen her crack a grin; she seemed more relaxed now they were outside.

Skandar followed her into the garden, confused. 'Aren't we supposed to be driving to the white unicorn? To Uffington? Isn't that where the helicopters land to fly new riders to the Island?'

The woman grinned at Skandar and he noticed that several of her teeth were missing. Something in her crooked smile made him feel even more nervous. 'You ask a lot of questions, don't you, Skandar Smith?'

'I just—'

The woman chuckled and patted Skandar on the shoulder. 'Don't you worry. I'm parked over here.'

'You parked your car in the communal garden? I don't think that's—'

'It's not a car exactly,' the woman interrupted, pointing straight in front of them.

And there, between the rickety old swings and a graffitied park bench, was a unicorn.

CHAPTER FOUR

THE MIRROR CLIFFS

Skandar almost ran the other way. Almost. Unicorns were absolutely, categorically *not* allowed on the Mainland. Ever. That was in the Treaty – it was one of the most important rules. Yet here one stood, in the communal gardens of Sunset Heights tower block in Margate. The woman – *the rider* – marched confidently towards the beast. The unicorn seemed much bigger up close, and it didn't look at all friendly. It was snorting, pawing at the ground with one giant hoof and swinging its white head from side to side, the razor-sharp horn atop its head looking more lethal than on any TV screen. To complete the ferocious picture there was fresh blood around its jaw.

'What did I tell you about snacking on the local wildlife?' the woman grunted, as she nudged aside the remains of something Skandar really hoped *wasn't* the ginger cat from Flat 211.

Fear and wonder fought in Skandar's mind at seeing a real

unicorn for the first time. 'Can you please tell me what's going on? You – it – that –' he pointed at the unicorn, unable to contain himself – 'is not supposed to be here.'

The unicorn's red-rimmed eyes narrowed when Skandar spoke, and a low growl escaped from deep within its belly. The woman stroked the great creature's neck.

'I mean,' Skandar dropped his voice to a whisper, 'I don't even know your name.'

The woman sighed. 'I'm Agatha. And this is Arctic Swansong – Swan, I call him. And, no, I'm not a Mainlander from the Rider Liaison Office.'

Agatha moved away from her unicorn and towards Skandar.

Skandar took a step backwards.

Agatha spread her hands wide. 'You don't trust me; that's fair enough.'

Skandar choked out something between a cough and a laugh. 'Of course I don't trust you! You phoned my school to stop me taking the exam, and now you tell me that I'm going to the Hatchery anyway? Why didn't you just let me sit the exam; surely that would have been simpler than –' he pointed at Arctic Swansong – 'all this?'

'You would have failed the exam, Skandar.'

Skandar felt like all the breath had left him. 'How could you possibly know that?'

Agatha sighed again. 'I know it's confusing. But I promise –' her dark eyes shone – 'I mean you no harm. All I want is to take you to the Hatchery tonight, so you can try the door at dawn. Like the others.'

'But why bother?' Skandar insisted. 'If I would've failed the exam, then I'm not going to be able to open the Hatchery door, am I? You've broken all the rules bringing your unicorn here – and for what?'

'The exam doesn't work exactly how you think,' Agatha murmured. 'Forget what you've been taught; the rules don't apply to you. You're . . . special.'

Special? Skandar didn't believe that – not really. He'd never been special in his whole life, so why would he start now?

But here Skandar was, with a unicorn right in front of him and an opportunity to get to the Hatchery. If this Agatha got him to the Island, and Skandar ended up opening the Hatchery door, what did all this matter? Once he started his rider training, nobody would care that he hadn't walked on to the chalk of the white unicorn with the other Mainlander hopefuls, hadn't flown to the Island the 'normal' way. Perhaps that was *their* chance, but this was his – and he was going to take it. After all, he'd spent his whole life trying to be like everyone else, and it hadn't exactly worked out for him so far.

So Skandar asked a different kind of question, one a brave person might ask. 'Are we going to ride Arctic Swansong?'

'Swan's plenty strong enough to carry two.' Agatha looked up at the sky. If she'd noticed the change in him, she didn't say. 'Speaking of which, we need to get going. Walk by me, and he won't mind you.'

Agatha steered Skandar towards the white unicorn. The creature watched curiously, making ominous growling noises in his throat. Now he was closer, Skandar's bravery swiftly disappeared. He gulped twice, three times. This couldn't be happening. It couldn't be real.

'I'll get on first, and then I'll lift you up behind me, okay? Just mind you keep your legs tucked in; Swan's partial to a kneecap every now and then.' As Agatha balanced on the iron railings and launched herself over Swan's back, her laugh was guttural, not unlike her unicorn's own growls.

Skandar's throat was dry, his forehead sweaty despite the cool night air as he climbed up on to the railings after her. He'd imagined riding a unicorn practically every day of his life, but it hadn't been like this. Not in the middle of the night, round the back of his tower block, with a woman who'd only told him her first name. And had Swan taking a bite out of his knees been a joke or a warning? But despite all that, as Agatha lifted him up on to Arctic Swansong's back, Skandar felt an enormous swoop of excitement in his stomach.

The unicorn's sides were warm against Skandar's jeans, each breath quivering against the insides of his legs. It was all going quite well until Arctic Swansong started to move – and Skandar almost fell off sideways. Luckily at the last moment he grabbed a handful of Agatha's leather jacket to steady himself.

'There's not much room in this garden,' Agatha called over her shoulder, 'so it'll be a pretty steep angle as we take off. Make sure you hold on tight round my middle; there's not much I can do if you fall off in mid-air – don't want all this trouble to be for nothing!' Her bark of a laugh echoed off the buildings.

The unicorn backed up against the furthest edge of the communal garden. And then they were galloping forward,

Swan's hooves pounding faster and faster on the dry summer ground. Skandar was painfully aware of how much he was bouncing on the unicorn's spine – he wouldn't have blamed Arctic Swansong if he'd thrown him off in protest. But that was the least of Skandar's worries, because he knew what was coming next. He should – it was his favourite part of the Chaos Cup.

Skandar forced himself to keep his eyes open as the unicorn's white-feathered wings unfurled and beat the air in a rhythm that quickened with every stroke. But they hadn't yet left the ground, and Skandar watched the railings at the other end of the garden getting closer and closer. He wasn't at all sure they'd make it, until—

With a stomach-churning jolt they were airborne, rising high over the fence, leaving the bench and the swings – and Skandar's home – far below them. Arctic Swansong pointed his horn towards the moon, and Skandar crouched forward on the unicorn's back, clinging on to Agatha for dear life. The unicorn's wings sounded like they were moving underwater as Arctic Swansong fought to take them upwards against air currents Skandar couldn't see. The wind howled past Skandar's ears and through his hair.

Once Arctic Swansong stopped his climb into the night sky, the unicorn's wingbeats were so smooth that it was almost comfortable to sit behind the mysterious Agatha. Skandar couldn't work her out: she seemed kind – with her easy laugh and her winking apologies – but there was something secretive, something dangerous about her, and Skandar knew that there was a good chance she was flying them straight into trouble. But these worries left his mind as his eyes caught on the seaside lights of Margate blinking below and disappearing into the distance. Skandar wanted to shout with joy, with fear – he wasn't sure from one wingbeat to the next.

Skandar soon lost track of time. There was only the dark and the wind and the unicorn's muscles rippling on either side of his legs.

'Look down there!' Agatha shouted as they dipped out of a cloud.

And it was a *long* way down, but he knew exactly what he was seeing. The white unicorn at Uffington shone brightly in the light of the moon on its hillside. Skandar still found it hard to believe that, for centuries, people on the Mainland had called it a white horse. It was only when the Island had revealed itself that the true origin of the chalk beast had been rediscovered.

Even with Agatha urging Swan in and out of the clouds to avoid being spotted, Skandar could see that the chalk was a hive of activity. Car headlights lit up the nearest road, torches flickered up the hillside and figures cast shadows on the white unicorn. Some would be Rider Liaison Officers, some police, some unicorn superfans, some journalists desperate for interviews from the new rider hopefuls. But others would be the anxious thirteen-year-olds themselves – waiting for the solstice sunrise and their turn at the Hatchery door. Skandar had imagined the moment so many times: the chalk whitening the soles of his shoes as he waited to fly to the Hatchery.

'Helicopters haven't arrived yet,' Agatha yelled without turning round. 'That's good; we'll beat them to the Mirror Cliffs.'

Skandar didn't know what the Mirror Cliffs were. But as the

ghostly shape of the unicorn disappeared behind them, Skandar felt a pang of sadness. He wasn't sorry he was on the back of a real unicorn – it certainly beat waking up and going to school tomorrow! – but he felt a swell of guilt for Kenna back in Flat 207. He'd write to her, tell her everything. If he became a rider, if he could open the door . . .

They flew on, the wind over the sea far too strong for conversation now. Skandar's hands were numb from cold, but he was very glad of his mum's scarf wound tightly round his neck. Aside from its warmth, it felt like she was with him somehow, keeping him safe.

Without warning, Swan descended towards the waves. Skandar squinted into the gloom for any sign of land, but it was just darkness and sea spray and the smell of salt. Skandar clenched his arms round Agatha even tighter, not understanding what was going on. Were they going to dive into the sea? Surely Agatha wouldn't have gone to all this trouble just to drown him? Margate was by the sea – there'd been plenty of water there! He closed his eyes for the impact.

But it never came. Judging by the crunch of the unicorn's hooves, they'd landed on some sort of gravel. The only light came from a single lantern at the end of a tiny wooden jetty a few metres away. Skandar looked down over Swan's outstretched wing and saw a pebbled beach, as the unicorn's ribcage moved up and down against his shoe from the effort of flying.

Agatha vaulted from her unicorn's back. 'And you too, Skandar – give him a rest,' she ordered, pulling him down roughly. Skandar landed on the beach with a thump.

Agatha crunched over towards the dark sea, the pebbles loud against the regular crashing of waves on the beach, and yanked the lantern from its fixing at the end of the jetty. As she and the light approached, Skandar thought he could make out flickering figures up ahead – another Agatha and Skandar and Arctic Swansong standing directly opposite.

Agatha saw Skandar's head snap up and chuckled softly under her breath. 'These are the Mirror Cliffs, and this is known as Fisherman's Beach. Very tricky to land a boat here if you don't know what you're looking for – just looks like the sea reflected back at you. And, of course, the currents do their best to stop boats getting close. Island sailors train for years before they master it. Mainlanders like to think they know all our secrets, but, truth be told, they only know the ones we want to share. You'll soon learn that.'

A new sound reached Skandar's ears above the crashing of the waves. In the lantern's light he saw the muscles in Agatha's face tighten with worry.

'That's the helicopters. We haven't got long. Now, listen. Do as I say, and you'll be fine. Follow me.' The sudden fear in Agatha's voice made Skandar's stomach turn over – she didn't sound like she thought everything would be fine at all.

Arctic Swansong growled at Skandar as they passed. It was disconcerting walking towards his own reflection, so Skandar kept his eyes on Agatha's back as they made their way right to the foot of one of the cliffs.

Agatha crouched down and Skandar did the same so he could make out her words over the sound of the sea.

'Do you hear that?' Agatha whispered. They were silent while Skandar listened. And then he did hear it: a low hum of voices coming from above.

'That's the Hatchery up there,' Agatha murmured. 'In a few moments those helicopters are going to land on the clifftop and drop off the Mainlanders.'

Skandar nodded.

'You need to get on to the clifftop, ready to join them. You need to mix in with everyone else, d'you understand?' Agatha said roughly. 'Anyone asks you any questions, you flew here in Blitzen.'

'Blitzen?'

'The Rider Liaison Office code-named the helicopters after Santa's reindeer. A sort of joke, I suppose. But, anyway, Blitzen's pilot is a friend of mine. She'll get your name on the right list.'

'Okay,' Skandar croaked, his brave resolve starting to crumble. 'Is Swan flying me up there?'

'Don't be ridiculous. I've got to get out of here. It wasn't exactly a sanctioned visit to the Mainland.' Agatha's patience seemed to be thinning as the helicopters whirred closer, but Skandar needed answers before she left him.

'But why did you bring me? I still don't understand!'

Agatha closed her eyes for the briefest of seconds. 'Your mother asked me to look out for you.'

Skandar's heart leaped. 'How? She's – she's dead. She died just after I was born.' He knew he should be used to it, but he still hated saying that out loud.

'She asked me a long time ago.' Agatha smiled sadly. 'Back when things were different.'

'But how did you even know her?' Skandar asked desperately. 'You're an Islander . . . aren't you? And if that's true, why didn't you come for Kenna last year?'

A helicopter hovered above and landed on the clifftop. Agatha continued as though she hadn't heard Skandar's questions. 'There are metal rungs built into the rock.' She moved the lantern closer to the cliff and tapped one, then another above it. 'That's the way up.'

Skandar swallowed hard. *Right. The Hatchery door.*

'Look, Skandar.' Agatha spoke very quickly now, her eyes flicking up to the sky every other second. 'Did you see the Weaver at the Chaos Cup? Did you watch it?'

'Yes,' Skandar murmured. 'Everyone watches the race.'

'The Island is trying to downplay it like always, but something's different in the Weaver. Something's changed. Coming out into the open like that? Risking being caught? I don't know what the Weaver's planning, but I'm sure of one thing. Now the Weaver has the most powerful unicorn in the world – the Chaos Cup *winner* – nobody's safe.'

Agatha's eyebrows knitted together in a deep frown, darkening her whole face. 'And if anyone tells you the Weaver won't bother with the Mainland, they're kidding themselves. You saw the Weaver pointing into the camera. That wasn't an accident. That was a threat.'

'But how do you know all this? And why are you telling *me*?' Skandar pleaded. 'I'd never even heard of the Weaver before the Cup.'

'Because I think you'll remember to care about the Mainland, even when you're a rider. I've been watching and I think that's the kind of person you are, the man you'll become. You're different, Skandar, and you've got a good heart. A better heart than mine.'

'But I'm not brave!' Skandar exclaimed. 'If you wanted a big-hearted hero, you should have brought Kenna; she's—'

Agatha's head snapped up to look at the sky where the lights of the helicopters illuminated the night. 'I've got to go – I can't have them catch me. I'm sorry. I hope we'll meet again one day.'

'Me too,' Skandar said, and he meant it, no matter how mistaken she was about the kind of boy he was. Without Agatha he would still be asleep in Flat 207.

'Oh, I almost forgot.' Agatha rummaged in her pocket and took out a glass jar. 'You might not need it, but better safe than sorry. Hide it,' she added, as Skandar tried to see what was inside. At a glance it looked like some sort of thick black paste. Skandar pocketed it.

A helicopter whirred over their heads and they both ducked further down, leaning into the cliff face. 'Go,' Skandar urged, seeing fear flash across her face. 'I'll be all right.'

'No doubt.' Agatha winked, then turned and ran across the beach, taking the light of the lantern with her. As she vaulted on to Arctic Swansong's back, she raised a hand in farewell, then flung the lantern into the sea, plunging the beach into darkness.

Another helicopter buzzed overhead and landed at the top of the Mirror Cliffs. Skandar didn't waste any time. He took a deep breath and began to climb.

He'd only managed a few rungs when there were shouts

below – angry and insistent. 'Dismount and put your hands up!'

The beach suddenly blazed with light. Agatha and Arctic Swansong were surrounded by unicorns, their riders' faces covered with silver masks. Skandar froze in helpless panic as Agatha and Swan tried to break through the circle.

Three of the masked riders dismounted, pulled Agatha from Swan and wrestled her to the ground. As the unicorn screeched for its rider, magic lit up the beach below – fire, water, air and earth attacks all directed at Agatha and Swan. The rider and unicorn crashed to the pebbles and were still.

Skandar stifled a cry of horror. He wanted to help them, but he knew he was no match for even one of those silver-masked riders. Realising how visible he must be, Skandar climbed faster and faster, until at last he reached the final rung. Skandar hoped beyond hope that Agatha and Arctic Swansong had just been injured and weren't— He couldn't even think it. Skandar launched himself, like a penguin on its belly, on to spongy green grass.

He got up and brushed himself down as quickly as he could, trying to make it look a bit less like he'd just flown on an illegal unicorn from the Mainland, witnessed an arrest and scaled the edge of a cliff. He was lucky. There were people absolutely everywhere and the line for the Hatchery door was easy to make out in the predawn glow; it snaked all the way down the centre of the grassy clifftop. Feeling like this was all far too easy, Skandar walked quickly towards the back of the line.

'Stop right there!'

Skandar's heart clenched. A young woman, dressed all in black except for a short yellow jacket, was approaching him. It was the standard uniform for all riders: black trousers, short black boots, black T-shirt and a jacket the colour of the elemental season. Skandar swallowed and tried to look like this wasn't the most unusual night of his entire life.

'Which helicopter did you come in?' she asked. 'I don't think I've checked your name.'

'Oh,' Skandar panted, trying not to sweat any more than he already was. The reindeer code name. Which one had it been? He tried to sing the beginning of 'Rudolph the Red-Nosed Reindeer' in his head to jog his memory, which felt odd in June – *Comet and Cupid, and Donner and* – 'Blitzen. It was Blitzen.' He said a silent thank you to Agatha, and hoped that his telltale blush would go unnoticed.

'And your name is?' She somehow managed to sound impatient and bored at once.

'Skandar Smith.' His voice caught on the 'S' of 'Smith' so he had to say it twice.

The young woman dropped her chin, unfolded a piece of paper from her pocket and miraculously ticked off his name. He stared at the top of her pencil, hardly daring to believe that he might actually pull this off.

'What are you waiting for?' she snapped. 'Get to the back; don't push in or wander off. It's almost sunrise.' Her hair swung over her shoulder as she turned away and Skandar spotted the gold flames of her element pin twinkling on her yellow lapel.

Skandar hurried to join the queue and looked up into the distance for the first time. The clifftop didn't stay flat for long. The people at the front were standing in the shadow of a green mound. He'd read that some thirteen-year-old Islanders actually camped out for days prior to the ceremòny, just so they could be among the first to try the door and reach the unicorns inside.

The Hatchery stood alone like a giant burial mound, its grassy top and sides just visible in the early-morning light. From this distance, Skandar could make out a large circle of granite cut into the side of the mound and lit by lanterns on either side. The Hatchery door. It looked very ancient. And very shut.

Skandar was chivvied forward by another rider in a black uniform so he was practically breathing down the neck of the person in front. There was a lot of shushing. Skandar felt a wave of nerves as he thought about the helicopters perched like metal birds on the cliff edge, waiting for those Mainlanders who failed to open the door and had to return home.

'Ouch!' Something thumped into Skandar's back. He spun round and found himself face to face with a girl. She had a short bob of straight brown hair and deep olive skin. She was staring back at him, her face shadowed by a heavy fringe, her dark eyes flinty. She didn't apologise.

'I'm Bobby Bruna,' she announced, cocking her head to one side. 'My actual name's Roberta, but if you ever call me that I'll push you over that cliff.' She sounded serious.

'Right. That's, um – yeah. I'm Skandar Smith.'

'I didn't see you at the white unicorn.' She narrowed her eyes at him suspiciously.

Skandar tried to keep his voice casual. 'I tend to blend in with the crowd.' It wasn't a lie exactly.

'I heard you say you were in Blitzen.'

'Yeah?' Skandar felt himself getting defensive, even though he didn't have a leg to stand on. Not even a toe. Not even a wart on the bottom of a toe. 'Are you spying on me?'

Bobby shrugged. 'Thought it wouldn't hurt to size up the competition.' Skandar noticed that her fists were clenched, purple nail varnish visible on her thumbs. 'But that's beside the point. You weren't in that helicopter.'

'I was.' Skandar could feel his neck getting sweaty under the scarf; he adjusted his rucksack nervously.

'You weren't,' Bobby said coolly. 'Because I was, and I didn't see you anywhere. And I would have remembered a name like Skandar.'

'I told you—'

Bobby held a palm up so it almost touched Skandar's nose. 'Please don't embarrass yourself by saying you "blend in with the crowd" again. My memory is practically photographic, and there were only four of us. Also, you're blushing.'

The white-hot panic that was sweeping through Skandar must have been obvious because Bobby put her hand back into her pocket. 'I don't care which helicopter you came in.' She shrugged. 'I just want to know why you're lying.'

'I—' Skandar began to say, but at that very moment there was a glint in the corner of his eye. The sky glowed pink as the sun rose over the Mirror Cliffs.

'It's starting,' Bobby murmured, and she turned away as a great cheer went up from the line – the round Hatchery door swinging back to admit the first new rider of the year.

CHAPTER FIVE

THE TUNNEL OF THE LIVING

Skandar and Bobby moved closer to the Hatchery door inch by inch. To Skandar's relief they didn't speak. He couldn't believe that the first person he'd had a proper conversation with on the Island already knew he was lying. Okay, so she thought he was just lying about the fact that he'd come in *her* helicopter, but it was only a matter of time, wasn't it? Until she raised the alarm?

Skandar forced himself to take a deep breath, like he did at school when Owen and his friends were being particularly terrible. Who cared if one person knew? Why would she bother herself with him? And maybe she wouldn't even be able to open the Hatchery door – or maybe *he* wouldn't and this would all be for nothing.

Skandar was still too far back to see what was happening outside the Hatchery, but every so often he heard a cheer, which meant someone had opened the door. Whenever there was a long silence, Skandar felt his stomach lurch at the thought of being turned away.

'Stop stressing,' Bobby hissed in his ear, when he forgot to step forward. 'They're mostly Islanders at the front. They basically all try out, remember? More of them get rejected, because more try out. Didn't they teach you anything at your school?'

Skandar didn't say anything, not wanting to prompt questions about the Hatchery exam he definitely hadn't taken.

As the line moved forward, Mainlanders who'd failed to open the door started being sent back towards the helicopters. Some were crying, some looked angry, and others kept their heads bent in disappointment as they trudged the length of the line.

Skandar tried to make himself look away, focusing instead on the top of the Hatchery. Now he was nearer, he could see that there were unicorns with riders on top of the mound. And they had silver masks – just like the riders who'd attacked Agatha!

'What are they doing up there?' Skandar blurted.

Bobby tutted. 'You're not the sharpest lemon in the tree, are you?'

'That's not even a saying, and I wasn't talking to you,' Skandar snapped. His nerves were getting worse; he could almost count the number of people ahead of him. Would those masked riders arrest him if they found out he'd never passed the exam? Was that what they were there for?

'So you were talking to yourself?'

'No, I was just . . . noticing.'

Bobby snorted and Skandar faced her, wondering if she was going to mention the helicopter again. But she didn't. Instead,

Bobby pointed at the unicorns. 'They're armoured guards. I was eavesdropping –' she dropped her voice to a whisper – 'and apparently they're here to protect us.'

Skandar gulped. 'From what?'

'Oh, I don't know, maybe that *Weaver* thing everyone's been talking about?' She rolled her eyes.

Now he was almost at the Hatchery, Skandar could see a stern-looking man with a clipboard to the right of the door, calling out names.

'Presenting Aaron Brent,' the man shouted. The long-legged boy in front of Skandar stepped forward, flicking his thick dark hair out of his eyes. Skandar felt a pang of jealousy; Aaron definitely looked more like a rider than he did. He could imagine the tall boy staring out from a Chaos Card. Aaron sauntered to the granite door and pushed his palm against it. Nothing. When that didn't work, he tried to pull at the round edge. Still nothing. He began kicking at the door in desperation.

After a few painful moments, the clipboard man put a forceful arm round Aaron's shoulders and moved him away. Skandar watched Aaron disappear back towards the cliffs.

'Approach.' Skandar heard the call and didn't move. His head was still spinning with the awfulness of Aaron being sent home, just like that. He shouldn't have come with Agatha; he felt like the lies were written all over his face. His legs started to shake.

'Approach,' came the voice again.

Bobby kicked his ankle. 'Go on!'

Skandar walked unsteadily towards the man. He was older than he'd looked from a distance. His black hair was peppered with grey, and he was so thin that his cheekbones dominated his sallow face. 'Name?'

'Skandar Smith,' Skandar said, his voice cracking.

'Could you repeat that? Quickly – we haven't got all day.' His voice was clipped and harsh.

'Skandar Smith.'

The man's wiry eyebrows knitted together in a frown. Skandar held his breath while the man looked for his name on the clipboard. What if there was something Agatha hadn't thought of? Maybe they knew, maybe they'd checked whether he'd sat the exam and—

'Presenting Skandar Smith!' the man boomed.

Skandar moved towards the Hatchery door, his legs like lead. He had a mad impulse to run back to the helicopters. That way he'd never know. He could always dream that he'd been destined for a unicorn because he'd never even tried the door. But he could feel the riders' eyes burning into him from above, and he had no choice but to reach out and place his palm on the cold granite of the Hatchery door.

For one heart-stopping moment, nothing happened. There was a roaring in Skandar's ears that had nothing to do with the sea thrashing against the Mirror Cliffs. He stared at the door, the disappointment so heavy his knees buckled, his shoulders slumped, and he started to step back and withdraw his palm. But as he did, there was a grinding of stone and a great creaking of ancient hinges.

Slowly but surely, the Hatchery door was opening.

Excitement exploded right from Skandar's toes to the tips of his fingers, and he wasn't taking any chances. As soon as there was enough of a gap, he squeezed through the round entrance and into the darkness beyond. He didn't look back.

The great door swung shut behind him. He was in! He'd done it! He was a rider. It didn't matter how he'd got to the Hatchery; all that mattered was that there was a unicorn in here somewhere, a unicorn that'd been waiting thirteen years for him, just like *he'd* been waiting. He hardly dared to believe it. Hardly even dared to think the word *rider* again in case it was suddenly taken away. Skandar collapsed on to the cold stone, put his head in his hands and let the tears – of relief, of tiredness, of happiness – fall.

Then he remembered that if Bobby opened the door, she would step right on top of his head. And although he'd only known her a very short time, he was pretty sure she'd trample straight over him.

Skandar scrambled to his feet, his eyes adjusting to the gloom. He was at the end of a long tunnel lined with flaming torches. He couldn't help but feel nervous. His textbooks hadn't said anything about the inside of the Hatchery; he'd assumed it would all be straightforward. Open the door, get an egg, hatch his destined unicorn – and boom! They'd be bonded for life, ready to start training. He hadn't expected a creepy tunnel. He hadn't expected to be alone. He wished Kenna was with him. Even though she hated small spaces, she'd have shouted silly things that echoed off the tunnel walls to make them laugh.

But there was no turning back now. Skandar started to make his way along the tunnel, fiddling with the ends of his mum's scarf. The only sounds were his breathing and the shuffle of his trainers. After a few steps, he noticed that the walls of the tunnel were roughened by markings cut into the stone. He leaned in for a closer look. There were words carved into the tunnel – but, no, not words . . .

'Names,' Skandar breathed, his whisper impossibly loud. Names were crammed into every visible space: the walls, the floor and even the ceiling. He wondered why they were there, who they belonged to. Skandar walked a few more steps and was surprised to read a name he recognised: EMA TEMPLETON – Kenna's favourite from the Cup this year. They were rider names! He looked eagerly for more he knew, but it was impossible – there were so many. Countless names swam in front of his eyes: FREDERICK ONUZO, TESSA MACFARLANE, TAM LANGTON.

Skandar almost jumped out of his skin at a scraping up ahead. It sounded like nails across a blackboard, the kind of noise that makes your teeth go numb and sends shivers down your spine. Bloodthirsty unicorns he was okay with. Ghosts? Not so much. Skandar squinted in the direction of the sound, but there was nobody ahead of him. He took a few more steps towards it, feeling like he should be doing the exact opposite.

At the source of the noise Skandar still couldn't see anything or anyone up ahead. There were just more names everywhere: ROSIE HISSINGTON, ERIKA EVERHART, ALIZEH MCDONALD and . . .

The grinding noise suddenly made sense. Tiny pieces of rock fell to the tunnel floor, as Skandar saw the final 'H' carve itself: SKANDAR SMITH. Skandar's name had joined the other riders' in the tunnel. Excitement bloomed in his chest. It was real; he was a rider; he had a unicorn to hatch!

He walked with more purpose now, and at last a door came into view at the end of the line of torches. It was an exact match in shape to the one outside, but this time – thankfully – it had a big round handle. Skandar strained as he pulled back the heavy stone, and he heard people – talking, laughing, giving instructions – and climbed out of the tunnel towards his new life.

Skandar noticed the heat first. The cool stone of the tunnel was gone, replaced by a cavernous space lit by hundreds of torches blazing in their brackets and a fire roaring in a deep pit in the rock floor. As Skandar's eyes adjusted to the brightness, he realised it was less like a room and more like a very wide corridor stretching to the left and right of the fire, where the other new riders were gathered. Hundreds of stalactites with ends like daggers hung above Skandar's head. Glittering white drawings of unicorns shone out at him from the walls, like cave paintings – though in the flickering light of the torches they looked almost alive.

Skandar stood a little distance away from the other riders, feeling nervous. He suddenly felt like everyone had made friends already and left him out, just like they did at school. Bobby hadn't come through behind him yet – Skandar didn't even know if she'd been able to open the Hatchery door. She was the only person he'd spoken to so far and he felt bad hoping that he'd never see her again, but then maybe his secret would be safe. Skandar took another step towards the other riders, telling himself not to worry. This was a new start.

He hovered on the edge of a conversation between some Islanders. It wasn't difficult to work out who came from where: the Mainlanders were furthest from the fire pit, looking tired and anxious, dressed mostly in jeans like Skandar and clutching hastily packed bags; the Islanders were closest to the fire: laughing, slapping each other on the back and wearing loose-fitting clothes all in black.

'The Tunnel of the Living was *super* underwhelming, if you ask me. The decoration was completely basic, and I really think we should be able to choose exactly where our names go.' The girl speaking had dark chestnut hair, freckles on her light pink cheeks and a slightly upturned nose, as though it was protecting itself from bad smells.

The Islanders around her looked fascinated by what she had to say. They kept nodding and saying things like 'You're so right, Amber'.

'What do you think you're looking at?'

It took Skandar a moment to realise Amber was speaking to him.

'I—' Skandar felt like he was back at Christchurch Secondary and his usual nerves blocked his throat; he could feel his mind going blank with worry as he fiddled with the end of his mum's scarf.

Amber fixed him with a patronising smile. 'And why are you wearing that ragged old scarf? Is it some odd Mainland tradition? I'd get rid of it if I were you. I'm sure it's *super* important to you to fit in with all of us Islanders. Top tip – we don't usually wear scarves indoors.' She smiled wider, but it was more like seeing a shark's teeth before it eats you. The Islanders around her sniggered.

'The thing about Skandar's scarf,' said a voice from behind him, 'is that he can take it off. Shame you can't do the same with your personality.'

There was a stunned silence, during which Amber's face turned the colour of a tomato.

Then Bobby simply marched off, giving Skandar little choice but to rush after her.

'Why did you do that?' Skandar groaned once they were out of earshot. 'They'll hate you now. And me probably! That Amber girl seemed really popular.'

Bobby shrugged, examining one of her purple nails in the light of the fire. 'I don't like popular people. They're overrated.'

Skandar certainly agreed with that. Owen had always been 'popular' and that hadn't meant he was kind or nice, or anything else you'd want in a friend.

'Thanks, though, for—' Skandar started, but he didn't have time to finish, because the man from the Hatchery door – clipboard under his arm – was standing opposite the fire, clapping his hands for silence. A round man and a woman with curly grey hair stood on either side of him, their faces lined and serious.

'For those of you who don't know,' said the clipboard man, his voice echoing off the cave walls, 'I am Dorian Manning, president of the Hatchery and head of the Silver Circle.'

'What's the Silver Circle?' Bobby whispered loudly to the Islander on her other side, but he shushed her.

'As Hatchery president, my main job is to oversee the proper execution of the Hatchery exam, the presentation of candidates to the Hatchery door and the hatching itself – along with these esteemed members of my team.' He gestured to the people standing on his left and right.

'I also oversee Hatchery security at all other times of the year. And, of course, there is the noble and perilous endeavour of delivering unhatched eggs to the Wilderness before they hatch into wild unicorns at sunset.' He sniffed loudly and puffed out his skinny chest, looking very pleased with himself. Skandar was liking him less by the second.

'But enough introductions. Congratulations are almost certainly in order. You are now officially riders of the Island, protectors of this land and the land across the sea. Somewhere in this chamber there is an egg for each one of you, an egg that appeared in this world when you did. A unicorn that's been waiting thirteen years for you to arrive.' A few people cheered, but they were quickly silenced by a stern look from the president, his tightening cheeks looking almost hollow in the torchlight.

'Without riders – without *you* –' he pointed dramatically at them all – 'your unicorns would be bondless – wild – a danger to us all. And racing them is how we, and our ancestors for thousands of years, have channelled their . . . energy into something good. But –' he held up a finger, eyes glinting in the torchlight – 'a word of warning. And I mean all of you, not just the Mainlanders. Unicorns, even when bonded, are fundamentally bloodthirsty creatures with a preference for violence and destruction. They are ancient noble beasts, and you must earn their respect, even as their destined rider. Now –' the president clapped his hands pompously – 'to business.'

The president and his two colleagues moved through the crowd, tapping new riders on the shoulder – seemingly at random – and asking them to follow. Bobby was tapped by the round nervous-looking man, while Skandar was tapped on the shoulder by Dorian Manning himself. He followed the president behind another boy who had straight black hair and brown glasses a shade lighter than his tawny skin. Every few steps the boy looked anxiously behind him, and pushed his glasses up his nose where they'd slipped down.

The president stopped in front of a row of bronze stands that reminded Skandar of giant test-tube holders. The eggs were clasped in thick claws at about his chest height and they were enormous; he'd once seen an ostrich egg on a school trip to the zoo, and these had to be at least four times the size. Skandar wanted to pinch himself; he was actually here in the Hatchery, about to meet his destined unicorn.

'Don't dally, don't dally! Gather round me,' the president said quietly, as though if he spoke any louder, the eggs might hatch all in one go. 'This is the first batch of twelve eggs due to be hatched this year. They've been expertly cared for by my team since they appeared in the bowels of the Hatchery. Every year, for thirteen years, the eggs have been moved up one level, closer to the surface, the baby unicorns growing inside them slowly but surely. And finally, in a moment, you will each take a place in front of one.' The president paused for breath.

Skandar's eyes widened in amazement. How deep *was* the Hatchery if there were that many floors underneath where he was standing?

Dorian Manning continued giving instructions. 'You must place your right palm on top of the egg. If nothing happens after ten seconds, step away and swap to the next egg on your right.'

Skandar wished he could get his sketchbook out and write this down – he didn't have the best memory for details – and he really wanted to ask what the president meant by 'if nothing happens'. What was supposed to happen? What if he missed it? But there didn't seem to be time; he was already talking again.

'And remember, when you feel the unicorn horn puncture your palm—'

Skandar gasped, and he wasn't the only one. It hadn't said this anywhere in his books; he'd just thought hatching meant . . . well . . . the unicorn would do it on its own once Skandar arrived.

'—that egg is going to start hatching immediately. Grab the egg as quickly as you can and then shut yourself in a hatching cell behind you.'

The new riders turned round to look. Along the wall opposite the egg stands, there were caves with half-open doors. Doors made from metal bars.

Skandar swallowed. He noticed that the other Mainlanders in his group looked just as worried; a Mainlander girl with long dark hair was muttering under her breath.

'Do *not* open those doors mid-hatching or before you've got a head collar and lead rope on your unicorn,' the president whispered, the flare of a burning torch making his green eyes flash wildly. 'Those eggs might not look that big, but, mark my words, the unicorns will start growing as soon as they're out. What we absolutely don't want is any escaped baby unicorns today – not on my watch! The havoc they could cause . . . It doesn't bear thinking about.'

Skandar was beginning to panic, and the president's dire warnings weren't helping. He wanted to ask a thousand questions. For starters, what was a head collar and where could he get one? But there was barely time to take a few deep breaths before the president was saying, 'Ready? Lower your palms when I tell you.'

So Skandar stepped into place and stared at the giant egg in front of him.

CHAPTER SIX

SCOUNDREL'S LUCK

The president's instructions swirled around Skandar's mind. *Ten seconds. Grab the egg. Puncture.* Would there be blood? Would it hurt? He felt very, very sick.

'Palms . . . down!' the president hissed.

The new riders lowered their hands on to the tops of the white eggs in front of them. The shell was warmer than Skandar had expected, and very smooth. He had to fight the urge to shut his eyes so that he wouldn't actually see the unicorn horn stab his palm. Excitement and fear were galloping through him side by side; he could feel his pulse beating in his neck. He waited. And waited. The egg didn't move.

'Stand back,' said the president. 'Nobody on the first try? Not unusual, not unusual. You must find the egg meant for you, after all. There are only forty-three of you in here this year, and over fifty eggs ready to be hatched.' The president sighed. 'It may well take until the last egg to find your unicorn. Patience, patience is needed.' Skandar didn't think the president sounded very patient as they all moved along one egg.

'Palms . . . down!' Now Dorian Manning had made it clear that finding an egg was down to fate, Skandar felt calmer. Three seconds in, there was a yelp from someone two eggs along. A few new riders, including Skandar, turned to stare. He recognised the boy as Zac; Skandar had seen him open the door.

'Keep your palms on those eggs no matter what,' President Manning warned. 'If you miss your egg, you'll have to go round again and we'll be here until next year's hatching! I certainly do not have time for that!'

Skandar tried to watch Zac without turning his head. Out of the corner of his eye he saw him lift the egg from its clasp and into his arms, sweat dripping down his deep brown forehead. Skandar could already hear the cracking of the shell as the unicorn began to fight its way out of the egg. Then Zac was stumbling under the egg's weight, and Skandar lost sight of him as the barred door of the hatching cell clanged shut.

'One down,' the president muttered.

They switched again, and again. Two more riders found their eggs in the first batch. They moved further along the chamber to the second batch. Skandar was standing right next to a Mainlander girl with long dark hair – he thought her name was Sarika – when the horn pierced her egg's shell. She didn't cry out, but he saw blood dripping from her palm as she carried the egg into one of the cells.

By the third batch there were four riders left, including Skandar and the boy with the black hair and glasses. Skandar had become so frustrated he was no longer afraid. Now each time he rested his hand on the hard surface of a shell, there was nothing he wanted more than to feel a sharp stab of pain.

'This doesn't seem like a particularly efficient way to find our unicorns,' the black-haired boy murmured a few eggs down.

Skandar stepped forward to the second egg in the line of twelve. The third and fourth had already gone from their bronze clasps. 'Palms . . . down!' cried the president from behind him.

Three heartbeats later, there was a loud crack under Skandar's hand and blinding pain surged through his right palm. Then, as though on autopilot – blood dripping from the centre of his hand – he lifted the egg up out of its bronze claw. It was heavier than he'd expected. Leaning the weight of the egg against his chest, Skandar staggered towards the hatching cell behind him. He could already see cracks spreading across the egg's surface, like ice breaking over a frozen lake. A piece of shell dropped to the floor just as he pulled the barred door shut.

The hatching cell was lit by one flaming wall torch. A rickety iron chair stood alone in the flickering light, a rope hanging over its back. Skandar suddenly felt completely out of his depth. He couldn't be responsible for hatching his own unicorn! What if he did it wrong?

Skandar's egg was quaking in his arms and his palm was bleeding all over the white shell. He needed to put the egg down, but it felt wrong to let it roll around on the cold stone floor. The trouble was there wasn't anything soft in sight except . . . He looked down at himself. His hoodie.

Skandar carefully kneeled down. Grateful that the sharp

horn was nowhere to be seen, he sat cross-legged, balancing the egg in his lap. He slipped his rucksack off and pulled his hoodie over his head. Steadying the egg with one hand, he spread the hoodie out on the floor and bunched it into a sort of nest. As an added barrier, he unwound his mum's scarf from his neck and placed it round the edge. He couldn't help grinning at how proud she'd be. *I promise you a unicorn, little one.* She'd whispered that to him as a baby – so Dad had said – and now here he was, about to hatch one!

It was a relief to put the egg down. Adrenaline had made it seem lighter than it actually was, but now Skandar could feel his arms aching.

Skandar watched the egg eagerly. It felt like his whole body was fizzing with excitement. He couldn't believe it. He was finally here. In only a few moments he'd be face to face with his destined . . . But the egg had stopped moving. *No need to panic,* he thought, panicking. Skandar tried to distract himself by investigating the contraption dangling from the back of the chair. It had to be the head collar and lead rope the president had mentioned, attached together with a metal clasp.

Skandar cast another worried glance at the egg. It was quivering but only very slightly. Occasionally a piece of shell would fall on to the hoodie or make Skandar jump by skittering across the hard floor. He could hear the odd noise from cells nearby but nothing recognisable, and certainly nobody shouting helpful step-by-step instructions. Skandar went to fiddle with the clasp of the rope, but immediately hissed in pain as the cold metal touched his punctured palm.

Skandar looked at his hand for the first time since he'd entered the cell. It wasn't bleeding any more, but the round puncture had turned a nasty dark red. Alarmed, Skandar moved closer to the torch burning in its bracket. Five lines glowed in the torchlight, growing out of the wound itself in the middle of his palm, creeping up towards the base of each of his fingers.

Skandar had always thought that riders had special tattoos on their palms. In fact, he was sure he'd read about it somewhere. It was how he'd recognised Agatha as a rider back in Margate. But it wasn't a tattoo at all; it was a wound. And it hurt – a lot.

The egg was still and silent now. Skandar wondered a little desperately if there was something he should be doing to help. He thought about chicks hatching. Did hens do anything to speed up the process? Other than sitting on their eggs, he didn't think so, and that didn't seem very sensible given the sharp horn. Anyway, unicorns weren't chickens, they were – well – unicorns.

He sighed and kneeled by the egg. 'Don't you want to come out?' he asked quietly. 'I wish you would, because it's pretty horrible and dark out here, and I'm all alone, so . . .' He tailed off, feeling ridiculous talking to an egg. It was a bit like talking to your breakfast.

There was a small shriek. Skandar looked around wildly. Then it happened again – and he realised it was coming from inside the egg itself. He kneeled closer. Unbelievably, the talking seemed to be working.

Skandar took a deep breath. 'Look, I want to meet you. I really do. We're going to be partners, you and me. I might need you to look out for me a bit because, well . . . I'm from the Mainland but you're from here so—' The egg shrieked again and a large piece of shell flew past his left ear.

'But I think that might be the least of our problems.' Skandar knew he was babbling, but the shell was breaking apart in front of his eyes. 'I didn't even take the Hatchery exam – don't tell anyone, will you? – but someone helped me get here and I'm worried I'll get found out. This girl – Bobby – she suspects. And also, there's this Weaver on the rampage, but maybe I should wait until you're a bit older before I tell you about that. Anyway, so I think I'm going to need you, and you're going to need me.'

The shrieking was constant now: somewhere between a horse's whinny, an eagle's cry and a human scream. The unicorn's horn broke clean through the egg for a second time: onyx-black, shining and – as Skandar already knew – very sharp. It moved from side to side, breaking away more of the shell. Then there was a loud crack and the whole top came off. Skandar grabbed the larger pieces of shell – slimy in his hands – and threw them across the room. He kneeled up, but just as his face loomed over the egg, the remaining shell cracked into two and fell apart.

The unicorn lay on its belly, four legs splayed out on the floor of the hatching cell, its ribs moving quickly up and down, the fine black hair on its body shining with sweat and slime. An ebony mane crowned its neck, the strands of hair tangled from the effort of freeing itself. It still had its eyes closed, but as Skandar stared at the creature in wonder, something strange started to happen. Its puny black-feathered wings crackled with electricity, the floor of the cell quaked, a white light flashed, a strange mist rose around its body, obscuring it from view, and—

'Argh!' Skandar jumped backwards, the pure joy of seeing his unicorn for the first time quickly turning to alarm. The unicorn's hooves were on fire; all four of them had just burst into flame. Skandar moved towards the unicorn to try to get the hoodie from underneath it, in the vain hope that he might be able to put out the fires. Was this supposed to happen? Or was he the only one with a spontaneously combusting unicorn? But as he started to pull on the corner of the hoodie, the unicorn opened its eyes.

Two things happened simultaneously as Skandar looked into those two dark eyes. He felt a balloon of happiness swell in his chest and a searing pain in his right hand. Breaking the unicorn's gaze, he raised his hand to his face in the dim light and saw that his wound was healing. But as it healed, the lines were lengthening, reaching the tip of each of his five fingers. At the same time, a thick white stripe was forming down the middle of the unicorn's black head. Their eyes stayed locked until the stripe had finished forming, and Skandar's hand had healed.

'Thanks?' Skandar said uncertainly, and the electricity, the quaking, the light, the mist and the fire all disappeared as though someone had flicked a switch. Boy and unicorn stared at each other. Skandar had read about the invisible bond between a rider and their unicorn, but he hadn't thought he'd be able to feel it: a tight pull in his chest, as though his heart strings were now connected elsewhere, outside himself. He was pretty sure that if you followed them, you'd find this little black unicorn's heart at the other end.

Then the unicorn broke the spell, letting out a tiny roar, but somehow Skandar wasn't afraid. Their bond made him feel safer than he'd felt in his life, like he'd opened the door to the cosiest room in the world and he could keep everyone else out and sit by the fire for as long as he wanted. He wanted to shout. To dance around the cell. To sing even. He wanted to roar like his unicorn, as it wobbled to its feet.

Skandar backed away in alarm. 'Are you sure you're ready for—' But the unicorn, *his* unicorn, was up and stumbling towards him. Skandar could have sworn it was already bigger; it almost reached his waist. He supposed the unicorns would grow a lot faster now they weren't cooped up inside their shells – they'd waited thirteen years, after all. The unicorn wobbled to a halt right in front of Skandar and gave a cry, its horn pointing directly at his hip. 'I don't know what you—' Skandar started to say, but then his gaze came to rest on his rucksack.

Keeping his eyes on the unicorn, Skandar unzipped the front pocket. Back home he'd grabbed a packet of Jelly Babies from Kenna's secret stash in her bedside table, just in case he got hungry on the journey. He fumbled with the packet, his newly healed wound still tender. The unicorn stepped closer and gave another shriek.

'All right, here you go,' Skandar breathed, taking out a red Jelly Baby and holding it flat on his good left palm. The unicorn sniffed, its nostrils expanding, and snatched the sweet out of his hand. The noise it made when it ate was a little unsettling. Like it was eating some*one* rather than some*thing*. It gave out growls of contentment as it chewed, so Skandar emptied a few more on to the floor and sat down on the chair to study his unicorn.

Its coat was completely black, except for the thick stripe of white starting below its horn, running between its eyes all the way down to its nose. Skandar knew for a fact – because he had once spent an entire week obsessing over a library book about unicorn colourings – that he had never seen a unicorn with a white blaze. Yet something about the mark seemed familiar.

Finished with its small supply of Jelly Babies, the unicorn headed straight for him again, its walking improving with every step. The president's words floated across his mind: *Unicorns, even when bonded, are fundamentally bloodthirsty creatures, with a preference for violence and destruction.* Maybe Mainland Skandar would have overthought his next move, asked his sister what to do, even tried to look it up in a book. But he was a rider now, and he felt proud of himself for maybe the first time in his life. And wasn't being a rider all about being brave?

So Skandar stretched out a hand and stroked his unicorn's neck, and as his skin came into contact with the unicorn, the strangest thing happened. Skandar found he knew his unicorn was male, and he knew his name: Scoundrel's Luck. Skandar loved it at once; it suited the little unicorn, but it also sounded like the unicorn names at the Chaos Cup. Like a name that could win one day.

Skandar continued to stroke the unicorn, who nickered softly, sounding a bit more like a horse. 'Nice to meet you, Scoundrel's Luck.' Skandar chuckled. 'How about Scoundrel for short?' The unicorn made a rumbling sound in its chest. Cautiously Skandar fed the unicorn another Jelly Baby from his hand, as he lifted the head collar over his horn and clicked the lead rope into place.

An ear-splitting human scream erupted nearby. At the noise,

Scoundrel's Luck screeched right into Skandar's ear, which didn't help matters, and started skittering all over the cell.

Another scream. Mind made up, Skandar pulled gently on Scoundrel's lead rope and urged him to walk towards the Hatchery cell door. He pushed against the bars and the door swung open for the boy and unicorn.

A third scream. Skandar followed the sound to a cell two doors down from his. 'Hello?' he said, his voice shaking a little. 'Are you hurt? Do you need help?'

There were three other children and three other unicorns already inside the hatching cell. The black-haired boy with glasses was holding on tightly to a blood-coloured unicorn. Skandar recognised Bobby too, with a light grey unicorn. The third rider was a girl with a cloud-like black afro, and she was backed into a corner by a shining silver unicorn. She had her head in her hands, sobbing between screams.

'Do you need help?' Skandar repeated more loudly, since nobody had looked away from the silver unicorn.

The boy with the glasses finally turned. He stared, open-mouthed, at Scoundrel's Luck. 'I think we do now,' he said, just as the girl in the corner looked up, pointed at Skandar's unicorn – and screamed even louder.

CHAPTER SEVEN

THE DEATH ELEMENT

Skandar took another tentative step into the hatching cell. The girl in the corner continued to scream – all four unicorns screeching along with the noise. The black-haired boy had frozen on the spot – still gaping at Scoundrel's Luck – while Bobby tried to calm her grey unicorn, its eyes red and rolling back in its head.

Skandar was very confused. This wasn't the kind of reaction he was used to when he walked into a room. People usually just ignored him.

'Can you shut up for a minute?' Bobby snapped at the screaming girl. 'I think my eardrums are going to burst!'

Bobby's eyes followed the girl's fearful gaze. She sighed. 'That's just Skandar. Sure, his name's more unfortunate than an elephant with diarrhoea, but he's not *scary*.'

'Oh, thanks,' Skandar spluttered. 'Nice introduction.'

Bobby shrugged. 'You're welco—'

'Quiet, both of you!' hissed the boy with the red unicorn.

'Flo's not pointing at him. She's pointing at his unicorn.'

Bobby frowned. 'Who's Flo?'

'*She's* Flo.' The boy pointed impatiently at the girl in the corner. 'And I'm Mitchell. But we don't exactly have time for polite introductions! There's an illegal unicorn standing right there, which must mean he –' Mitchell jabbed a finger at Skandar – 'is an illegal rider.'

Skandar was so shocked that he looked over his shoulder, just to check that there wasn't another rider and unicorn standing behind him.

Mitchell waved his arms about wildly, seeming even more enraged by their inaction. His minutes-old unicorn strained on its lead rope, trying to escape its rider's flapping. 'That's no ordinary blaze. It shows the unicorn is allied to *the fifth element.*' Mitchell's voice had dropped to a whisper.

Bobby narrowed her eyes at Mitchell. 'We might be Mainlanders, *Mitch*,' she said, 'but we do know there are *four* elements, not five. Everybody knows that.'

Mitchell ignored her. His eyes were flicking between Skandar and Scoundrel, as though he was deciding whether to make a run for it.

'There are officially four elements, you're right,' Flo said gently, her soft voice carrying in the awkward silence. She still looked terrified of Scoundrel's Luck, but at least she'd stopped screaming.

Bobby jutted her chin out at Mitchell. 'See.'

He shut his eyes and muttered something under his breath.

'But there used to be five. There *is* a fifth element,' Flo continued more bravely. 'Though we're not supposed to say that. Riders, I mean, or anyone on the Island. The Mainland don't know anything about it; it was banned before the Treaty and—'

'What's it called?' Bobby's eyes were hungry for the secret.

Flo looked anxiously around, as though she was worried somebody might be listening. 'Spirit.' It was barely a whisper.

'Flaming fireballs!' Mitchell hissed at Flo. 'Are you mad? Saying it out loud? In here – the most sacred place on the whole Island? We have to do something; we have to tell a sentinel about *him* – about *that*!' Mitchell jabbed a finger from Skandar to Scoundrel.

Skandar wasn't going to wait around to find out who or what a sentinel was. He'd just about had enough of being pointed at. He cleared his throat. 'If nobody needs help, then I'm going back to my hatching cell.'

'You can't go anywhere with him looking like that,' Flo said very quickly and quietly. 'They'll kill you both.' She gestured to Scoundrel's Luck, who was trying to bite the back of Skandar's trainer.

'What are you talking about?' Skandar said, shaking his head. 'He was only born about seven minutes ago! He hasn't done anything wrong. Maybe *I* have –' he tried to avoid Bobby's gaze – 'but not him. Scoundrel's Luck is just a baby. Look at him.' Scoundrel had started snapping his teeth at the shadows cast by a burning torch; his jaw clunked against the wall as he got too close.

'He. Has. A. Spirit. Wielder's. Blaze. On. His. Head!' Mitchell burst out, unable to contain himself any longer.

'Come again?' Bobby said, just as Skandar asked, 'What's a spirit wielder's blaze?'

'That white mark,' Mitchell said, exasperated. And in his effort to convince everyone, he pointed so close to Scoundrel's head that the unicorn tried to bite his finger. 'It's a sign that you two will be allied to the spirit element. You don't see it on Silver Blade.' Mitchell jabbed a finger at the silver unicorn. 'You don't see it on Red Night's Delight –' he pointed at his own blood-red unicorn – 'and you don't see it on this grey one either.'

'Her name is Falcon's Wrath,' Bobby said irritably. '*Grey one*, honestly.'

Flo crossed her arms and turned to Mitchell. 'That's not necessarily true. It might just be a mark.' She gestured to Skandar. 'He might wield a different element – not spirit at all.'

'Just a mark!' Mitchell spat. 'Are you willing to risk the safety of the entire Island on the off-chance it's *just a mark*?'

A flash of doubt swept over Flo's face, but she didn't uncross her arms.

Mitchell raged on. 'Did you miss the Chaos Cup last week? Or was it just me who saw the Weaver storm the arena on a wild unicorn and STEAL THE MOST POWERFUL UNICORN IN THE WORLD?'

'What does a mark on Scoundrel's head have to do with the Weaver?' Skandar asked slowly. 'What does any of this have to do with New-Age Frost going missing?'

'Forking thunderstorms!' Mitchell exclaimed. 'Do they teach you nothing on the Mainland? Did you not *see* the Weaver at the Chaos Cup?'

Skandar pictured Kenna and Dad standing with him in front of the TV and the face of the Weaver, the paint from hair to chin.

'The white stripe,' he murmured.

'It's the Weaver's sign,' Flo said. 'The Weaver is a spirit wielder.'

'But what's so bad about the spirit element?' Bobby huffed.

'The Weaver uses it to kill!' Mitchell's face contorted in frustration. 'Is that bad enough for you? Unicorns, riders – anyone in the way!'

'That can't be true,' Bobby scoffed. 'It isn't possible for a rider – for anyone – to kill a unicorn. Not even this Weaver person . . . thing.'

Skandar was nodding. 'That's right! We learned about it in our Hatchery lessons. That's why you need riders from the Mainland – because the wild unicorns can't be killed. And neither can the bonded—'

'Actually, there are two ways to kill a bonded unicorn,' Mitchell interrupted loudly. 'Kill their rider – and they die too. Or –' he swallowed – 'use a spirit wielder.'

There was silence.

'IT'S THE DEATH ELEMENT!' Mitchell half shouted.

Bobby now looked mildly concerned. 'So this Weaver maniac can use the death slash fifth slash spirit element *and* has the most powerful unicorn in the world?'

'Everyone's really scared,' Flo said, her brown eyes filling with tears.

'Okay, great,' Mitchell said sarcastically. 'Now we've all established how bad the fifth element is and that the Weaver is the greatest threat facing the Island and Mainland since forever, can we please report *this* spirit wielder to a sentinel?' Mitchell looked at Flo pleadingly.

'No,' Flo said stubbornly, Silver Blade snorting as if in agreement. Skandar saw her trying to hide how much the unicorn's sudden noise had made her jump.

'We have to! The unicorn's a danger; this Skandar character's a danger! He shouldn't have passed the exam! How did he even get here? Have you thought about that?'

Skandar could feel Bobby's eyes on him. She could mention the helicopter at any moment and make everything even worse. *Please*, he begged in his head. *Please, don't say anything.*

'It doesn't matter,' Flo said. 'He's here now. And I'm not going to be the one who sends them to their deaths. I couldn't live with myself.'

'But you hatched a silver,' Mitchell whined. 'You can't be mixed up in this! They won't let you in the Silver Circle if you help a spirit wielder.'

Fear flashed across Flo's face, but then she gathered herself. 'Skandar and Scoundrel's Luck haven't done anything to me. I'm not running to one of those masked guards. But you're right – I do have a silver unicorn. Do you really want to cross me, Mitchell? Make an enemy of me and Silver Blade at age thirteen?'

'No, I . . .' Mitchell tailed off, but he obviously couldn't help himself and carried on. 'But even if we don't tell a sentinel, everyone is going to see the blaze as soon he leaves the Hatchery. There's no way to hide it.'

'Actually, I think there is,' Skandar said, suddenly

remembering the jar Agatha had given him. He took it from his pocket and unscrewed the lid.

Mitchell stared as Skandar dipped a finger into the jar's black liquid and showed them his fingertip. 'Do you think this'll help?' he asked. 'To cover the blaze – for now? Until this is all worked out and I'm a fire wielder or an air wielder or something?' Skandar tried to keep his voice steady. If Agatha had known that he'd need this, what did that mean? And who even *was* Agatha anyway?

'Where did you get that?' Flo asked, confusion in her voice.

Skandar didn't know how to answer. He wasn't sure saying he enjoyed painting was going to cut it.

'Didn't you find that in our helicopter?' Bobby said, and gave Skandar the tiniest wink.

Mitchell stared at Bobby in disbelief, but before he could ask another question, he was knocked over by Red Night's Delight, who'd angered Falcon's Wrath by ripping out a chunk of her mane. Bored of their riders' discussions, the unicorns had started to cause havoc. Red, Falcon and Scoundrel were skittering about and shrieking all over the hatching cell, while Silver Blade stood imperiously in a corner and roared if the others got too close.

When Skandar and Bobby finally managed to catch Scoundrel's Luck, it turned out he did *not* like having his blaze touched. The whole operation wasn't helped by Mitchell just standing with his arms crossed, telling them they'd all be locked up for assisting a spirit wielder and it was the end of their riding careers, and probably their lives, because Skandar and/or his unicorn would kill them all in their beds.

'Mitchell, would you just shut up?' Bobby shouted, rubbing the last of the ink into the blaze. She had volunteered to get her hands covered in the stuff because she'd said it would be too suspicious if Skandar's were stained black. He'd tried to argue with her, but hadn't managed to get a word in edgeways.

Flo looked like she was swiftly regretting her decision and kept staring nervously around the hatching cell. She seemed very on edge again – her silver unicorn kept letting out low growls, making her yelp into her hand. Her eyes welled with tears every time she even looked at Silver Blade.

'Are you all right?' Skandar ventured. After all, Flo had been screaming *before* he'd arrived.

Flo had just opened her mouth to answer when they were interrupted by an almighty rumbling sound. The wall directly opposite the barred door was shaking violently.

What now? Skandar thought hopelessly. This hadn't exactly been the triumphant arrival to the Island he'd been dreaming of.

All four unicorns were skittering about in fear, the new riders struggling to keep hold of them as they shrieked and snorted, their sharp horns swinging dangerously in the enclosed space. It wasn't until sunlight seeped into the dark cell that Skandar understood: the wall was moving upwards. It was the way out.

As the wall disappeared completely, the screeching of forty-three newly hatched unicorns reached their ears. The sound was deafening, like the brakes of a thousand trains.

Over the din Mitchell was shouting, 'Just go! Move! We're in the wrong cell anyway. If we get going, they won't notice!' He disappeared into the dazzling sunlight with Red Night's Delight.

Skandar didn't have time to ask exactly *where* they were going, as Bobby hastily pressed the jar of ink into Skandar's hand.

'Just act normally and everything will be fine,' Flo said kindly, as she led her silver unicorn into the mid-morning sunshine. 'You can't even tell.'

'You coming or what?' Bobby asked Skandar, as she pulled Falcon's Wrath after Flo.

'Thanks, by the way,' he mumbled awkwardly. 'You know, for the helicopter thing.'

'Oh, stop.' Bobby rolled her eyes and punched Skandar on the arm. It reminded him of something Kenna might do, and made him feel a little less like everything was going wrong.

A line of young unicorns snaked ahead of Scoundrel. More guards in silver masks – Skandar had worked out that *these* were the sentinels – were largely failing to keep them all on the path. Something about being outside had reminded the unicorns that they were elemental creatures, full to the brim with a fresh supply of magic. Dust swirled in the air and mixed with sparks and explosions. Water sprayed from horns, hooves burned black marks into the grass, trees along the way fizzled with electricity, and craters cracked open in the path ahead. Riders yelped in pain as they found themselves caught in the elemental crossfire, clinging to lead ropes in desperation as their unicorns reared and bucked and swiped their horns through the air.

Scoundrel's Luck was no exception – the baby eating sweets in his hatching cell seemed long gone. As Skandar attempted to follow the line, Scoundrel tried to bite his fingers and kicked out at his leg. Flames lit up his tail and sparks landed and burned the back of Skandar's hands. Scoundrel's eyes were rolling between black and red and, like many of the other unicorns, he was frothing at the mouth. Skandar hoped this was a sign of excitement rather than the unicorn wanting to eat him. As if he could hear Skandar's thoughts, Scoundrel snapped his teeth dangerously close to his rider, grazing his hip with his incisors. Great – maybe the unicorn really *did* just want to eat him.

Skandar looked over his shoulder. Flo and Mitchell were walking their unicorns side by side along the path behind him, right at the back of the line. Bobby was ahead now, interrogating an Islander and leading Falcon beside her. Skandar couldn't help feeling left out, even though he knew that was probably the least of his problems right now. He'd hoped it would be different on the Island. He'd thought having a unicorn in common might help him make friends.

Instead, it seemed he and Scoundrel might be allied to an illegal element he'd never even heard of. Skandar swallowed down his disappointment, making himself concentrate on Scoundrel's Luck as he snapped at a low-flying bird. At least he had his unicorn – and the bond that made his heart feel twice as big.

As the line of unicorns ahead of him disappeared round a turn in the path, the smell of something rotten hit Skandar's nostrils. It smelled like a mixture of dead fish washed up on Margate beach and Dad's breath after he'd drunk too much beer.

Two yells pierced the air. 'HELP! HELP!'

Skandar turned Scoundrel as he recognised Mitchell and Flo's voices.

Between him and the two Islanders was an enormous wild unicorn.

The shock hit Skandar like a bucket of icy water. Time slammed to a halt. His brain kept short-circuiting: *run, freeze, scream, run, freeze, scream.* The wild unicorn was a monster. It blocked the path, swinging its giant head from side to side: mouth gaping, teeth sharp and jagged, breath rancid. Unlike Skandar's unicorn, its horn was ghostly – transparent. The wild unicorn was terribly thin, its bones visible under its dapple-grey coat. An open wound gaped on its flank, flies buzzing around the blood.

Flo and Mitchell's unicorns were squeaking fearfully, but – like their riders – they seemed unable to run. Skandar looked around wildly for a sentinel, but they had all passed the turn in the path ahead.

The wild unicorn let out an excruciatingly high-pitched shriek and fired electricity from its horn at a silver birch tree just to the left of Mitchell's arm. The tree's trunk and branches disintegrated, its leaves curling and dying before they'd even hit the ground. Flo screamed in terror, flinging her hands over her ears. Skandar didn't think that the wild unicorn would miss again. And if what he'd been taught about wild unicorn magic was true, then Mitchell and Flo's injuries would never heal – if they survived the attack at all.

The wild unicorn bellowed and the sound rattled through Skandar's ribcage. Wild unicorns were allied to all the elements, so there was no telling how it might attack next. The rotting grey monster lowered its deadly horn, pointing it straight at Flo and

Mitchell, and something in Skandar unfroze.

'Hey! Oi!' Skandar shouted and waved a hand in the air, the other firmly gripping Scoundrel's rope. 'Over here!'

He didn't know what made him do it. He had never been a brave person. Whenever Owen had demanded he hand over his lunch or his homework or a Chaos Card, he'd done it without putting up a fight. Kenna had always been the brave one. But Kenna wasn't here.

'What's he doing?' Mitchell whined, as the wild unicorn growled and turned towards Skandar instead.

Its eyes locked with Skandar's, and he was surprised by what he saw there. Anger – yes – but so much sadness too. It stopped snarling, green gunge dripping from its half-open mouth. Scoundrel let out a tiny snarl of his own as the wild unicorn searched Skandar's face, almost like it was looking for something. Skandar didn't think he'd ever seen a creature so lost. Then it reared on its back legs, flapped its tattered grey wings, and kicked out at the air in front of it, in front of Skandar. Scoundrel roared back, although his baby sound was swallowed up by the wild unicorn's bellow. Skandar didn't even think to duck. He just braced for impact.

But it never came. The wild unicorn's hooves hit the rocky path with a loud thump. Skandar opened his eyes just in time to see it turn and gallop away.

Skandar's legs began to shake all the way from his thighs to his ankles. He collapsed to the ground, drew his knees to his forehead and shut his eyes. A loud, anxious screech echoed above his head. 'All right, boy,' he muttered. 'I'll be up in just a—'

This didn't satisfy Scoundrel, who sniffed his rider's head before chewing on a clump of his hair.

Skandar winced, but the unicorn took absolutely no notice. 'Ow, that hurts a bit actually.'

Mitchell was murmuring frantically to himself somewhere above Skandar. 'A wild unicorn! On the path? Right there! I can't believe he did that. I can't believe a spirit wielder would— It doesn't make any sense.'

'You complete and utter idiot, Skandar!' Bobby's voice sounded distant, though still very cross. 'Can I not leave you alone for five minutes? Did you really just shout "oi" at a wild unicorn?'

'You know, Roberta—' Mitchell's voice was still shaky.

'Don't call me Roberta!' Bobby snapped.

'You know, *Bobby*,' Mitchell emphasised. 'I think that's the first sensible thing you've said since I met you.'

'And haven't the hours just flown by?' Bobby said sarcastically.

'Please be quiet!' Flo's voice was soft but insistent. There was an awkward pause, during which Skandar tried – and failed – to shake a little less obviously. 'Can't you see he's not okay?'

Skandar sensed the three of them lean a little closer. He opened his eyes.

'I'm al-al-all right,' he managed to say.

Flo crouched down, her face full of concern. Skandar could feel Silver Blade's warm breath on the back of his neck; it wasn't exactly making him feel calmer.

Mitchell shoved Flo out of the way. 'Get up!' he hissed. 'Get up before anyone sees!'

'I didn't do anything . . . did I?' Skandar asked, bewildered.

'Well, you must have done something! Why didn't it attack?' Mitchell was practically pulling his black hair out. He turned to Flo. 'I told you we should've turned him in! He's a spirit wielder; they're connected to the wild unicorns. Look at the Weaver—'

'Are you for real?' Bobby said, but Flo spoke across her.

'Instead of accusing him, Mitchell Henderson, maybe try thanking him?'

Mitchell looked aghast.

Flo had both hands on her hips. Silver Blade snorted round her elbow. 'We've barely said a nice word to him, and he just saved our lives. Or did you not notice that?'

'But—'

'I don't know about you,' Flo dropped her voice, 'but that means a lot more to me than some stupid prejudice against spirit wielders, just because one of them went bad.'

Mitchell bit his lip, looking anywhere but down at Skandar.

'Well, *Mitch*,' Bobby said, clearly enjoying herself. 'We're waiting.'

Mitchell scowled at her and took a deep breath. 'Thanks, I guess,' he murmured in Skandar's direction. 'For being stupid enough to risk your life and get that monster away from us.'

Flo sighed. 'Well, I suppose that'll do. And, Skandar, I think maybe you *should* actually get up. We might get in trouble for being so far behind.'

Flo and Bobby both reached down and pulled him to his feet. Before Skandar had even finished brushing off the dust from his jeans, Mitchell had marched off with his red unicorn.

'Charming,' Bobby said, shaking her head at his rapidly disappearing back.

'Urgh, it still reeks of that wild unicorn.' Skandar wrinkled his nose. 'Why are they like that? The rotting flesh, the smell, the –' something squelched under his trainer – 'gunge?'

Flo gazed sadly at the dead leaves where the tree had stood. 'For ever is too long for anything to really live. That's why the wild unicorns look the way they do. Why they're rotting away. Our unicorns get their immortal life spans compressed when they bond with us, but wild unicorns? Their lives are stretched out too long. So they're living but they're also dying – for ever. There's no escape. They can't even be killed by a *spirit wielder.*' She whispered the illegal words, shivering despite the June sunshine. 'All they think about is blood and murder. That's all they have. Some of them can't even fly any more.'

Skandar felt impossibly sad. Dying for ever sounded awful; no wonder the wild unicorn had seemed so lost. Then he remembered something that made him feel even worse.

'Mitchell said that spirit wielders have a connection to wild unicorns . . .' Skandar stopped, seeing the pained expression on Flo's face.

'I really don't know that much about the fifth element; we're not supposed—'

'Well, you definitely know more than us,' Bobby interrupted. 'So spill.' She put a hand on one hip, Falcon's rope in the other.

The conflict between breaking the rules and being fair to Skandar played across Flo's face. Finally, she screwed up her eyes and spoke very quickly under her breath. 'You saw the Chaos

Cup – the Weaver wasn't just *riding* a wild unicorn. The Weaver wielded that wild unicorn's magic, like they were bonded. And everyone says the Weaver used the fifth element to do it – please don't ask me how; I don't know,' she added nervously. 'The Weaver has been using the spirit element for evil since before we were born. That's why the Island decided it was too dangerous to be allowed. But I can tell my parents are really scared this time – all the adults are. They think the Weaver's planning something big.'

'So you're basically saying that if Skandar turns out to be a spirit wielder, everyone's going to think he's in on the Weaver's plan and best mates with all the rotting wild unicorns?' Bobby asked bluntly.

'That's exactly what I'm saying.' Flo swallowed. 'Anyway, let's stop talking about it. I don't like scary stuff, and the Weaver is about as creepy as you can get. I even find bonded unicorns a bit . . .' She cast a nervous glance at Silver Blade, who was snapping at flies.

Bobby rolled her eyes. 'Come on, we'd better catch up.'

Skandar and Scoundrel walked behind the others as they rejoined the line. And with every step along the rocky path, there was one thought in Skandar's head. *Please don't let me be a spirit wielder, please don't let me be a spirit wielder.*

CHAPTER EIGHT

THE EYRIE

'Look up!'

'Did you see that?'

'In the sky!'

Cries of excitement echoed along the line of riders. A winged shadow passed over Skandar's head and he too looked up. The sky was filled with unicorns: swooping and diving, shrieking and roaring to the babies below them. They were definitely bonded unicorns – their horns were coloured, unlike the wild unicorn Skandar had just met. He had to fight the urge to duck as the older unicorns flew lower and lower, as though they were daring each other downwards. Scoundrel, Falcon and the other baby unicorns had grown quickly – from the size of a large dog to a small pony in only a few hours – but they were still less than half the size of the older unicorns. The fearsome beasts flying above his head – combined with worries about the spirit element *inside* his head – meant Skandar was feeling very jumpy.

Then Skandar really did jump, as Falcon zapped Scoundrel with electricity from her horn. The black unicorn was forced to leap sideways, and Falcon walked serenely round a puddle on the path. The grey unicorn hadn't wanted to get her hooves wet! Bobby's brown hair skimmed her shoulders as she shook her head, exasperated. 'Unbelievable. I've ended up with a killer unicorn that doesn't like getting dirty.'

Skandar watched as Scoundrel's Luck stared at the unicorns above, his horn pointing up to the sky. His eyes flashed from red to black as they followed the unicorns flying above him; his tiny wings flapped as though he wanted to join the older creatures in the air.

'That might be a bit dangerous for you yet,' Skandar said, laughing. The unicorn showed what he thought of that by lifting his head and squirting water out of his horn, right into Skandar's eyes.

'Argh, seriously?' Skandar yelped, as Bobby howled with laughter.

Scoundrel flapped his wings and looked at his rider mischievously from under his eyelids. Skandar was beginning to think his unicorn had quite the sense of humour.

The line began to move again, but Skandar couldn't help looking up every few seconds, as more and more unicorns joined the display above his head. Some coasted in the light breeze, others played boisterously with each other, and still others fought in the air so elements exploded like fireworks.

Skandar was so busy looking at the sky that he barely noticed that they were climbing steadily up the side of a rocky hill until he found himself out of breath. As the uneven path snaked its way round the enormous mound, Skandar spotted the occasional fenced-off area – some had scorch marks scarring the grass, others had deep cracks in the earth itself, and in one the grass was waterlogged and greener than the rest. He couldn't work out what the grassy plateaus were, until he saw the hoof prints.

'Training areas?' he puffed to Scoundrel, as the unicorns in front came to a halt on the steep slope, their progress blocked by the most enormous tree Skandar had ever seen.

Its gnarled bark climbed up towards the sky, but it wasn't until Skandar tipped his head right back that he saw that the branches opened out into a vast canopy. The leaves weren't only green like he'd been expecting. They were a mixture of deep reds, cornfield yellows, emerald greens, sea blues – and in some places gleaming whites, poking through to break up the chorus of elemental colours.

Either side of the giant tree was a high wall, though Skandar couldn't actually see anything that resembled bricks underneath the tangle of extremely odd-looking plants and flowers. To the right of the tree the wall decoration reminded him of photos he'd seen of the Great Barrier Reef – the orange and pink plants looked exactly like the coral that grew there, at the bottom of the sea. To the left the wall was blanketed in moss and dark creepers, snails and giant slugs. Skandar even thought he could see the occasional vegetable poking out between brambles. What *was* this place?

Two silver-masked sentinels on unicorns guarded the giant tree. As the new riders surged closer to the trunk – their unicorns jostling each other, horns dangerously close to stomachs – one of the sentinels dismounted. She placed her palm on the trunk – the same gesture Skandar had used on the Hatchery door that morning. He gasped as a line of flame burned in a circle and a portion of bark swung back, leaving a space big enough for the new riders and their unicorns to walk through one at a time.

Skandar heard excited muttering from Mainlanders and Islanders alike. The young Islanders clearly hadn't been here before either, and Skandar felt glad they all seemed to be in the same boat for once.

'Welcome to the Eyrie.' Flo grinned as Skandar's head and then Scoundrel's horn came through to meet her on the other side of the entrance.

Skandar looked up and stopped dead. Nothing could have prepared him for this. The Tunnel of the Living had been something; the Hatchery chamber had *really* been something. But this? Of course he'd known a rider training school existed. And that it would probably be an improvement on a normal school – maybe with stables or unicorn statues or really nice food with unlimited mayonnaise. But he hadn't expected *anything* like this.

The Eyrie was a fortified forest: the trees had armour. Or that was what it looked like from the ground, as Skandar and Scoundrel made their way through the dark warren of trunks. Wood and metal collided – the natural with the man-made. Metal ladders cascaded from low-hanging branches, thick trunks supported treehouses that resembled iron fortresses – nothing like the wooden ones Skandar and Kenna had wished desperately for when they were little, along with a garden and a dad who'd want to build them one.

The treehouses had multiple levels built upwards into the high canopy in higgledy-piggledy towers. Some were stacked eight storeys high, others stretched so far back into the treeline that it was impossible to see where they started and ended. The treehouses were an explosion of grey in the sea of green, though many had brightly coloured graffiti on their walls: blue for water, red for fire, yellow for air and green for earth. Skandar tried not to wonder what colour the spirit element was linked to.

People were crowded on to bridges made from metal cables, connecting one treehouse to the next at every level. The bridges glinted in the early-afternoon sun as they swung between boughs. Everywhere he looked – on cable bridges, on platforms, at treehouse windows – young faces stared down at the new riders and their unicorns below, chattering, laughing and pointing.

Skandar inhaled the earthy fragrance of the forest; he could almost taste the freshness in the air. The view of the Island from the treehouses must have stretched for miles – the Eyrie's hill-home was the highest point Skandar could see, the trees perched on the crest like guardians. In the sky – just visible through the greenery above – unicorns soared, casting winged shadows. And Skandar knew that he'd never quite be able to capture the magic of it, even if he drew a thousand pictures in his sketchbook.

So despite everything – despite the Weaver, and the spirit element, and Scoundrel's hidden white blaze – Skandar smiled. 'You're not in Margate any more,' he murmured, trying to take it all in.

'Talking to yourself again, are you?' Bobby came up beside him with her grey unicorn, and Flo with her silver one. Shouts of 'Silver unicorn!', 'Look, a new silver!' and 'There she is!' came from the bridges suspended above them. And Skandar had to agree that Silver Blade was magnificent. He had never even imagined a unicorn of such a colour back on the Mainland: liquid metal, his horn like a lethal carving knife.

'So, um, what happens now? Lunch?' Skandar asked hopefully, his stomach rumbling. Scoundrel growled back at it suspiciously.

Flo laughed, but she was clearly bothered by all the attention. 'I'm not sure . . . We're walking the fault lines at sunset so I guess they might give us food before that—'

'We're going to find out our allied element today?' There was a wobble of worry in Bobby's voice.

Flo nodded and pointed through the trees ahead. 'The Divide is over there – where the fault lines meet. Can you see?'

Skandar squinted through the shadowy trunks as officials rolled a golden hoop into the centre of a grassy clearing. It thumped as they dropped it on to the hard ground and then moved it to the right, then a little to the left, until they were satisfied.

'The Eyrie was built around the Divide because it helps our unicorns access their full elemental potential,' Flo continued. 'It's sort of good because they teach us everything here. Elemental theory, sky-battle training, race etiquette, even stuff for if we win the Chaos Cup and become Commodore one day . . .' She tailed off as people called to her from a metal bridge, all waving red flags decorated with flames.

Skandar had read about 'the Walk' and he knew it involved a new rider and unicorn standing on the Divide, the place where the four fault lines – fractures in the fabric of the Island – met. The fault lines were fabled to be the source of the Island's magic, running across the Island and dividing it into four zones: fire, water, earth and air. The ceremony Flo was talking about would determine which element they would wield. Their 'best element', as Miss Buntress had put it in class. Skandar checked the ink on Scoundrel's blaze again – hopefully it would be enough to stop anyone else thinking he was a spirit wielder.

A young woman with cropped black hair, light olive skin and a welcoming smile approached the new riders and unicorns as they sheltered nervously among the trunks. As well as the gold spiral of her air pin, her yellow jacket was customised with patches of different textures, an intricate metal feather and five pairs of wings stitched on to its right sleeve. With relief, Skandar also noticed the wire basket full of sandwiches hooked under her arm.

'Hello! Hi! I'm Nina Kazama.' She waved to get everyone's attention. 'I'm in my final year of training here at the Eyrie – originally from the Mainland, like some of you.' She winked at nobody in particular. 'I'm going to be showing you to the stables so you and your little unicorns can rest before sunset. Follow me, Hatchlings!'

'Hatchlings?' Bobby asked indignantly.

'That's what we call riders in their first year at the Eyrie.' Nina beamed as she offered each rider a sandwich. 'Second years are Nestlings, third are Fledglings, fourth are Rookies and fifth years – that's me – are Predators, or Preds for short.'

'Oh, hello, Florence!' Nina gave Flo an awkward one-armed hug round Silver Blade, who was leaving a puddle of bubbling lava behind in every hoof print. The silver unicorn looked very affronted by the invasion of his personal space.

'Florence's dad is a saddler,' Nina explained to the Hatchlings nearest her. 'Shekoni Saddles – best in the business. Count my lucky lightning bolts every day that he chose me and Lightning's Mistake for one of his saddles.'

Flo somehow managed to look embarrassed and proud at the same time.

Nina started walking, gesturing for the Hatchlings to follow.

Skandar passed by Mitchell, who was moaning, 'Oh, Red, what are you doing?'

The unicorn was refusing to walk, and her head was tucked under one of her small wings, almost like a toddler putting their hands over their eyes to hide themselves.

Skandar had to hand it to Nina. She was about the most enthusiastic person he had ever met. As they weaved between the trunks, she didn't stop talking.

While Nina explained about the healer treehouses, one specialising in rider injuries and the other for unicorns, Bobby mumbled something about her being suspiciously cheerful. Skandar, however, was staring around in wonder as he polished off his second sandwich, very pleased to detect mayonnaise in the filling. Excitedly he listened to Nina pointing out the post trees – five fat-trunked trees labelled *Hatchling*, *Nestling*, *Fledgling*, *Rookie* and *Predator*, each one dotted with holes. He couldn't wait to write to Kenna.

'So we can write to our families on the Mainland?' someone asked.

Nina nodded. 'Though you mustn't reveal too much about the Hatchery or the Eyrie,' she warned. 'And definitely don't mention the Weaver. The Rider Liaison Officers get a bit funny about things like that.'

Skandar found himself walking beside a boy with blond curls and a pale white face. He looked very anxious, although his unicorn was behaving well enough. 'Are you from the Mainland too?' the boy asked.

Skandar nodded. 'I'm Skandar.'

'Albert.' The boy's smile only half worked. 'I'm not so sure about this place, you know. First the palm stabbing, next this sunset Walk in front of the whole Eyrie, and then there's the nomad thing.'

'What nomad thing?'

Albert dropped his voice, and Scoundrel hissed at the whispering. 'Apparently the instructors here can kick us out – at any time! – if they think we're not up to becoming a rider like the ones at the Chaos Cup. They can declare us a *nomad* and then we have to leave the Eyrie for ever. Just like that!'

'Are you sure?' Skandar couldn't believe he now had something else to worry about. So if he didn't get killed for being a spirit wielder, he still might get thrown out of the Eyrie?

'Don't worry about that.' Nina had overheard. 'No Hatchling will be declared a nomad just yet – the instructors want to give you a chance to prove yourselves. You haven't even walked the fault lines!'

'But –' Skandar couldn't help asking – 'what on earth do you do if you're bonded to a unicorn and you're not allowed to train at the Eyrie any more?'

Nina tried to reassure him. 'As a nomad, you'd learn another trade – one that requires a unicorn. And, of course, just like the Chaos Cup riders, as a nomad you'd be summoned to the Mainland once a year to recruit Mainlander riders. There are thousands of nomads, and they all lead fulfilling lives with their unicorns. It's not that bad!'

But Skandar didn't think Nina sounded entirely convinced.

Nina stopped abruptly by an arched opening in the Eyrie wall, and the riders all had to hang on to their unicorns' ropes to slow them down.

'This is the west door of the stables – between the fire and air quadrants. You'll notice that the wall to the right of the door has fire-based plants, more reds and browns, as well as plants from hotter places, like cacti. To the left you've got air-related stuff like long grasses and dandelions, more yellows like buttercups and sunflowers. Helps to let you know which elemental quadrant you're in if you get lost. There are four doors into the wall, and this is the one that's closest to the Hatchling stables. Come inside.'

Skandar was amazed as they followed her through the archway and into the Eyrie wall itself. The sound of unicorns echoed off the stone. All the hairs stood up on his arms, as though his body was telling him he was walking into a predator's den. Shrieks, rumbles, bellows, cries, whinnies – every sound Skandar had ever heard at the Chaos Cup and more besides. He felt a little shaky.

'Hatchling stables are just down here,' Nina said, leading the way. Lanterns shone softly above iron stables along the inner side of the wall, and unicorn horns of different colours stuck out over the doors, their occupants hissing menacingly at the newcomers as they passed.

Nina waved to a couple of riders as they bolted their unicorns' stables, chattering away as she walked. 'The unicorns are free to roam in the day – when they're not training. They like to fly over the wall and eat the grass and small animals on the rocky banks below the training school. It's good to remember they have their whole own thing going on – friendships, disagreements and worries. But this keeps them safe at night. If things got really bad, there'd only be four entrances to guard.'

'Safe from what?' Skandar asked nervously, though he could guess the answer.

'Wild unicorn stampedes, or even lone wild unicorns when they're really little. And then, of course, there's the Weaver.' Nina shivered. 'The Weaver's never managed to get inside the Eyrie to take any of the unicorns-in-training. There are sentinels stationed at the entrance, and they patrol all four walls. But who knows? The Weaver had never stolen the Chaos Cup winner before either.'

Nina fell silent for the first time since she'd handed out the sandwiches. 'Anyway, here we are.'

They'd reached a line of stable doors that were wide open, beds of straw set out inside. Each had an iron water trough and a feed bucket full to the brim with grisly looking meat. Scoundrel's Luck was making a frightening guttural sound in his throat and pulling on his rope, desperately trying to get into the nearest stable. He kicked out, and Skandar yelped as his fingers were hit with an electric charge. 'Ouch!'

Nina laughed. 'Aww, so cute! I forgot they do that when they're little. Lightning's Mistake prefers sizzling entire trees now.'

Skandar was puffing, trying to hold Scoundrel back from the bloody meat, and he could see Albert, Flo and Mitchell having similar trouble. 'Oh, gosh! Sorry!' Nina exclaimed. 'Go ahead, let them into any stable. Whether they're babies or fully grown, when they smell blood there's no stopping them.' Skandar let go of the rope just before Scoundrel pulled him into the stable wall.

'Best leave them alone while they're eating,' Nina said quickly to the Hatchlings. 'Shut the doors behind you. There are hammocks round the corner so you can have a rest before sunset too if you like. It's been a long day so far, am I right?' She waved goodbye cheerfully, making her way back along the line of stables.

'And it's not over yet,' Mitchell muttered, appearing at Skandar's shoulder as the other Hatchlings left their unicorns. 'We have a problem.'

'Come to turn him in, have you?' Bobby said, raising her eyebrows.

'No, I haven't,' Mitchell hissed at her. He spoke to Flo as she left Silver Blade and joined their anxious huddle. 'Have you thought about what's going to happen when Skandar steps into that circle?'

'Don't they just tell you which element you'll be best at and send you on your way?' Bobby cut in.

'Surely with the blaze hidden, we'll be okay?' Skandar said. 'Why would they assign me an illegal element?'

'Argh – *Mainlanders*! They don't *choose* an element for you.' Mitchell clenched his jaw as though he was trying not to shout. 'Flo? The Walk? Have you thought about it?'

'I – well, I don't know,' Flo said, sounding worried. 'Is it different for – for people like Skandar?'

'*Of course* it is.' Mitchell groaned. 'My father was just chosen for the new Commodore's Council of Seven, so he has lots of inside knowledge. He happens to have explained to me *with relish* how no wielder of the fifth element could step on to the Divide unnoticed.' Mitchell paused dramatically. 'The four fault lines ignite at once. Boom!'

The other three all looked at Skandar, who busied himself stroking Scoundrel's black neck over the stable door. He didn't trust himself to speak. He didn't know how cracks in the ground could possibly 'ignite' – but however it happened, 'boom!' didn't sound very subtle.

'He might not be a spirit wielder,' Flo said timidly. 'You don't—'

'He's a spirit wielder,' Mitchell interrupted. 'The white blaze is evidence enough, but what happened with that wild unicorn makes it undeniable. As soon as Skandar steps on to the Divide at sunset, those lines are going to go up like a beacon so—'

'I thought you didn't want anything to do with me,' Skandar said bluntly.

'Skandar, he's trying to help—' Flo started, her expression pinched and upset.

'Wh-what? I'm not *helping* him, I'm just pointing out; well . . .'
Mitchell blustered.

Skandar sighed. 'I know you're all worried about getting
into trouble. You really don't have to help me, okay? Seriously,
I'm not your problem.' Skandar knew he needed all the help he
could get; Flo's warning from the Hatchery was still ringing in
his ears – *they'll kill you both*. But he didn't want them getting into
trouble because of him. The image of Agatha and Swan lying
unmoving on the beach flashed across his mind.

Gathering himself, Mitchell took a menacing step towards
Skandar, though the effect was kind of ruined by his blood-red
unicorn burping a smoke ring over her stable door.

'Oh no you don't!' he said, grimacing. 'Don't you try to keep
the upper hand. You saved my life, and I don't want to owe a
spirit wielder anything. I'm helping you and that abomination –'
he pointed at the black unicorn – 'through the Walk, but then
we'll be even, do you hear me? No debt between us. Finished.
Over.'

'That's fine with me,' Skandar said quietly. 'But I don't see
how – if I *am* a spirit wielder – we're going to hide this igniting
thing you keep going on about.'

Mitchell raised both black eyebrows. 'We're not going to hide
it,' he said. 'We're going to cause a distraction.'

Bobby snapped her head up. 'What do you mean *we*?'

CHAPTER NINE

THE FAULT LINES

Mitchell's plan was not a good one. But unfortunately it was the only one they had. As the other riders snoozed in their hammocks or chattered nervously about which element they'd be allied to, Mitchell whispered frantic instructions and Skandar tried not to throw up.

Just before sunset, the riders led their unicorns into the Eyrie's clearing. The golden ring shone on the Divide at its centre, marking the place where the four fault lines met. Officials buzzed around making sure head collars were properly fastened and lead ropes secured. Skandar watched nauseously, as a group of spectators unrolled a green flag that said EARTH WIELDERS ROCK over the side of a bridge.

All he could do was hope that the three young riders – whom he'd met only hours before – could cause enough of a distraction to shield him and Scoundrel from arrest and almost certain death. Part of him still hoped it wasn't true – that there was no such thing as the spirit element – but something about the concern in Flo's face and the grim resolve in Mitchell's as the four of them had separated had made his heart sink. And then, of course, there were Agatha's words: *Forget what you've been taught; the rules don't apply to you.* Had she known he was a spirit wielder? Was that what she'd meant by 'special'? Why had she brought him?

Skandar couldn't see Mitchell or Bobby any more, their unicorns blending in with the other newborns. But he couldn't miss Flo, with Silver Blade blindingly bright in the sunset's embers. Bells started to ring. Skandar looked up at the sound, and realised that the bells were in the trees, hanging from branches above the treehouses.

Moments later, Aspen McGrath marched into the clearing in a golden cloak embroidered with blue thread, like rivers running through gilded fields. As the winner of the Chaos Cup, she was the new Commodore of Chaos, the official head of the Island.

Whispering erupted around the clearing, as well as up in the trees. Skandar wondered if the Commodore would usually ride into the Eyrie on a unicorn, if she should have been sitting proudly astride New-Age Frost – the unicorn the Weaver had stolen. Despite his scarf, he felt the hairs on the back of his neck stand up. If he was a spirit wielder like the Weaver, what would Aspen McGrath do to him if she found out? To Scoundrel's Luck?

Officials lowered a metal platform from a tree to Skandar's right and Aspen stepped deftly on to it, not even putting out a hand for balance as it was hoisted higher.

Aspen McGrath's voice was clear when she spoke, despite the

unmistakable strain etched into the lines of her pale freckled face. Skandar thought she looked like a completely different rider from the one who'd passed under the finishing arch only days ago; it was impossible to imagine that look of triumph now.

'As new Commodore of Chaos, it is my great pleasure to welcome all you new riders and unicorns fresh from the Hatchery. I especially welcome the Mainlanders among you for having the bravery to accept the call of a place you have never visited, to a way of life you can only have imagined.' There was a lukewarm round of applause.

Aspen continued, spreading her arms wide. 'These new riders have many obstacles before them and much to learn. This is a –' she paused to find the word – '*challenging* time for the Island. We all have a responsibility to root out the evil that showed itself again only last week, and took –' she swallowed – 'and *stole* New-Age Frost from us.'

There were scattered shouts of agreement from the bridges and treehouses. Skandar felt like his heart was beating at ten times its normal speed.

There was raw emotion in Aspen's voice as she spoke. 'Many of us have become complacent in the fifteen years since the Weaver bonded to a wild unicorn and cut short twenty-four innocent lives. Since the deaths of those unicorns, the Weaver has hidden away in the Wilderness like a villain in a fairy story, hovering on the edge of myth and reality. Children might have whispered to each other that they saw a black shroud, a rider at the rear of a wild unicorn stampede. Murmured about unusual disappearances and unexplained deaths. But did any of us really believe? And if we did, did any of us truly fear the Weaver, more than we did the wild unicorns?' Aspen slammed her fist against the metal cable holding up the platform, the sound reverberating through the clearing.

'But there will be no more pretending, no more closing our eyes to the danger. The Weaver has come out of hiding and so must we. I vow to you as your Commodore, in this special place, this place all us riders call home despite our different elemental allegiances. I vow that I will hunt down the Weaver and bring New-Age Frost home. Whatever the Weaver is planning, I will fight it to my very last breath. I will fight it as fiercely as the bond still sears in my chest. The death element has allowed the Weaver to torment this island for too long. Will you help me protect the Island? Will you help me hunt down the Weaver and crush the death element for good?'

Cheering and applause erupted from every tree and the shrieks of unicorns bounced off the walls of the Eyrie. Skandar couldn't bring himself to join in. With the bone-rattling sound of the crowd stamping their feet in approval, the Eyrie suddenly felt like a cage filled with predators – and he and Scoundrel's Luck were the prey.

'But why do I choose the Walk as the time to tell you all this?' Aspen continued, strands of her red hair blowing about in the breeze. 'It is because I want you new riders to remember that in time, with training, you will have power beyond your wildest dreams. You are privileged to hold at the end of your ropes the most fearsome beasts this world has ever known, creatures that can bend the very elements to their will. You share in that power, and all that I ask of you is that you use that power for good.'

Skandar was sure he felt the weight of those words more heavily than any other rider. If he really was a spirit wielder, like the Weaver, would that mean it was impossible to use his and Scoundrel's power for good? Would it make him into a monster too?

The bells were ringing again and four people emerged from the crowd, settling themselves at the ends of the cracks in the ground at four equal points from the gold circlet of the Divide. Each wore a different coloured cloak: red, blue, yellow or green.

Two silver-masked sentinels escorted the first rider and her nut-brown unicorn to the edge of the gold circle. Aspen called their names: 'Amber Fairfax and Whirlwind Thief.' It was the girl who'd sneered at Skandar's scarf back in the Hatchery. She looked very confident standing there in front of all the other riders, waving at someone in the crowd. A bell rang out sharply, and Amber led Whirlwind Thief on to the Divide.

It happened almost immediately. Lightning crackled and sparked down a fault line on one side of the Divide. Like writhing snakes, tendrils of electricity wrapped themselves round gusts of wind as they exploded out of the ground, the long grass blowing this way and that. The lightning gusts picked up debris as the howling grew louder and miniature tornadoes swept up and down the fault line. Amber didn't look so relaxed now, but Skandar watched as she vaulted on to her unicorn's back and encouraged Whirlwind Thief out of the safety of the gold circle. What was she doing?

Amber braced herself against the tornadoes, her back bent

low, but Skandar saw her laugh out loud as she realised the wind wasn't touching her at all. Amber and Whirlwind Thief reached the yellow cloaked figure at the other end of the line, who congratulated Amber and handed her a gold pin. Huge cheers exploded from a group of riders on a bridge between two trees. They waved yellow flags – displaying the spiral symbol of the air element – in celebration.

Skandar felt sick to his stomach. This? *This* was the famous Walk? Aside from the very alarming detail that they were expected to actually *ride* their unicorns down a fault line, what on earth was going to happen when he and Scoundrel stepped into that golden circle? How would any distraction be big enough to cover up *all four* fault lines igniting like the air line had for Amber? Mitchell's plan was never going to work.

The more riders he watched walk the fault lines, the worse Skandar felt. And it wasn't just that he was terrified of being found out – he felt jealous of the other new riders too. He wanted to be normal. He wanted to be an air, water, earth or fire wielder. But instead, here he was worrying about the spirit element – an element he hadn't even known existed, an element that the Commodore of the Island wanted to root out and destroy.

It wasn't long before Aspen McGrath called, 'Mitchell Henderson and Red Night's Delight.' Almost as soon as the boy and his unicorn stepped on to the Divide, the fire line ignited. Two roaring waves of fire rose up out of the crack in the earth and crested, forming a long tunnel of flame along the fault line. Mitchell and his red unicorn were barely visible through the inferno, until – all at once – he emerged, coughing, shrouded in smoke. He slipped clumsily down from his unicorn's back and the red-cloaked official handed him a fire pin. There was a roar of triumph from the fire wielders in the crowd and a waving of red flags. Skandar thought that an allegiance to the fire element was about right for Mitchell. His anger at Skandar seemed to flare up quick and hot, out of control – like flames in a dry forest.

After Kobi Clarke joined the water wielders with his unicorn, Ice Prince, it was Flo's turn.

A hush went through the crowd. Even Aspen McGrath's voice sounded slightly awed. 'Florence Shekoni and Silver Blade.'

'I heard she didn't even want to try the door,' a girl standing near Skandar was saying to the sandy-haired boy next to her. Her long black hair fell in curtains on either side of her light brown face, so it was difficult to see her expression, but Skandar noticed the flames of her fire pin already pinned to her chest.

'Her dad's that famous saddler. I heard she wanted to stay apprenticed to him,' the sallow-faced boy said.

'And then she gets a silver unicorn. Unbelievable,' she replied. 'First one in years as well.'

'Look, Meiyi.' The boy tutted and pointed across the clearing. 'She can barely manage him.'

Skandar stopped listening and looked over to the Divide. Flo was struggling with Silver Blade, his hooves catching fire as she pulled him inside the gold ring.

The ground quaked beneath Skandar's feet, making everything blurry. A few smaller trees toppled over, throwing up earth. Someone screamed – none of the other Walks had caused disruption outside the fault lines. Flo scrambled up on to

Silver Blade's back, holding his silver mane for dear life. Soil and rock exploded out of the earth line on all sides as she galloped along it. Flo jumped from Blade's back as quickly as she could once she reached the man in the green cloak. As he passed over her gold earth pin, he wiped tears from his cheeks.

Conversations erupted all around Skandar.

'Has there been an earth-allied silver before?'

'So unusual!'

'Did you feel the power of that magic? It's great news – especially with the Weaver gaining strength.'

The number of riders waiting to walk the fault lines was rapidly decreasing. And then finally – inevitably – it was Skandar's turn. As Aspen called his name he felt as though the whole clearing was holding its breath; even the leaves paused their rustling. Skandar hurriedly checked that Scoundrel's blaze was still completely covered, as the sentinels came to escort him to the Divide. He'd never felt so afraid: for himself, for Scoundrel, for Bobby, for Flo. Even for Mitchell. How much trouble would they be in if someone realised they'd helped a spirit wielder get into the Eyrie? Every step Skandar took was harder than the last, as his feet carried him closer to the fault lines that would expose his true elemental allegiance.

Skandar hovered outside the gold ring, waiting for the signal he'd agreed with the others. His heart was beating so fast that he thought even Aspen up on her platform might be able to hear it. The sun had gone down, but even in the gloom he could feel eyes on him from every treehouse, every window, every bridge. It was taking too long. Maybe Mitchell had bottled out? Maybe after Aspen's speech about the Weaver he'd decided it wasn't worth it? Maybe Flo and Bobby had taken Mitchell's side?

'Come on, Scoundrel,' Skandar murmured. 'Let's just get it over with.'

An ear-splitting scream pierced the air. Flo's voice was high-pitched and terrified. 'The Weaver! The Weaver's taken Silver Blade. Please, help!' Aspen McGrath vaulted down from her platform, sprinting over to Flo, Mitchell and Red Night's Delight. Bobby was nowhere to be seen. Mitchell was bellowing. 'Help! The silver unicorn is missing! Stop the Weaver now!' *Stop the Weaver* were the words Skandar had been waiting for.

Just as they'd planned, there was immediate and absolute pandemonium. Hatchling unicorns around the fault lines blasted elements into the dark clearing – sparks and smoke and debris swirling – as their riders pulled them in all directions, desperately trying to run away from the threat of the Weaver. Screaming and shouting erupted from the bridges and platforms in the Eyrie's trees and anyone who wasn't running for cover or panicking had their faces turned towards Flo and Mitchell.

Amid the mayhem, Skandar tugged a little on Scoundrel's rope, lifted a foot and stepped into the golden ring.

All four fault lines exploded to life at once, just as Mitchell had warned. Flames roaring, waves crashing, a hurricane building, the earth shaking. Skandar barely had time to notice the white glow from the ground under his feet before launching himself on to his black unicorn's back. It wasn't easy, even though Scoundrel was a lot smaller than Arctic Swansong – and he balanced precariously on his stomach before eventually managing to swing his leg over the unicorn's back.

Scoundrel slashed his horn through the air, turning his head this way and that, so Skandar had to try to grip with his knees. Scoundrel didn't seem to know what to do with his wings – the two lumps of feathered muscle kept banging into his rider's feet. But they couldn't stay within the circle; the white light was growing brighter beneath them.

Skandar plunged his hands deep into his unicorn's black mane and held on as tightly as he could. Having watched some of the other riders do the same, he pressed his feet into Scoundrel's sides so the unicorn careered out on to the water line. Water made the most sense to Skandar of all the elements: he'd grown up by the sea, he'd rather get a bit wet than electrocuted or scorched by fire or swallowed up by the earth, and – if Dad was to be believed – water had been his mum's favourite element.

As soon as Skandar was off the Divide, the other three fault lines ceased their magic, making Skandar look exactly like any other water wielder. But Scoundrel was not going with the plan. He was no fool – he knew they weren't water-allied. He tried to turn on the line, the waves breaking and splashing around them so they were soaked to the skin.

'Please, boy,' Skandar begged, putting his wounded palm against the unicorn's damp neck. 'You've got to trust me.' Scoundrel's Luck seemed to understand – he stopped trying to turn and hardly flinched as waves crashed over them, threatening to wash them from the line.

Halfway along, Skandar noticed that the woman in the blue cloak hadn't joined the rest of the riders in their search for Silver

Blade and the Weaver. She was turned away – watching Aspen with Flo and Mitchell – but she hadn't moved from her position at the end of the water line, still ready to give her next water pin. Skandar felt a jolt of fear – he and Scoundrel were wet through, and if they'd truly been water-allied the waves wouldn't have touched them.

As Scoundrel approached the blue-cloaked figure, Skandar was desperately trying to come up with an excuse for being drenched, but his mind was jammed with fear and exhaustion. He couldn't even see Scoundrel's head to check if the ink had washed off. Surely they hadn't gone through all that for nothing? Mitchell's plan had actually worked, but now was he going to lose everything just because they'd got wet?

Then, by some miracle, Skandar felt his legs grow warm as Scoundrel became hotter and steam began to rise off the unicorn's back.

'Clever boy!' Skandar whispered. Scoundrel was drying them both! He pressed the sleeves of his wet hoodie against the unicorn's hot skin, ran his warm fingers through his hair, put his face in the steam—

'Dismount!' the blue-cloaked woman commanded as Scoundrel reached her. She had short silvery grey hair styled into spikes as sharp as her voice. 'Quickly! I don't want to alarm you but there's a chance the Weaver has breached the Eyrie.'

Skandar tried to look very alarmed.

'You're burning up.' The woman frowned at him with startlingly blue eyes. They swirled dangerously, like whirlpools. 'And so is your unicorn.'

'Umm, yes,' Skandar mumbled. 'I think we just galloped quite fast down the line.'

'Well, yes, it is very exciting that you and Scoundrel's Luck are water-allied. What a year for a rider to become a water wielder.'

She looked over her shoulder at the pandemonium in the clearing, and then spoke very fast. 'I am the water instructor here at the Eyrie, and oversee water-element training for all Hatchlings. Now you've been identified as a water wielder, you will answer to me. Is that clear? You may call me Instructor O'Sullivan.'

'Yes, Instructor.' Skandar met her piercing gaze. He couldn't believe Mitchell's plan had worked! He could barely keep a smile off his face.

'Your pin,' she said abruptly, dropping a gold object into his outstretched hand. 'Wear it with pride. Now I must go and help . . . My goodness!'

A silver unicorn galloped towards his rider, a trail of fire blazing behind him, the ground of the clearing cracking underneath his hooves. People cried out with relief, and some even started clapping as Silver Blade flapped his wings and came to a sharp halt in front of Flo.

'False alarm.' Instructor O'Sullivan sounded relieved as she watched Flo throw her arms round Blade's silver neck – probably, Skandar thought, to hide the fact she wasn't actually crying.

Aspen McGrath was now back up on her platform. 'An understandable reaction given recent events; can't be too careful. Now let's get back to it. There can't be many to go. Roberta Bruna and Falcon's Wrath!'

'We did it, boy!' Skandar whispered into Scoundrel's black ear.

He held out the water droplet pin, and Scoundrel sniffed, then tried to snatch it with his teeth. Skandar chuckled with relief.

Falcon's Wrath was calm and collected stepping on to the air line, the onslaught of forked lightning and gale-force winds barely making her blink. But Skandar didn't pay much attention to Bobby's Walk; he was distracted by the smarting of his Hatchery wound against the gold pin. Skandar counted the lines: one up each of his five fingers. He held his palm up to his face. Five lines. This was one place they couldn't hide the spirit element.

'Hmm,' said a voice very close to Skandar's left ear, making him jump. 'Turns out the Weaver didn't steal Blade after all. Who'd have thunk it?'

Skandar grinned at Bobby. But the smile dropped from his face when he saw the welts up and down her bare forearms.

'Was that Silver Blade?' he whispered, horrified.

'Burned me, didn't he? The monster.' Skandar didn't think she sounded upset at all. 'I could barely hold him. I thought you were never going to get Scoundrel down that fault line. I'd rather have Falcon any day; even if she is just boring grey, rather than oh-so-exciting silver.'

But Skandar felt terrible. 'I'm so sorry, Bobby. I'm sorry about getting you involved in all of this. It's not like you asked to be standing behind me in the Hatchery line.'

'Jeez. Calm down, will you? They're just burns. They'll heal.'

When Skandar looked gloomily at the ground, Bobby whacked him – far too hard – on the back. 'Being friends with you is certainly going to keep things interesting around here. I say, keep it up.'

'Are we friends?' Skandar asked her, completely taken by surprise.

'Look, just cheer up and put your pin on, will you? I can't bear to look at your miserable face any more.' But Bobby grinned at him.

Skandar uncurled his fingers and fastened the gold pin to his black hoodie. At least he looked like he belonged, even if nothing was further from the truth.

And one friend was a whole lot better than the none he'd had on the Mainland.

The Walk was over and night had truly fallen. Only the Hatchlings were left in the clearing. The older riders had disappeared into their treehouses, while the Commodore had left the Eyrie accompanied by the ringing of bells.

The four instructors – each still wearing an elemental cloak – stepped on to Aspen's platform, their shadows dancing in the lantern light. Instructor O'Sullivan clapped for silence; Skandar noticed a long angry scar shining on her neck.

'We have one last thing to ask of you before you get into your hammocks for a well-earned rest,' she boomed. Many of the young unicorns were messing about on their ropes, baring sharp teeth at each other and flapping their wings aggressively.

Instructor O'Sullivan ignored the chaos. 'You may have walked different fault lines; you may be wearing different pins. But here at the Eyrie you train in all four elements. Your allied element will always be your strongest, your focus. However, the most successful riders are those who develop skills in all four. We have found that the best way for riders to share that knowledge is to live together in quartets – one rider allied to each element, sharing a single treehouse.'

The Hatchlings began to whisper and edge towards their friends. Instructor O'Sullivan held a hand up for quiet. 'I know many of you – especially the Mainlanders – have only just met. But this is your chance to make lasting friendships with wielders of different elements. Choose wisely. You have five minutes to form your quartets.'

Skandar felt like he was back at school, standing on the edge of a freezing football pitch and waiting to be picked for a team. He'd never been awful at sports, but he'd always been unpopular, and he wasn't tall or muscly enough to cancel that out. Bobby had said they were friends, but did that stretch to living in a treehouse together? He wanted Kenna here so badly – she would have broken all the rules just so they could be together.

'Skandar! Hello? Anyone in there? Honestly, it's like talking to an armoured tree.' Bobby's voice reached his ears.

'Oh.' Skandar turned to see Bobby with Falcon, and Flo with Blade, beside him.

'We were wondering if you wanted to be in our quartet?' Flo asked timidly.

Skandar had a horrible feeling they were teasing him. That this was some kind of joke.

But Flo hurried on. 'It's just . . . I'm earth, Bobby's air, and you're—'

'Pretending to be water,' Skandar finished, completely stunned. 'Wouldn't you rather be with somebody else?' He desperately wanted to be in their quartet, but he didn't want them asking just because they felt sorry for him.

Flo said, 'Not really.'

Bobby laughed. 'Oh, *Flo's* had plenty of offers, don't you worry! I tell you, it's been an absolute nightmare fighting them off. *"Please, Florence Shekoni, will you be in our quartet? It'd mean the world to us, Flo. A silver unicorn in our quartet would be everything."'*

'Don't,' Flo said quietly. 'I don't like everyone staring at me.'

Skandar couldn't believe it. They'd chosen him – an illegal spirit wielder – over all the real water wielders. He tried to hide his grin; this would never have happened on the Mainland.

Bobby was all business. 'Now we just need to find a fire wielder. Although we could just try to wing it and see if we end up as a three? There's an odd number of riders here; we'd have more treehouse space!' she said excitedly, adding, 'I snore, so it's in your interests, Flo. You can share with Skandar if it gets too loud. My parents say I sound like a pot-bellied pig.'

Skandar laughed. He liked how Bobby didn't seem to care what anyone thought of her. He'd have never admitted to snoring, let alone sounding like a pig.

'There must be a spare fire wielder somewhere,' Flo mumbled, squinting at a nearby group. 'We should at least try to find someone else, since the instructor told us to.'

Bobby rolled her eyes. 'Do you always do what you're told?'

A frown knitted into Flo's dark brown forehead. 'Yes. Don't you?'

'Well, it'll have to be me, won't it?' Mitchell Henderson emerged from the shadow of a tree with Red Night's Delight.

'Oh, great, it's the angry one who thinks you're going to bring about the end of the world,' Bobby whispered very loudly to Skandar.

'I thought you hated me?' Skandar asked, open-mouthed.

'I can't say I'm particularly excited about the idea of sharing a treehouse with – with – someone like *you*,' Mitchell said, 'but logically it's the only option. If a different fire wielder joins your quartet, how will you hide your secret from them? And then we'll all get thrown in prison for helping you into the Eyrie.'

'He's not wrong,' Bobby said. 'Annoyingly.'

Mitchell sighed, looking extremely pained. 'It's the only way.' And as if to emphasise the point, Red let out a long loud fart, ignited her back hoof, then kicked her leg up to set the fart on fire.

The four riders were still coughing and spluttering through stinking smoke when the red-cloaked instructor approached.

'Nothing like a bit of flaming flatulence on a summer evening,' the instructor said, chuckling. 'Ah, excellent. So we have Florence, earth; Roberta, air –' Bobby made a face – 'Mitchell's one of my fire wielders, and Skandar's a water wielder, I believe. A complete quartet!'

As the smoke cleared, Skandar noticed the instructor's ears. Flames danced around their outer edges.

'That's a seriously impressive mutation, Instructor Anderson,' Bobby said in an awed voice.

In his Hatchery lessons, Skandar had learned all about riders mutating. During their training, part of a rider's appearance changed for good, becoming a bit more, well, magical. Skandar thought it was almost as though the unicorns were giving riders their very own elemental gift – something to say, 'this is *my* rider' – since, unlike the bond, mutations were visible. He and Kenna had spent hours and hours imagining what would happen to them if they became riders.

Instructor Anderson laughed and the flames flickered playfully against the black skin of his bald head. 'I don't like to boast, but the *Hatchery Herald* did feature me on their front page when I mutated. Must have been a slow week for news.' He winked. Then, with a flourish, he produced a map from inside his cloak. 'Now, your quartet's treehouse will be . . . Ah yes. From the west door you'll find it seven ladders up, four bridges across, second platform to your right. Easy!'

Skandar was about to ask Instructor Anderson to repeat it again but he'd already swept away to the next group of four, his red cloak billowing out behind him.

The new quartet led their unicorns back through the west door of the stables. The unicorns were much quieter now; most were snoozing and snoring – there was only the odd shriek or growl as Skandar and Scoundrel passed. Skandar noticed a makeshift sign fixed to the outside of a stable door. SCOUNDREL'S LUCK, it read, with a scribbled water symbol underneath. Seeing it made Skandar feel even worse – he couldn't help but wonder what the symbol would have been for spirit.

Mitchell led Red Night's Delight into the stable right next door.

'Looks like we're neighbours,' Skandar called to him, trying to make an effort. If they were going to be in the same quartet, surely Mitchell couldn't hate him for ever?

But Mitchell completely ignored him. He bolted Red's stable door and stalked away without a word.

'What a day,' Flo breathed, as she came to lean over Scoundrel's stable door. 'I feel like I haven't even had a chance to meet you properly.' She held out a hand. 'Hello, I'm Flo. It's great to meet you. And there's absolutely nothing unusual about my unicorn.'

Skandar shook her hand over the door. 'Hello, Flo. I'm Skandar, and there's absolutely nothing unusual about my unicorn either. Nothing illegal to see here.'

She grinned. 'Does your family call you Skandar? Or do you have a nickname? Skandar sounds quite . . . epic?'

'My sister, Kenna, calls me Skar,' he replied. Even saying her name made him miss her. He'd send her a letter as soon as he worked out how.

'Can I call you Skar?' Flo asked tentatively.

Skandar smiled at her. 'Sure.'

'I'm sorry about the way Mitchell's being to you.'

Skandar sighed. 'I think he really hates me.'

'I'm sure he doesn't hate you!' Flo said encouragingly. 'It's classic fire wielder stuff; the saying goes that they're quick to judge and flare up in anger. He hates the idea of you, that's all.'

Skandar choked out a laugh. 'Well, that makes me feel loads better.'

Flo looked troubled. 'Oh dear. It really was meant to help! You see, his dad's on Aspen's Council of Seven – he's one of the water wielders the Commodore trusts the most. And you heard Aspen, her every act this year is going to be about finding the Weaver, getting New-Age Frost back and destroying the fifth element. Mitchell's dad must believe in all that – must really hate spirit wielders – or he wouldn't have made it on to the Council. It would be hard for Mitchell to unlearn all that in a few hours, just because he'd met you.'

'You don't hate spirit wielders, though, do you?' Skandar asked hopefully.

'My mum and dad, well, they believe in giving everyone a chance. And so do I. My dad says that fairness is something a lot of earth wielders are known for. Finding out Silver Blade and I are earth-allied was the only part of this whole day that's made any sense. I just wish Blade was a bit less, well, scary.'

'Thanks, Flo,' Skandar breathed. 'And don't worry about Silver Blade – you hardly know him yet. He'll calm down.'

'I hope so,' she murmured. 'Are you coming to see the treehouse?'

Skandar hesitated. For some reason he didn't feel ready just yet. He'd lived in a high-rise flat all his life, in the middle of a Mainland town. He'd never even had his own stairs. This was the first time he would live in a house, in a place where the stars were framed by trees not buildings. Never mind the unicorns – that was overwhelming by itself. And somehow with the spirit element, and the Weaver, and Mitchell and all the questions Skandar had about Agatha, adding a new home to all that just seemed too much tonight.

'I think I'm going to stay with Scoundrel for a bit,' Skandar mumbled, expecting Flo to argue.

But she didn't. She nodded, smiled and Skandar thought perhaps she understood.

Once she'd gone, Skandar ran his hand along Scoundrel's neck. 'Do you mind if I stay in here with you? Just for a while?'

Skandar made his way to the back of the stable and slipped down against the cool black rock. Scoundrel followed his rider, stared down at him for a few seconds, and then collapsed in a heap himself on to the straw, resting his horned head on Skandar's knee. A sleepy wasp flew right past Scoundrel's nose. Skandar readied himself to stand up and run away. But in a split second Scoundrel had caught it between his teeth and swallowed it. It felt like a good omen. Scoundrel ruffled his wings and squeaked contentedly. Skandar felt his own happiness overflow too, as though he'd just sprinted into his sister's arms for the best hug in the universe. It was like the bond was magnifying his feelings, making them unicorn-sized. The world was bigger somehow. What he could do, what he could feel – in that moment anything felt possible.

Skandar's worries about Mitchell and the spirit element drifted away as he looked into his unicorn's eyes. They didn't need to speak to understand each other – the bond connecting their two hearts did all the talking for them. Skandar knew he'd do anything to protect Scoundrel. Somewhere under his black coat – between those spindly wings – was an elemental power that could get them both killed. But Skandar was never going to let anyone harm Scoundrel's Luck. Ever.

CHAPTER TEN

SILVER TROUBLE

After that first night, Skandar and his quartet spent a couple of days getting used to the Eyrie. Skandar's heart sang every time he looked at the treehouse he now called home. It was nestled a few trees in from the Eyrie's outer wall. At only two storeys high it was one of the smallest treehouses around – nothing like some of the steel giants he'd climbed past when he, Flo and Bobby explored the swinging walkways – but it was easily recognisable: its roof came to a sharp point, with a small round window just visible behind a leafy branch on the upper level. In the evenings Skandar liked to sit on the metal platform outside the entrance, filling his sketchbook with drawings of Scoundrel and listening to the new night-time noises – the chirruping of crickets, the hoot of an owl, the rumble of unicorns from deep within the wall, the occasional burst of excited rider chatter.

But the Hatchlings soon discovered that the Eyrie was not

the kind of place that would allow them to laze – and in Bobby's case snore – away the days in their hammocks. The first training session arrived far too quickly, and Skandar found his hands shaking with nerves as he got Scoundrel ready in his stable.

Like the other newly hatched unicorns, Scoundrel had been causing havoc in the Eyrie grounds. Watching the young unicorns from his treehouse window, Skandar now understood why the place was built like a fortress; it was completely normal for the young unicorns to reduce bushes to ash, electrify armoured trees with lightning bolts, or knock unsuspecting riders from their feet with miniature cyclones. And Scoundrel was being more difficult than ever today. He snorted sparks on to Skandar's hands and whipped up an icy wind between his wings that made Skandar's skin burn and freeze in quick succession.

'Can you just keep still?' Skandar begged, as the unicorn threw his head around. 'Don't you want to do fire magic together?'

Skandar heard a scoff from the stable next door. Mitchell was watching him.

'What?' Skandar shot over the stone wall.

Mitchell shrugged, leading Red Night's Delight out of her stable. 'Oh, nothing. Just wondering if the reason you're struggling with that bridle is because *you're not even supposed to be here.*'

'Keep your voice down!' Skandar hissed, scaring Scoundrel, who walloped him with one of his feathery wings. Skandar had tried not to let Mitchell's continued unfriendliness get to him, but it was very hard sharing a room with someone who would barely speak. And Skandar felt more on edge than ever about being a spirit wielder now he was facing his first real training session.

'Are you coming?' Flo asked Skandar, emerging from the stable on his other side. Blade snorted sparks imperiously into Red's tail as Mitchell and his unicorn stalked past.

'You go,' Skandar called over the door. 'I'll wait for Bobby.'

A few moments passed, and there was still no sign of Falcon emerging from her stable.

'Bobby? Are you ready?' Skandar's voice echoed around the cool dark stone.

No answer. Skandar wondered if Falcon was insisting on having her hooves polished again, since the unicorn was so particular about her appearance.

Scoundrel shrieked after Red Night's Delight, impatient to leave with her. Unlike their riders, the black and red unicorns had developed a close friendship already. Scoundrel and Red had been making all sorts of mischief around the Eyrie together, from strategically dropping dung in front of passing riders (it was *not* rainbow-coloured) to exploding multiple trees with a mixture of the fire and air elements, creating something halfway between a firework display and a raging bonfire. They seemed to have a similar sense of humour, though Scoundrel definitely provided the brains behind their schemes, and Red, well, she provided the enthusiasm.

Skandar went to peer over Falcon's door. Like all the other Hatchling stables, the makeshift sign stating the unicorn's name and elemental symbol had now been replaced with an engraved brass plaque.

He couldn't see Bobby at first, only Falcon tearing a goat carcass limb from limb. Then he spotted a figure in the straw at the back, knees pulled up to her chest, struggling to drag air into her lungs.

Skandar rushed into the stable. 'What's up? Are you okay? Are you hurt?'

'What . . . are . . . you . . . doing . . . in here . . . Skandar?' Bobby said as crossly as she could through rasping breaths.

'Umm . . .' Skandar tried to look anywhere but at the tears running down Bobby's face. 'I was waiting for you. I . . .' He trailed off. He couldn't leave her like this, but he also knew she'd be mortified that he'd seen her crying. He couldn't quite believe it himself.

'Oh, that's . . . nice of . . . you,' she gasped out.

Bobby's wheezing made Skandar remember something. This had happened to Dad once, right in the middle of the supermarket, after hearing he'd been fired from another job.

Skandar jumped up, sprinted round to the supply cupboard and rummaged through drawers until he found a paper bag tucked under a tail comb.

'Here,' he said, rushing back and offering it to Bobby. 'Breathe into this.'

Skandar stood awkwardly in front of her as – slowly but surely – Bobby's breathing returned to normal.

'Urgh,' she choked out, putting the bag on the straw beside her.

'Are you all right? Was that a panic attack?'

Bobby started shredding a piece of straw. 'I used to get them all the time. Before the first day of school, exams, birthday parties, Christmas Day, sometimes just for no reason at all. I can't really explain why.'

'It's okay – you don't have to . . .' Skandar mumbled.

She got to her feet. 'This is the first one I've had on the Island.'

'Today's a big day, with the first real training session and all that,' Skandar said lamely. 'I couldn't eat any breakfast.'

Bobby shrugged. 'Even with mayonnaise? Now that *is* a big deal.'

'Oi!'

'Come on, we should get going.' She pulled Falcon away from the bloody goat remains.

Skandar looked sideways at her. 'You know you're going to be fine, Bobby, right?'

'No, Skandar.' She poked him in the chest. 'I'm going to be the *best*.'

Skandar opened Falcon's stable door, and from behind him Bobby whispered, 'Skandar, don't tell anyone, okay? I don't want people to know.'

'Okay,' he murmured back.

And then if it hadn't been Bobby, he could've sworn he heard her say 'thank you'.

Both unicorns were unsettled as they began their long trudge through the Eyrie's tree-trunk entrance, past the sentinels and down the steep hill to the training grounds. Falcon snatched something from the grass and it squeaked loudly. Scoundrel strained against his lead rope, looking around, sweat pouring off him, his eyes turning from black to red to black again. Skandar reached out to stroke his neck and—

'Ouch!' Skandar rubbed his arm, which throbbed from a sharp electric shock.

Bobby laughed. She was obviously feeling better – and he was glad.

'Falcon looks very lovely – did she have you up half the night brushing her again?' Skandar shot back, knowing it would annoy her.

'Nothing wrong with being deadly *and* beautiful,' Bobby said, and she turned Falcon's head towards Skandar. The unicorn's nose, mouth and chin were all dripping with fresh blood. 'Poor little bunny, didn't stand a chance.'

'Do you think Amber Fairfax is in our training group?' Skandar asked, changing the subject. The forty-three new Hatchlings had been split into two groups, and they'd train with those riders and unicorns for the rest of the year. As well as Amber, Skandar had been hoping Mitchell might have been put into the other group. But unfortunately quartets stayed together. Always.

'I *know* she is,' Bobby answered. 'I saw her this morning prancing around telling everyone about how great she was going to be at fire magic.'

'Brilliant,' Skandar muttered sarcastically.

The path wound down around the Eyrie's hill, until they finally reached the lowest of the five levels. Now he knew how far it was, Skandar couldn't wait until Scoundrel's wings developed enough so they could fly up and down instead. The

Hatchling plateau encircled the grassy hillside, with the four elemental training grounds round the edge, like points of a compass. The fire training ground was on one side, cut into the slope of the Eyrie's mound. Skandar noticed its lightly singed red pavilion.

Instructor Anderson was already there, sitting astride his unicorn, Desert Firebird. The young unicorns looked like toys compared to the dark bay giant. Firebird snarled as Albert – the Mainlander boy who'd told Skandar about nomads – let Eagle's Dawn skitter too close.

'Line up, and keep to your quartets so the fire wielders are spread out – summoning the fire element will come easiest to them.' The flames at the tips of the instructor's ears danced. 'If that's a line, then I'm a water wielder – straighten up, Hatchlings! Ignore the elemental blasts, if you can.' On Skandar's left, as if to test the point, Silver Blade roared and shards of ice flew from his mouth with enough force to stick into the baked soil of the training ground. Flo quivered in fear.

'Welcome to my favourite place on the whole Island.' Instructor Anderson grinned at them. 'I have the great honour of taking your first-ever training session. Throughout the year the instructors will be teaching you how to ride and fly, as well as summon, fight and defend yourselves with all four elements – all in preparation for the Training Trial.'

There was an outburst of nervous chatter.

Instructor Anderson chuckled. 'Yes, yes, as the Islanders among you already know –' Bobby made an annoyed face – 'the Training Trial is a miniature version of the Chaos Cup that you'll compete in at the end of your Hatchling year. Your families will be invited to watch – yes, yours too, Mainlanders. You must finish above the bottom five in order to continue your training here at the Eyrie.'

'What happens if we don't?' a Mainlander boy called Gabriel asked, sounding worried.

'Those riders will automatically be declared nomads and leave the Eyrie.' Instructor Anderson looked a little more serious than usual, the flames on his ears at a low smoulder.

'*Five* of us?' gasped Mariam, shock all over the Mainlander's olive face.

Skandar was just as horrified. It was one thing having the instructors *decide* to declare you a nomad during the year, but automatic expulsion?

'Spluttering sparks! No need to look so gloomy. The Training Trial is still almost a year away!' Instructor Anderson smiled at them reassuringly. 'First things first. On my signal I want you to mount your unicorns.'

There was a piercingly high whistle. Nobody moved.

Instructor Anderson laughed from his belly. 'That was the signal, in case you were wondering!'

Skandar stared at Scoundrel's back. It wasn't that far up yet, not like a fully grown unicorn. But he'd grown since the Walk and it was still *up*.

On Scoundrel's other side Mitchell was point-blank refusing to mount Red Night's Delight. 'Isn't Instructor Anderson going to talk us through this? Before we just go and jump on?'

'I don't think that's his style,' Bobby murmured, as she vaulted neatly on to Falcon's back. She looked absolutely delighted with herself.

'How did you do that so easily?' Mitchell demanded. 'Talk me through the exact steps!'

Skandar knew he didn't have long until Scoundrel joined in with the elemental blasts, so he decided to swallow his fear. He couldn't exactly be a rider without ever training his unicorn. Hopping, he launched himself on to his stomach, caught hold of Scoundrel's reins with one hand, and then swung his leg round so he could sit up straight.

Now he was on, the nerves hit Skandar all at once. Scoundrel must have felt them too. The unicorn started to quiver, his muscles tense. He was bunching himself up from behind, and swinging his horn around so much that Skandar felt like he was sitting on an unexploded bomb. Scoundrel's wings stretched out and back again in his anxiety, the sinewy muscles and feathers whacking painfully into Skandar's knees.

While Flo was begging Blade to stand still – he didn't appear to have any patience for his rider – Mitchell had scrambled on to Red Night's Delight, though the unicorn didn't seem at all happy about it. Red kept kicking out backwards, so Mitchell had to hold on to her neck to stop himself being catapulted off.

At the other end of the now non-existent line Skandar saw Old Starlight break ranks and gallop across to the red pavilion at the opposite side of the training ground – his rider, Mariam, clung to her unicorn's neck for dear life as water gushed from Starlight's horn. Gabriel's unicorn, Queen's Price, was bellowing at the top of her lungs as an earth elemental blast cracked the ground under her hooves. Zac's unicorn, Yesterday's Ghost, was attempting to kick Rose-Briar's Darling in the flank, which was enraging Meiyi – her angry shouts adding to the shrieking and roaring of the excited unicorns. Poor Albert had already fallen off Eagle's Dawn.

'You'd think *Instructor* Anderson might actually do some instructing at this crucial moment,' Mitchell grumbled, still wobbling on his unicorn's back as she did a kind of pirouette on the spot.

'Aww, is baby Mitchy-titch scared?' Amber called. 'Do you want your *super*-important daddy to come and save you? Why don't you just declare *yourself* a nomad, then you can spend more time hanging out alone?'

'Shut up!' Mitchell called back, although his response was slightly undermined as Red farted, loud and long, and kicked two flaming hooves back to light it. This seemed to be the unicorn's party trick. Mitchell started coughing at the putrid smoke now swirling around him, as Amber sat laughing from Whirlwind Thief's back.

Skandar saw a tear running down Mitchell's cheek. He rode Scoundrel forward protectively until he was blocking Mitchell from Amber and her brown unicorn. The laugh died on Amber's lips.

Then Skandar felt it. An itch in his palm. He looked down at his Hatchery scar. It was glowing white. The same light he'd seen on the Divide, the same light he'd seen the Weaver use just before the darkness fell at the Chaos Cup. The white light of . . . the spirit element?

The realisation emptied Skandar's chest of air, like he'd been winded. Panicking, and unable to stop the glow, he jammed his right hand into the pocket of his new yellow jacket. Slowly, dreading the worst, Skandar looked up, expecting Whirlwind Thief to be standing right in front of him. But Amber was gone. Skandar looked wildly around the colourful mass of writhing magic-blasting unicorns, trying to see the triumph on her face that would surely mean she knew his secret.

Then, as though someone had pressed a mute button, the young unicorns fell silent. Instructor Anderson's palm was turned to the sky, held above his head. Desert Firebird's hooves glowed like hot coals, tendrils of smoke rising from the grass, and Instructor Anderson's palm glowed bright red to match. The glow grew brighter and brighter until he thrust his palm towards the sky a second time and a column of fire exploded from his hand. Both rider and unicorn were very still, although Skandar could see sweat pouring down Instructor Anderson's bald head. Then the column of fire hit a distant point in the sky above them, and the flames fanned outwards and down towards the edges of the training ground like a cascading firework.

The riders were now enclosed within a burning dome. They could no longer see the Island beyond the hill, and the trees of the fortified Eyrie were blurred by flames. It looked like the world was on fire. Instructor Anderson slowly lowered his arm and rode Firebird towards the Hatchling line. The column disappeared, but the dome remained in place. Skandar was struck by the smell of the strong magic – a mixture of smouldering bonfires, freshly struck matches and lightly burnt toast. Kenna would have loved this. Whenever they'd talked about which element they would be allied to, she'd always said fire.

Instructor Anderson interrupted his thoughts. 'Now that's done, we're good and ready to start your first fire session,' he said cheerfully, as though he'd just handed out worksheets, rather than created a dome of fire with his bare hands.

'Your unicorns are tapped into the fire source created by Desert Firebird.' Firebird bared her teeth at the sound of her name. 'They won't be able to summon any other kind of magic.'

Skandar could have cried with relief. He pulled his hand out of his pocket and gingerly uncurled his fingers. The white glow had thankfully disappeared.

'The idea is that it'll be easier for you to share, and ultimately influence, your unicorn's power. Any fool can sit on a unicorn and let it blast off whatever element it feels like – your unicorns have been doing that by themselves since they hatched. But those are just elemental blasts – they have no fixed form. Think of blasts as your unicorns blowing off steam or messing around. Before riders bonded with them that was all unicorns could do.'

Instructor Anderson rode Firebird along the line, her great brown wings held gracefully at her sides. 'It is your job as a rider to learn magic – offensive and defensive – and to share that knowledge through the bond. Think of your unicorn as an intelligent power source. And by summoning elements along the bond and into your palm, together you have the power to control the elements completely. As you progress, your unicorns will learn to mirror and complement the magic you summon with their own. So you see, you won't just share their magic – you can mould it.' Instructor Anderson's voice was full of wonder.

Firebird stopped, her golden brown horn facing the Hatchlings. Skandar saw Sarika's black unicorn, Equator's Conundrum, take a few steps back in fear.

Instructor Anderson continued. 'Fire magic is the least subtle of the elemental types. I say this with love, as the Eyrie's fire instructor. It is volatile and highly dangerous. This is why we spend our first training session teaching you a degree of control.

'While we're on that subject –' Instructor Anderson cleared his throat – 'if any of you injure yourselves and draw blood, you will need to leave the training ground immediately. I do like a joke, but I am deadly serious about this. No rider here has the control needed to stop a unicorn that smells human blood. Your own won't attack you, but another rider's unicorn won't hesitate.'

'Oh no, oh no, oh no,' Flo was muttering over and over on Skandar's left. So much steam was rising off Silver Blade that he could barely see Flo's face.

'Now, I want you all to face your right palms upwards – the one with your Hatchery wound. Just rest that palm on one of your thighs . . . that's it. Try not to think in words but picture your palm glowing red, flames leaping into your hand. Shutting your eyes sometimes helps.'

Skandar felt very stupid sitting there on a dangerous magical beast with his eyes closed.

A cry of victory came from Skandar's right. Bobby was stretching out her palm and showing it to Instructor Anderson. 'That's flaming brilliant!' he joked. 'Well done. It's very rare for an air wielder to be the first to summon fire.'

This seemed to irritate Amber. 'How is she doing it already? She's not even *from* the Island!'

'As we say on the Mainland,' Bobby called, 'if the cape fits, swish it.'

'Urgh, what are you even talking about?' Amber turned away.

'Bobby, since when do we say that on the Mainland?' Skandar asked, staring jealously at the flames dancing in her palm. If he thought *I want flames to come out of my hand* any harder, he would pass out.

Bobby winked. 'These Islanders think they know everything. Doesn't hurt for them to think we have our own Mainlander stuff too.'

'This doesn't make any sense,' Mitchell huffed to no one in particular. 'I read that—'

'Weren't you listening?' Bobby crowed. 'We can't communicate with our unicorns *in words*.'

'I *was* listening—' Mitchell started, but Bobby had already lost interest as flames began to dance up her arms.

Skandar tried to do what Bobby had said. He placed his own palm at the base of Scoundrel's smooth neck and visualised flames appearing there. His palm itched. He opened one eye and felt a jolt of excitement when he saw that his Hatchery wound was glowing bright red. He took a deep breath and imagined harder.

'Skandar, you're doing it! You're doing it!' Flo squealed. Skandar's eyes flew open, and there – sure enough – were little dancing flames in his hand. The fire magic didn't burn him but he felt a pulsing sensation in his Hatchery wound, almost like a heartbeat, as it flickered in his palm. Scoundrel screeched very loudly and flapped both wings, pleased that he'd done the right thing. Skandar got a second dose of happiness that filled his chest up like a balloon, and he wondered whether his emotions weren't entirely his own any more.

'Yes!' Skandar leaned down to pat Scoundrel on his sleek black neck. 'Yes, that's right, boy. We did it!'

Once they'd summoned their first flames, the Hatchlings improved quickly. The main difficulty was keeping their unicorns under control. Skandar saw at least four people fall off as their unicorns reared, bucked or just randomly galloped across the ground. A boy called Lawrence flew right over the ears of his unicorn, Poison Chief, and Skandar himself was almost dislodged as Scoundrel reared up to snap at a low-flying bird for an early lunch.

Despite all the chaos Instructor Anderson was as relaxed as anything, riding up and down the line giving tips. As the last exercise of the class, they threw the flames towards the ground – in preparation for learning fireball attacks next time.

Skandar was concentrating so hard that only Flo's scream made him realise something had happened.

A few metres away Silver Blade was suspended in the air, rearing, his front legs up high as his wings beat furiously. Flo was still on his back, hanging on to his silver mane, but a towering column of flame enclosed them. Blade's eyes were glowing red, black smoke streaming out of his nostrils and curling round his horn.

Instructor Anderson was shouting something up at Flo, but

Skandar could barely see her through the flames. All the other riders had stopped their fire magic too and were looking at Blade in horror. The inferno around Blade and Flo was so hot that Skandar's cheeks began to smart, his eyes watering from the heat and smoke. Skandar blinked away the bright light, trying to make out his friend on her unicorn's back.

Flo's arms were still wrapped round Blade's neck as he roared down at Desert Firebird, flames erupting from his mouth, but Firebird stood her ground and bellowed back. After a few agonising seconds, the column disappeared and Blade landed heavily on the ground.

Instructor Anderson looked very worried as he helped Flo down from Blade's back.

'Get back to your practice, riders!' For the first time he sounded stern, the flames growing tall over his ears. Skandar saw him putting an arm round Flo's shaking shoulders, before sending her and Blade back to the Eyrie.

Skandar could hardly concentrate for the rest of the session. By the time Instructor Anderson dismissed the Hatchlings they were a sorry-looking crowd. Almost all of them had fallen off, most had dirt or ash across their faces, and some even had singed hair or eyebrows. When they reached the Eyrie, Skandar was determined to find Flo and ask her if she was okay, but for some reason there was a big crowd outside Silver Blade's stable.

Skandar recognised Mabel – an Islander's – voice. 'You're so lucky! Sarika, come look at this.'

Flo was standing with her back pinned against the stable door.

'Unbelievable! Though I guess metal makes sense for the

earth element. How did it happen?' Zac was asking her, blocking Skandar's view.

Closer to the stable, Skandar was just able to hear Flo's whisper of a reply. 'I don't know. It just . . . did.'

He pushed through the crowd towards Flo, intending to rescue her from whatever everyone else was gawping at. But when she came into view, he stopped dead.

Her black cloud of hair was shot through with silver.

Later that evening, Skandar returned to the treehouse alone. He'd overheard Instructor Anderson telling Zac the domes would come down after the Earth Festival in a couple of months' time, and he was worried. The domes were a bit like learning to ride a bike with stabilisers – and without their steadying influence Skandar would almost certainly fall off.

Not to mention, now he'd seen how visible Flo's mutation was, he was terrified about getting a spirit one. So, as soon as Scoundrel was safely in his stable after training, Skandar had snuck off to visit all four elemental libraries to see if he could find anything that might help him hide the spirit element.

The treehouse libraries were very beautiful – each was built to look exactly like a book had been placed, half open, across the top, its spine creating the topmost edge. They were grand, with multiple storeys, and decorated for their particular element. The water one, for example, had chairs and shelves forged in the shape of waves, and its walls were covered inside and out with paintings of water wielders using their power.

There Skandar had found the four elemental scriptures: *The*

Book of Fire, The Book of Water, The Book of Air and The Book of Earth. But the libraries didn't seem to have one word about his banned element, and Skandar couldn't help worrying whether Agatha bringing a spirit wielder to the Island had anything to do with the Weaver's plan.

Skandar hung up his yellow jacket by his treehouse door. Three more jackets – green, red and blue – were safely tucked away upstairs, ready for the Earth, Fire and Water festivals that marked the move from each elemental season to the next. The Hatchlings' jackets were very plain compared to those of the older riders, who customised them in their own styles – covering rips with patterned patches, studding sleeves with painted metal or stitching over scorches with elemental designs. All Skandar's jacket had was a single stylised pair of wings on the right arm, symbolising his first year at the Eyrie.

The quartet's treehouse was unusually quiet apart from the crackling of the wood-burning stove, its chimney flue reaching up and out into the Eyrie. Skandar had been hoping to talk to Flo – he hadn't even managed to ask her if she was okay, let alone talk to her about mutating. But despite his concern for Flo, his fear that Amber had seen his white palm and his own worries about mutating, Skandar felt happiness bloom as he looked around.

He loved the four squashy beanbags in the elemental colours, he loved the bookcase filled with essential unicorn reading, and he even liked the heavy stone box that acted as their fridge. But most of all he loved the trunk that went through the centre of the treehouse. Metal rungs stuck out from the bark, spiralling round and round as a ladder to the upper level. From the top, he could look out of the tiny round window, and see across the Eyrie and the Island for miles. It felt safe in the treehouse. It felt like home.

That reminded him. Skandar grabbed his sketchbook and pencil from the bookshelf to write to Kenna. He couldn't tell her anything about the spirit element just in case the Rider Liaison Officers were checking the letters, but he could draw the treehouse and tell her all about the fire training and about Flo's mutation and – he felt a swing of guilt in his stomach – ask how she was coping alone with Dad. He wrote down the first things that came into his head.

Dear Kenn,

I miss you so much! And Dad. But you more (PS if you're reading this out to him don't say that bit). How's everything going? How's school? How's Dad? Sorry – so many questions. It's just weird not being able to talk to you. I don't think we've ever gone a whole day without talking – have we? I can't believe I'm writing this (from a treehouse – I've drawn you a picture!), but I'm now officially a unicorn rider. My unicorn is called Scoundrel's Luck. Scoundrel for short. Do you like the name? He really loves Jelly Babies (oh yeah, I kind of took a packet from your stash before I left – sorry!). This is probably too much to ask, but could you maybe send me more? I'm not even sure if they have them on the Island. Although *they do have mayonnaise, which obviously I was worried about . . .*

Flo climbed down the rungs of the tree trunk, making Skandar jump.

'I didn't know you were here!' he said cheerfully, although his smile faltered when he looked at her face. 'What's wrong?'

She dropped down on to the green beanbag nearest the fire, and Skandar couldn't help but notice the silver in her hair, flickering in the firelight.

'I couldn't control Blade today, Skar,' Flo said very quietly. 'I thought he was going to kill me.' Her voice caught on the last two words.

'But you're bonded,' Skandar tried to reassure her. 'He wouldn't hurt you!'

'You don't understand,' Flo choked out. 'This is exactly why I was so upset when he hatched. The thing is, I never really wanted to be a rider at all; I wanted to be a saddler. I could have been apprenticed to my dad – I was already helping him – and –' she took a deep breath, rushing on – 'my twin brother, Ebenezer, he'll get to be a saddler; the Hatchery door didn't open for him. And I would have been really happy with that and I know that's hard for Mainlanders to understand, but I didn't want to try the door, not really. I know that sounds selfish.' She took an enormous breath.

'But then you hatched Silver Blade?'

'Yes!' She exhaled. 'And that made it all even worse.'

'Why?'

'I'm not saying I don't love him. I do. I can't not. We're bonded;

we came into this world together. He's been waiting thirteen years for me . . . but – he's a silver unicorn.'

'I don't—'

'Silvers are special on the Island, Skar. They're really powerful; they're deeply connected to the magic of this place. But there's never been a silver winner of the Chaos Cup. And what happened today is why. Their magic is so strong it often works against them. The worst thing is that everyone is so *happy* for me! So proud. A silver hasn't hatched on the Island for a long time; I'll be the first new member of the Silver Circle in years – it's this elite group for riders with unicorns like Blade. And once I start going to their meetings next year, there'll be so much *expectation.*' She choked on the last word.

'The Silver Circle controls the sentinels, right?' Skandar thought of Agatha and Arctic Swansong down on Fisherman's Beach.

'Exactly!' Flo threw up her arms. 'They guard the Island. The Circle have all this power and they like to use it. The Commodore of Chaos and Council change every year, but the Silver Circle members don't – Dorian Manning has been in charge for ages and he's got a son with a silver unicorn too. And now I have to be part of all that. I don't even get a choice.'

Skandar hadn't heard her speak this much about herself before – it was like all the words had been coiled up inside. 'I'm sorry it hasn't gone the way you wanted,' he said gently. He knew what it looked like when your dreams got shattered – Flo had that same defeated sadness in her eyes as Kenna. Flo knew, just as he was beginning to understand, that the bond changed everything. It connected two souls, two hearts – for ever. And now Flo could never abandon Silver Blade and follow her dream to become a saddler.

She sighed. 'I'm trying to be brave, but three of the last ten silvers accidentally killed their own riders – and themselves. A bonded unicorn can't survive their rider's death.'

Skandar gasped. 'What? Why would they kill their own riders?'

'Not on purpose. But they've got so much power and if their elemental blasts get too out of control and they hit the rider . . .' Flo shook her head.

A shadow appeared high up on the tree trunk. Mitchell was listening.

Skandar ignored him. 'Then why is everyone so obsessed with silver unicorns? At the Walk everyone was really excited about Blade.'

'They're a symbol that the magic is still strong within the unicorn population. So right now, with the Weaver, a unicorn like Blade gives everyone hope.'

'What do you mean?'

'Silvers are too strong for a spirit wielder to kill,' Mitchell said from a rung halfway down the trunk.

'I didn't want to tell him yet!' Flo crossed her arms, frowning up at Mitchell. Then she turned to Skandar with pleading eyes. 'I didn't want you to think we can't be friends. You know, because you're a spirit wielder and I'm a silver. I didn't want it to change anything.'

'Flo, I'm not planning on killing *any* unicorns. To be honest, finding out I won't accidentally kill Silver Blade is the best news I've had all day.'

'It's not a joke, Skar. Before they outlawed the spirit element, the Silver Circle and the spirit wielders were the two most powerful groups on the Island. There was this ancient rivalry . . .'

Skandar shrugged. 'So what? We're friends, that's the end of it.' He couldn't help feeling rather pleased that Flo had kept this secret because she cared about their new friendship too much to risk it.

'That's what your kind always say. And then you come for us in the night with your death element.' Mitchell's voice was full of doom.

'I'm not *a kind*, Mitchell,' Skandar said sadly. 'I'm a person just like you. I wish you could see that.'

The treehouse door clanged open and Bobby marched in. She didn't say hello but went straight to the cold box, lifting out ingredients. They were all captivated as she spread butter, then raspberry jam, then Marmite – which she must have brought from the Mainland – on to a piece of bread. She finished off the odd mixture with a slab of cheese, folded the bread over and took a bite. Noticing them all watching her with varying levels of disgust, Bobby swallowed her first mouthful. 'It's an emergency sandwich,' she explained.

'What's the emergency?' Flo asked politely, staring at the ingredients all over the counter.

'I'm hungry – obviously.'

Then the sky outside exploded.

CHAPTER ELEVEN

ISLAND SECRETS

The explosion wasn't loud enough to be inside the Eyrie, but it wasn't far away. Bobby – closest to the door – threw it open and rushed outside. Skandar followed, Flo and Mitchell behind him. Night had fallen, dark and inky; the lanterns of the capital, Fourpoint, blinked at the base of the Eyrie's hill. The quartet stood on the bridge between their treehouse and the next, staring out across the Island. Yellow smoke billowed in the gloom.

Mitchell shook his head gravely. 'Air wielder.'

BANG!

This time Skandar saw the whole thing. Something like a firework exploded into the dark, belching red smoke in its wake. The sky glowed a mixture of red and yellow.

'What is it?' Sarika asked, the light of the smoke dancing across her brown eyelids. The rest of her quartet had joined Skandar's by the rail.

Mitchell's face was bleak, as were Flo's and Mabel's. Mitchell recited, as though from a textbook: 'Sentinels guard the Island's key strategic locations: the Hatchery, Fourpoint, the Mirror Cliffs and so on. When on patrol, each sentinel attaches a cord from their jacket to a distress flare on their saddle. If the rider leaves their unicorn's back, the flare explodes in the colour of their element.'

'Pfft. So two sentinels just fell off their unicorns?' Bobby scoffed. 'That's what all the fuss is about?

'Sentinels don't fall off, Bobby. Not unless –' Flo swallowed hard – 'not unless they're dead. The flares are designed to alert other sentinels to a fatal attack, a gap they need to fill in the line of defence.'

'But who's doing it?' Gabriel demanded, his face pale and ashen. 'Who would attack two sentinels?'

'I can think of someone,' Mitchell murmured, as he rummaged for something in his pocket.

There were more riders out of their treehouses now. Lanterns lit up worried faces; questions bounced off the armoured trunks.

'SILENCE!' Instructor O'Sullivan swept on to a bridge nearby, her blue cloak billowing out behind her in the night breeze. 'Silence, please.' She was breathing heavily through her nose. 'Fourpoint has just signalled to the Eyrie that all is well.'

'But how—' Sarika started.

'The two sentinels who lost their lives tonight have been replaced by new guards.'

'What were they guarding, Instructor O'Sullivan?' Zac asked, his voice shaky.

'Who attacked them? Are our families at risk?' Mabel demanded.

'It was the Weaver, wasn't it?' Bobby asked, but it wasn't really a question.

Instructor O'Sullivan sighed. 'We suspect that to be the case. But there's no need to worry yourselves. Worry more about my training session tomorrow. Bed, NOW!' However, there was no hiding the strain etched across her face.

Once Instructor O'Sullivan had moved on to calm the next group, Mitchell pushed to the front rail of the platform. He had something in his palm. He kept looking down at it, and then up at the coloured smoke in the distance.

'Umm, Mitchell, what are you doing?' Skandar asked tentatively.

Mitchell held up a finger, as though asking for quiet.

'Is that a compass?' Bobby asked, trying to peer into his hand.

He snapped the object shut and turned to the rest of his quartet. 'Correct, Roberta. It is a compass. And it's confirmed exactly what I suspected.'

'What?' Skandar asked.

'Those flares went off directly above the Mirror Cliffs. And do you know what the sentinels on the Mirror Cliffs are guarding?'

Flo gasped just as Bobby and Skandar shook their heads.

'The Mainland,' Mitchell said darkly.

Skandar's whole body tensed as an image of the Weaver flew into his mind, the wild unicorn's ghostly horn lit by the moon. *Kenna. Dad.*

'Why wouldn't Instructor O'Sullivan tell us that?' Flo wondered aloud.

'I suspect they didn't want to cause panic.' Mitchell shrugged. 'All the adults are worried about what the Weaver's planning, and if it involves the Mainland then . . .'

'You might be wrong,' Bobby countered, although her voice had a note of worry in it. 'That compass thing doesn't exactly look advanced.'

Mitchell shrugged. 'Compasses don't have to be advanced – they're good at what they do. *Direction*. I'm just telling you what it told me.'

Skandar turned to face Mitchell. 'If you're right, what happens if the Weaver kills *all* the sentinels in the defence line? What if the Weaver breaks through to the Mainland?'

It looked for a moment like Mitchell was going to say something reassuring, but then his mouth set in a grim line. 'You tell me, *spirit wielder*.'

Skandar crossed his arms. 'You don't have to hate me, you know. Just because your dad wouldn't like us being friends. You're allowed to have different opinions. You're allowed to believe I'm not like the Weaver.'

'No, I'm not,' Mitchell snapped, and turned back to their treehouse alone.

One Saturday evening a few weeks later, Skandar entered the Trough, where the riders ate all their meals. It was a cavernous treehouse built between dozens of trees, their trunks lining both long sides. Tables and chairs were dotted around on large circular platforms, which perched in the branches at different levels all the way up to the high roof. The riders would collect food on a tray from the long table at floor level, then clamber about to find a place to eat. Once Skandar had got used to balancing his tray and climbing a ladder at the same time, the tables felt cosy, nestled high among the leaves and branches. The only thing to watch out for were the squirrels, who loved trying to steal from their plates.

Flo waved down at Skandar from one of the high platforms, pointing at an empty chair beside Bobby, and he felt a rush of happiness. Back on the Mainland, nobody had ever saved him a seat.

Flo and Bobby were chattering away about mutations when Skandar joined them. Apart from the recent sentinel attack, mutations were all the Hatchlings had been able to talk about since Flo's hair had changed. Skandar wasn't sure which made him more worried. While the other Hatchlings were trading theories about what the dead sentinels had been guarding, all Skandar could think about was what Agatha had told him on the beach: *You saw the Weaver pointing into the camera. That wasn't an accident. That was a threat.* But a threat of what? What was the Weaver planning to use New-Age Frost for? And was Mitchell right – did the Weaver's plan include attacking the Mainland?

And if that wasn't enough to worry about, when it came to mutations, Skandar was not at all excited about what might happen to *him*. A spirit mutation may well give him away just as much as the Divide. True, at the moment, there wasn't much danger of him using the spirit element with the domes in place. He and Scoundrel were throwing tiny fireballs or jets of water at targets, and summoning gusts of wind or minor tremors in the ground, just like everyone else. What kept him up at night was the idea of the domes coming down – and that white glow returning to his palm. Besides revealing his secret, could he accidentally kill a unicorn with it? Spirit was nicknamed the death element, after all.

'Have you seen Gabriel's hair?' Bobby rolled her eyes.

Flo was much more enthusiastic. 'He mutated in earth training earlier – I saw the whole thing!'

Gabriel was sitting on a nearby platform, with Zac and Romily. His dark brown hair had turned to stone, and now resembled the tight curls of a Greek statue. The colour matched the light grey of his unicorn, Queen's Price, exactly.

'He's really *rocking* that look.' Bobby laughed at her own joke. 'Get it?'

'Sarika and Mabel mutated this week as well, don't forget,' Flo added.

Skandar had not forgotten. Sarika's mutation was, Skandar had to admit, very cool – all her fingernails looked like they were constantly on fire. Mabel's was pretty good too – the freckles on her arms now sparkled like ice crystals. He couldn't help but feel slightly jealous.

'Theirs aren't as impressive as mine,' Bobby boasted, pushing up the sleeves of her yellow jacket. Much to her delight, Bobby had been the second Hatchling to mutate. Tiny slate-grey feathers had sprouted from her wrists to the tips of her shoulders. She smoothed them down fondly before going back to her slice of apple pie.

'Are you excited for your Mainlander class tonight?' Flo asked.

'Definitely,' Skandar said, as Bobby scoffed in disgust.

'We don't need *extra* classes.' She spat the word as though it were poisonous. 'I'm better than all the Islanders in training – no offence, Flo.'

'Well, I'm glad it's happening,' Skandar insisted, keeping his voice low. 'That way I can ask the instructor whether they know anything about the sentinel attacks.'

'Oh, Skar! I don't know if that's a good idea,' Flo whispered back. 'What if the instructor suspects something about you being a you-know-what?'

'I won't be obvious,' Skandar said. 'I just want to find out if Mitchell's right. If the Weaver's trying to get to the Mainland.'

'But—'

'My family are there; Bobby's family are there,' Skandar said firmly. 'We at least deserve to know what the Weaver's planning.'

'I'll keep an eye on him, don't worry.' Bobby poked Skandar with her spoon.

Amber suddenly started speaking very loudly from a nearby platform. 'The Mainlanders don't have a clue, of course, but it's that Joby Worsham who's teaching them. They're in for a shock – apparently he's barely human, let alone a rider.'

The rest of her quartet – Meiyi, Alastair and Kobi – were listening wide-eyed. Flo and Skandar had nicknamed them 'the Threat Quartet' because they were always being nasty to someone. Amber flipped her loose chestnut hair over, so it was all on one side of her head. Skandar had seen other girls she hung around with doing that too – he wasn't sure what was cool about having a lopsided hairstyle.

'I've heard of him!' Meiyi half whispered. 'My mum says I shouldn't go anywhere near him. You never know when someone like that's going to lose it completely.' She made a loud shivering noise.

Kobi fiddled with the braid above his ear. 'When my brother was training at the Eyrie a few years ago, he saw Worsham one night. Apparently he was walking across a bridge right at the top of the Eyrie muttering to himself like some sort of mad ghost. Like he was looking for something.'

Just then Albert dropped a plate as he climbed down from his table, and both Kobi and Alastair jumped.

'Yeah, well, I know something *super* twisted about Worsham that'd honestly make your skin crawl,' Amber boasted.

The others begged her for details, but Amber mimed zipping her mouth shut. 'All I'm saying is that having someone like that *inside* the Eyrie?' Amber raised her eyebrows. 'My mother says she's always been against Worsham teaching here. I mean, why would you want new riders being taught by a person whose unicorn has been killed? It's not exactly a good example.'

Flo rose abruptly from the table, her dark eyes shining with anger. Skandar and Bobby looked at each other in confusion, before following her down the ladder and out of the Trough.

'I can't believe how unkind Amber is sometimes,' Flo spluttered, as soon as they were on the metal platform outside.

'Who was she talking about?' Skandar frowned. He hadn't understood the conversation at all.

'Instructor Worsham. He's teaching your Mainlander classes,' Flo explained, her face sad. 'People gossip about him because –'

she dropped her voice – 'well, because he doesn't have a unicorn any more. She died.'

Bobby shrugged. 'People are dumb. Especially Amber, and she hasn't even mutated yet – no offence, Skandar. So this instructor has no unicorn; what's there to gossip about?'

Flo sighed. 'If a unicorn dies, the bond breaks. But a rider keeps living.'

'But if I die, Falcon dies *with* me, right?' Bobby checked.

'Exactly – she's linked to your lifespan as her rider. But you aren't linked to hers. If a unicorn dies, their rider is left behind and, well, they're not quite the same as they were before. Imagine having all that power, all that magic, all that *love*, and then it all being taken away – and your unicorn with it. It's no wonder it changes a person. Makes them less . . . whole.'

Skandar thought that perhaps he'd experienced the tiniest fraction of what Flo was talking about before, when he'd come home without taking the Hatchery exam. He knew how he'd felt then, when he'd only lost the *idea* of bonding with a unicorn. The *dream* of becoming a rider. Now he could sense his connection with Scoundrel's Luck in every heartbeat. Sometimes he even thought he felt the unicorn's emotions. His mind gravitated towards the unicorn, like a compass point he'd be lost without. Skandar suddenly had a horrible image of himself walking the swinging bridges of the Eyrie at night, looking for something he was never going to find.

Skandar pushed on the door of Instructor Worsham's treehouse, his heart beating a bit faster as it creaked open on rusty hinges.

Sarika, Gabriel, Zac, Albert and Mariam were already inside, sitting on beanbags, giant pillows and fluffy rugs in silence. They all looked a little frightened: Sarika was fiddling anxiously with the steel bangle on her wrist, Albert was biting his lip, and Gabriel was so pale he looked like he might faint. Skandar wondered if they'd heard about Instructor Worsham from Amber too.

Instructor Worsham himself was sitting on a purple beanbag and staring out of a small window, as though he was unaware of his visitors.

'Bit young for a ghost, isn't he?' Bobby whispered to Skandar, as they sat down on a fluffy orange rug – the only space left in the small living room.

Bobby might be blunt, but Skandar had to admit she had a point. Instructor Worsham's blond hair was tied in a high tangled ponytail and he didn't look any older than thirty.

Instructor Worsham suddenly seemed to notice them all in his treehouse and cleared his throat. Several of the Mainlanders gulped.

But when Instructor Worsham spoke his voice was kind, even if his blue eyes were sad and unfocused. 'Officially –' he smiled at them – 'I am Instructor Worsham, but please just call me Joby. You may have noticed that you are all Mainlander Hatchlings.' He gestured at them sitting in front of him. 'I am not from the Mainland, but I have studied it in great detail, and have become an expert since Mainlander riders first graced our shores. Please don't try to work out how old that makes me.' Nobody laughed.

'The point of this class,' he continued, ignoring the awkward silence, 'is that there'll be things in your training – in your social life even – that you'll come across and won't fully understand, given that you were born on the Mainland.' He opened his hands wide. 'I think it's reassuring to remember that thousands of years ago the first unicorn riders – the ancestors of Islanders today – came from every corner of the Earth, so the Island was new to them once too. But until you Hatchlings settle in I'm here to translate. How does that sound?'

Silence. Most of the Mainlanders still looked terrified. Albert was looking anywhere but at Joby's face, as though he hoped the instructor wouldn't notice him if he didn't meet his eye.

Joby sighed, and Skandar had never heard a sound so steeped in sadness. 'I take it from the fact that you all seem so scared of me that someone has talked to you about my history.'

Nobody answered.

'Right.' Joby grimaced, and then began talking in a monotone, as though he'd told the story many times before. 'Just like you, I successfully opened the door to the Hatchery in my thirteenth year. Just like you, I hatched an egg and was marked by my unicorn's horn –' he held up his right palm to show his Hatchery wound – 'and just like you, as all riders are, I was bonded to my unicorn. Her name was Winter's Phantom.' Joby's voice broke, and it took a moment for him to be able to carry on. Skandar hardly dared to breathe.

'During my first year of training at the Eyrie – a Hatchling like you – Phantom was k-k-killed. And I have been alone ever since.' Joby clutched at his chest through his creased white T-shirt, as though suddenly in pain. If Skandar hadn't known that a rider–unicorn bond wrapped itself directly round your heart, he might have thought Joby was being dramatic. But the place he was clutching at, clawing at, was his own heart, the exact place his bond with Winter's Phantom should have been.

Albert and Sarika had tears running down their faces. Even Bobby looked slightly perturbed.

Joby shifted his weight on the beanbag, trying to compose himself again. 'I am not a ghost or a spectre. I am not mad or unhinged. The scariest thing about me is that I'm not so unlike you. My mutation might have faded, but I'm still a rider in here.' He touched his chest again. 'The only difference between me and all of you is that your bonds are whole, while mine never will be again.'

Skandar could feel his bond with Scoundrel searing at the very thought that they could be separated for ever. He found – for the first time – that if he concentrated on that feeling in his own chest he could almost feel his unicorn's presence. He could sense the unicorn's personality somehow: the cheekiness, the intelligence, the playfulness, the edge of elemental power, the greed for Jelly Babies. It was there inside himself. And almost without meaning to, Skandar murmured, 'I'm really sorry, Instructor Worsham.'

Joby turned his haunted blue gaze towards him and smiled. 'Thank you, Skandar.' The other Mainlanders murmured similar words until the mood in the room lifted just a little.

Joby stood up. 'Now, you're not here to learn about me. You're here to learn about yourselves, your unicorns and the Island. Any questions? Remember, you can ask me anything. Anything at all.' Seven hands exploded into the air, and he laughed, clearly relieved.

'How likely is it we'll be declared nomads?' Zac asked, sounding worried. 'Surely since us lot are Mainlanders, we're at a disadvantage already?'

Joby looked like he wished he'd chosen someone else first, but he answered all the same. 'It's very rare for any Hatchling to be declared a nomad before the Training Trial.'

'But then they kick out five of us!' Albert wailed, colour leaching from his pasty face.

Joby smiled sadly at them, placing a hand on his chest where he should have been able to feel his bond. 'You have to remember that it's the bond that's important. Being a rider isn't just about training in the Eyrie or the glory of qualifying for the Chaos Cup.'

Bobby made a grunting sound of disbelief.

Joby continued. 'Without the bond the Island would be a deadly place to live – elemental blasts destroying crops, wildlife, people. But the unicorns have us – their riders – and it's only the wild ones that cause any real destruction. Why do you think the Chaos Cup is called the Chaos Cup? It was invented to show the strength of the bond, to demonstrate how riders can control the chaos.'

Joby answered question after question, from things like visiting the elemental zones, and whether they'd get time off training for Diwali, Hanukkah, Christmas or Eid, to the availability of Mainland snacks in Fourpoint. Occasionally, though, Joby would lose his train of thought or stare out of the window and forget he was in the middle of a sentence. As the class began to draw to a close, Skandar asked a question that had been bothering him since the Hatchery door had opened at his touch, and hoped it wouldn't give anything away.

'Instructor Worsham, erm, Joby,' Skandar stuttered. He could feel the telltale blush that seared his cheeks whenever he was trying to hide something. 'How do the questions in the Hatchery exam help the Island decide who should try the door? And, also, there are quite a few Mainlanders who get sent back, so . . .'

'Well –' Joby looked uncomfortable again – 'the thing is, Skandar, the real test isn't the written exam at all. The reason a person with a bond attends every exam, and shakes every candidate's hand, is that they can recognise a potential new rider. Don't ask me how they know, but they do. They make mistakes sometimes, but a rider will have felt a connection with every single Mainlander here.'

'So the Hatchery exam is actually just about destiny and *magic*?' Bobby made 'magic' sound like a swear word.

Albert shook his head. 'They could have at least told us.'

'The Island likes its secrets,' Joby said sheepishly.

Sarika stuck up her hand. 'Can you tell us about this fifth element? The one the Commodore mentioned in her speech. I know we're not supposed to ask about it, but . . .' She let the question hang in the air hopefully.

'You're right: you're not supposed to talk about it.'

Sarika shifted awkwardly on her fluffy rug.

'But no doubt the Hatchling Islanders all know about it; their parents will remember . . .' Joby closed his eyes for the briefest of seconds and looked more haunted than ever as he continued.

'The fifth was known as the spirit element. Over a decade ago, the Weaver used it to bond with a wild unicorn. The twenty-four innocent lives our Commodore mentioned in her speech were the first the Weaver cut short. They're known as the Fallen Twenty-Four – twenty-four unicorns killed across different Chaos Cup qualifying races. Twenty-four bonds severed on the same day, the riders left to live out a half-life without their unicorns. It was an act of unimaginable cruelty. It's been illegal to be a spirit wielder ever since.'

Joby's voice was low. 'After the Fallen Twenty-Four, all the known spirit wielders were imprisoned. Partly because the Council didn't know which one of them was the Weaver, and partly because they were afraid that more spirit wielders would use their element for evil. Spirit is the only element capable of killing a bonded unicorn – like it did my Winter's Phantom.'

There was a long silence. 'But how do they stop spirit wielders trying the Hatchery door?' Albert asked in a panic. 'How do we know there isn't one in the Eyrie right now?'

Skandar tried as hard as he could to keep his face blank, but he could feel sweat dripping down the back of his jacket. His cheeks burned hotter than fire magic.

'Well, for Mainlanders it happens at the Hatchery exam,' Joby answered. 'At the same time as riders can detect if you might be destined to open the door, they also get a vague indication of elemental power. It doesn't always match the result at the Walk, but if a rider shakes a child's hand on the Mainland and gets any sense of the fifth element, that child will automatically be failed. On the Island we do similar checks.'

Skandar suddenly understood what Agatha had done. She'd known he would have failed the Hatchery exam as soon as the invigilating rider shook his hand! By not allowing him to take it, Agatha had saved him from being disqualified as a spirit wielder. She'd given him a chance at the Hatchery door. And maybe that was why Kenna had failed the exam too! She, like countless other potential spirit wielders, hadn't had an Agatha to help her. But why had Agatha helped Skandar? It seemed a lot to risk on a promise to his mum.

'Well, that's good,' said Mariam, who was almost being swallowed by her large beanbag. 'I'm glad. Spirit wielders shouldn't be allowed unicorns. Just look what the Weaver did to those sentinels!'

Joby said nothing, his empty eyes wandering back to the window. Skandar stared at the pattern on the carpet and fiddled with the water pin on his lapel. The Weaver, the Fallen Twenty-Four, the spirit element. All fundamentally linked. He felt sick.

Fifteen minutes later, Skandar and Bobby dawdled as the other Mainlander Hatchlings left Joby's treehouse.

Instructor Worsham noticed, his blue eyes resting on them as he plumped up a lime green pillow. 'Was there something else you wanted to ask?' His voice was kind.

'Umm, yes, sort of,' Skandar blurted. 'It's about the sentinels that were killed a few weeks ago.'

Joby sighed and put the pillow down. 'A tragedy.'

'Well, I thought maybe that the smoke was coming from the Mirror Cliffs? And somebody told me that the cliff sentinels guard the Mainland, so I guess I'm asking—'.

'Whether the Weaver was trying to break through to the Mainland?' Joby finished for him.

'Yes.'

Joby leaned against the central trunk of the treehouse. 'Officially we don't know where those sentinels were killed. But unofficially –' Joby picked at a piece of bark – 'you're quite right. I can't see the sense in lying to you.'

Skandar felt panic rising in his chest. 'But doesn't that mean the Mainland is in danger? Doesn't that mean someone should be doing something?'

'You don't need to worry about that. Our new Commodore is determined to hunt down the Weaver. Determined to find New-Age Frost, of course. Though that would be a lot easier if they hadn't locked all the spirit wielders up. It's ironic really, but I reckon it'd take a spirit wielder to stop the Weaver. Not a popular opinion around here, but there you have it.'

Skandar almost choked. 'What do you mean? What do you think the Weaver's planning? What could a spirit wielder do to help?'

Bobby kicked Skandar hard in the back of the leg.

Joby's eyes clouded over, obviously realising he'd gone too far. 'How would I know?' he said sharply. 'And there's no use thinking about it anyway – there aren't any true spirit wielders left. As our Commodore reminded us, spirit is the death element. In fact, we shouldn't really be talking about it at all.'

'No,' Bobby growled, 'we shouldn't.' She practically dragged Skandar to the door.

'You look after yourselves,' Joby murmured, his eyes curious as he turned and closed the door behind them.

Back at the treehouse, Skandar was pacing around and around. 'So Agatha helped me get on to the Island by stopping me taking the Hatchery exam. By flying me here herself.'

'I still can't believe I did all that revision for nothing,' Bobby grumbled.

'And now we know she was right about the Weaver's plan somehow involving the Mainland.'

Flo was still preoccupied with the question Skandar had been asking himself ever since he'd seen a fully grown unicorn by his tower block.

'But who *is* Agatha?' she asked. 'I still don't understand why she'd help you get on to the Island. Was she just being kind?'

'Or maybe,' Bobby said darkly, 'she's working *for* the Weaver?'

Flo shivered. 'Why can't you just assume Agatha was doing something nice?'

'But it makes sense, doesn't it?' Bobby insisted. 'The Weaver wanted Skandar – to help with the spirit element or whatever – so sent this Agatha person to get him.'

'I've told you,' Skandar said, exasperated. 'Agatha warned me *against* the Weaver! And if the Weaver wanted me, why didn't Agatha just take me straight to a lair or whatever?'

Flo giggled. 'The Weaver doesn't have a lair. The Weaver lives in the Wilderness – with all the wild unicorns.'

'Full-on creepy villain style,' Bobby said, sounding almost impressed.

'But the most important thing we found out from Joby–' Skandar walked another circle of the treehouse – 'is that a spirit wielder might be able to stop the Weaver. If Joby's right, then maybe Agatha brought me here because I could help?'

'But the spirit element is illegal, Skar,' Flo said sadly. 'If you try to help, then you and Scoundrel will be thrown in jail – or worse. Agatha can't have wanted to bring you just so you'd get arrested.'

A clang came from above their heads. They all looked up.

'I completely forgot Mitchell was here,' Bobby breathed.

'Do you think he heard?' Skandar whispered. 'About Agatha?'

'We were talking so loudly.' Flo had her hand to her mouth.

In a panic Skandar pulled himself up the rungs of the tree trunk two at a time, and threw open the door of their bedroom.

Mitchell looked startled. He was sitting on the floor and trying to hide something under his leg.

Skandar saw the edge of a card, a flash of colour. 'Have you been going through my things?' he demanded, all thoughts of Agatha forgotten. 'Those are my Chaos Cards,' he said, stepping closer.

'They were under your hammock. I was interested to see what the Mainland— We-we don't have them here. I like the stats,' he spluttered, clearly embarrassed.

Skandar sighed and sank down next to Mitchell on the floor. 'I like how the unicorns look so realistic, even though they're drawings. I wish I could sketch like that – with all that detail.'

Mitchell picked up another card, depicting Sunset's Blood – the unicorn bonded to Federico Jones. 'Exactly! The details are fascinating. The wing beats per minute are particularly interesting when you compare past Chaos Cup winners—' Mitchell cleared his throat, stopping himself from saying more. 'But I'm sure you're just here to tell me not to say anything about your illegal flight to the Island. Don't bother. It would link me to you, and that's the last thing I want.'

Skandar tried not to look too relieved.

Mitchell stood up all of a sudden. 'You know, I was really excited to meet riders from the Mainland. I couldn't wait to be in a quartet – three other people essentially guaranteed to be my friends! I just wanted a new start. And then you turn up and ruin everything.'

Skandar got to his feet too so they were eye to eye. 'Think about how I feel! I wanted to be a unicorn rider more than anything. Then it turns out I'm allied to an element I didn't even know existed! I have no idea what I'm going to do when the domes come down! And now, apparently, it turns out Scoundrel and I might actually be able to help stop what the Weaver's planning – whatever that is. But if we do – we're dead. Oh, and my room-mate hates me. How's that for everything being ruined?'

Mitchell climbed into his hammock, his face terribly sad. 'We can't be talking like this. If you get found out and my father thinks I've helped hide a secret spirit wielder . . . He's the Justice Representative on the Council, for goodness' sake – he's in charge of imprisoning riders like you! He'd be so disappointed; he'd never speak to me again. And I have our family name to think about. You're dangerous.'

Skandar shook his head. 'Do you know what I think? I think the real Mitchell Henderson is someone I'd one hundred per cent want as my friend. But the one he pretends to be for his dad? I'm not so sure.'

He left to rejoin the others – sad and disappointed and scared.

But as he climbed down the trunk he felt a pulse of happiness that made him feel a little less miserable. *Scoundrel?* he wondered. Perhaps the bond could summon more than magic.

CHAPTER TWELVE

MUTATION

Much to Bobby's annoyance, the Hatchlings had not been allowed to attend the Earth Festival at the beginning of August, when everyone had swapped their yellow jackets for the green of the earth season. According to the instructors, it had coincided with a crucial point in their training, although Bobby had insisted this was 'very convenient'. So she was delighted when, as the autumn leaves began to fall from the armoured trees, a notice went up announcing that Hatchlings would be able to attend the Fire Festival in a few weeks' time.

Skandar couldn't wait to go either, but Flo was less keen.

'They're really noisy and busy, and there are people everywhere,' she said as they made their way to the post trees after breakfast. 'I'd rather just stay here than fight through the crowds.'

Bobby shook her head. 'Absolutely no way are we staying here. I've heard there are fireworks *and* food stalls. Nothing's keeping me away.'

Flo laughed. 'Bobby, you couldn't be more of an air wielder if you tried.'

'What do you mean?' Bobby asked suspiciously.

'My mum says air wielders are extroverts. And they like change, and dancing, and noise – so basically they really love parties, whereas earth wielders . . .'

'Would rather just stay home with a good book and a chocolate biscuit?'

'Exactly.' Flo grinned, as she twisted open her green-and-gold capsule. Skandar was used to the system now. Each rider's hole in the tree held a metal capsule. His was half gold, half blue – for the water element – and he had to twist it open to check for letters. If he wanted to send a letter, he had to place the capsule with the blue side facing outwards to show something was inside. It was simple and colourful – the capsules cheerfully decorated the trunks like jewels.

Skandar took his time over opening his own capsule, stuffing a package from Kenna into his pocket. He always felt awkward during conversations about elements and personality. He'd heard all sorts about the other element types: fire wielders were imaginative, burning with ideas, quick to anger; water wielders were forgiving, adaptable, problem-solvers. Nobody seemed to know – or want to discuss – what spirit wielders were like, and comparing his own personality to other water wielders seemed fake and wrong. And the libraries were no help – even Bobby and Flo had searched with him. They'd flicked through the four elemental scriptures, as well as pages and pages of other books, for even a mention of the spirit element – anything to help Skandar for when the training domes came down. But there was nothing.

Flo gasped as she read the letter clutched in her hand.

'What is it?' Skandar asked quickly, thinking immediately of a sentinel attack. His dreams were still haunted by thoughts of the Weaver breaking through and somehow reaching Kenna and Dad – though all had been quiet on the cliffs since their first week.

'My mum and dad's friend – a healer. She's gone missing from Fourpoint.'

'What do you mean "missing"?' Skandar asked, his voice low.

Flo was still staring down at the letter. 'Dad says she was taken during a wild unicorn stampede two nights ago. There are lots of whispers about it being the Weaver.'

'Why the Weaver, though?' Bobby asked. 'People can go missing for lots of reasons.'

Flo's voice was so quiet Skandar could barely hear her. 'Apparently there was this white mark on the healer's treehouse. A white stripe of paint. You know, like the one on the Weaver's face.'

And Scoundrel's head, Skandar thought darkly.

Flo turned the letter over. 'Dad seems really worried. People used to blame it on the Weaver when riders and unicorns disappeared near the Wilderness, but they could just as easily have been attacked by wild unicorns. The Weaver's never actually taken someone from their treehouse before. Never left a mark.'

Skandar couldn't help himself imagining a white mark appearing on the window of Flat 207; a rotting wild unicorn with madness in its eyes; the Weaver's shroud flapping in the wind off the sea; a hand reaching out for Kenna, asleep in bed.

Flo pointed at the letter. 'My dad says he doesn't think the Island should be having *any* festivals right now. Maybe we shouldn't go to the Fire Festival after all.'

Bobby rolled her eyes, but Skandar didn't think it was as convincing as usual.

A little while later, they were lining up their unicorns on the earth training ground, when Amber rode past Scoundrel, Falcon and Blade – flicking her hair aggressively – followed by the rest of the Threat Quartet. She stopped Whirlwind Thief right in front of them.

'Hi, Skandar.' Amber wiggled her fingers at him. 'Have you heard the *super* good news?'

Bobby squinted towards her. 'I think you've got something gross on your head, Amber? Oh no, that's just your mutation. My apologies.' Bobby mock-bowed. A white star crackled on Amber's forehead – matching her unicorn's white marking.

Skandar disliked Amber as much as Bobby did, but he wished Bobby could ignore her instead of baiting her. He was still worried Amber had seen his palm glow white in their first training session.

'It's so cute how you Mainlanders don't know anything that's happening around here! I'm surprised you can tell one end of a unicorn from the other.' She let out a high fake giggle.

Skandar saw Bobby tighten her grip on Falcon's leather reins.

Flo pushed Blade forward to intervene. 'I'm not sure I know what news you're talking about either, Amber,' Flo said softly, 'and I'm an Islander born and bred. How about you explain what you mean?' Smoke curled ominously out of Blade's nostrils.

Amber suddenly looked awkward. Flo had only been trying to keep the peace as usual, but because she was a silver she had an authority that worked on everyone.

'The domes are coming down today.' Amber's teeth glistened shark-like in the sun.

Cold fear crept up Skandar's spine. He'd been hoping for some warning; he'd thought he had more time!

Flo gasped. 'Now? In this earth session?' Having Silver Blade able to summon all the elements wasn't exactly good news for her either. Flo often struggled to control Blade during training – his magic was overwhelmingly strong – but it was much worse for Skandar, who felt about ready to vomit over the edge of Scoundrel's wing.

'Why do you wear this all the time?' In a flash Amber had ridden Thief forward and grabbed a fistful of Skandar's black scarf, half choking him. Scoundrel screeched in protest, and tried to bite a chunk out of the chestnut unicorn's shoulder.

'Don't!' Flo cried out. 'It was his mum's. It's the only thing he has of hers.'

Skandar stared at Flo in disbelief. After years of being tormented by Owen, Skandar knew it was a mistake to reveal any piece of personal information to a bully. Sure enough, Amber looked like she'd won the Chaos Cup.

'So we have something in common do we, *Skan*dar?' She spent too long on the first half of his name, making it sound silly. 'My dad died heroically in a fight with about a hundred wild unicorns, but you don't see me moping around with his old things. It's super pathetic.' She let go of the scarf, and Skandar almost fell sideways off Scoundrel.

'Or maybe you're hiding something *under* it. Perhaps . . . a mutation. Hmm?'

'Skandar hasn't mutated,' Flo said, and Blade let out a low growl. 'And – and if your dad really did die a hero, then I don't think he'd be very proud of the way you treat people sometimes. It's not very kind.'

Amber's face twisted in anger and she rode Thief to the other end of the line, trailed by the rest of the Threat Quartet.

'Always a pleasure,' Bobby called after her, doffing an imaginary cap.

'Do you think that was too harsh of me? Her dad *was* killed by wild unicorns, and she must be sad about it, but she does always change the number of wild unicorns that attacked him, so I'm not sure—'

'She knows,' Skandar interrupted as soon as Amber was out of earshot.

'Knows what?' Flo and Bobby asked together, riding Falcon and Blade closer to Scoundrel.

Skandar dropped his voice so nearby riders wouldn't hear. 'Amber knows I'm a . . . you-know-what. Didn't you hear what she said about the domes coming down, about hiding a mutation under my scarf? Why else would she say that?'

Flo frowned. 'Hmm. But surely she would have reported you by now?'

'Maybe she's enjoying torturing you before she does it.'

'Bobby!' Flo cried. 'Don't say that!'

'I'm a truth-teller.' Bobby shrugged. 'I can't help how honest I am.'

Instructor Webb blew his whistle from Moonlight Dust's back. Skandar still wasn't used to the moss of the instructor's mutation that crept between the wispy hairs on his balding head. 'Today we will attempt some simple sand shields. In a sky battle you would create this barrier to protect yourself from incoming attacks. Useful, yes? Three easy steps. Summon earth to the bond and turn your right palm outwards.' He flipped his hand so the riders could see the green glow. 'Lift your elbow, so your fingers point to the left. Then swipe up and down in the air in front of you.' Instructor Webb's deeply wrinkled face disappeared behind a solid wall of sand. The magic smelled like newly dug soil, pine needles and sun-baked rocks.

'But there isn't an earth dome yet, Instructor Webb,' said Albert, sitting astride Eagle's Dawn a few unicorns down.

Instructor Webb chuckled, his shield collapsing as he dismounted. 'No more domes now, little Hatchlings. You will have to strike out on your own, like birds from the nest. All the instructors have agreed that you're ready.'

'It'll be all right,' Flo whispered to Skandar, and he managed to jerk his head in a nod.

Skandar kept flicking his eyes down to his palm to check that it was still his natural shade of pasty white. The palms of other riders in the line began to glow bright green, and Skandar had no choice but to take a deep breath. He imagined the fine sand of the shield and the smell of the earth magic. He let out an enormous sigh of relief as his palm glowed green like everyone else's, and he swiped his arm upwards to attempt the defensive move.

But without warning, Scoundrel galloped around the training ground at breakneck speed. Skandar pulled on Scoundrel's reins and dug his fingers into his mane, desperately trying to cling on. And through his fingers Skandar could see the ghostly white glow of the spirit element. 'No, Scoundrel! No! We can't!'

Skandar tried with all his might to will his palm green again, but out of nowhere he felt a stab of rage so fierce that it blurred his vision. He knew then for certain that Scoundrel was angry with him, furious that Skandar had tried to block the spirit element. As they came full circle, the black unicorn reared, fire bursting from his mouth, water pouring out of his front hooves into the sky as he kicked them up and outwards. Soon the whole line of riders was soaked through.

Scoundrel's sides were slick with water and sweat, and the insides of Skandar's legs slipped and slid so he was barely able to grip. Instructor Webb called for Skandar to pull up. When it didn't make any difference, he blew his whistle, but this only made Scoundrel wilder. The unicorn zoomed past the instructor and knocked him off his feet, as Moonlight screeched with anger.

'Please, Scoundrel! STOP!' Skandar shouted as he clung on, reins now abandoned, his arms locked round the unicorn's neck as a last resort. Scoundrel snarled and tried to bite at his rider's hands in irritation, a white glow lighting the black feathers on his wings. Skandar cried out in fear and desperation when he saw it, begging, pleading, but there was no stopping

Scoundrel. An icy gale whistled around his wings, stinging Skandar's cheeks. Suddenly Skandar's whole chest felt like it was fit to burst, like he'd swallowed too much air. The smell of the spirit element filled his nostrils – a cinnamon sweetness with a leathery edge.

Then, without meaning for it to happen, Skandar stopped thinking about the earth element altogether. And for a few glorious seconds the joy Skandar and Scoundrel felt, as the spirit element filled the bond, eclipsed all thoughts of death or the Weaver. They could do anything. This was their element. Summoning it was easier than breathing. Colours exploded around the line of riders – reds and yellows and greens and blues. A ghostly ball of glowing white began to build in his palm – and somehow Skandar knew that if he threw it, he could use it to attack, to defend, to win races . . . But then Scoundrel turned sharply, his left wing colliding with his rider's leg, and Skandar remembered.

'Scoundrel, I can't!' he howled over the wind, tears streaming down his face. 'We can't! I'm so sorry. We might kill a unicorn! I don't know—'

Scoundrel dipped a shoulder and threw Skandar sideways. He hit the ground hard. Scoundrel reared over him, kicking out at the air above Skandar's head with his hooves, as they billowed sparks and smoke. Skandar covered his head, afraid that the unicorn would trample him in his determined fury.

A mound of soil rose up out of nowhere – shielding Skandar from Scoundrel – and Instructor Webb approached, now safely back on Moonlight Dust, and wheezing with the effort of galloping towards him. The wispy-haired instructor dismounted and pulled Skandar up off the ground. He looked angrier than Skandar had ever seen him.

'Scorching sandstorms! That unicorn is out of control!' he cried, his voice uncharacteristically harsh. 'He's a danger to you and your fellow riders.' He jabbed a finger at Scoundrel's Luck, who was now growling, his eyes flashing black to red to black. 'Take Scoundrel back to the stables and for goodness' sake calm him down. I thought he was going to kill both of you.'

Instructor Webb squinted at Skandar. 'Are you hurt, boy? What's that on your arm?'

While the old instructor searched in his green cloak for his glasses, relief flooded Skandar as he realised that Instructor Webb hadn't seen him use the spirit element. Skandar looked down at his arm. The green sleeve of his jacket had ridden up over his elbow. He turned his palm upwards and stared at the inside of his left forearm. It was as though someone had taken a brush and painted a white stripe from the inside of Skandar's elbow to his wrist. But the weirdest thing was that the white was translucent. He could see the tendons and bones of his arm through the skin. He made a fist and saw all the muscles tense. Scoundrel rumbled happily behind him.

'A burn, is it? Let me have a look.' Skandar began to offer his left arm to the instructor when – *WHAM*. Someone shoved Skandar sideways.

'Instructor Worsham! What are you—' Skandar was so stunned he couldn't even finish his question.

Instructor Webb opened and closed his mouth.

'Apologies. I noticed that Skandar's hurt. I'll take him to a healer.'

The old man looked shocked, afraid even. 'But – but what are you doing down here? It's highly irregular. Highly irregular indeed. Yes, Instructor Worsham. I suggest you return to your treehouse.'

A shadow crossed Joby's face and he looked much scarier than he did in their Mainlander classes. 'I'll take Skandar to the healer treehouse on my way,' Joby said stiffly. 'Come on, Skandar. Scoundrel can go back to the stables with Moonlight Dust.'

'I'm not leaving him—' Skandar started, trying to reach for Scoundrel's reins, but Joby shoved him in the back, away from the other Hatchlings.

'Do *not* stop walking,' Joby whispered from behind him. 'Pull your sleeve down and do not stop until you get to my treehouse. Do you understand?' Scoundrel screeched in alarm, as his rider moved away up the Eyrie's hill.

'O-okay.' Fear started to eclipse Skandar's adrenaline. Had Joby finally become unhinged by the grief of losing his unicorn, like Amber and her friends had hinted all those weeks ago?

Back at the Eyrie, Joby slammed his treehouse door behind them and rounded on Skandar. 'What in the name of all five elements were you playing at?'

'I, um, what?' Skandar stammered.

Joby's blond ponytail swung from side to side as he paced. 'I know you're a spirit wielder!' he shouted. 'I saw all the fault lines ignite for you. I wasn't fooled by that Weaver stunt; I'm assuming your friends were responsible for that!'

Skandar didn't say anything. His head buzzed with panic. The treehouse felt like it was swaying, vibrating. What had he done?

'And then today you decide to use the spirit element in *training*? What were you thinking? It's only because Scoundrel knocked Webb over that he didn't notice!'

'I didn't mean to!' Skandar couldn't stop himself. It was too late now anyway. He was done for. Joby was going to tell everyone; he and Scoundrel were going to be . . . He couldn't even think it.

'I didn't mean to,' Skandar said more quietly. 'But Scoundrel was pulling towards it so strongly. I didn't even realise I was doing it, and then—'

'Arghhh.' Joby tugged at the end of his ponytail, jerking his head back in anguish. 'We can't even be talking about this, Skandar!'

'You brought me here!' Skandar protested. 'I was fine. I wasn't hurt—'

'If I hadn't pulled you away, Instructor Webb would have seen your arm.' Joby was in front of him suddenly, pulling up the sleeve of Skandar's green jacket.

'This,' Joby hissed, 'is a spirit wielder's mutation.'

Skandar stared down at his arm, the tendons and bones visible underneath. The white stripe reminded him of Scoundrel's blaze – and the mark painted on the Weaver's face.

'You're going to have to keep it hidden at all times,' Joby muttered, dropping his arm. 'Do you know how difficult that's going to be?'

'What's the point?' Skandar said dejectedly.

'What's the point?' Joby spat. 'What do you mean "What's the point?"'

'You're going to report me, aren't you?' Skandar asked flatly. 'We're spirit-allied; we're illegal – and now you know, so . . .' He shrugged.

Joby stared at Skandar as though he'd hit him. 'Report you?' He frowned. 'Skandar, I—' He sank down on to a beanbag, all the anger going out of him. 'I'm not going to turn you in.'

Skandar's heart beat very fast. 'Why not?'

Joby sighed. 'Because I'm like you. I'm a spirit wielder. Or, at least, I was.' Then, for some inexplicable reason, Joby removed the boot from his left foot and peeled off a mustard-coloured sock.

'There,' Joby said, lifting his foot. 'It used to look more like yours – they fade, you see, if your unicorn dies. But you can still see the resemblance.'

At first Skandar thought Joby's foot was just oddly pale, but as he looked more closely he could faintly spot tendons, ligaments and bones underneath the surface of the skin. In some places new skin had knitted together so you couldn't see the mutation at all, creating a patchwork of different shades.

Skandar stared at him. 'But you said your unicorn was killed by a spirit wielder.'

'She was!' Joby exclaimed, the anguish ringing in his voice, his eyes roving around the room madly. 'I was a spirit wielder Hatchling when the Weaver first appeared and killed those twenty-four unicorns during the Qualifiers. The Silver Circle started rounding us up and before long . . . all our spirit unicorns were dead.'

'But how did they kill Winter's Phantom without killing you? Spirit wielders are the only riders who can do that, aren't they?'

Joby swallowed. 'The Silver Circle gave all the spirit wielders an "opportunity" to be spared – but only one took the bait. They told her she had a choice: die along with all the spirit wielders or help the Silver Circle kill our unicorns and take our power. They called her the Executioner.' He wiped away a tear. 'What you have to understand is that before the spirit element was outlawed, the spirit wielders and the Silver Circle were the two most powerful groups of riders on the Island. They hated each other. Recruiting the Executioner was the Silver Circle's perfect revenge.'

Joby took a deep rattling breath. 'I suppose she saved my life, the lives of all the spirit wielders, but –' he shook his head – 'I can't ever forgive her for taking Winter's Phantom from me. Look what I've become – I'm nothing without Phantom, worse than nothing! You can't let it happen to you, to Scoundrel's Luck.' Joby's eyes shone with manic determination. 'You must not use the spirit element, Skandar. Ever.'

'I don't *want* to use it. It's the death element! I'm too scared I'll kill a unicorn. I didn't want to use it today, but it was so hard to stop. I don't want to be like the Weaver—'

'Listen to me.' Joby kneeled in front of Skandar, like he was begging. 'Spirit wielders – like you, like me – have the ability to kill bonded unicorns, but that isn't going to just happen. If a spirit wielder wants to kill a unicorn, they have to really mean it. Do you understand? Don't torture yourself thinking you could accidentally kill a friend's unicorn, okay?'

Relief flooded through Skandar so strongly that his knees

almost buckled. He nodded. He wasn't dangerous – unless he wanted to be.

'Like the other four elements, spirit is in every unicorn, in every rider,' Joby continued. 'But nobody teaches it – nobody uses it any more – so riders won't understand it, even though it flows through their bonds. I'm not telling you to stop using the spirit element because it's evil. I'm telling you to stop because the Silver Circle *will* kill you if they find out what you are. Aspen McGrath is desperately looking for someone to blame for these sentinel deaths. They won't spare either of you.'

'But I couldn't control Scoundrel today – I couldn't stop spirit coming into the bond.'

'You must learn to block it. Imagine another element as strongly and as forcefully as you can.'

'That's what I was trying to do!' Skandar cried. 'But it didn't work!'

'You have to learn to focus,' Joby spat. 'Your mind, your will, has to be strong. You must fight Scoundrel – you can't give in.' Joby stood and began to pace, more energetic than Skandar had ever seen him. 'How are you hiding Scoundrel's blaze?'

'Ink to start with, but now I'm using black hoof polish,' Skandar explained.

'Who else knows?' Joby demanded.

'Bobby Bruna, Flo Shekoni—'

Joby froze. 'With the silver?'

'She won't say anything. We're friends.'

'A silver and a spirit wielder. Dangerous.'

Skandar ignored this. 'Oh, and Mitchell Henderson.'

'*Ira* Henderson's son? He's on the Council!' Joby exclaimed in disbelief. 'Are you serious?'

'Oh, and possibly Amber Fairfax. She's the one I'm most worried about,' Skandar mumbled quickly, expecting Joby to fly off the handle.

Instead, Joby just waved his hand dismissively. 'She won't say anything.'

'Have you met her?' Skandar asked sarcastically. 'Of course she will!'

Joby faced him. 'She won't want to be linked to a spirit wielder. She won't want the Council asking her questions, and she won't want her face splashed all over the *Hatchery Herald* with yours.'

'Why not?' Skandar spluttered. 'Being in the Island newspaper sounds exactly like the kind of thing Amber would love!'

'Her father, Simon Fairfax, is in prison.'

'She said he was killed by wild unicorns!' Skandar was furious. His mum was *actually* dead – how could Amber lie about her dad like that?

Joby let out a humourless bark of laughter. 'Well, I expect she and her mother would prefer that. No, Skandar. Simon Fairfax is a spirit wielder. Like us.'

Questions exploded in Skandar's brain, colliding with each other like birds fleeing a herd of hungry unicorns. He asked the first one that reached his mouth. 'Why aren't you in prison with Simon Fairfax? With the other spirit wielders.'

'They decided to show me some *mercy*.' Joby's laugh was hollow. 'I was the youngest spirit wielder in the Eyrie; they didn't think I could do much damage with my unicorn dead. They let me read books on the Mainland and I became so knowledgeable that they let me teach the Mainlander riders when they arrived. But I'm not free; I haven't been free since the day they took Winter's Phantom. I expect things might change after today, though. No more sneaking out to keep an eye on your training after the stunt I pulled with Webb.'

There was a clang on the bridge outside and they both looked up. 'Listen to me, Skandar. Do *not* use the spirit element again. Do *not* speak to me about the spirit element again. And, for goodness' sake, never let anyone see that mutation.'

'But there's so much I want to ask! If the spirit element won't hurt anyone, then maybe it can help? You told me before that spirit wielders would have been able to stop the Weaver – what did you mean? Do you know what the Weaver's planning? Maybe I can help? Someone brought me to the Island, Joby – maybe that's why?'

Joby was already herding him towards the door, as though terrified someone was going to arrive. 'With people going missing and sentinels exploding, if anyone finds out you're spirit-allied, it won't matter if you're trying to help or not.'

'But I need to learn more. What about the Mainland? What about my family?'

'Even if you could help, that doesn't mean you should. The fifth is called the death element for a reason, Skandar. Don't let it kill you too.'

And Joby shut the door in Skandar's face.

CHAPTER THIRTEEN

CHOCOLATE CUSTARD

Shaking with a mixture of shock, terror and disappointment, Skandar stomped back to his treehouse, swinging across dangerous gaps between the platforms and jumping down ladders four rungs at a time. He couldn't believe Joby – the only spirit wielder he'd ever met – was refusing to help him or say more about the Weaver. In the safety of his room he tore open the package from Kenna he'd collected from the post tree that morning, hoping it would calm him down. A bag of Jelly Babies thumped on to the rug beneath his black boots as he read.

Skar!

I can't believe you're doing elemental magic already. I guess your favourite class must be water, because you're allied to it, right? So proud of you, little bro. I actually think you're really brave riding

a real unicorn. Okay, so I have a list of questions —
prepare yourself. I want to know EVERYTHING!
So does everyone at school. I'm practically famous
now because of you — they all want to know about
Scoundrel, your training, how well you're doing.
They want me to talk about you in assembly. Don't
worry, I'll describe the look on Owen's face in
GREAT detail in my next letter!

 PS Hope the Jelly Babies aren't too squashed.

Skandar screwed the paper into a ball. He couldn't answer
any of her questions – not with the truth anyway. He didn't
feel brave at all, especially with Joby's warnings ringing in
his ears. The only thing that was keeping him from tears was
concentrating on the sensation of the bond in his chest, tingling
and alive – Scoundrel's way of telling him: *We've always got each
other, even if the whole world is against us.*

Finally, beaten by hunger, Skandar headed to the Trough for
lunch, bumping into Mitchell just outside.

'Are you a nomad? Did Instructor Webb throw you out? What
did Instructor Worsham say?' Mitchell seemed oddly concerned
for someone who thought Skandar was evil.

'No, not this time. Close call, though.'

Mitchell frowned. 'Oh. That's good. It-it would look bad, you
know, for our quartet, if you were made a nomad this early.'

'Right,' Skandar said, thoroughly confused.

'You dropped this,' Mitchell said abruptly, handing Skandar

his mum's scarf. 'Down on the training ground.'

Skandar's hand went to his neck immediately – he couldn't believe he hadn't realised. 'Thank you, Mitchell. That's actually really—'

'I'll be going, then,' Mitchell said, and hurried inside.

A few moments later, stomach rumbling, Skandar was about to pick up a plate when he spotted Mitchell again. He was choosing between desserts and Amber was approaching him, flanked by the rest of the Threat Quartet.

Skandar heard Amber's high faux-sweet voice. 'Still no friends, Mitchster?'

'Go away, Amber,' Mitchell muttered, not looking up.

'What's wrong? Don't you want to play with us?' black-haired Meiyi cooed at him.

'Look, I just want to eat my food. I'm not bothering anyone. Hey, Kobi, give that back!' He'd snatched away Mitchell's bowl of dessert, and was holding it out of his reach. 'That's mine!'

'No. It's. Not,' Amber growled at him, pushing him three times in the chest.

After the day he'd had, something inside Skandar snapped. Suddenly Amber was every girl who'd told Skandar he was weird, and every boy who'd ever said his dad was a loser and that he'd end up the same way. But he wasn't the old Skandar – trapped in a school with no friends and needing Kenna to stick up for him. He was a rider now. He had Flo and Bobby and Scoundrel's Luck – and he wasn't going to put up with bullies any more. Especially ones who lied about their parent being dead.

Skandar strode towards Mitchell. The Threat Quartet were

so busy laughing that they didn't even see him coming. He got behind them and lifted Mitchell's bowl of chocolate custard right out of Kobi's hand.

'Hey!' Kobi shouted. The others stopped laughing.

'You've got a nerve,' Amber snarled, taking a step towards Skandar.

He started to panic. He hadn't thought this through any further than stopping them bullying Mitchell. So as the Threat Quartet closed in, he used the only weapon he had and flung the contents of Mitchell's bowl towards them.

Chocolate custard hit Amber right between the eyes, a large blob landed on Kobi's head, and Meiyi ducked to the ground, screaming that it was in her hair. Only Alastair remained unscathed. He started towards Skandar, fists clenched. But Skandar had an idea.

'Lay one finger on me or Mitchell,' Skandar hissed as menacingly as he could, 'and I will set Scoundrel's Luck on you. Even if it's the last thing I do before we get kicked out of the Eyrie.'

The Threat Quartet glowered at him.

'You saw him in training today.' Skandar shrugged. 'Try it. See what happens.' He was amazed his voice was steady.

The quartet looked nervously at each other, unsure of their next move. Skandar decided to leave them to it. But he had one last thing to say. He stepped closer to Amber, who was rubbing custard off her upturned nose.

'If you do anything,' she hissed under her breath, 'I'll tell everyone—'

'I dare you,' Skandar growled, his voice low. 'And when I get to prison, I'll be sure to say hello to your dad.'

Amber opened and closed her mouth like a goldfish. 'He's not there,' she finally croaked, and her lie helped Skandar ignore the twinge of guilt he was feeling for using her secret to keep himself safe.

He stepped away and grabbed a plate as though nothing had happened. His ears were hot and his heart was beating wildly, but he piled up some food and ladled more custard into Mitchell's bowl. When he turned back, the Threat Quartet was gone.

'More dessert?' Skandar asked Mitchell, and couldn't help grinning at the expression on his face.

'Forking thunderstorms! I cannot *believe* you just did that. That was – that was the BEST thing I've ever seen in my *life*.' Then Mitchell started to laugh, and Skandar – who'd never seen him smile before, let alone laugh – joined in.

'The chocolate on Amber's face,' Mitchell wheezed. 'I can't tell you how long I've dreamed of something like that happening.'

There was a sort of coughing noise from behind Skandar. Bobby and Flo were standing behind the laughing boys, shaking their heads.

'You're going to *set Scoundrel's Luck on them*?' Bobby raised an eyebrow. 'Did I really just hear you say that?'

Mitchell smiled at her, tears of laughter in his eyes. 'That's right! What was it, Skandar? *Before we get kicked out of the Eyrie*?'

Bobby nodded appreciatively. 'Badass.'

Flo did not look happy. 'Skandar –' it was the first time she hadn't called him Skar since their first night and it made him stop laughing – 'you can't go around saying things like that. Someone might think you're serious – you could get declared a nomad. Not to mention someone might think you're actually dangerous!'

'Didn't you see what happened in training today?' Skandar said quietly, looking into her concerned face. 'We *are* dangerous.'

Flo started wringing her hands. 'I know, Skar, but maybe keep the death threats to a minimum?'

Skandar smiled at her. 'I'll do my best. But I'm telling you, it'll be a struggle.'

And this time all four of them collapsed into fits of giggles.

A few weeks later, Skandar woke early. He made his way down the tree trunk, threw some logs into the stove, and wrote a letter to Kenna. Telling her how he was feeling always made him feel better, as though she was sitting right next to him and tucking her hair thoughtfully behind her ear as he wrote.

Kenn,

I don't want to lie to you – things aren't fine here. Scoundrel isn't really himself at the moment and our bond doesn't seem to be making any difference at all. He's biting and bucking and screeching and, to be honest, I can barely control him most of the time. Other riders are afraid of him, and some have even said we should be chucked out of the Eyrie. But I'm scared it's my fault.

Skandar didn't just *think* it was his fault; he knew it was. But he couldn't risk mentioning his constant battle to stop the white light spilling into his palm. Or the guilt he felt when he blocked it or the rage that vibrated in his chest from Scoundrel. What did it matter if they could feel each other's emotions if their bond felt less like a connection and more like a tug of war? Things had become so bad that Skandar had tried to seek out Instructor Worsham for advice a few times after Mainlander classes, but Joby had practically shoved him out of the door.

You know I told you how Scoundrel liked messing around with Red in the clearing, or splashing water at Falcon to annoy her or chewing my hair? Well, he doesn't really do that any more. And he's gone off Jelly Babies – even red ones. I wish you were here, Kenn. There's so much more I want to tell you. Miss you more than ever. Skar x

He enclosed a sketch he'd drawn of Scoundrel rearing up, then climbed down to the post tree. On his way back Skandar felt a questioning tug on the bond – an unexpected pulse of happiness from Scoundrel trying to cheer him up – so instead he changed direction and headed to the stables.

Skandar practically jumped out of his skin when he arrived. Hammers clanged on metal, hot iron sizzled, and lively conversation bounced around the wall alongside the usual shrieks and calls of the unicorns.

A boy was standing by Scoundrel's stable with his arms crossed and eyebrows raised. He was only a little older than Skandar, with golden-brown hair and mismatched eyes: one brown, one green. He didn't look very happy.

'Does this monster belong to you?' he asked Skandar crossly.

Skandar wasn't sure what to say. Smoke was curling out of Scoundrel's nostrils and he had blood from his breakfast smeared around his bottom lip.

'He's shocked me twice, sent a fireball at my leg and practically chased me from the stable with a water jet. Is that normal?'

'Scoundrel's a bit lively at the moment,' Skandar said sheepishly – the understatement of the century.

'Well,' the boy grumbled, 'don't let me regret choosing you.'

'Choosing me?'

'I'm his blacksmith.'

'Ohhh.' Skandar had dreamed about this back on the Mainland. Growing up, he'd drawn countless sketches of unicorns in armour, imagining what his own might look like. All young unicorns were fitted with a full set of armour to protect them during sky battles. The riders' armour would protect both themselves and – because of the bond – the lives of their unicorns.

'Sorry, I didn't realise.' Skandar practically had to shout over the noise of metal on metal. 'It's just you seem quite—'

'Young?' The boy put his hands on his hips. 'Yeah, so what if I'm an apprentice blacksmith? Is that a problem?' He leaned against the stable door, scowling. He was wearing a dark green polo shirt, brown trousers and short brown boots. Like all the other blacksmiths, he was also wearing a very grubby leather apron with a belt full of tools at his waist. The boy was probably only a year older than him, but somehow he made Skandar feel like a baby.

'No, no, it's no problem. I'm just sorry about Scoundrel trying to blast you,' Skandar mumbled.

'Well, it might be better now you're here,' the blacksmith said gruffly. 'I'm Jamie Middleditch.' He stuck out a hand, which was even grubbier than his apron.

'Skandar Smith,' Skandar replied, feeling like this was all oddly formal.

'I know,' Jamie replied, taking a measuring tape out of his apron pocket. He looked at Skandar expectantly.

'Oh yeah. Of course. I'll go in first, then?' Skandar said, grabbing a brush and feeling awkward under the boy's mismatched gaze.

'Right you are,' Jamie said, though this time there was a ghost of a smile on his lips.

Scoundrel snorted a stream of water that Skandar had to dodge as he entered. The unicorn's black coat fizzed with electricity, his ever-growing wings flapped aggressively and some of the feathers ignited.

'It's going to be that kind of day, is it?' Skandar sighed, raising his eyebrows at Scoundrel. He put a hand to the unicorn's hot black neck and tried to calm him.

'Now?' came Jamie's voice from the stable door.

'Why not?' Skandar called, and then murmured quietly to Scoundrel: 'This is Jamie. He wants to make armour for both of us; to protect us when we battle the other unicorns. Please, *please* try not to kill him.'

Jamie approached and Scoundrel's nostrils flared red. Skandar braced himself for an elemental blast. But it never came. Jamie was singing under his breath to the unicorn: a soothing melody. The unicorn lowered his neck, sniffed Jamie's boots and then his blacksmith's apron. Jamie put out a hand to stroke the unicorn's head.

'Stop!' Skandar said suddenly, afraid the blacksmith would notice Scoundrel's blaze.

Scoundrel and Jamie both stared at him in surprise. Skandar thought quickly. 'He doesn't like his head being touched. Sorry. I should have warned you.'

'No problem,' Jamie said, and stroked the unicorn's neck instead.

Skandar looked on in astonishment. Just the other day, Flo had tried to stroke Scoundrel's nose, and he'd tried to bite her finger off. 'Scoundrel never lets anyone else near him, let alone—'

'We smiths have a gift.' Jamie smiled at the unicorn. 'I like him when he's not trying to fry me.'

'Same,' Skandar said, and both the boys chuckled.

As Jamie unrolled his measuring tape and Scoundrel playfully attempted to bite the end of it, a question began to form in Skandar's mind.

'Have you heard much about the Weaver recently?' He'd never really met an Islander who didn't live in the Eyrie before, and wondered what he could glean from Jamie. 'We saw the sentinel flares from up here, but we don't get much news.'

Jamie had his back to Skandar, as he held the tape against Scoundrel's leg. 'They like keeping you safe and worry-free up here in your metal nest, I bet. They don't like you having distractions.'

'I heard about a healer being taken,' Skandar blurted, remembering the letter Flo had received from her dad earlier that month. 'And do you know if anyone has seen New-Age Frost?'

Jamie motioned for Skandar to join him by the stable wall furthest from the door. 'No sign of New-Age Frost, but there are a lot more people missing now,' he said quietly.

Skandar waited.

'Since the Chaos Cup there've been more wild unicorn stampedes than ever. And everyone knows the Weaver is behind them, driving the beasts out of the Wilderness. But every time there's a stampede, more of us go missing.'

'More of you?' Skandar asked.

Jamie shivered. 'No *rider* has been taken. They're all like the healer you mentioned – normal Islanders. Non-rider Islanders. Like me.'

'How many missing people are there?' Skandar asked, horrified.

Jamie sighed heavily. 'A shopkeeper, a bard, a saddler's apprentice, a tavern owner and at least two blacksmiths. Can you imagine? We sort of thought we were safe from the Weaver, not being riders, you know?'

'I don't understand why the Weaver would take people, though.'

'Me neither.' Jamie shrugged. 'Although there've been whispers about experiments.'

'What kind of experiments?'

'No idea. Might just be talk.'

'Is anyone trying to find the missing people?' Skandar asked indignantly.

Jamie's laugh was hollow. 'Aspen McGrath is desperate to work out what the Weaver's planning. But apparently she's more focused on finding New-Age Frost than the missing Islanders. Sure, the Council's been putting up signs everywhere, asking people to report anything suspicious to them, but it hasn't done any good so far.'

Skandar tugged down the sleeve of his green jacket to make sure his mutation was fully covered.

'If you ask me, our Commodore is blinded by losing New-Age Frost. The Weaver's planning something big, I'm sure of it. Bigger than stealing New-Age Frost, bigger than the Fallen Twenty-Four. The Weaver's never killed sentinels before. You need to be careful.'

Jamie patted Scoundrel's neck, and the unicorn screeched appreciatively. 'Don't want Scoundrel's armour getting into the Weaver's creepy hands.'

Skandar watched Jamie measuring for a while and holding up pieces of metal against Scoundrel's legs. 'When will the armour be ready?' Skandar was thinking that it might be quite useful to protect him *from* Scoundrel if things carried on the way they were.

'After the Fire Festival,' Jamie said, straightening up.

Skandar remembered something Jamie had said earlier. 'Umm . . . what did you mean when you said about choosing us?'

Jamie grinned. 'The instructors sent over a file on all the unicorns – and we had to pick one.'

'And you chose Scoundrel's Luck?' Skandar asked, incredulous. 'He's not exactly got the best record for behaving himself recently. It's not his fault,' Skandar added. 'He's just a bit . . . different.'

'Well, Skandar, I know what it's like to be different.' Jamie sighed. 'My whole family are bards – they sing for a living – but I always wanted to be a blacksmith. Being different, it takes guts. And guts is what it takes to win the Chaos Cup. That's why I picked you and Scoundrel.'

'You got all that from our file?'

Jamie laughed. 'It made for *very* entertaining reading. You fall off quite a lot, don't you?'

Skandar groaned.

'But you get back on,' Jamie said more kindly. 'That's why I chose you.'

He brandished the measuring tape at Skandar. 'Your turn!'

That evening the sound of raindrops echoed across the roofs of the Eyrie like hands slapping steel drums. Each treehouse had its own special rhythm to add to the cacophony that filled the night air. But not even the rain could dampen Skandar's spirits. It was the Fire Festival tomorrow, and he would be riding Scoundrel's Luck into Fourpoint for the first time. And, best of all, he'd be going with his friends. Sure, now the domes were down, Skandar's training sessions were filled with the terror of being discovered as a spirit wielder, but somehow he felt protected by the four metal walls of their treehouse. Before the chocolate custard incident, Skandar hadn't realised that his spirit element worries had been magnified by Mitchell's behaviour towards him. Now the treehouse felt like a completely different place. Even more like home.

'Can I see it again?' Bobby demanded, interrupting Skandar mid-sketch.

Skandar pulled up his green sleeve so his skeletal mutation was visible. He clenched his fist, and Bobby stared at the muscles and tendons moving under the skin, the bones shining.

Over in the corner, Mitchell shielded his eyes as though the mutation would blind him.

Bobby rolled her eyes. 'Oh, stop.'

'Excuse me!' he protested. 'I've only been vaguely okay with this whole thing for about five minutes so I'm sorry if it's going to take me a little longer to get used to a spirit wielder's *actual* mutation.' He looked back down at his book.

'What are you reading?' Skandar asked, trying to keep the peace.

'My mother sent me this fascinating book on unicorn saddles.' Mitchell held it up to show Skandar the cover. 'She's a librarian for the Council.' He sounded proud – not scared, like when he talked about his dad.

'So would she know about *The Book of Spirit*?' Skandar asked, unable to stop himself.

Mitchell winced and shook his head. 'She works for the water library.'

But Bobby was interested in something else Mitchell had

said. 'When do we get saddles?'

'Not until we're Nestlings,' Flo answered. 'Dad says he's going to embarrass me when he brings his designs to the ceremony next year.' She smiled as though picturing the conversation.

'Well, it can't come quickly enough,' Bobby moaned, shifting around on her beanbag. 'My bum has more bruises than an apple crumble.'

'What does that mean?' Flo asked politely. 'Is that a Mainland expression? Don't you think it's interesting being in a quartet with two Mainlanders, Mitchell? Everyone on the Island knows each other, so it's a really nice change to be surprised by things.'

'Well, don't listen to Bobby!' Skandar was trying not to laugh. 'That is *not* something we say on the Mainland.'

'You never let me have any fun,' Bobby grumbled.

'What are you drawing, Skar?' Flo asked, getting up.

Skandar felt himself blushing as she peered over his shoulder. He'd drawn the quartet with their unicorns. Red and Scoundrel were exploding a tree together, with Mitchell and Skandar taking cover nearby. Bobby was grooming Falcon's mane – the unicorn always insisted on looking her best. And he'd drawn Flo smiling up at Blade, with one hand on his neck.

Flo burst into tears; Skandar put the sketchbook down hurriedly. 'Did I draw you wrong? It's for my sister. I was going to send it with my letter, but I don't have—'

'No, Skar, it's – it's beautiful.' Flo hiccoughed. 'It's how I wish Blade and I looked at each other, but we just don't have the same connection as the rest of you. I see you together and it's like you were moulded for each other. Mitchell, Red keeps you warm when you sleep in her stable – she glows like coals; I've seen her do it!' She turned to Bobby. 'And Falcon might be a princess, but she understands that you're competitive so she always tries her best for you. And, Skar –' Flo heaved in a breath – 'you said yourself that you can already feel Scoundrel's emotions! That doesn't usually happen until Fledgling year!

'You fit each other, you all feel the love in the bond. But Blade doesn't even like me; he never has. He doesn't understand why I'm afraid of him.'

In a completely uncharacteristic move, Bobby got to her feet and hugged Flo. 'It'll get better. I'll help you, okay?'

Flo wiped away some tears. 'But I can't—'

'DON'T give up!' Bobby looked at Flo fiercely. 'Because if you do, you'll have me to answer to. And believe me, Florence, I can be much scarier than a silver unicorn.'

'I don't doubt that,' Mitchell mumbled to Skandar.

Skandar laughed under his breath. But as he watched Bobby wrap her arms tighter round Flo, he thought she was actually a lot less scary than she would ever let on.

BANG! There was an explosion outside.

Skandar ran to the door and threw it open, Bobby close behind. They rushed to the rail of their platform and stared out into the distance. Sure enough, green smoke was rising again over the Mirror Cliffs.

'Was that another sentinel flare?' Flo's hand flew to her mouth as she and Mitchell joined them.

'An earth wielder's flare,' Mitchell said, his voice soft and sad.

BANG! Another explosion echoed around the Eyrie. Yellow smoke this time.

BANG! Now red smoke mixed with the yellow and green over the Mirror Cliffs so it looked more like a billowing bonfire. Skandar knew he should have been thinking of the families and friends of the dead sentinels, but an image of Kenna's terrified face burst into his mind.

Other riders were out of their treehouses now and standing on bridges, pointing to where the sentinels had fallen. Mainlander voices – from Hatchlings to Preds – were the loudest.

'That's definitely the Mirror Cliffs!'

'The Weaver's trying to get to the Mainland!'

'Was that three?'

'One after the other?'

'Surely the Weaver's broken through?'

'We need to do something!'

'Has Fourpoint signalled?'

Several chaotic minutes later, torches flared down in the clearing, the light reflecting off the trees' armour. The Eyrie instructors were shouting as they rode through the forest. 'The Mainland is safe. The line has been held. The Mainland is safe.'

'But how long is it going to be safe for?' Skandar said, as they collapsed on to beanbags back in the treehouse. 'We can't just wait around up here while the Weaver gets closer and closer to attacking the Mainland!'

Bobby nodded, her eyes alight with the same fire as Skandar's. Their families were on the Mainland, unprotected. This was different for them.

'What are you saying?' Flo asked, full of trepidation.

But Skandar was looking at something else. A piece of newspaper poking out of Mitchell's book. He grabbed at it.

'You've lost my place!' Mitchell complained.

Skandar was staring at the front page of the *Hatchery Herald*, hardly able to believe his eyes.

'What is it? What's wrong?' Flo asked.

'Agatha's alive,' Skandar croaked, and he pointed at a black-and-white photograph under the headline: BACK BEHIND BARS: EXECUTIONER'S ESCAPE ENDS.

'That's her?' Mitchell asked urgently. 'The woman who flew you to the Island . . . is the Executioner? The one who betrayed the spirit wielders? Who killed all their unicorns? Who killed *Joby's* unicorn?'

'Are you sure?' Flo asked, squinting at the picture. 'Are you sure, Skar?'

'Certain,' he said. 'I remember those marks on her cheeks. I thought they were burns – but it's her. It must be her spirit mutation.'

There was a beat of silence.

'Why would the Executioner bring you here?' Bobby asked, her brow crinkled.

But an idea was forming in Skandar's mind. Agatha was a spirit wielder like him. Agatha had brought him here. She would have the answers he needed.

'Mitchell, your dad's in charge of the imprisoned spirit wielders, right?'

Mitchell looked very wary. 'Yes . . .'

'Can you get me into their prison?'

Mitchell's eyes widened behind his glasses. 'Sorry, you want to go where?'

'Joby won't talk to me about the spirit element. He's too afraid. But Agatha . . . She knew somehow that the Weaver was going to attack the Mainland. She helped me get here. I need to know why. And even if she won't help me, there's a whole bunch of spirit wielders there who might be able to tell me how to control the spirit element. Maybe they know more about what the Weaver's up to?'

'It's too dangerous,' Flo said immediately. 'She's the Executioner, Skar!'

'But she helped me before! And she'll be behind bars; what can she do?'

Mitchell looked like he might be sick. 'But what about my father? What if he—'

'You can't have it both ways, Mitch,' Bobby said bluntly. 'Either you want to help Skandar or you don't. Choose.'

'Well, I don't think it's as simple as that,' Mitchell blustered. 'You're asking me to break into a prison! Have you checked the libraries? Maybe if I helped, we could find . . .'

Skandar was already shaking his head. 'They don't have anything on the spirit element. Look, it's not just about Agatha or the Weaver's plan. If I don't learn how to control the spirit element, to hide it, I'm not going to be training in the Eyrie much longer. Scoundrel throws me off practically every day. They'll declare me a nomad for sure, and even if I make it to the Training Trial there's no way I'll finish above last place. Please, Mitchell. I wouldn't ask if there was any other way.'

'Well, I do have one suggestion . . .' Mitchell mused.

'So you'll do it?' Skandar asked.

'You've all gone mad!' Flo cried.

Skandar looked at her. 'You don't all have to come. I can just go with Mi—'

'No way!' Bobby shouted, as Mitchell said, 'Absolutely not; it'll take all four of us.'

'I'm coming,' Flo said quietly. 'I just want someone to write down that I said this wasn't a good idea.'

'It's going to take some serious planning.' Mitchell was already getting to his feet. 'I'll need you all in attendance at our first Quartet Meeting.'

'I think people usually just call it a chat,' Bobby said.

He narrowed his eyes at her. 'This is serious.'

'Fiiiine. When is it?'

'Now,' Mitchell said forcefully. 'If we're going to get away with this, we need to break into the prison when the sentinels – and my father – are busy.'

'Busy with what?' Skandar asked.

'The Fire Festival.'

'But that's tomorrow night!' Flo exclaimed.

'Yes,' said Mitchell. 'Exactly.'

CHAPTER FOURTEEN

THE FIRE FESTIVAL

Overnight the rain had turned to snow, so on the morning of the Fire Festival the tree bells woke the riders to a sparkling-white Eyrie. From their round treehouse window, Skandar looked out over roofs, bridges and treetops weighed down by the new snowfall. The Eyrie glistened in the early-November sunshine, white powder partially burying the armour round its tree trunks, and it was as though Skandar had woken up to a different world – a winter wonderland rather than a training school.

Flo was absolutely beside herself with excitement. Snow was rare on the Island – and even rarer before the fire season – so when Mitchell and Bobby clambered sleepily down the tree trunk, Flo was already wrapped up in a coat, scarf and gloves.

'Come on! Hurry up! We can go to the training ground before our water session – before this melts. I want to show Blade. Maybe it'll help him relax a bit.'

'How is it,' Bobby groaned, 'that you're so enthusiastic about everything? It's exhausting.'

'Not everything.' Flo dashed right up to Bobby. 'Just snow! Don't be so boring, Bobby.'

'You're going to regret calling me boring when I annihilate you in a snowball fight,' Bobby growled. 'It snows every year in the Sierra Nevada in Spain, where my mum grew up. My grandparents still live there, so I've got serious skills.'

Flo looked delighted.

Mitchell was by the fire, leaning over a map of Fourpoint.

'Hey, are you coming?' Skandar asked.

'Well, I'm not sure. The plan for the prison isn't quite finished, and we have to be properly prepared—'

'But the snow!' Flo pleaded, pulling him to his feet. She laughed, trying to make him go round in a circle. His glasses fell right down to the end of his nose as they spun. 'I'm a silver. You have to do as I say,' Flo joked.

Mitchell looked flustered but pleased, a blush creeping up his brown skin. 'I have heard snowball fights are quite fun,' he said thoughtfully. 'How about me and Bobby versus Skandar and Flo?'

'How come you get Bobby?' Flo moaned.

'Oi!' Skandar cried.

'To be fair,' Flo said, opening the door of the treehouse and crunching out on to the snowy platform, 'we do have a silver unicorn and a spirit unicorn on our side. It's pretty even.'

But in the end the unicorns weren't much help with the snowball fight. They were just as excited as Flo about the strange cold substance all over the ground of the clearing. Falcon's Wrath took a while to let her mane down, carefully melting the snow beneath her hooves so she didn't get them wet, but when Scoundrel careered into her, trying to play, she forgot all about it. Red got so overexcited that she ended up losing control of her legs and getting her horn stuck in a snowdrift. Scoundrel tried to pull her out by her tail, which made Flo and Bobby fall about laughing. Even Silver Blade joined in, rolling over in the snow on his back and moving his wings from side to side.

'Oh, look, a deadly snow angel,' Skandar joked; his cheeks hurt from laughing.

'Snow unicorn, surely?' Mitchell corrected him, and Skandar threw a snowball in his face.

Flo sighed, as they watched Blade relaxing in the snow. 'I wish he was always like this.'

For a whole hour they were just four normal Hatchlings messing about with their unicorns. Skandar completely forgot to worry about breaking into the prison, or whether Agatha had brought him to the Island for good or bad. He didn't think about New-Age Frost or the Weaver or the dead sentinels or all the missing people. He even forgot to dread the upcoming water training – terrified that he'd lose his fight with Scoundrel and reveal their true element. Instead, Skandar threw himself into snowdrifts, attempting to hide from Scoundrel – who tried to tug off his black boots as soon as he found him, making Skandar howl with laughter.

The fun came to an abrupt end when the unicorns – clearly hungry from all their play – decided to catch a variety of animals that had been driven out of their holes and nests by the weather, dragging the dead creatures through the snow to eat them. The effect was rather smelly and gory, the white snowdrifts turning pinkish red, and the riders didn't really fancy making snowballs after that. And things got even more raucous when the other Hatchling unicorns arrived for training and joined the bloody feast.

Instructor O'Sullivan eventually restored order, shouting instructions over the howl of the icy wind whipping around the Eyrie's hill. 'Today you'll be summoning waves with water magic. Waves are useful in attack or defence because of the sheer amount of water they generate. For example –' Instructor O'Sullivan always gave examples – 'I once saw a rider use the air element to electrify a tidal wave so large, it took out half the unicorns in the Chaos Cup.' Skandar sometimes wondered whether Instructor O'Sullivan was the rider in all her examples.

Her demonstration made it look so easy: astride Celestial Seabird, she held her glowing blue palm outwards and quickly tipped her fingers down and then up again in a smooth curve. A perfect wave crested and troughed through the air above the training ground, breaking in a frothy crash at the opposite end.

'Your turn,' she barked.

Bobby and Mitchell managed to make small waves almost immediately, along with many of the other Hatchlings. Gallons of water poured from Blade's ears and nostrils as Flo tried to explain calmly to the silver unicorn what a wave was.

'Skandar?' Instructor O'Sullivan approached on Seabird. 'Let me see what you and Scoundrel can do. I've seen many a water wielder of mine use waves to secure themselves an excellent place in the Training Trial at the end of the year. How are yours doing?'

Skandar took a deep breath and concentrated with all his might on the water element, pushing all thoughts of spirit from his mind. He imagined the water element's aromas of mint, salt and wet hair filling his nostrils. His palm glowed blue. Perhaps Scoundrel understood. Perhaps they were going to be all right. Shakily Skandar lifted his palm the way Instructor O'Sullivan had demonstrated and—

Scoundrel screeched and reared on his back legs, higher and faster than he ever had before. The unicorn's anger erupted in Skandar's own heart. Fury that his rider never let him use his allied element. Scoundrel's wings snapped out, jolting Skandar's thighs, and Skandar was thrown from his unicorn's back, hitting the soggy grass of the training ground with a squelch. Scoundrel, calmer now that Skandar wasn't actively trying to block the spirit element, looked curiously at his rider on the ground, as though he was surprised to see him there.

Instructor O'Sullivan vaulted from Seabird's back in an instant. 'Don't move,' she ordered. 'Are you hurt?'

'Just winded,' Skandar gasped out, clutching his chest. 'I think I'm all right.'

Instructor O'Sullivan sighed with relief. 'Could be a broken rib. Much better than a broken neck.' She surveyed him. 'But I'll take you up to the healer treehouse myself.'

'You don't need—'

'I'll decide what I do and don't need to do, Skandar, thank you,' Instructor O'Sullivan snapped, grabbing Scoundrel's reins. 'You will ride Celestial Seabird.'

'No, please,' Skandar begged. But she wouldn't take no for an answer.

It was the most humiliating thing that had happened to Skandar since he'd arrived on the Island. The rest of the class hung back, whispering, as Instructor O'Sullivan led Scoundrel's Luck back up the hill, Skandar clutching his chest and balancing on Seabird beside her.

The great tree entrance of the Eyrie opened for Instructor O'Sullivan in a whirl of water.

'I want to show you something,' she said, her voice unusually soft.

After walking through the armoured trunks of the Eyrie for a while, Instructor O'Sullivan stopped and pointed out a tree that was set apart from the others.

Skandar blinked in confusion. The trunk was sparkling in the late-afternoon sunshine.

'What is it?' Skandar dismounted from Seabird and stepped closer; the bark was studded with gold metal.

'If a rider is declared a nomad, the Eyrie has their elemental pin smashed into four pieces.'

Skandar leaned in with horrified fascination. Sure enough, he could make out tips of gold flames, a broken spiral, a solitary rock, half a water droplet – all hammered into the trunk.

'A quarter is given to each remaining member of the nomad's quartet,' Instructor O'Sullivan explained, 'and the fourth piece is brought here and hammered into this tree, as a reminder that they once trained among us.'

'Why are you showing me this?' Skandar asked, starting to panic, words tumbling out of his mouth. 'Are you – I can't be declared a nomad! Being a unicorn rider is all I ever wanted. I promise I'll try harder. I want to race, I want to race for my dad, my sister . . . my mum. She loved the Chaos Cup and I thought maybe one day I could compete, maybe one day I could make her proud. I'll try harder, I promise. Please give me another chance!'

Instructor O'Sullivan held up her hands, the sunlight catching her Hatchery scar. 'I'm not declaring you anything. Not yet. I brought you here because I think you have real potential.' She pointed at the tree. 'I don't think becoming a nomad would be the right path for you and Scoundrel's Luck. Your magic is battle-worthy – I saw it when the domes were up. But I won't put the other Hatchlings at risk. To be blunt, your recent training sessions have been a disaster. So understand this as a warning: unless you get Scoundrel's Luck under control, I'll have no choice but to ask you to leave the Eyrie. And I don't want that for one of my water wielders.'

'We'll do better,' Skandar mumbled. 'Scoundrel was just so angry with me.' Instructor O'Sullivan turned sharply away from the tree. 'Do you mean you thought he was angry, or you felt his anger? The two are different.'

'I-I think I can actually feel his emotions,' Skandar stuttered. 'I definitely felt his rage today. And if I'm sad about, erm, something, then I can feel him almost nudge my chest, like he's checking if I'm okay. He sends me happy feelings, like his heart is trying to make my heart smile again. Is that . . . normal?'

'This is exactly what I'm talking about, Skandar!' Instructor

O'Sullivan's eyes swirled wildly. 'That's very impressive. It's very advanced for you to be feeling emotions in the bond. It shows real strength in your connection.' She stroked Scoundrel's black nose. 'You need to work harder for both of you. Remember: if he's scared, you can be brave for him. The bond lets you support each other. We'll make a water wielder of you yet.' She patted Skandar on the shoulder, but her final words only made him feel worse.

Suddenly, getting answers from Agatha seemed more important than ever. Because he could never be a water wielder, no matter how hard he tried.

Later that afternoon, all the riders in the Eyrie put on their red jackets and set off for the Fire Festival. There were unicorns everywhere, and the air reeked of sweat and magic. Skandar had become used to the smell of the elements since he'd started training. They smelled nothing like the magic of the wild unicorn he'd faced on the way to the Eyrie, which was rotting and rancid, like warmed-up death. Bonded magic was different. Each element smelled a particular way to an individual rider – so water magic smelled different to Skandar than it did to the rest of his quartet. Though now, all mixed together, Skandar thought they smelled tangy – like oranges and smoke.

Once the tree gate was opened, the older riders didn't stay around for long, their unicorns taking off into the sky in a symphony of screeching and flapping. Skandar wondered what it would be like to learn to fly Scoundrel in a few weeks' time, and felt a fizz of excitement – until he remembered that there was a very good chance Scoundrel would throw him off mid-flight.

In all the chaos Red belched in Falcon's direction. A bubble of smelly ash popped, splattering across the grey unicorn's neck.

'How many times have I told you to stop Red from doing that?' Bobby shouted, brushing burp ash out of the feathers on her arms. 'You know how Falcon feels about bodily functions!'

'It's perfectly natural,' Mitchell said calmly.

'No, it's . . .' Bobby tailed off, which was unusual for her. Skandar thought her olive skin looked pale, and her fringe stuck to her forehead as though she'd been sweating. Skandar wondered if she'd had another panic attack, but he didn't think she'd want him checking she was okay in front of the others.

As they rode their unicorns away from the Eyrie, Flo kept casting worried looks at Scoundrel.

'He'll be fine,' Skandar called over reassuringly. 'He's in a great mood today. Aren't you, boy?' Skandar stroked Scoundrel's black neck. 'Ouch!' The unicorn zapped him with a tiny electric shock.

'Hilarious,' he murmured under his breath, and Skandar would have sworn – if unicorns could laugh – that the bond was vibrating with it.

They rode on, further from the Eyrie than they'd ever been. In the sky above, unicorns flew from east to west, their wings catching the late rays as though they were racing the sunset. From the ground you couldn't even tell if they were bonded or wild. Skandar felt the bond fizzing around his heart, as Scoundrel made strange squeaking noises and sent Skandar jolts of his excitement. Skandar tucked his scarf more tightly round his neck. He wished his mum could have seen him riding Scoundrel. Wherever she was, he hoped she could see the unicorns too.

Skandar assumed they were now entering Fourpoint, but it wasn't like any town he'd seen on the Mainland. On either side of the road the trees exploded in a carnival of colour. Whether a treehouse was single-storey and modest, or built like a higgledy-piggledy tower into the sky, scarlet reds clashed with canary yellows, piercing sky blues with leaf greens – even the trunks and branches of the trees were decorated with fabric. Skandar thought it was sort of nice that there was no elemental separation here – it reminded him of living in his quartet.

Further along, the tree-lined street had shops that looked far more interesting than any Skandar had seen in Margate. Many had gold swirling signs and window displays dedicated to all things unicorn, rider and racing. The shopfronts were on the ground so that customers could wander in from the pavements, but as Skandar stared into a healer's shop specialising in fire-based injuries, he realised that the shopkeeper lived in a treehouse above. Looking down the line of trees, he saw that the same was true of NIMROE SADDLES, BETTY'S BRUSH BARN, the OINTMENT AND OILS EMPORIUM and THE BRILLIANT BOOT COMPANY. Having seen elemental blasts up close, Skandar completely understood why the Islanders had built their homes off the ground. Bonded unicorn blasts were bad enough, but – remembering the video from his Hatchery classes – he shuddered to imagine how dangerous a stampeding wild unicorn herd would be.

'Do you trust him?' Bobby asked Skandar, interrupting his thoughts.

'Who, Mitchell?'

'Yes, Mitchell, obviously,' Bobby hissed as Falcon shrieked along with her. 'What if he's leading us into a trap? Have you thought about that?'

'No, I—' Skandar started.

'You throw one bowl of custard and suddenly he's all "Let's have a Quartet Meeting". Don't you think it's a bit suspicious? He wouldn't be seen dead talking to you a few weeks ago and now he's breaking you into a prison?'

Skandar shrugged. 'You think everyone's up to something.'

'Everyone *is* up to something, Skandar.'

'No, they're not!'

'Look at you.' Bobby gestured at him, reins still in her hand. 'Frankly you look like a pretty pathetic, powerless Hatchling, but you're actually an illegal spirit wielder riding a spirit unicorn, having been brought to the Island by the escaped Executioner. Oh, and your unicorn has a blaze that you've been hiding since you got here, which exactly matches the one painted on the face of the Weaver – the most evil rider there's ever been.'

'Keep your voice down!' Skandar urged her, though as Scoundrel turned his head this way and that, snorting sparks at his new surroundings, he checked the hoof polish was still covering the unicorn's blaze. He had to admit Bobby had a point. Only a few months ago, she'd shown him that despite appearing to be the most extroverted air wielder around, she was fighting her own demons on the inside. Perhaps people were more like elements than he'd realised. With fire you didn't just get sparks or billowing flames – there was a lot in between. And a gentle breeze and a hurricane couldn't be more different. Perhaps belonging to an element didn't just show you were one kind of person at all – elements, like people, were made up of all sorts of visible and invisible pieces.

Skandar hoped Bobby would've one day told him about her panic attacks if he hadn't discovered them by accident – it was easier to understand her now, somehow, like he'd seen her whole face, rather than some of it being obscured by shadow. And it didn't make her less of an air wielder at all.

Bobby shrugged. 'I'm just saying. Look how much you're hiding. I don't trust anyone, especially not snooty Mitchell Henderson.'

'Fine,' Skandar said. 'But what choice do we have? If I can ask Agatha about controlling the spirit element, it might save me, save Scoundrel. And aren't you worried about your family back on the Mainland? What if Agatha knows something about the Weaver that Aspen McGrath doesn't? What if she can help? What if *I* can? This is the only plan there is, Bobby!'

'Well, I don't like it,' she grunted, as electricity crackled across Falcon's feathery grey wings. 'If you're wrong about Mitchell, he's sending us into the simplest trap imaginable. We're walking into an *actual* prison.'

As the Hatchlings left the main road, Fourpoint became a dark warren of old shops, wooden stalls and treehouse taverns – the streets far too narrow for all the unicorns and red-clad Islanders trying to squeeze through. They reached Element Square just as the sun was going down and torches were being lit around four stone statues at its centre.

Unicorns filled the square, the sound deafening and the smell of magic overpowering. The statues resolved themselves into shapes as they rode closer: flames for the fire element, waves for water, a jagged rock for earth and a lightning bolt for air. Before Skandar could wonder whether there'd once been a spirit statue, five unicorns streaked across the sky above them, flames billowing from tails, manes and hooves. They flew in zigzags and loops and dived down to the square, making the crowd gasp with delight.

'It's the Flaming Arrows!' Flo shouted excitedly to Skandar and Bobby. As if they had heard, the acrobatic riders fired sparks, fireballs and flames into the dark above in beautiful shapes. The air smelled to Skandar like fire magic always did – bonfires, lit matches and overdone toast. Skandar wished Kenna could have seen it – she'd always loved fireworks and this was a thousand times better.

On the ground in a long fenced-off area was a line of flaming torches. At either end stood a fully armoured unicorn, moonlight catching the shades of metal as their riders waved at the gathered crowd.

Someone raised a flag at the centre of the line and the unicorns galloped at full tilt towards each other – one on either side of the line of torches. Skandar saw the riders' palms glow – one green, one red – and shining weapons appeared in their hands.

The fire wielder summoned a bow and arrow made entirely of flame. He drew back the fiery string to loose the arrow as the two unicorns were about to pass each other. But then the earth wielder summoned a sword of sand, and as she cut through the air it caught the flaming arrow and extinguished it. The heavy sand slammed into the fire wielder's chest just as the unicorns passed each other at full gallop. The crowd cheered.

As the unicorns slowed to a trot – now at opposite ends – the referee held out a flag with a two on it and waved it towards the earth wielder.

Mitchell noticed Skandar watching and shouted over the noise. 'Do you have jousting on the Mainland?'

'Not like this!' Skandar called back excitedly.

'We'll learn to summon weapons next year,' Mitchell said. 'There's a Nestling jousting tournament.'

'Is that Nina Kazama?' Flo was trying to squint at the next pair. And, sure enough, the Pred who'd shown them around on their first day was putting on her helmet to compete.

Flo sighed. 'Isn't she great? Dad says he thinks she's in with a chance of qualifying for the Chaos Cup.'

Skandar pushed Scoundrel forward for a better view and found himself stuck behind a couple of Islanders on foot.

'If you're serious, take this. Let me know, d'you hear? And don't tell a soul,' said a man with auburn hair, pressing a piece of paper into a blonde woman's hand. As she took it, Skandar saw the flash of a symbol: a wide arc with a black circle beneath it, cut through from top to bottom with a jagged white line. He peered over Scoundrel's folded wing, trying to make out the words.

'Are you okay?' Flo asked, as the two strangers moved out of the silver unicorn's way.

'I just saw . . .' Skandar frowned. What *had* he seen? He pulled his mum's scarf tighter round his neck against the cold.

'Come on,' Mitchell urged. 'It's time.'

'Can't we have some food first?' Bobby demanded. 'Flo said there are stalls selling all sorts of—'

Mitchell cut her off. 'We don't have time. The plan, remember? We're already behind schedule.'

Bobby looked like she wanted to punch him.

They left Element Square and rode past a bard singing a beautiful song about flames and destiny, and then food stalls selling fire-themed delights: one announced VAL'S VOLCANO CHILLI – SO SPICY YOUR MOUTH WILL EXPLODE; another sold CINDER TOFFEE with shovels to remove the chunks straight from a smouldering fire. The air was filled with delicious smells, and Skandar really wished they could stop when he saw one stall selling FLAMING CHOCOLATE.

Along from the food stalls, you could buy red jackets, paintings of famous fire unicorns, red scarves and – inexplicably – live salamanders as pets. The quartet pushed their unicorns past smiling Islanders holding lanterns or torches and dressed head to foot in red. Scoundrel kept turning to bite the toe of Skandar's boot, his horn dangerously close to his rider's shin – the unicorn had become obsessed with eating shoes – but he was otherwise behaving himself. Every so often, Islanders stopped to gawp at Silver Blade.

With each winding turn, the crowds thinned out. Away from the hubbub of Element Square, the streets soon became dark and deserted – with the festival in full flow, everyone was out enjoying themselves. But Mitchell didn't slow Red Night's Delight until they were right on the edge of Fourpoint.

'We're here,' he announced unnecessarily. Above them a giant boulder was suspended in mid-air. Metal chains stretched out from four towering trees and wrapped round the middle of the stone, holding it up in the moonlight. Its surface was grey and smooth, and it looked . . . impenetrable.

Four sentinels stood directly underneath the prison. Their unicorns were as still as statues, just like the ones guarding the Eyrie entrance. It looked like Mitchell had been right – the others were all busy with the Fire Festival tonight.

'Time for stage one, Roberta,' Mitchell murmured.

Bobby scowled at him and dismounted Falcon's Wrath, giving her reins to Skandar so she and the other three unicorns could hide out of sight in a small copse.

'Remember to be polite,' Flo whispered after her.

Skandar heard Bobby's voice loud and clear. 'Greetings, your tincandescent silveriness-esses.'

'What's she playing at?' Mitchell moaned. 'They're not even real words!'

Bobby cleared her throat importantly. 'The Justice Representative requires your immediate assistance in Element Square.'

The sentinels remained still.

The one on the black unicorn spoke first. 'It's against our orders to leave the prison unguarded.'

Bobby stood up straighter. 'Reinforcements are on the way. Never fear – I shall remain here until they arrive.'

Another sentinel snorted with laughter atop his chestnut

unicorn. 'Are you even a rider? Where's your unicorn?'

'Are you questioning Ira Henderson's authority?' Even though this was the plan, Mitchell still cringed at the sound of his dad's name.

The sentinel stopped laughing. 'You are not Ira Henderson.'

Flo and Skandar exchanged worried glances. This was the moment of truth.

Bobby barked the one word they hoped would make all the difference.

'Riptide!'

The effect was immediate. Within seconds, all four unicorns were galloping away.

With the sentinels gone, Skandar, Mitchell and Flo rode their unicorns out of the copse, leading Falcon with them.

'That worked really well,' Flo whispered in surprise.

'Worryingly well,' Bobby murmured, giving Skandar a significant look.

'I don't know why you were all so worried. I knew that was my father's emergency code word.' Mitchell shrugged. 'I told you – if you have a book in your hands, nobody ever suspects you of eavesdropping.'

'And if you make your friend do the talking, nobody ever suspects you of breaking into a prison.' Bobby raised an eyebrow at Skandar. 'Anyway, shouldn't we get on with stage two before they realise there's no emergency?'

Flo gazed up at the prison. 'But how are we supposed to get up there?'

'Good point.' Bobby looked up too. 'I like a challenge but that must be at least fifty metres high!'

'And where's the door?' Skandar said, his eyes searching the unblemished stone surface of the prison. With a jolt he realised that the four chains were each tinged with one of the elemental colours; he felt more like an illegal spirit wielder than ever.

'My father taught me how to get into the prison in the event of his untimely death. To fetch his belongings, papers, that sort of thing.' Mitchell puffed out his chest.

'In the event of his untimely death?' Bobby mouthed at Skandar.

'It was almost fatherly of him.' Mitchell sighed. 'A real bonding moment.'

'But how do we do it?' Flo urged. 'Why are you so relaxed?'

'There's a plan – so I'm relaxed.'

'But surely those sentinels are actually going to find your father any minute?'

'Okay, okay,' Mitchell said crossly. 'Just trust me, will you? Now the guards are gone, it's not really that difficult to get inside. See those four chains – elemental magic will open the prison. It will work best if we pick the chain that matches our element, and throw magic at it. If we all do it at the same time that should work.'

'You didn't tell us this in the Quartet Meeting,' Bobby hissed.

'It wasn't necessary prior information.'

'Umm, Mitchell,' Skandar said. 'Small problem. I'm a spirit wielder, remember? Not a *water* wielder.'

'You don't have to actually *be* a water wielder; just summon the magic,' he said impatiently.

A few moments later, the quartet were in position under the hanging prison. Flo, Bobby and Mitchell's palms were already glowing green, yellow and red, but Skandar had decided to wait until the last minute to summon his water magic. He was hoping it would reduce the time he had to fight Scoundrel over the spirit element.

Mitchell started to count down. 'Ten, nine . . .'

'Okay, Scoundrel.' Skandar leaned forward to whisper near his unicorn's ear. 'If you ever want to be able to use the spirit element, I need you to let the water element through.'

'Six, five . . .'

'Just for a few seconds. Please, boy. I'll give you an entire packet of Jelly Babies. I'll catch you a bird. I'll let you play with Red after training.' Skandar knew Scoundrel couldn't understand him, but he hoped he could get a sense of his desperation through the bond.

'Two, one . . .'

Skandar summoned the water element, his palm glowing blue. Scoundrel screeched.

'NOW!' Mitchell shouted, and the sky exploded with flames, electricity, rocks and . . . a fountain of water.

'Yes, Scoundrel!' Skandar cheered, as the water hit the chain above his head.

The four chains started to glow brightly with their elemental colours, the magic spiralling in and out of the metal links up towards the rock of the prison and then—

WHOOSH!

A door opened in the very bottom of the boulder above their

heads and a metal ladder shot down like a lightning bolt, the pointed ends thumping into the ground at Mitchell's feet.

Mitchell didn't give them time to celebrate. 'Let's hide the unicorns in the copse again. Just in case the sentinels come back quicker than we expect.'

Now they had a clear path into the prison, Skandar felt his nerves return. Mitchell had told them the sentinels only guarded the outside, but what if he was wrong? His heart hammered with every step up the ladder. He hated leaving Scoundrel below. And what Bobby had said kept circling his mind too – *Do you trust him? Do you trust him?* What if Skandar had led himself – and his friends – into a trap? Was Skandar being naive to think that Mitchell was now his friend? The fire wielder might have got them into the prison, but what if he wasn't planning to let them out? What if he was helping his father catch another spirit wielder?

Skandar felt even worse once they were inside. It was a spooky place – their footsteps echoed off the rounded rock walls, and small torches burned in brackets, making their shadows flicker and split as though they were being followed. Mitchell led them quickly along a corridor where portraits of fearsome-looking unicorns stared down at them. Some showed bloody sky battles, while others depicted triumphant unicorns with their opponents on the ground, defeated. The scenes became more grisly as the quartet hurried down a passage, following the curved outer wall of the boulder round to the cells. Skandar wondered if the defeated riders were supposed to be spirit wielders.

'I think I should speak to Agatha alone,' Skandar whispered, as the inner wall gave way to metal bars.

'That wasn't the plan,' Mitchell argued. 'I made a checklist of questions and—'

Skandar sighed. 'I know. But I'm worried that if we all try to talk to the spirit wielders, they won't tell us a thing. Why should they trust us? But Agatha knows me.'

'Are you sure, Skar?' Flo asked, putting a hand on his shoulder.

He nodded. He could already hear the prisoners murmuring up ahead.

'We'll wait here for you.' Mitchell sounded as though he was recalibrating the plan. 'We'll keep watch for the sentinels coming back. Remember – you haven't got long.'

The further Skandar walked, the darker it became, and the distant voices grew louder.

'Agatha?' he called.

No response.

'Agatha? Can I talk to you?'

Still nothing.

Skandar felt his heart sink. She wasn't here after all. He'd have to ask the other spirit wielders; maybe they'd know where to find her? Maybe they could help? Skandar racked his brains for something, *anything* to get them talking. And then he realised. How could he have forgotten Amber's dad?

'Simon Fairfax, are you there?'

The voices behind the bars stopped abruptly.

'He isn't here,' a high-pitched voice called back. 'As you very well know. As the Commodore knows.'

'What do you mean he isn't here?' Skandar asked, heart hammering.

'Who are you?' a gruff voice called. 'You sound very young.'

'I'm . . .' Skandar hesitated. Agatha would have known who he was, but revealing his identity to these strangers felt too dangerous.

'I'm not a guard. But I can't tell you who I am. I'm sorry. I wish I could.'

There was a murmur of interest. Shadows moved behind the bars, refusing to resolve into faces. 'Well, whoever you are, Simon Fairfax isn't here,' someone rasped, their low, gravelly voice echoing through the bars. 'Here's the truth for you, laddie. The truth they're not telling you or anyone. He was never caught. The Executioner killed his unicorn, yes, but Fairfax has never set foot inside this prison. And still the Commodore asks us who the Weaver is.'

Skandar's heart started to race. Could that be true? Could it be Amber's dad? He opened his mouth to ask another question but stopped himself. The code word stunt with the sentinels could only buy them so much time – there was more he needed to ask.

'Is the Executioner here?' Skandar asked shakily. 'Is Agatha in this prison? Do you know where she is – or Arctic Swansong?'

'We do not speak those names here!' somebody shouted.

'Who *are* you?' the old voice croaked again.

Skandar ran, sprinting further round the curve of the boulder, hoping he'd circle back to the others, but nothing looked familiar. Hardly any moonlight shone through the barred prison windows. Skandar didn't like the dark. At all. He stopped. He couldn't even hear the spirit wielders now. Was he lost? This had been a mistake. A *huge* mistake. He'd put Scoundrel's Luck in danger, and for what? And Amber's dad? If Amber's dad was the only other free spirit wielder, could that really mean he was the—

'Skandar,' a frail voice called out. 'Wait.' A hand reached through the bars a little way ahead. A pale hand with gnarled knuckles, as though its owner had been in a fight.

'Agatha?' Skandar stopped abruptly. 'Is that you?'

'I thought I heard your voice! What in the name of all five elements are you doing in here?'

'Looking for you,' Skandar whispered, facing the bars. 'I called out, but I thought you weren't here. The others wouldn't tell me anything about you. Are you okay?'

'I'm not in with the rest of them,' Agatha breathed. Skandar could just about make out her outline in the shadows. 'They've locked me in a separate cell. I'm not exactly popular here. But why are you looking for me?'

Now he'd found her, Skandar wasn't sure where to start.

'You're a spirit wielder,' Agatha said.

'How did you . . . ?'

'Had a hunch,' she said, and Skandar thought he could detect the ghost of a smile in her words.

'The spirit element. How do I hide it? How do I control it?' Skandar asked desperately. 'I've tried blocking it, but it's not working and I'm going to be declared a nomad any—'

'Let it into the bond alongside another element.' Agatha spoke quickly. 'Blocking can work but I'm assuming you're having problems with your unicorn?'

Skandar swallowed. 'He hates me when I don't let him use the spirit element.'

'He doesn't – he just doesn't understand. Let the spirit element in and it should help you control the element and your unicorn's reaction.'

Skandar wanted to sink to his knees with relief, but he didn't know how much longer he had. How long would it take for the guards to come back? What if Mitchell's dad came to investigate?

'The Weaver,' Skandar asked urgently, trying to remember what Joby had said. 'Is there some way a spirit wielder can help get New-Age Frost back? Is that why you brought me to the Island? Is there something I can learn to do, to help against the Weaver?'

There was a pause. 'I don't know for sure. I don't know exactly what the Weaver's planning, but it'll be about the bond, Skandar. It always is with the Weaver. And you can see them.'

'*See* bonds? No, I can't!' Although as soon as he said it, Skandar remembered those strange coloured lights when he'd mutated. Had those been the bonds of the other Hatchlings?

'You'll be able to soon. If you let the spirit element in. That's why only a spirit wielder can stop the Weaver. Only spirit wielders can see bonds.'

'But can't you—' His heart was beating so fast that he could feel the skin on his chest moving against his T-shirt. He had so many questions, but there wasn't enough time. And he had been half hoping Joby had been wrong – that he wouldn't be able to help, that the Weaver wouldn't be his responsibility after all.

'It has to be you, Skandar. I can't do it; I'm not strong enough.

And, anyway, they have my unicorn. I'm so sorry. It has to be you.' Agatha sounded more pained than ever.

'But how am I supposed to learn about the spirit element? Use it? There's nothing in the libraries; they'll throw me in here if they find out – or worse. Nobody out there will help me!' Skandar said desperately, his voice rising.

'Take this. They locked it in here with me – they think it's as dangerous as I am.'

A thick white leather-bound book appeared through the bars. It was just light enough for Skandar to make out a symbol – four entwined gold circles. Embossed gold lettering on its cover said: *The Book of Spirit*.

'Take it,' Agatha rasped, and Skandar reached out for the fifth and final volume of the elemental scriptures. It weighed heavy in his arms.

Skandar couldn't help but flick through its pages at random, reading snatches.

Spirit wielders have the ability to amplify their use of other elements, meaning they can rival those allied to fire, water, earth and air when battling them in their own element . . .

Whilst spirit is not a particularly strong offensive element, its defensive capabilities are unparalleled across the other four element types . . .

Spirit was a real element! And it sounded pretty great! He was holding a book that acknowledged there were five elements, not four! He flicked through a few more pages.

Those allied to the element of spirit have an affinity with wild unicorns that can be explained by their link to the bond, which is unmatched by wielders of other elements. Wild unicorns sense the strength of the spirit element in its wielders and have an interest and respect for it that they do not show for other . . .

Spirit-allied unicorns have the ability to transform and take on the appearance of the elements themselves . . .

Agatha was speaking again. 'Find the spirit den. There should be more books there, more information about the spirit element. Learn as much as you can.'

'What's a den?' Skandar asked, but just as Agatha was about to answer a siren started wailing.

'Go! Go! You have to go!' Agatha urged, but as she said it she grabbed Skandar's wrist and pulled him closer to the bars.

Her voice was rough, desperate. 'Please don't kill the Weaver, Skandar. Do everything you can to stop whatever the plan is, but please—'

'What?' Skandar asked over the squealing siren.

'I'm begging you. Don't kill the Weaver.' And then she released him, her arm disappearing from between the bars as though it had never been there.

In a frenzy Skandar sprinted back towards his friends who were looking wildly around for him, their hands over their ears. Skandar's immediate thought was that the sentinels had returned and set off an alarm. But then Flo and Mitchell yelled, 'STAMPEDE!'

CHAPTER FIFTEEN

STAMPEDE

'Flaming fireballs!' Mitchell cried as Skandar reached them. 'Is that *The Book of Spirit*?'

'Could we maybe delay book club while we try not to DIE?' Bobby shouted, as they headed for the exit, her face set in a grimace against the stampede siren's incessant wailing.

Outside, a deep bellowing filled the night, accompanied by the thundering of hooves and the sound of distant screaming.

'We need to get to the unicorns!' Flo cried, as she jumped the last few rungs and landed on the ground.

'What *is* that?' Bobby choked out.

There was a horrifying smell. Skandar had come across it once before on his first day on the Island – the stench of living death. The stampede was getting closer.

Skandar sprinted as fast as he could towards Scoundrel's hiding place in the trees. The black unicorn screeched with delight as he spotted his rider, electricity crackling across his folded wings in greeting.

The thundering of hooves had become so loud that Skandar half expected to see wild unicorns approaching the prison as he vaulted on to Scoundrel's back. He tried not to listen to the human screams that were mixed in with the bellows and shrieks of the wild unicorns.

'Get on! Get on!' Mitchell shouted, even though he was the only one still on the ground, struggling to untie Red's reins from a tree.

Scoundrel sniffed the air, and Skandar felt a squeeze of fear from him through the bond. 'Don't worry.' He stroked the unicorn's dark neck. 'I'll get you out of here.'

Mitchell galloped through the twisting deserted streets, leading the way on Red Night's Delight. Skandar hoped Mitchell could tell better than him which direction the wild unicorns were coming from. When they met a dead-end at some forges – sheets of metal abandoned, hammers cast aside – Skandar started to panic. He tried to focus on the comforting pull of the bond on his heart, *The Book of Spirit* under his arm, and Scoundrel's regular breathing, but the sound of the stampede was so overwhelming that it felt like they'd meet it at every turn as they fled through Fourpoint.

The tiny streets emptied them on to Element Square. The four stone statues loomed eerily large with the crowds gone. The smell of wild unicorns was so strong that Skandar had to breathe through his mouth to keep from gagging. Bellowing filled his ears.

Skandar tried to urge Scoundrel's Luck onwards across

the square but the unicorn started to back up. The other three unicorns were doing the same, elemental blasts brewing beneath their skin. Red's back had started to smoke. Scoundrel's fear filled their bond, magnifying Skandar's own.

'What's wrong with them?' Flo said, desperately trying to urge Blade forward.

'That,' Bobby said flatly, and pointed to the opposite edge of the square.

The wild unicorns had arrived.

Flo screamed, making Blade rear up on his back legs. Scoundrel kept turning on the spot, flapping his wings. Skandar reckoned they had less than thirty seconds before they'd be flattened by the stampeding herd.

'Fly! We have to fly!' Bobby yelled.

'Don't be ridiculous!' Mitchell shouted back. 'We haven't even had our first flying lesson yet. It's not due for weeks.'

'I can't; *they* can't yet!' Flo screamed.

'If we stay on the ground, they'll catch us. Wild unicorns aren't as good at flying as bonded unicorns. They might not try to follow; they might go for an easier target,' Bobby insisted, already gathering up Falcon's reins and crouching low on her back.

'Might?' Mitchell spluttered. 'You're willing to risk this on probability?'

'Let's go!' Bobby shouted to Falcon's Wrath, ignoring Mitchell. The unicorn pointed her grey horn directly at the oncoming monsters . . . and galloped straight for them.

'This is absolute madness!' Mitchell cried.

'They're going to collide!' Flo squeaked, one hand over her eyes.

But they didn't. Falcon's grey wings snapped outwards, beating fast, and lifted her clean off the ground, high above the wild unicorns, and into the sky. Bobby's whooping echoed around the square.

All talk of madness forgotten, Mitchell urged Red Night's Delight towards the stampede. Flo followed closely on Silver Blade, and Skandar and Scoundrel's Luck brought up the rear. Skandar watched as Mitchell crouched forward and Red unfurled her thickly feathered wings, kicked up her front legs and attempted to take off. But both legs crashed back down again – she couldn't seem to lift herself off the ground.

'Come on, Red!' Skandar muttered under his breath. Skandar heard Mitchell yell in fright as he looked up at the ever-closer stampede, but then Red flapped her wings, once, twice, and on the third beat her four hooves rose off the ground and into the air.

Blade was next, and it was as though he'd been waiting for this moment. Right in front of Scoundrel's nose the silver unicorn beat his wings and rose gracefully upwards. Flo clung to her unicorn's neck in terror – Skandar was almost certain that she had her eyes shut – but, for once, the unicorn looked after his rider and lifted them both smoothly into the sky. And then Skandar was urging with his legs, wishing with his heart, begging Scoundrel to do the same, to lift them both away from danger.

Skandar felt Scoundrel's wing joints move near his knees, and his black wings spread wide, wider than Skandar had ever seen them. The dark feathers caught the wind, as Skandar pressed his legs into the unicorn's hot sides, urging him faster. *The Book of Spirit* was tucked under Skandar's arm, but his muscles were failing, and Scoundrel's gallop was too uneven. It slipped. Skandar grabbed a fistful of pages, but it was too heavy – the pages slid from his grasp, until the book was hanging by just one page. And with another jolt from Scoundrel, the page ripped at the corner and *The Book of Spirit* crashed to the ground.

'No!' Skandar screamed. But there wasn't time to think about whether he'd ever get it back. Scoundrel angled his wings upwards – his breathing uneven and ragged – as he galloped full tilt towards the wild unicorn stampede, the creatures so close that Skandar could see their skeletal faces, the slime dripping from their eyes and noses. He abandoned the reins and threw his arms round Scoundrel's neck, crouching as low as he could to lessen the resistance of the air. And just when Skandar thought they might not make it, he felt his stomach jolt as Scoundrel's hooves left solid ground.

Skandar's head felt suddenly light, his eyes refusing to accept the view of the sky through the gap between Scoundrel's two black ears. The night air roared around Skandar, buffeting him this way and that, lifting his hair off his forehead. He felt at that moment the least ordinary he'd ever felt in his life. He was a superhero. A wizard. No, better – a unicorn rider. Scoundrel soared upwards into the dark sky, leaving the stampeding monsters below him. And, as Bobby had predicted, they didn't attempt to follow.

Skandar had never gone so quickly from pure terror to unbridled joy. Flying was wonderful. Flying was everything. It was nothing like his journey with Agatha and Arctic Swansong. It was different to fly on his own unicorn, to share the sky with the one he had always been destined for. It didn't feel scary or dangerous, or any of the things Skandar had expected. It felt right. After all, the bond told him that if he fell, Scoundrel's Luck would catch him.

The quartet's unicorns formed a diamond shape: Bobby at the front, Flo and Mitchell on the sides and Skandar at the rear. He grinned so much as Scoundrel cut through the air that his teeth ached with the cold. This was finally something Skandar could write to Kenna about that was absolutely, completely true. No secrets, no spirit element – just flying. Skandar's black scarf rippled out behind him and he was so glad Kenna had given it to him, so glad that a small piece of his mum could fly with him tonight.

The unicorns called to each other gently, their whinnies carrying on the wind. Skandar wondered whether Bobby knew the way back to the Eyrie – but as Scoundrel glided under the stars, he realised he didn't particularly care. Agatha's words came back to him as they flew: *Let the spirit element in*. It couldn't hurt up here, could it? Letting spirit into the bond just for a moment?

The white of the spirit element glowed in Skandar's hand and Scoundrel let out an excited roar as the tips of his feathers glowed white to mirror his rider.

Then Flo's voice, suddenly urgent, reached him through the wind. 'Look! Down there!'

'What exactly are we looking at?' Mitchell called back.

But Skandar had seen something between Scoundrel's black feathers that made his blood run cold.

At the back of the herd of wild unicorns, galloping its way out of Fourpoint, was a unicorn that differed from its skeletal companions. Where their muscles were wasting, his were strong; where their wings were weak, his looked capable of anything; where their skin was rotting, his was unblemished; and where their horns were translucent, his was solid grey.

New-Age Frost. And on his back sat the Weaver, black shroud billowing out behind, face shining with a solid white stripe.

'There's someone else sitting behind the Weaver!' Bobby yelled. 'There are two people on New-Age Frost's back!'

'He looks familiar,' Mitchell shouted. 'I'm sure I've seen him before – but he's too far away. Flo, do you recognise him?'

But as Skandar squinted down at the figure, white spirit magic still shining in his palm, he saw something else. A shining white cord connecting the hearts of New-Age Frost and the Weaver. A bond. Had the Weaver somehow managed to *bond* to New-Age Frost? Was Aspen's bond still there? Or had it broken? How was that even possible?

Skandar looked up to tell his friends, but he was distracted by colours flashing around them too. A red cord between Mitchell and Red, yellow between Bobby and Falcon, and green between Flo and Blade. He looked down at his own chest . . . but there was nothing. Perhaps spirit wielders couldn't see their own bonds? He felt wonder and fear galloping through him. Agatha had been right. Using the spirit element *did* allow Skandar to see riders' bonds. He looked back and saw the Weaver's bond to New-Age Frost shining as together they drove the wild unicorns back towards the Wilderness. But did that mean Agatha had been right about everything? He shivered, her words playing through his mind: *It has to be you, Skandar.*

It wasn't long before they were outside the Eyrie entrance. Landing wasn't half as much fun as flying through the air. Scoundrel had ploughed into the hill at great speed – skidding and sliding in the mud – as Skandar clung on to avoid being catapulted over the unicorn's head.

Once they were all safely on the ground, Bobby hurried to put her palm on the knot of the great tree trunk, hoping the sentinels guarding it wouldn't ask any questions, when—

'Desert dust storms! Did you four *fly* here?'

Instructor Webb was silhouetted against the outline of the Eyrie wall. He appeared to be wearing a dressing gown made entirely of moss; it matched the clumps on his head perfectly.

None of them answered him.

'Well? I'm assuming you know there was a stampede at the Fire Festival?' he spluttered. 'An entire Hatchling quartet missing, presumed dead. That's how our minds work nowadays. Five sentinels were killed tonight. Five! And two more Islanders taken by the Weaver. Didn't you see the smoke?'

'Is the Mainland safe?' Skandar asked.

'Yes, boy, but what about you four? Worried sick, we all were. A silver taken by the Weaver – my goodness, can you imagine? It's unthinkable!'

The Eyrie entrance opened in a whirl of water, and four more people marched through, their shadows dancing against the fire plants of the wall.

Skandar recognised three of them. Instructor O'Sullivan looked furious, fists clenched at her sides. Skandar had heard a rumour that the permanent cut on the instructor's neck had happened while fighting off three wild unicorns. And by the fierce way her whirlpool eyes were swirling, he would have bet a litre of mayonnaise she could have fought off at least ten more. Instructor Anderson looked more disappointed than angry, the flames flickering despondently around his ears. And Instructor Saylor – the glamorous air instructor – appeared serene, though all the veins on her arms were pulsing dangerously with electricity.

Skandar didn't recognise the fourth person. A man with light brown skin and a long dark plait stood silently between the instructors. One braid was blue and alive, running down his back like a waterfall.

'We're done for,' Mitchell croaked as the group headed straight for them. Skandar had never seen Mitchell look so afraid; even his fingers were shaking.

'What's wrong?' Skandar whispered. 'Who is that?'

'My father,' Mitchell rasped. 'He must know. About the prison break-in. About you. About . . . everything. Why else would he be here?'

Skandar felt all the breath leave him. Instinctively he held on tighter to Scoundrel's reins. He wouldn't let anyone take him. He wouldn't be like Joby. He'd die before—

'Mitchell?' It was Instructor Anderson who spoke first. His voice was calm, concerned even. 'I'm afraid your father has come to share some bad news.'

'Wha— Bad news?' Mitchell turned to face his father. 'Is Mother okay?'

'Your cousin, Alfie,' Ira Henderson barked impatiently. If he'd been concerned by his son's suspected disappearance he didn't show it. 'Your cousin has been taken by the Weaver. I thought you ought to hear it from me before the blasted *Hatchery Herald* reports it tomorrow.' His deep brown eyes, so like Mitchell's, flashed in the darkness. 'If anyone asks you to comment, say nothing. We must avoid further shame being associated with the Henderson name.' There was not even a hint of warmth in the councillor's face.

'Yes, Father,' Mitchell mumbled.

Bobby, Flo and Skandar exchanged glances. *Mitchell's cousin? Was he the person riding with the Weaver?*

Ira Henderson turned to Instructor O'Sullivan. 'I must be going. I've been kept waiting long enough. We're moving the Executioner to a new location tonight.' He dropped his voice lower, but Skandar could still just about hear him. 'Share this information no further, but *The Book of Spirit* has been stolen. My code word was used to send the sentinels away from the prison tonight. I'll be honest with you, Persephone, we fear that someone is helping the Weaver from inside the Council. Who else would have access to such classified information?'

Skandar willed himself not to look at Mitchell.

Instructor O'Sullivan shook her head in disbelief. 'Surely not!'

Ira cleared his throat. 'The Eyrie must be on high alert. I'll be sending more sentinels. Tonight.'

With a final cursory glance at the group Ira Henderson swept away into the night, without even a word of goodbye to his son.

Ira Henderson's departure was followed by the worst telling-off of Skandar's life. But luckily the instructors had no evidence to disprove the quartet's story of getting left behind when the siren sounded. They were sent straight to bed with dire warnings ringing in their ears.

Of course, they didn't actually go to bed. Once the friends were settled on beanbags, and warming their hands by the stove, Skandar told them what he'd found out – from Simon Fairfax never being caught, to seeing the bond between New-Age Frost and the Weaver. He left out one detail, though – the one that scared him the most: *It has to be you, Skandar. I'm so sorry. It has to be you.*

After he'd finished, Mitchell stood up abruptly and climbed to their bedroom.

'Do you think he's okay?' Flo asked, the golden rock cluster of her earth pin twinkling. 'I can't believe his cousin's been taken. Alfie's an apprentice at Martina Saddles, one of my dad's rivals – my brother knows him!'

'His dad didn't exactly break the news gently,' Bobby said through a mouthful of emergency sandwich. The jam and Marmite oozed between the cheese. Skandar still didn't understand where she got the bread from.

But Mitchell came back down the ladder almost immediately,

carrying a large rectangular object under one arm.

'Is that . . . a blackboard?' Bobby asked incredulously.

'Correct, Roberta.' Mitchell produced a piece of chalk with a flourish. 'I didn't have time to get it out for our last Quartet Meeting. But now we can start doing things properly.'

Mitchell cleared his throat. 'Welcome to our second-ever Quartet Meeting, called at twenty-two hundred hours.'

'Twenty-two hundred hours?' Skandar mouthed at Flo, who whispered, 'Ten o' clock,' and stifled a giggle.

'I'm going to need a bigger sandwich,' Bobby muttered.

Mitchell pushed his glasses back up the bridge of his nose and tapped his chalk on the board. 'What do we know? We know the Weaver has somehow created a bond with New-Age Frost. We know the Weaver is killing the sentinels guarding the Mainland. We know the Weaver is stealing people – non-riders.' Mitchell swallowed. 'People like my cousin, Alfie.'

'We also know that the Silver Circle never caught Simon Fairfax,' Flo added.

'If you ask me, it makes total sense that Amber's dad is the Weaver,' Bobby said. 'She lied about him being dead, for goodness' sake. Who does that?'

'And she isn't a very nice person,' Flo volunteered, and then looked immediately guilty.

'I agree.' Mitchell nodded, and drew a line between the word *Weaver* and Simon Fairfax's name. 'He's definitely our top suspect.'

'Should we tell anyone that?' Flo asked. 'Or ask Amber?'

Skandar sighed. 'I don't see how we can. The only reason

Amber hasn't told anyone I'm a spirit wielder is because she doesn't want people knowing about her dad. If we go around saying Simon Fairfax is the Weaver, she'll have nothing left to lose. Plus the spirit wielders said Aspen doesn't believe it's Fairfax.'

'Also –' Bobby snorted – 'how are we going to say we found out?' She put on a mock-low voice. 'So, er, we were just hanging out at the spirit wielder prison for absolutely no reason at all and we happened to speak to—'

Flo grimaced. 'All right, all right.'

Skandar jumped in. 'We also need to find out—'

'Why Instructor Webb has a dressing gown made of moss?' Bobby grinned, then took another bite of her emergency sandwich.

'Er, no,' Skandar said. 'We need to find the spirit den, whatever that is. Especially now this is all I have left of *The Book of Spirit*.' He held out the ripped corner of the page he'd tried to hold on to. It only had half a sentence on it – *wild unicorn and mend* – which was completely unhelpful. 'I guess we could go back to Fourpoint to look for it?'

'Too dangerous,' Mitchell said immediately. 'At least the dens are in the Eyrie.'

'It'll be difficult to find them,' Flo said. 'They're really hidden.'

'But you know what they are?' Skandar asked excitedly.

Flo nodded. 'I mean, I don't know *where* they are, but I've heard of them. The dens are four – well five, I guess – underground spaces in the Eyrie, dedicated specifically to the wielders of each element. We're allowed in them next year if we make it through the Training Trial. The Mine for earth wielders, the Hive for air, the Furnace for fire and the Well for water.'

'That. Is. AWESOME!' Bobby said, her eyes bright.

'I do like the sound of the secret entrances,' Flo continued. 'A Nestling was telling me that you have to find a specific tree stump and it takes you underground. And if you're not allied to a den's element, the entrance won't let you in.' She frowned. 'But finding exactly the right tree stump for the *lost* spirit den? It won't be easy.'

Mitchell looked troubled. 'But should we really be trusting Agatha? I mean, she's the Executioner, Skandar. She killed all the spirit unicorns! *Scoundrel's* a spirit unicorn.'

'I don't see what other choice there is,' Skandar said slowly. 'I have to learn as much about the spirit element as I can. And the spirit den seems like a pretty good place to start.'

Skandar knew then that he had to tell them the one thing he'd been holding back. They were his friends, and they were the only people on the whole Island who might be able to help him.

Skandar took a deep breath. 'Joby was right, though. He was right when he said it'd take a spirit wielder to stop the Weaver. Agatha told me the same thing. And when I saw the Weaver's bond to New-Age Frost, I knew they were both telling the truth. Only a spirit wielder could have seen that new bond. So I have to find out what the Weaver's planning . . . and stop it. It has to be me.'

'But why you?' Flo demanded. 'You've only been in training five minutes!'

Mitchell spluttered. 'I don't think you're quite up to taking on the Weaver. And let's not forget we don't even know for sure who that is! Agatha probably meant someone older, like a Chaos Cup rider. Maybe she meant herself? Not you, not a Hatchling!'

'Scoundrel and I are the only spirit-allied unicorn and rider left. The only pair that are free anyway. There isn't anyone else,' Skandar whispered, and the truth of it weighed heavy. 'Just me and Scoundrel's Luck.'

There was silence. An owl hooted outside their treehouse window.

'Oh, great!' Bobby cried. 'So it's *still* all about you, then? How about giving one of us a turn?'

Despite everything, Skandar burst out laughing, then Flo, Bobby and Mitchell joined in. Skandar's friends closed their arms round him in an enormous hug that he thought might just have enough love in it to save the world.

⁓

Later that night, Mitchell didn't blow out the lamp straight away. He started a conversation instead. This had never happened before – he was usually very particular about getting the right amount of sleep.

'Skandar, I just wanted to say, I know I wasn't exactly friendly back before the custard . . . It's— I—'

'It's okay,' Skandar mumbled from his hammock.

'No,' Mitchell said roughly. 'It's not. It's not your fault you're a spirit wielder. And all you've been is kind to me when I've spent basically the whole time treating you like—'

'Like people have always treated you?'

'Not people.' Mitchell rubbed his eyes behind his glasses. 'Mostly my father. He— As you probably noticed he's not exactly the kind and caring type. But I've always tried to make him proud of me anyway. Make him notice me. He and my mother stopped living together when I was small, and whenever it was my father's turn to look after me he was always so busy all the time, you see?

'Even now, nothing I do ever seems to be worthy of his attention. I mean, he didn't even suspect that it could be *me* who'd shared his code word! That's how little he notices me. And whenever I *do* try to talk to him, he has this disappointment in his face, even though he's barely listening to what I say. So I've spent my whole life trying to live up to the name of Henderson, trying to get his approval. Nothing else was important, not even making friends.'

'Mitchell, that's awful—'

'But since I met all of you, I'm beginning to deduce that there could be more to life than trying to prove to my father that I'm worth his time. You see, it's hard to make friends when your own father doesn't think you're interesting. I didn't really think anyone would want to be my friend. And then you get actual bullies like Amber and it sort of confirms the theory.'

Mitchell sighed. 'And my father really hates spirit wielders, Skandar. I mean, his dream job is imprisoning them! When I was little, he even tried to pretend to me that there'd never been a fifth element at all. So being associated with you, well . . . that would be the ultimate way to disappointment him. To confirm I'm worthless after all.'

'Mitchell,' Skandar said gently, 'you are *not* worthless.'

'But it's not an excuse,' Mitchell rushed on. 'Just because he hates spirit wielders, it doesn't mean I have to hate them too. I understand that now. And I know you, and you're nice, so it makes me think that maybe I was wrong about all the others.'

Skandar laughed. 'I saved your life on the way to the Eyrie, you saved mine on the fault lines, and all you can say is that I'm *nice*?'

Mitchell blushed the colour of his element, and Skandar felt bad. 'We're friends, Mitchell. Okay? That's what's going on here. We're friends. I look out for you; you look out for me. And breaking us into the prison today was seriously brave with your dad and everything.'

'I haven't really had much experience at being a friend,' Mitchell mumbled.

'Me neither,' Skandar said. 'But I think we're doing all right so far.'

'You think?'

'Yeah.' Skandar got up and blew out the lamp. 'Just do me a favour, and don't start going on about how I'm going to bring an end to the Island again, okay?'

Mitchell chuckled. 'Deal.'

'Skandar?'

'Yes, Mitchell?'

'If we find out what the Weaver's planning, you're going to want to try to stop it, aren't you? Even if it's dangerous?'

Skandar had never had the power to change anything about his life back on the Mainland, but maybe he could change something here. He thought about what Joby had said: *Even if you could help, that doesn't mean you should.* But Skandar didn't agree with that at all. How could he hide up in the Eyrie while other people were in danger?

So – into the darkness – he said, 'I think so, yeah.'

Skandar didn't voice the other reason he wanted to find out more about the spirit element, because he didn't think Mitchell would understand. Mitchell was an Islander. Mitchell was a fire wielder who had opened the door to the Hatchery and hatched a red unicorn. He knew who he was. But Skandar didn't feel like he fitted anywhere yet. Not on the Mainland, not on the Island. Skandar had never even known his own mum. And all he knew about his allied element so far was a few snippets from *The Book of Spirit* and the evil acts of the Weaver. Finding out more about spirit might just be his chance to learn more about himself – to have a chance at belonging. And maybe once he did, he might be able to change things.

Mitchell yawned. 'Is being someone's friend always this exhausting?'

CHAPTER SIXTEEN

SKY BATTLES

The news that more sentinels were being stationed at the Eyrie spread faster than a wildfire attack, from Hatchlings right up to Preds. But the Weaver wasn't the only thing the young riders had to talk about. As December became January, the Training Trial – and the reality that the bottom five in the race wouldn't get to stay in the Eyrie – suddenly seemed a lot closer than before.

Luckily, what Agatha had told Skandar at the Fire Festival had been right. If he summoned a combination of spirit and whichever element he was *supposed* to be using into the bond, he was just about able to control Scoundrel. On better days Skandar could summon air, water, earth and fire magic like everyone else. It was nowhere near good enough to avoid being declared a nomad at the end of the Training Trial, but at least he wasn't going to get kicked out just yet.

If that wasn't enough to think about, soon all the Hatchlings were flying – though Skandar, Flo, Bobby and Mitchell still felt pretty smug that they'd flown *before* their first lesson. Once he'd had a few sessions, Skandar was proud to discover that Scoundrel's Luck was really fast – one of the fastest fliers in their year. And learning how to take off and land neatly, how to lean into the wind and read the air currents – was a welcome distraction from the Quartet Meetings Skandar and his friends held practically every night.

Finding the spirit den was proving to be just as tricky as Flo had warned. Mitchell spent hours searching the libraries for old maps of the Eyrie, but every time he thought he'd identified a book that might be useful, the pages referring to the spirit den had been torn out. One evening he was reduced to tears when he was faced with yet another dead end, and Skandar thought perhaps Mitchell was a lot more worried about his cousin Alfie than he was letting on.

Meanwhile Flo and Bobby climbed the swinging bridges of the Eyrie, searching the elemental quadrants for any clues they could find. They even tried asking older riders – Mainlanders and Islanders – about their own dens, but all they got were secretive smiles: 'You'll find out next year,' a Fledgling told them. 'You have to pass the Training Trial first,' one Rookie sang in a patronising sing-song voice.

Skandar searched on the ground, but it felt sort of stupid looking for a tree stump in the Eyrie – the whole place was full of trees. He tried to knock on Joby's door, but the spirit wielder wouldn't even answer, and made sure he was never alone with Skandar after Mainlander classes.

When they weren't searching for the spirit den, the quartet went around in circles, sorting through everything they knew: Agatha was the Executioner, Simon Fairfax was alive and free, sentinels were exploding, non-riders were disappearing, the Weaver had somehow bonded to the most powerful unicorn in the world, the Mainland was a target and – most importantly of all – only Skandar could stop the Weaver's plan. The trouble was, they still didn't fully understand what that was.

One late-February morning, a few weeks into the water season, Skandar pulled on his blue jacket, put on his mum's scarf and headed in the direction of the post tree. He found a letter from Kenna inside his half-blue capsule and hoped that reading her words would make him feel less worried about her and Dad, make him feel like their lives were far removed from the cliff sentinel deaths and the Weaver's plan – even though he knew they weren't safe at all.

Dear Skar (and Scoundrel),
You asked for some news from me so here it goes. I've been chatting online – it's kind of a group that helps people like me, people who missed out on being riders and can't, well, can't really get used to the idea of it not happening. I don't want you to feel bad because it's not your fault. But sometimes I feel like I'm living in black and white instead of colour. I can't help seeing unicorns everywhere. I

can't help dreaming about them. And the trouble is,
when Dad has a good day now, all he really wants to
talk about is you, and Scoundrel's Luck. And some
days I love talking about that, but some days, well,
I don't . . .

Sadness and guilt filled Skandar's chest like he was drowning
in it. He'd been so caught up in trying to find the spirit den that
he hadn't written to Kenna very much at all. From the stables a
querying pulse nudged on the bond – Scoundrel's way of asking
him what was wrong. But as he made his way to the wall before
training, all Skandar could think about was how Kenna might
have been destined for a unicorn, might even have been training
as a Nestling in the Eyrie right now. About how if she'd been
identified as a spirit wielder, she would have failed the Hatchery
exam automatically. About the cruelty of allowing spirit unicorns
to hatch wild and die for ever. And about how that was all the
Weaver's fault.

There was a dark shape outside Scoundrel's stable.

Skandar crept closer, his heart beating furiously until the
shape resolved itself.

'Jamie!' Skandar called in welcome. 'Everything okay?'

But then Skandar saw Scoundrel's Luck. The unicorn was
barely recognisable. A shining black breastplate sat snugly
across Scoundrel's chest, protective metal guards ran from
his knees to his lower legs, chainmail protected his stomach,
and a metal skull cap covered his ears. He looked just like the

armoured unicorns at the Chaos Cup.

Scoundrel shrieked his hello. Skandar thought he sounded very pleased with himself.

Jamie was looking sideways at Skandar, waiting for his reaction. 'It's all element-resistant. Any smith who says armour can be completely element-*proof* is lying.'

'He looks unbelievable!'

'Like, unbelievable in a good way?' Jamie's voice was shaking. Skandar hadn't realised how nerve-racking this was for the apprentice blacksmith.

'In a very good way,' Skandar reassured him.

Out of habit Skandar checked to make sure Scoundrel's blaze was still covered with polish. He felt suddenly deflated. Here in the stable Scoundrel's Luck looked like a champion, but could Scoundrel ever win a race if he wasn't allowed to use his allied element properly?

Skandar's own armour fitted him perfectly. The chainmail on his arms and legs gave him flexibility of movement, and the breastplate wasn't too heavy and allowed him to wear his blue jacket underneath – keeping his mutation hidden – with enough space to breathe.

They walked out of the wall together, winding through the Eyrie's tall trunks, avoiding the biggest roots: Skandar clinking in his armour on one side of Scoundrel and Jamie on the other, holding Skandar's visored helmet.

'Did you see those giant ice unicorns at the Water Festival?' Jamie asked, though his voice was gloomier than usual.

'I couldn't make it – too busy with training,' Skandar lied.

They'd spent the whole day of the festival in front of Mitchell's blackboard.

'Well, you missed out. I went with my friend Claire, and we—' Jamie suddenly broke off, unable to finish the sentence.

'Jamie? What is it? What's wrong?'

'She, well, the Weaver took her.' Jamie's voice was very sad. 'I still can't believe I didn't hear anything. We live in the same treehouse with the other apprentice blacksmiths at my forge. Her room is right next to mine – and I didn't hear a sound. Next thing I know, there's a stampede siren and I run to her room. She's not there. I run outside, and there's the white mark on the outside of our treehouse. The Weaver's mark.'

'I'm so sorry,' Skandar murmured.

Jamie sighed. 'The weirdest thing was that it was almost as if she knew something was going to happen. She even gave me a present the night before – an iron unicorn she'd made down at the forge. Like she was saying goodbye or something. Must have been a coincidence, I guess.'

Skandar knew exactly what Mitchell would say: *I don't believe in coincidences.* Mitchell's cousin and now someone from Jamie's own treehouse? It felt like the Weaver was getting closer and closer.

'And we can't get the mark off the treehouse. We've tried everything. And all I can think whenever I see it is, what if I'm next? That's how everyone's thinking nowadays.'

'I'm really sorry about your friend.' Skandar put a hand on Jamie's shoulder.

'Me too,' he said, then changed the subject. 'Are you going to take that scarf off? It might not fit under your armour.'

'Oh, I—' Skandar hesitated. He knew it was silly but he'd taken to wearing it for good luck. He needed as much of that as he could get lately.

'I mean, if you really want to wear it, I guess you could squeeze it underneath.' Jamie caught the end, testing the scarf's thickness between his fingers. 'Where did you get it? Fourpoint?'

'It was my mum's,' Skandar said quietly.

'Huh.' Jamie frowned. 'Interesting. You're a Mainlander, aren't you? This scarf looks Island-made.'

'I don't see how it can be,' Skandar murmured, fiddling with the name tape Kenna had sewn in.

'Anyway,' Jamie said. 'I'd better go. I want to get a good seat.'

'For what?' Skandar asked, as Jamie gave him a leg-up. Scoundrel was almost too tall to mount without help now.

'Sky battles, of course! What did you think you were wearing the armour for? A fashion parade?'

As soon as Scoundrel landed on the Hatchling plateau, butterflies rushed into Skandar's stomach at the sight of all the other armoured unicorns. They really did look like the unicorns he'd watched on TV all his life. Red looked magnificent in rust-coloured armour. Falcon looked terrifying – her armour included a metal helmet, her horn protruding from a hole. Blade's silver armour reflected the spring sunshine so brightly that it hurt Skandar's eyes.

The unicorns weren't confined to one of the four elemental training grounds like usual. Both training groups – all forty-three Hatchlings – were milling about on the grassy plateau, their elemental blasts obscuring the view of the Eyrie with magical debris. All four instructors were huddled together on their unicorns in the middle of it all.

Skandar felt the nerves really hit him when he noticed seating at the edge of the earth ground, like a miniature version of the seats in the Chaos Cup arena. Some of the Islander Hatchlings were waving over at the stands and calling out. He wondered if Flo or Mitchell's families were there, and suddenly felt a little sadness mixed in with all the butterflies. He wished Kenna and Dad could be here to see him in his armour and smile proudly like the Islander families sitting there in the spring sunshine. He would have to wait for the Training Trial to see them.

As he passed by on Scoundrel, Skandar spotted Joby, who was looking out across the plateau, his blue eyes clouded and a deep frown carved into his brow. The other Islanders had left large gaps around where he was sitting. Clearly the suspicion of riders without unicorns went further than just the Eyrie.

Scoundrel was snorting anxiously and the ends of his wings flicked and sparked. He felt heavier and more dangerous in his armour, and the chainmail under his stomach clinked against Skandar's black boots. Skandar turned the unicorn in a tight circle, trying to keep him under control. As he watched Instructor O'Sullivan hammering a sign saying START near the air training ground, he noticed a bright blue bond stretching all the way back to Celestial Seabird at the other end of the plateau. Skandar blinked, then made his palm into a fist, urging the spirit element away. He needed to concentrate. He needed to fight it.

Instructor Saylor, the air instructor, blew her whistle, encouraging the riders to line up. Skandar was so distracted by seeing unicorns he didn't usually train with that he barely had time to get Scoundrel straight before the instructor blew her whistle again for silence.

'We will be starting sky battles today,' she called to them, riding North-Breeze Nightmare up and down the line. She was the youngest instructor by far, and the most glamorous, with bouncy honey curls and a yellow cloak embroidered with air spirals. Her voice was always calm and soft, though when she was irritated the veins in her arms and neck would crackle and spark like forked lightning. Today she was using her calmest voice, which somehow made Skandar feel even more nervous.

'Over the last few months we've been teaching you elemental attacks and defences – all to prepare you for sky battles. In the Training Trial being able to win a battle may be the difference between remaining at the Eyrie or leaving as a nomad. You cannot rely on being a fast flier; you have to be able to use your elemental magic to protect and improve your position.'

'Pssst.'

Red appeared by Scoundrel's right shoulder. Mitchell's eyes were shining with excitement, which Skandar found very strange. Mitchell absolutely hated surprises, and having to battle each other was the biggest, most unwelcome one yet.

'Did you see my father's here to watch?' Mitchell blurted. 'I can't believe he actually came all the way up from the prison. To watch *my* first sky battle. The Eyrie must have written to the Islander families, and he's here. For me! Can you believe it? Look!'

Skandar had never seen Mitchell this enthusiastic, not even when Amber had ended up with custard on her face. He followed the direction of his friend's outstretched arm and saw Ira Henderson with his waterfall braid. He wore the same unamused expression Mitchell did when Bobby was annoying him.

'Do you mind being a bit quieter?' Flo said shakily from Blade's back. 'I think you might get in trouble if you keep talking, and I really need to hear what the instructors are saying.'

Mitchell muttered an apology; Bobby rolled her eyes.

'You'll be battling in pairs,' Instructor O'Sullivan now said, her voice harsher than Instructor Saylor's. 'The rules are—' she paused – 'well, there aren't really any rules. You may use any combination of elements, but I would advise that you use your allied element where you can. First one to the finish wins.'

The flames around Instructor Anderson's ears flared as he laughed. 'You all look worried. Don't be. This'll be great fun!'

'Fun?' Mariam whispered nearby, her brown eyes fearful. 'What if I have to battle Flo and Silver Blade?'

Skandar felt his stomach drop. Were they actually going to do this? What if Scoundrel threw Skandar off in mid-air? What if he lost his sky battle so abysmally that the instructors immediately declared him a nomad? He felt even worse when he noticed healers arrive – with *stretchers*.

Then, as Instructor Saylor read out the pairs, things got even worse. 'Skandar Smith will battle Amber Fairfax.'

Skandar groaned. 'Forty-two other Hatchlings, and of course it had to be her.'

Bobby and Albert battled first. Skandar could see poor Albert's hands shaking on his reins before the whistle even sounded. For a moment Eagle's Dawn was a picture, her white tail flowing through the air, until . . . *WHAM!* Bobby summoned a tornado from her palm and launched it through the sky towards her opponent. The force tore at Eagle's wings and blew her wildly off course. Skandar could see Albert desperately trying to put up a water shield.

'Do you think she's going to electrify that?' Flo worried, as the water shimmered prettily in the air. But instead the tornado splashed Albert's own magic at him, and pushed Eagle further upwards away from the finish. Bobby landed Falcon, and galloped over the finishing line. Almost immediately the wind dropped again and Albert looked very embarrassed as he trotted Eagle along the length of the plateau alone.

'Well done!' Skandar and Flo called to Bobby, as she rode Falcon back to their quartet.

Bobby shrugged. 'Oh yes, well, I was always going to win. Congratulate me when I've won the Training Trial.'

Other pairs were more equally matched. Sarika and Alastair fought a furious mid-air battle, circling each other halfway along the course.

'Go on, Sarika!' Skandar cheered. 'Go on!'

Fire erupted in the sky above, and suddenly Dusk Seeker was spiralling downwards, Alastair hanging on to Seeker's neck. They landed awkwardly and Alastair was thrown to the ground.

Sarika landed Equator's Conundrum just before the finish and galloped over the line, the flaming fingernails of her mutation dancing in the wind.

Flo gasped. 'Look at Dusk Seeker's wing.' It was still on fire.

'I think Alastair's bleeding,' Skandar said.

Equator's Conundrum was salivating, trying to turn back to where Alastair had fallen. Dusk Seeker stood protectively over her rider as other unicorns sniffed the air and growled hungrily. Just in time, healers streamed on to the ground and whisked a white-faced Alastair away on a stretcher.

'Amber Fairfax and Skandar Smith!' Instructor O'Sullivan called.

'Use the fire element,' Mitchell advised. 'Statistically you'll have an advantage.'

'Just try your best,' Flo encouraged.

Bobby grinned. 'Give her hell.'

At the starting line Whirlwind Thief growled and pawed her hooves on the ground. Scoundrel bared his teeth, and snapped at her, jolting Skandar. The edges of the unicorns' breastplates scraped against each other, their wings colliding.

'You're going down, spirit wielder,' Amber hissed.

Skandar gritted his teeth. 'Actually, I'm going *up*.'

When the whistle sounded, Scoundrel rose higher and faster than Thief, his wings beating furiously either side of Skandar's legs. Skandar braced himself against the air currents, trying to get used to the new weight of his armour. Like he'd been attempting for weeks, he imagined the spirit and fire elements working side by side, the white and red mingling in his mind. But there was no more time. In the air below, Amber's palm glowed a dark forest green, and sharp rocks flew towards Scoundrel like hundreds of tiny missiles. Skandar was completely taken aback. He'd been expecting Amber to use air – her allied element – but she'd chosen earth instead.

Scoundrel roared in challenge and Skandar felt the pull of the spirit element stronger than ever before, stronger even than when he'd mutated. It was as though a balloon was expanding inside his chest, as though the power of the element was growing from the centre of the bond itself. 'Scoundrel!' he warned.

'Still wearing Mummy's scarf, I see.' Amber had followed her missiles upwards, but as Scoundrel dodged them all the anger Skandar had been suppressing bubbled to the surface.

'How can you live with yourself? How can you go around saying your dad's dead when he's not?'

'He's a spirit wielder!' Amber shouted coldly. 'It would be better if he was dead.' More rocky missiles flew from her palm.

Skandar was dimly aware of a white glow as he screamed back over the flapping of Scoundrel's wings. 'Don't you dare say that! You don't know what it's like to have a dead parent. You don't get to say you'd prefer it. You have no idea what you're talking about!'

He pointed Scoundrel downwards, trying to outfly Amber and her rocks, but she chased him through the air, her star mutation sparking on her forehead. 'Are you lost without your mummy, little spirit wielder? Do you wish she—'

Skandar lost control. The spirit element was suddenly all Skandar could feel in the bond, in the world. It was in his head, under his skin, in every breath. Spirit smelled different from the other elements; its cinnamon-sweet magic danced on his tongue. The magical link between him and Scoundrel was humming in recognition. *Give in. Give in. This is the element you're destined for.* And Skandar saw – clearer than ever – a shimmering yellow line running from Amber's heart – her palm still glowing green – to the centre of Thief's chest.

Some instinct made Skandar stretch out his own palm. Scoundrel screeched with excitement, and Skandar's heart sang as the unicorn's emotions collided with his own. For a fleeting moment he didn't care if they were seen; he didn't think about Joby's warnings. He knew what to do. For the first time he knew exactly how to use his magic. A ball of bright *something* left his palm and surrounded the yellow cord coming from Amber's heart. She didn't see it coming. Her palm stopped glowing green, and the earth missiles dropped from the sky.

The words from *The Book of Spirit* floated into Skandar's mind: *Whilst spirit is not a particularly strong offensive element, its defensive capabilities are unparalleled across the other four element types.* Is this what it meant? Did he have the ability to stop a rival rider's magic inside the bond?

Amber cried out in confusion, and Skandar realised what he'd done, what he'd risked. He had to use another element; he had to make it look like he was battling like everyone else.

Horrified, Skandar summoned the fire element as quickly as he could, but something had changed. The magic came easily, but he could still feel – still smell – the spirit element. Scoundrel roared, fireball after fireball exploding from his mouth.

Amber regained her composure and switched to water, firing a succession of jets. Her eyes filled with panic as she realised they weren't strong enough to resist Scoundrel's firestorm. Skandar was shooting flames from his palm now too. Then suddenly Amber pointed at Scoundrel and yelled in fear.

Skandar looked down. Scoundrel's neck had turned to flame under his armour, and his flanks were swiftly following suit. Manes and tails usually sparked with elements, but not whole bodies. This wasn't normal. This didn't happen. Then the words he hadn't understood at all in *The Book of Spirit* suddenly made sense: *Spirit-allied unicorns have the ability to transform and take on the appearance of the elements themselves.* But he couldn't let Scoundrel turn to flame. Even at this height everyone would be able to see; everyone would understand what that meant . . .

'Scoundrel! Easy, boy!' Skandar called to him.

Scoundrel bellowed and sent another fireball at Thief. Amber's water shield came far too late and she had no choice but to swerve. Skandar took his chance and gathered up Scoundrel's reins, and they flew as fast as they could towards the finish. Scoundrel hit the ground and crossed the marker seconds before Whirlwind Thief.

'Dismount!' Instructor O'Sullivan barked. Skandar's heart was beating fast under his breastplate. Had she seen? Had anyone else?

'Well done, Skandar. You won this battle.'

Skandar sagged with relief; if she'd seen him use the spirit element, he was pretty sure she wouldn't have been congratulating him.

'Better luck next time, Amber. That water shield needs a little work, no?'

Amber hung her head.

'Shake hands, please,' Instructor O'Sullivan ordered.

Amber barely touched Skandar's hand before she stomped away in disgust. Skandar didn't doubt that she knew exactly what had happened in the air.

'That was a very strong fire attack for a water wielder,' Instructor O'Sullivan observed. 'You looked fire-allied up there.'

Skandar tugged the sleeve of his blue jacket down nervously. But Instructor O'Sullivan didn't say anything else.

'You beat Amber! It was almost as good as your legendary custard toss.' Bobby and Falcon were standing close to the raised seating. Flo was turning Blade in tight circles nearby to keep him under control. 'I think you might even deserve an emergency sandwich.'

'Oh no, it wasn't that impressive,' Skandar said quickly. 'No sandwich necessary.'

'Suit yourself. By the way, since when did you get so good at fire? Have you been training in secret? You could have invited me!'

'Keep your voice down!' Skandar urged. 'I'll tell you afterwards.'

Bobby frowned at him but didn't push it. 'Mitchell's battling a water wielder girl called Niamh from the other training group. That's Snow Swimmer.' Bobby pointed at a white unicorn on the starting line. 'He'd better win. We'll never hear the end of it if he doesn't.'

'His dad's watching and everything.'

'No, he isn't. He left fifteen minutes ago.'

'Already?'

'Yeah. Before your sky battle with Amber.'

The whistle sounded and Red Night's Delight soared into the air. But Skandar and Bobby were immediately distracted by a loud conversation behind the stands.

'It was pathetic, Amber; it really was. I'd be surprised if they even let you in the air den next year. The Hive is for serious riders.'

Skandar felt his hair stand up on end at the nastiness in the woman's voice. Owen used to call him pathetic at school.

'But, Mummy, Skandar didn't play by the rules; he—'

'All I'm hearing are excuses,' the voice boomed. 'In my first sky battle I was over the line in ten seconds.' Then, very quietly: 'Maybe there's more of that revolting spirit wielder father in you than I thought.'

Bobby winced at the harsh words.

'I'm sorry, Mummy. I'll work on my transitions between elements. I'll try harder, I promise.'

The woman sniffed. 'You'd better. Or I'll be suggesting you're declared a nomad myself.'

Skandar heard Amber stifling a sob. 'Let's go,' he whispered, and they moved their battle-tired unicorns away as quickly as they could.

'I guess that explains why Amber's a bully,' Bobby said once they were out of earshot.

Skandar could hardly take it in. 'Yeah, and I bet it wasn't her idea to pretend her father died in a wild unicorn attack either.' He couldn't believe he was feeling sorry for Amber of all people.

Just then a red unicorn came galloping towards them. Skandar could tell it was Red Night's Delight, not only because Scoundrel shrieked happily to his friend but because she was farting cheerfully between every stride. 'Did he see? I won!' Sweat was dripping from Mitchell's forehead as he removed his helmet, then wiped his glasses. 'I took Niamh down with that huge fireball; it was almost wildfire. I'm going to find him!'

Skandar and Bobby looked guiltily at each other. Not only had Mitchell's dad left before his sky battle; *they* hadn't watched it either.

'Er—' Skandar started.

But Bobby ploughed in. 'Mitchell, your dad didn't see your sky battle. He, um, had to leave for a Council of Seven meeting. Some kind of prison emergency.'

Mitchell's face fell. 'He – he didn't stay to watch?' Skandar could tell from Mitchell's voice that he was swallowing back tears.

Bobby shook her head, and Skandar tried to arrange his face to look like it wasn't the first time he'd heard about a prison emergency.

'He said he thought Red's armour looked really good, though,' Bobby volunteered. 'I mean, not as great as Falcon's obviously, but still like a Chaos unicorn.'

Mitchell's eyes looked a little less hopeless. 'He did?'

Bobby nodded, and a happier Mitchell went to wash Red down by the pavilion.

'That was really nice of you, you know,' Skandar murmured to Bobby.

She shrugged, threading strands of Falcon's grey mane through her hands. 'Being let down, especially by parents, really is the worst.' She hesitated. 'For ages my parents didn't accept that my panic attacks were real. They thought it was attention-seeking.'

'Are they still like that now?' Skandar asked tentatively.

Bobby shook her head. 'Nah. They got there in the end, but I think Mitchell and his dad might have a bit further to go before they're as comfy as cookies in a jar.'

Skandar burst out laughing. 'Oh, not this again! As comfy as cookies in a jar? Even the Islanders aren't going to believe that one.'

'Actually, I taught it to Mabel last week when she was going on about Islanders mutating earlier than Mainlanders. And now she's taught it to all her friends.' Bobby looked delighted.

A little while later, Bobby, Skandar and Mitchell sat on their unicorns to watch the final pair: Flo and Blade battling Meiyi and Rose-Briar's Darling.

'Come on, Meiyi!' Amber called as she passed. She turned in their direction with a sickly sweet smile. 'Your friend might be a silver, but everyone can see she's *super* scared of her own shadow. She doesn't deserve Silver Blade – I wouldn't be surprised if they mixed up the eggs and she was never supposed to hatch him.'

'It doesn't work like that!' Mitchell half shouted once she was safely out of earshot.

'Back to her old self, then,' Skandar murmured to Bobby, but she wasn't listening. She was watching Flo fumbling with her helmet by the grassy starting line.

'She looks like she's going to vomit,' Bobby observed.

Even in her bright silver armour, there was no hiding the look of pure terror on Flo's face.

'I wonder if they would ever make a nomad of a silver,' Mitchell mused.

'Mitchell!' Skandar turned to him, shocked. 'Don't say that! She'll be fine!'

But they needn't have worried. As soon as Instructor O'Sullivan blew her whistle, Silver Blade took off like a bullet, one second ahead of Rose-Briar's Darling. It was enough. Flo turned Blade sharply in the air, her palm glowing green, and before Briar's back hooves had even left the ground, a mound of thick mud smashed into her, accompanied by a thick flurry of sand. With her opponent dazed, half blinded by the sand and land-bound, Flo created a barrier of earth that surrounded Briar and Meiyi, sealing them in a muddy prison, unable to take off. Satisfied, Flo pivoted her silver unicorn in the air and was a blur of blinding silver as she crossed the finishing line.

The spectators cheered louder than for any of the other sky battles. The only person who didn't was Bobby, her dark eyebrows knitted in a frown.

'I don't like this new connection between Flo and Blade. It's been there since he saved her from the stampede. If they stay on form, I'm never going to beat them in the Training Trial.'

'Skandar?' Instructor Worsham had appeared in front of the

three friends. He was looking at Skandar and he looked furious. 'A word?'

The instructor led him and Scoundrel over to the blue water pavilion. Joby looked terrible, tormented even – like he hadn't slept in days.

'What were you playing at, using the spirit element in a sky battle? Some of those spectators are *Council members*! What if they'd noticed Amber's earth magic dying in the bond? It was lucky you were battling so high in the air, but still – it was completely reckless!'

Skandar tried to explain. 'I didn't mean to. I found a way to let spirit into the bond so that Scoundrel doesn't go wild. I just lost control, that's all. But it worked eventually – I could feel the elements working side by—'

'Eventually isn't good enough, Skandar! You're clearly not skilled enough to combine them, so you have to keep blocking it!' Joby looked crazed; spit was flying everywhere as he struggled to keep his voice low.

'It's difficult, okay? You don't understand!' Skandar could feel himself losing his temper. 'You never had to hide the spirit element. You never had to stop your unicorn from using it. It's not as easy as just blocking it. Scoundrel knows he's spirit-allied – if I keep blocking the spirit element, it's going to send him mad, wild. This is better.'

'The Silver Circle, the Commodore of Chaos, the Council – they'll all want you dead if they find out. Skandar, please. You have to understand.' Joby looked like he might hit Skandar, or burst into tears, and he couldn't decide which.

'I do understand,' Skandar said, pushing Scoundrel away from Joby. 'I understand that you're too afraid to risk helping me. That's up to you, but I'm going to get into the spirit den no matter how long it takes—'

'How do you even *know* about the den?' Joby asked, incredulous. 'And going there is completely reckless! It's right in the middle of the Eyrie's clearing. You'll be found out! You'll be seen! You're risking everything. And for what?'

'I can't live like you do,' Skandar said sadly. 'I can't spend my life pretending to be something I'm not. And I'm not going to hide up in the Eyrie and do nothing, when there's a chance I can stop whatever the Weaver's planning.'

As he rode Scoundrel away, Skandar suddenly realised what Joby had said: *It's right in the middle of the Eyrie's clearing.* Miraculously, at last, he knew exactly where the spirit den was.

Skandar was so eager to get back to his friends, to tell them the good news, that he didn't look back at Joby. He didn't see the expression on the spirit wielder's face turn from devastation to determination.

CHAPTER SEVENTEEN

THE SPIRIT DEN

The day of the Chaos Cup Qualifiers arrived. For everyone else in the Eyrie, it was the day they'd watch the heats to see which riders and unicorns would take part in the Chaos Cup later that year. The Hatchlings were particularly looking forward to it as a break from worrying about the Training Trial that would happen in a few weeks' time. But since the Eyrie would be deserted, for Skandar's quartet it was the day they'd chosen to search for the spirit den.

Unfortunately Mitchell seemed to be finding it harder than he'd anticipated to miss the Qualifiers. When the Eyrie bells rang for the start of the day, he was already awake in his hammock, looking wistfully up at the treehouse ceiling. He sighed dramatically. 'You know, I almost prefer the Qualifiers to the Chaos Cup itself; there's so much more to see.'

Skandar got up to avoid him, and met Bobby at the top of the trunk. She was just as bad. 'I can't believe we're going to miss the actual Qualifiers for the actual Chaos Cup!' she moaned. 'What if Joby was wrong? What if the spirit den isn't even there?'

'You don't have to come with me,' Skandar said, like he'd said to Mitchell upstairs. 'I can look for it on my own – I'll be all right.'

'Don't be ridiculous,' Bobby said and turned to glare out of the window at Sarika, Niamh and Lawrence, who were crossing a nearby bridge, faces painted with their favourite riders' colours. Bobby continued to scowl at them, adding, 'You can't do this on your own, Skandar. You can barely get yourself dressed. Have you even combed your hair this morning? It's sticking up everywhere – you look like a mad scientist.'

Flo looked like the worst day of her life had dawned when she came down in her pyjamas, so Skandar took himself off to see Scoundrel. At least *he* wouldn't complain that he wasn't allowed to watch the Qualifiers. Skandar took advantage of the quiet moment to add a line to his latest letter to Kenna, while Scoundrel tried to bite the back of his shoe. Something Jamie had said had been bothering him.

PS Kenn, what do you know about the scarf you gave me? Jamie, Scoundrel's blacksmith, told me it looked Island-made. Maybe Dad knows where Mum got it from? When/if he's in a good mood, could you ask him?

By noon the Eyrie was as deserted as Skandar had ever seen it. He couldn't bear to wait any longer. The quartet crossed the network of swinging bridges together and climbed down to the ground. In the shadow of a tree on the edge of the clearing Skandar spoke, keeping his voice low. 'I think we should start from the centre and work outwards.'

Flo jumped in alarm as a bird passed overhead.

'I'm bored of planning,' Bobby complained. 'Can't we just go already?'

'Classic air wielder,' Mitchell tutted. 'So flighty.'

'On three,' Skandar said, 'we run to the Divide as quickly as we can and try to find the stump. One. Two. Three!'

They sprinted to the centre of the clearing and began to search where the four cracks in the earth crossed. Skandar got down on his knees and sifted his fingers through the spring grass, mainly finding soil and the occasional earthworm.

His knuckles rapped on something hard. Excited, Skandar felt the grass around it, and followed its circular form. It was a very low tree stump surrounded by long grass and overgrown with creeping plants.

'I think I've found something!' Skandar called to the others, who were also on their hands and knees nearby. Mitchell and Bobby rushed over, Flo dragging her feet behind them.

'That's a tree stump all right,' Mitchell confirmed, feeling through the grass as well.

'Hate to be the voice of doom –' Bobby had her hands on her hips – 'but what if it's *just* a tree stump?'

But Skandar's palm had caught on something cut into the top of the stump. He pushed the grass aside. His heart beat wildly as he recognised a sign in the wood – four entwined circles.

'I think this is it,' he breathed – hardly believing it – and leaned back to show the others the mark. 'This is the symbol from *The Book of Spirit*!'

'Are you sure you want to go in?' Mitchell asked. 'Do we really trust Agatha?'

'It could be dangerous,' Flo added.

Skandar frowned up at them from the ground. 'That was the whole point of this. The whole point of missing the Qualifiers—'

'You might find out that the spirit element really *is* as bad as everyone says,' Bobby said, 'and it might not give us any clues for defeating the Weaver. It might make you feel even worse.'

'You have no idea what it's like! Any of you,' Skandar blurted out. 'Even Joby makes me feel like being a spirit wielder is something dirty, something to be ashamed of, like I shouldn't be allowed in the Eyrie, even though I hatched a unicorn. My family are all the way on the Mainland, and I've never even known my mum. All I want is to belong somewhere, just for a few minutes, to have a chance at finding out how I might use my element for good. But if you're not okay with that any more, you don't have to come.' He was breathing hard as he finished talking.

Mitchell patted Skandar awkwardly on the back. 'We're coming. But, just so you know, you definitely belong in our quartet.'

Bobby raised her eyebrows. 'That's quite emotional for you, Mitchell.'

'It's a simple fact. I mean, if he's declared a nomad, then that's a different story—'

Bobby waved her hand in his face. 'Shhh, don't ruin it.'

Flo closed her eyes, took a deep breath and nodded at Skandar.

For his first try, Skandar put his Hatchery wound against the symbol in the wood. Nothing. He searched round the edges of the stump with his fingertips, trying to feel if there was an opening. There was none. As Skandar tried to think how the entrance might work, he absent-mindedly traced the circular grooves of the symbol, as though he was sketching.

A great groaning of wood filled the clearing, and rusted metal handles sprang from the stump. 'Hold on!' Skandar shouted to the others.

Just in time, the quartet bunched in a tight circle on top of the grass-covered base, and it plunged down into the dark. All four of them screamed at the top of their lungs, like they were on a roller coaster. Skandar's stomach swooped and his cheeks wobbled at the sheer speed of the drop into the abyss.

After a whole minute of plummeting through darkness, the stump came to a shuddering halt and Skandar stumbled off it, coughing up a mixture of earth and dust. As the stump creaked back to the surface, he opened his eyes. The place was so dark it didn't make any difference.

Mitchell groaned over the sound of Flo's whimpering. 'I think I'm going to be sick.'

The sound of a match being struck echoed in the pitch black. A sudden flare of brightness lit up Bobby's face. 'You would make terrible explorers,' she said smugly, moving over to a torch bracket on the wall. The flame caught and light filled the domed cavern. 'Fancy not bringing matches on an adventure like this! Amateurs.'

Once, the black marble of the circular room must have been beautiful. But no longer. Messy scrawls in white paint – words, diagrams and crossings-out – covered every surface: the walls, the floors, even the trophy cabinet. In places the writing became so spiky and illegible that it looked like it'd been done by a toddler with a piece of chalk.

Skandar turned to his friends, their eyes wide with fear and confusion. 'I don't think it's supposed to be like this,' he croaked, guilt creeping in. 'Look –' he gestured to an empty bookcase – 'I reckon whoever did this stole all the books too.'

'It's clear who did it,' Mitchell said darkly, pointing at the wall directly opposite them.

It only took a second for Skandar to work out the word painted on the wall; he couldn't believe he'd missed it before.

Weaver, Weaver, Weaver – squashed between the white diagrams and strings of unintelligible words.

'I *really* don't like this,' Flo whispered. 'What if the Weaver comes back? What if there's another way in?'

'Don't be ridiculous,' Bobby snapped at her, though there was fear in her voice too.

Skandar was examining the walls. 'The paint looks old,' he said slowly. 'Like, really old. Look – it's flaking.'

'Do you think it's a warning?' Mitchell asked shakily.

But Skandar was looking at a sequence of diagrams and barely heard him. The first was of a person reaching out to touch a unicorn's neck, with a word scrawled across the top – *find*. In the second diagram someone else was drawn beside them, light coming from the second person's palm and twisting around to form lines joining the unicorn with the first person's heart. Above them was the word *weave*. In the third diagram the first person was sitting astride the unicorn, palm outstretched, with *bond* written across it.

'I think I know why the Weaver's been stealing people.' Skandar's voice sounded hollow as it echoed around the marble walls.

'How?' Mitchell snapped. 'What have you seen?'

All three of them rushed over to look at the three diagrams.

'I don't understand,' Mitchell said. 'They're just stick people and . . .'

Skandar hadn't gone into much detail about how he'd used the spirit element against Amber and Whirlwind Thief. He'd never described how he'd reached out with his spirit magic and extinguished the earth element Amber was using to battle him – how his power had taken hold of her shimmering yellow bond. He'd been worried what they might think.

But now he explained. He told them what he thought he was seeing in the diagrams. The first person was a non-rider. The second was the Weaver – with the ability to see bonds. The unicorn was a wild one, with a telltale transparent horn. The Weaver was – as the name suggested – weaving the human and unicorn souls together. The Weaver was mimicking the bond.

'Jamie mentioned experiments,' Skandar said grimly. 'He told me there were rumours the Weaver was experimenting on non-riders. And it's this! This is what the Weaver's doing with them! The Weaver did it with a wild unicorn, then New-Age Frost, and the next stage must be other people, other unicorns.'

'Trying to find out how the bond works,' Mitchell murmured half to himself. 'Bonding non-riders to wild unicorns? You think this is what's happened to Alfie? To Jamie's friend? Is it even possible? I've never read—'

'But why would the Weaver draw this evil plan all over the walls?' Bobby interrupted. 'Surely that's a bit idiotic? Though since the Weaver *is* Amber's dad, then that isn't surprising, I suppose . . .'

Flo shushed Bobby, as though she was worried the Weaver might be listening.

'We're talking about the Weaver here!' Mitchell rasped, pulling at his black hair in frustration. 'Nobody knows if the Weaver is even human any more; it's hardly surprising there hasn't been a logical decision-making process!'

Flo was still looking at the drawings when she spoke. 'I think you're right, Skar. This has to be why the Weaver wanted New-Age Frost. The most powerful unicorn in the world? His magic would be much easier to control than a wild unicorn's. Maybe the Weaver thought it would help speed up these experiments? Maybe New-Age Frost has already helped do . . . *this*?' She gestured at the wall.

'But why? *Why* would the Weaver want to do this?' Mitchell demanded.

'Isn't it obvious?' For once Bobby actually looked scared. All the grey feathers were standing up on her arms. 'Simon's building an army.'

'Don't call the Weaver Simon!' Mitchell snapped. 'That theory is unconfirmed!'

'The Mainland,' Skandar said, his heart beating very fast. 'Why didn't I see it before? The Weaver doesn't just want to attack the Mainland. Think about it: if the Weaver takes this army there, then *Mainlanders* could be bonded to wild unicorns. People like my sister! With a wild unicorn army that big, the Weaver could take the Mainland *and* the Island.'

The image of the Weaver pointing into the camera at the Chaos Cup flickered across his mind. What had Agatha said? *That wasn't an accident. That was a threat.*

'No, no, we mustn't get carried away!' Mitchell protested. 'Okay, so the Weaver's killing the cliff sentinels – which looks bad.'

'It doesn't just look bad! It *is* bad,' Skandar spluttered. 'The Weaver's preparing—'

'But the Weaver's only abducted a handful of people so far,' Mitchell said forcefully. 'Even if the experiment has worked on people like –' he gulped – 'my cousin, there's no way there are enough of them yet to break through to the Mainland – not with the sentinels, the Silver Circle and the Chaos Cup riders to stop them.'

'And all of us riders in the Eyrie,' Bobby said fiercely.

But despite their brave faces Skandar felt his heart sink. Visiting the spirit den was supposed to have been about finding out how to help. About proving to his friends that spirit wielders had once been just like those allied to other elements. About showing that he could do something good with the spirit element. But, like always, they were back where they'd started – the Weaver using it for evil.

'We have to go to Joby,' Flo said firmly. 'Surely he'll want to help if he knows the Weaver is building an army? He can't ignore that! If the Weaver's a spirit wielder and able to make these false bonds, maybe there's a way Skandar can reverse it? Maybe Joby can actually help for once?'

It took a moment for Skandar to work out how to get back to the surface. Where the stump had been, a tree trunk stretched up into the gloom. It was Flo this time who found the spirit symbol in its bark. As soon as Skandar traced the circles, the trunk began to creak downwards until it resembled a stump once again. Skandar and his quartet held on to the handles tightly, as they were propelled back up to the clearing's surface.

Thankfully, the Eyrie was still deserted. Bobby – in full adventurer mode – declared there was no time like the present and that they should go to see Instructor Worsham straight away. But Skandar was worried. Joby hadn't exactly been pleased when he'd discovered Skandar was searching for the spirit den. He hoped the spirit wielder would understand. This was about more than Skandar and Scoundrel – this was about the safety of both the Island and the Mainland. This was about whether the Weaver was capable of creating an army.

Within minutes, Skandar was hammering on Joby's door. 'Instructor Worsham?' he called. 'Are you in there? It's Skandar! I need to ask—'

The door swung open.

'Joby?' Skandar called. 'Are you in here?'

'Skar, we shouldn't go in if—' Flo warned, but Skandar was already inside the living room with its beanbags and rugs.

'What if he's asleep?' Flo hissed at Bobby as she climbed the metal rungs up the tree trunk.

'He's not here!' Bobby called down a few seconds later.

Skandar spotted a door off the main living area that was slightly ajar. If it hadn't been cracked open, he might have just thought it was part of the metal wall.

Skandar pulled it wider to let light in from the rest of the treehouse. 'Joby? Are you okay? Are you in here?'

Bobby, Mitchell and Flo had joined him on the threshold. Joby was nowhere to be seen. The only thing inside the tiny room was a table with a map spread across it.

Mitchell took a step towards the map. 'Where is this?'

Bobby laughed as she approached the table too, with Flo and Skandar closely behind. 'I love knowing things you don't, Mitch. It's the way you get this little line in your forehead – that's when I know I've—'

Skandar cut Bobby off, putting Mitchell out of his misery. 'It's the Mainland.'

'Leaping landslides!' Flo breathed. She picked up two tubes of rolled-up paper. 'There are loads more maps here too. Do you think Joby drew all of these?'

'I guess so.' Skandar unrolled another map and a piece of paper fell to the floor. It looked like a leaflet. Skandar picked it up and turned it over. It had a symbol on it. He was sure he'd seen it before. Skandar stared down at the paper for a few seconds, trying to remember and then – he had it! The arc and circle symbol he'd seen being passed between two Islanders at the Fire Festival. 'Hey, look at this!'

They heard the door of the treehouse open. 'Quick!' Flo squeaked, and they rushed from the tiny room as Skandar shoved the leaflet into his jacket pocket.

The living room was now *very* occupied – but not by Joby.

'Howling hurricanes!' exclaimed Dorian Manning. The Hatchery president and head of the Silver Circle was accompanied by all four elemental instructors, who looked just as surprised to see Skandar's quartet, as they were to see the adults.

Mitchell snapped out of his shock first. 'We're looking for Instructor Worsham,' he announced. Skandar thought his voice sounded a little sneering, like it used to before they were friends.

'Why aren't you at the Qualifiers with everyone else?' It was Instructor Saylor. Though her voice was calm as she searched Bobby's face, her veins crackled and sparked under her skin.

'We—'

'This is all highly irregular. Perhaps they know something? Perhaps they were *involved*?' boomed Dorian Manning.

'Or,' said Instructor O'Sullivan, looking like she was

struggling not to roll her whirlpool eyes, 'perhaps they can tell us if they've seen anything that could help us *find* Joby Worsham. I'm worried about him; he's not been himself lately.'

'Joby's missing?' Skandar asked.

Dorian Manning cut across him: 'I think we all know where he's gone, Persephone!'

'I don't think we do, Dorian,' Instructor O'Sullivan replied coldly.

'No sign of the fugitive, no sign of a struggle, no mark –' Dorian Manning gestured around the treehouse – 'and a spirit wielder missing from the place he's never supposed to leave. I think we can make a very good guess at where – or should I say *whom* – he's run off to. I always said we should have locked him up with the others. And now look what's happening – with the sentinels and all these disappearances we're facing a crisis worse than the Fallen Twenty-Four!'

'You think Joby's gone to the Weaver voluntarily?' Skandar asked.

Mitchell stamped down hard on his foot.

'Aha! So they *do* know something!' Dorian Manning cried triumphantly.

Flo stepped towards Dorian Manning, the silver in her halo of hair catching the light from the treehouse window. 'President Manning,' she said softly, 'it's my fault we're not at the Qualifiers. I overslept and I didn't want to risk taking Blade out alone with the Weaver so active. The rest of my quartet stayed with me. We heard that Instructor Worsham was here too, so Skandar and Bobby came to ask him some questions about, umm, the Island.' There were barely gaps between any of Flo's words. She gulped in an enormous breath.

'That seems a reasonable explanation to me, wouldn't you say, President Manning?' Instructor Anderson smiled around at them, the flames over his ears dancing.

Instructor O'Sullivan shooed the quartet out before Dorian Manning could say otherwise. 'Off you go, the lot of you.' But in the doorway the water instructor murmured, 'Do you think maybe you could at least *try* to keep your heads down? First the Fire Festival and now this?'

'Yes, Instructor,' they replied, trying to look innocent.

They turned to go. But as they did, Mitchell shouted in fear.

Instructor O'Sullivan was back over the threshold in a second, Dorian Manning and the other instructors close on her heels. 'What is it?'

The little crowd gathered outside Joby's treehouse and stared at the thick white stripe down its metal wall.

'There you go, Dorian,' Instructor O'Sullivan hissed. 'He was taken – just like the others.'

When they reached the safety of their treehouse, Skandar was already talking as he shut the door. 'I think President Manning was right. I don't think the Weaver abducted Joby.'

'Of course it was the Weaver.' Mitchell flopped down on to the red beanbag. 'We saw the evidence. The white mark was right there on the side of his treehouse.'

'But look at this.' Skandar pulled the leaflet he'd taken from Joby's out of his pocket.

WERE YOU DISAPPOINTED
AT THE HATCHERY DOOR?

HAVE YOU DREAMED OF HAVING
A UNICORN BUT BEEN TOLD THAT
IT WAS NEVER YOUR DESTINY?

HAS YOUR UNICORN DIED AND
LEFT YOU LOST AND ALONE?

DO YOU FEEL IT'S UNFAIR THAT
THOSE WITH BONDED UNICORNS
HAVE ALL THE POWER?

We're here to help.

We're here to break open the Hatchery.

We're here to ensure every person
feels the magic of the bond.

BECAUSE EVERYONE DESERVES A UNICORN.
AND EVERY UNICORN DESERVES A RIDER.

JOIN US.

Then it dawned on Skandar what the symbol he had seen at the Fire Festival meant. His horror echoed in his voice as he explained to the others: it was the arc of the Hatchery mound, with the circle of the Hatchery door beneath it. And the door was broken open from top to bottom – cracked with a jagged white line.

The leaflet had been torn at the bottom, so it was impossible to tell who 'us' was, or who you were supposed to contact if you wanted to join up.

Mitchell snatched the leaflet from Skandar's hands and read it again.

'Just think about it,' Skandar said carefully. 'The first time I ever asked Joby about the Weaver's plan, he knew enough to tell me that spirit wielders could have stopped it. And he knew where the spirit den was, so maybe he saw the drawings on the walls, the diagrams of bonds being weaved? And then there's this leaflet – I bet the Weaver's behind it. I think Joby was fed up with being stuck in the Eyrie. I think he wanted what the Weaver's offering. I think he wanted—'

'To be a rider again,' Flo said, finishing his sentence, her eyes sad.

'And Jamie told me that his friend Claire seemed to know that the Weaver was coming for her. He said she was almost saying goodbye the night she disappeared.'

'So maybe,' Flo continued, 'maybe the white marks aren't marking out victims. Maybe they're an *invitation*. Maybe they're telling the Weaver they want to be taken.'

Mitchell looked up from the leaflet and there was a tear

rolling down his cheek. 'I was only little when Alfie tried the Hatchery door, but I remember – I remember how upset he was. He *really* wanted to be a unicorn rider and then it was all over. He hasn't written to me since I started training here. Maybe my cousin was given one of those leaflets and wanted the chance to be bonded to a unicorn?'

'A *wild* unicorn!' Bobby cried. 'Who would want that, for goodness' sake?'

'You don't know what it's like to have the bond taken away, to have to live without your unicorn,' Skandar said grimly. 'None of us do. But Joby did, and he was barely keeping it together.'

'Those maps Joby had of the Mainland,' Mitchell said suddenly. 'They were really detailed.'

'This is bad,' Bobby said, eyes wide. 'Joby's a proper geek about the Mainland – it's all he's had to do for the past decade. I bet he knows everything Simon needs: quiet places to land wild unicorns so they won't be spotted, populations of towns, castles to take as strongholds – that kind of thing.' Her voice was shaking.

The treehouse window lit up with a flare of green light, as if to make Bobby's point. Another sentinel was dead. Mitchell didn't even bother to tell Bobby not to call the Weaver Simon.

In the uneasy pause that followed, Skandar remembered the manic look in Joby's eyes after the first Hatchling sky battles. He'd looked like a person tormented by a choice. And in the end he'd decided he couldn't pass up the chance to have a bond again. A bond only the Weaver could give him, even if the Mainland was the price.

'I'm sleeping in the stables tonight,' Skandar announced. 'I'm not leaving Scoundrel down there alone.'

The others agreed, and after grabbing blankets from their hammocks the four young riders went to spend the night with their unicorns.

But Skandar didn't go to sleep. He couldn't stop sketching the figures he had seen on the walls of the spirit den. *Find. Weave. Bond.* Time was running out. The Weaver had Joby. And Joby knew that Skandar was a spirit wielder.

Had Joby really been afraid to help Skandar? Or had he been scared of Skandar learning too much?

Because even though Skandar now knew that the Weaver was bonding people to wild unicorns, he had absolutely no idea how to stop it.

CHAPTER EIGHTEEN

THE TRIUMPH TREE

The next few weeks passed in a blur. The Training Trial was getting dangerously close and Skandar was almost at breaking point. Nightmares about the Weaver's wild unicorn army flying to the Mainland kept him awake at night, and every training session felt like a tightrope walk as he tried to suppress enough of the spirit element so it didn't show, but let enough into the bond so that Scoundrel didn't throw him off. The bonds between other riders and unicorns flashed all around him as they practised racing – red, blue, green and yellow – and he had to pretend he couldn't see them.

It didn't help that the Hatchlings started splintering off into elemental groups before and after training sessions. The fire wielders would discuss new fire attacks they'd tried. The earth wielders would discuss how to improve their performances. The air wielders would go over and over the effectiveness of their lightning shields. Skandar tried to join in with the water wielders, but it was no use. Instead, he retreated to the stables alone, feeling sharp stabs of jealousy and flicked through his sketches of the Weaver's diagrams.

Unsurprisingly, given all his distractions, Skandar kept losing sky battles – not just against Flo, Bobby and Mitchell, but against everyone. And in their practice races he almost always finished in the bottom five. He didn't need anyone to tell him that if things stayed this way, he'd be out of the Eyrie by the end of the year. And, right now, the idea that there would be a full arena watching him at the Training Trial – including Kenna and Dad – filled Skandar with cold dread.

But it wasn't just Skandar who was stressed out. Most of the Hatchlings were spending hours in the four elemental libraries reading up on attacks, defences and anything else that could help them finish above the bottom five in the Training Trial. There were actual physical fights over some of the rarer books, as well as tears when sky battles were lost or won. By the time the Air Festival arrived at the beginning of May, the Hatchlings were studying and training so hard that not one of them thought about attending.

Amber was being meaner than ever, especially to Mitchell, and took every opportunity to criticise his magic. And Mitchell was being very hard on himself too. Whenever he lost a sky battle or finished low down in a practice race, he'd spend hours obsessing over his mistakes.

'It's okay to get things wrong sometimes,' Flo had said to him one day, after he and Red had lost a particularly ferocious sky battle against air-allied Romily and Midnight Star.

'I should have launched my flamethrower attack more quickly. It was so sloppy.' He'd kicked a beanbag. 'And I *still* haven't mutated! It's only me and Albert left who haven't!'

Flo had tried to soothe him again. 'It's okay, Mitchell.'

'It's not,' he'd snapped at her. 'Not when you're Ira Henderson's son.'

A few weeks later, the atmosphere in the Eyrie became even more depressing when Albert – who struggled to stay on his unicorn's back in almost every race – was declared a nomad. Though Albert told everyone he was relieved that he wouldn't have to compete in the Training Trial, when the time came for him to leave the Eyrie – for his fire pin to be smashed into pieces – Skandar couldn't even bring himself to go down and say goodbye. He didn't want the images in his head: Albert riding Eagle's Dawn under the elemental leaves of the Eyrie entrance for the last time; the pieces of Albert's pin being handed to his fractured quartet; the fragment of gold flame sparkling in the trunk of the Nomad Tree. But try as he might to block it out, Skandar still heard the hammering when it came. The short, sharp taps of metal on metal seemed to echo all night.

Then, all too soon, there were no more training sessions standing between the Hatchlings and the race that would determine whether they'd stay in the Eyrie. The unicorns had been given the day off and were dozing in their stables; the riders themselves only had one thing left in their timetables.

At three o' clock sharp, Skandar, Bobby, Flo and Mitchell gathered in the clearing with the other Hatchlings and waited for Instructor Saylor. Looking round at all the familiar riders, Skandar thought about the Training Trial the next day. They would be competing in front of the Island, in front of their families and racing to keep their place in the Eyrie. Today they were all Hatchlings together – tomorrow they'd be rivals.

The air instructor arrived on her grey unicorn, North-Breeze Nightmare, and gestured gracefully for the Hatchlings to follow her through the trees.

'Where are we going?' Bobby complained, stomping on a twig. 'I need to go over my tactics. Can't we have an Eyrie tour another time? Like, *after* the most important race of our lives?'

'I couldn't agree more,' Mitchell said, and Skandar almost tripped over a root. Bobby and Mitchell agreeing happened about as often as Amber giving out compliments.

'I hope we're not going to the Nomad Tree,' Skandar murmured to Flo. A reminder that there was a very high chance he'd be thrown out tomorrow was the last thing he needed.

'I think that's the other way,' Flo replied, looking at the nearby wall. 'The Nomad Tree is in the water quadrant, but this is air – look at the plants.' Flo was right. There were buttercups and sunflowers growing in bright yellows over the wall, along with tall rustling grasses and dandelions spreading their fluffy seeds in the light breeze. As Skandar watched, two silver-masked sentinels rode their unicorns along the top.

Instructor Saylor stopped North-Breeze Nightmare at the foot of a thick tree trunk and smiled reassuringly at them.

'I promise you there are no tests today. But it is tradition that on the eve of the Training Trial, Hatchlings are brought to visit this tree – known as the Triumph Tree – in the hope that it will inspire them to race their hardest tomorrow. Which quartet wants to go first?'

Bobby's hand shot into the air.

Mitchell sighed. '*Such* an air wielder.'

'Wonderful!' Instructor Saylor cried, and her unicorn snorted along with her.

As the quartet reached the foot of the tree, Skandar realised that unlike many of the other trees in the Eyrie there was no ladder to climb. Instead, there were wooden steps hewn into the trunk, which spiralled round like a staircase.

'As you climb,' Instructor Saylor called to them, 'you will see metal plaques hammered into the trunk. They record the winner of every Training Trial since the First Rider founded the Eyrie. When you reach the top, dare to dream – dare to dream that your name will join theirs.'

There was a hushed murmuring among the other Hatchlings and Skandar started to feel nervous as he followed Bobby and Flo. He wasn't expecting to *win* the Training Trial, but all this talk wasn't exactly helping him forget that by this time tomorrow it would all be over.

Every few steps Skandar stopped to read the simple metal plaques. But the higher they climbed, the more he noticed that some had been wrenched away. Not far from the top, Skandar stopped by one gap and turned to Mitchell.

'Do you know why some of these plaques are missing?' Skandar asked him, unable to keep his curiosity to himself.

Mitchell looked suddenly awkward. 'Well, I think probably

they were the spirit wielders.'

Skandar blinked. 'You mean, any spirit wielder who won their Training Trial has just been . . . erased? That's – that's so –' Skandar struggled to find a word bad enough – 'unfair.' It was unfair that all the spirit wielders were blamed for the Weaver's crimes. It was unfair that all the spirit unicorns had been killed and parted from their riders for ever, the bond torn away from them. It was unfair that there were people out there – Mainlanders and Islanders – who could have opened the Hatchery door if they'd only been given the chance, whose unicorns were abandoned to die for all time. It was unfair that spirit wielders' achievements were just written out of history. It hit him all at once – the horror, the cruelty of it all.

'I'm sorry, Skandar,' Mitchell said.

But Skandar was pointing at the nearest gap. 'Who would this have been? Do you know? Do you remember any spirit wielder names?' Somehow it seemed important to remember someone, anyone, who had wielded his element and triumphed, especially today, before his own Training Trial.

'I mean, judging by its position in the tree, I guess it might have been Erika Everhart?'

'Who's Erika Everhart?' Bobby asked loudly, stopping on the highest step on the trunk to turn round.

'Everyone knows who Erika Everhart was!' Flo said, half laughing from the step above Skandar. But at the furious look on Bobby's face she rushed on. 'Everyone loved her. She was the youngest rider ever to win the Chaos Cup. She won it twice, and then – it was so tragic – the third time, well, her unicorn,

Blood-Moon's Equinox, was killed – it must have been another spirit wielder.'

'Was that common?' Bobby asked.

'Not really,' Flo said. 'It was before we were born, but my parents told me that Everhart's third Chaos Cup was one of the dirtiest they'd ever seen. There was sky battle after sky battle, and Blood-Moon was killed.'

'Erika Everhart?' Skandar murmured.

'Yes, Skandar, keep up!' Bobby said impatiently.

He traced the mark left by the plaque on the trunk with his finger, and at last he remembered. 'I knew I recognised the name!' he exclaimed. 'I saw it in the Hatchery. In the Tunnel of the Living.'

Mitchell said, 'That's impossible,' just as Flo said, 'You can't have done.'

'Why?' Bobby and Skandar said together.

'Because Erika Everhart died, Skar,' Flo said softly. 'After Blood-Moon was killed, she couldn't handle it any more and she—'

'Threw herself off the Mirror Cliffs,' Mitchell said bluntly. 'She couldn't live with the grief apparently.'

'And the Tunnel of the Living only shows riders who are still alive,' Flo said.

'But I saw her name; I'm sure I did!'

'If she's alive—' Mitchell started.

'She *is* alive!' Skandar yelled.

Instructor Saylor's voice floated up to them from below. 'What's going on up there? Time to give others a turn, please!'

Mitchell didn't move, his face very serious. 'If Erika Everhart

is alive, then she was an extremely talented spirit wielder –
maybe the best there ever was. If Erika Everhart is alive, then it's
highly likely that she's – that she's the Weaver.'

Bobby frowned. 'But what about Simon—'

BANG! BANG! BANG! BANG!

Confusion. Screaming. Coloured smoke swirling on every side.

The quartet scrambled off the top of the staircase and on to
the nearest swinging bridge. Skandar grabbed the closest hand
he could find. Mitchell's. Mitchell grabbed Bobby's hand. Bobby
grabbed Flo's.

'Is everyone all right?' Skandar's voice shook. It was difficult
to see through all the smoke, but they'd just made it to the nearest
platform when—

BANG! BANG! BANG! BANG! The flares from the fallen
sentinels filled the sky above the Eyrie's walls, the colours
mingling like the leaves of the entrance tree.

'What's happening?' Flo cried.

'I can't tell!' Skandar shouted, as other riders called to each
other across the walkways.

'It's the Eyrie sentinels,' Mitchell said, coughing in the smoke.
'I'm sure of it. But I don't think it's just the Weaver out there –
those explosions happened on all sides. At the same time.'

Skandar gasped. 'You mean you think the Weaver's brought
an army?'

Just then Instructor O'Sullivan's voice reached them, even
through the explosions. 'INSTRUCTORS! GUARD THE STABLES!'

'I'm going to Falcon!' Bobby shouted. 'I'm not staying here
while the Weaver's soldiers take her!'

Skandar's breath caught. *Scoundrel.* They threw themselves down the nearest ladder and ran towards the west door of the wall – but there was a unicorn blocking their path.

'What are you doing down here?' Instructor O'Sullivan was astride her unicorn, Celestial Seabird. 'Get back to your treehouses. The Eyrie is secure.'

'Then why are you guarding the stables?' Bobby asked a little rudely.

'It is not your place to question me, Roberta. It is a precaution until we're sure the threat has passed. The Eyrie sentinels have already been replaced.'

'The threat won't pass!' Skandar said, unable to bear Instructor O'Sullivan's reassurance. 'The threat won't pass until the Weaver is caught. Don't you understand?'

Instructor O'Sullivan's blue eyes swirled dangerously. 'Skandar, you're a Hatchling. The best thing you can do right now is return to your treehouse and get some sleep. The Training Trial is tomorrow.'

'Erika Everhart,' Mitchell said desperately. 'We think Erika Everhart might be the Weaver.'

'What are you talking about?' Instructor O'Sullivan snapped at him. 'Erika Everhart died years ago. Enough is enough. I suggest you get out of here before I declare you all nomads right now.'

'You know what this means,' Skandar said, as soon as they entered their treehouse. The others collapsed on to beanbags but he couldn't keep still.

'It's as we suspected,' Mitchell said, turning to pull books from the bottom shelf behind him. 'The Weaver is building an army and now its soldiers are attacking the sentinels.'

'But why would Simon attack the Eyrie and just leave?' Bobby asked.

'Roberta, enough with the Simon!' Mitchell cried.

'I don't think that was the plan,' Flo whispered. 'I think the Weaver wanted our unicorns. The instructors were guarding the stables, weren't they?' She shivered.

'What for? To kill them? To bond them?' Bobby asked, the feathers on her arms standing up.

'We need proof,' Mitchell said from among his pile of books. 'We need proof that Erika Everhart is alive. Maybe then we could go to Aspen. She clearly needs more than suspicion: she didn't even believe the spirit wielders about Simon Fairfax.'

'But doesn't Skandar need to be careful?' Flo asked. 'If he reveals himself as a spirit wielder . . .'

'He'll be erased like one of the riders on those missing plaques,' Bobby said, her voice gloomy.

'We don't need Skandar to do anything just yet,' Mitchell said. 'First we need to know for sure that Everhart's the Weaver.'

'I hate to be the sensible one,' Bobby said. 'But how do we find Erika Everhart? She's clearly the queen of hide-and-seek if she's managed to disappear for this long.'

'And it's the Training Trial tomorrow,' Flo said nervously. 'Shouldn't we wait until after . . .'

'I suppose we should probably make some plans first.'

Skandar listened to them and felt his temper rising, his

worries – about everything from the Weaver abducting Kenna, to Scoundrel being taken by a wild unicorn soldier – suddenly rising to the surface. 'Come on! If we don't do something now, the Weaver's going to keep killing sentinels, keep stealing people and keep building this army. Oh, and after that, don't forget we're talking about a wild unicorn army that can fly to the *unprotected* Mainland! Where the Weaver can bond my family, Bobby's family, the whole Mainland, to wild unicorns! And kill anyone who stands in the way! We can't keep stalling! We can't keep waiting for someone else to do something!'

'The Weaver isn't your responsibility, Skar,' Flo said softly. 'It's not your fault!'

'No!' Skandar was still shouting, not caring that he made Flo flinch. 'But it means my entire elemental family is dead or in prison. I'm the only one who can help. I'm the only one who can see bonds, maybe try to understand what the Weaver's done – even reverse it! But I'm just sitting around in a treehouse waiting for disaster to strike. Mitchell's right: if Erika Everhart is the Weaver, we need proof before Aspen will believe us. But we can't wait until after the Training Trial – we need it now.' Skandar was breathing hard. He didn't know if he sounded brave, arrogant or just plain stupid – he didn't care any more.

'Flaming fireballs! Will you calm down?' Mitchell put his hands in the air. 'We get it.'

Flo stood up suddenly from her beanbag. 'I can't believe I'm actually suggesting this, but there might be a way to know for sure whether Erika is dead or alive.'

'How?' Skandar asked, but Flo was looking at Mitchell.

She gulped. 'The graveyard.'

'Yes!' Mitchell cried, also standing up. 'Blood-Moon's Equinox!'

'Can one of you Islanders please explain what's going on here?' Bobby growled. 'I hate it when you do this!'

'We know where Erika Everhart's unicorn is buried,' Flo said, her eyes shining. 'If we want to find Erika, there might be a clue there.'

'In a graveyard?' Skandar forgot to be cross for a second. 'Check the writing on a gravestone or something?'

But Flo was already shaking her head. 'It's a special kind of graveyard. You'll see.'

CHAPTER NINETEEN

THE GRAVEYARD

The Eyrie was still in complete disarray when the quartet snuck off for the graveyard before sunset. After a short flight, Scoundrel, Red, Falcon and Blade landed by the edge of a wood, and the quartet made their way through the trees. Blade was out in front – he always liked to be the leader of the group, even if Flo didn't.

'Next year, can there please be less of –' Bobby gestured around – 'all *this*?' Falcon's wings fizzed with an electric current, mirroring her rider's frustration.

'I thought you liked drama? I thought I kept things interesting?' Skandar joked, even though his stomach was turning over and over with nerves. He really hoped the graveyard could give them something – anything. The attack on the Eyrie sentinels had really shaken him. It felt like the Weaver was always two steps ahead.

'Interesting or not, I don't want to get blasted by a wild

unicorn army,' Mitchell said bluntly, before going back to consulting a map.

After a while, the trees thinned out again and they approached a simple wooden gate.

'This is it,' Mitchell and Flo whispered at the same time.

Bobby dismounted to open the latch, but as she passed behind Red Night's Delight, the unicorn squeaked out a fart, kicked up a flaming hoof and set it alight.

Bobby coughed. 'That unicorn has a problem. This is a graveyard! Have some respect.'

Red burped at her and a smoke bubble burst in mid-air.

Mitchell just shrugged – he'd long given up trying to control Red's habits.

Skandar was a little disappointed that there wasn't a more impressive entrance. The graveyard where his mum was buried on the Mainland had an elaborate wrought-iron gate. One of his first memories was Kenna showing him the metal roses and birds twisted into the bars.

But here there were no graves at all, only trees. Hundreds – maybe thousands – spaced evenly apart. At least, Skandar thought they were trees.

Some had trunks blanketed with algae that looked like it belonged in a pond rather than on a tree, with seaweed for leaves, and pink and orange flowers like sea anemones swishing eerily in the breeze.

Others had leaves in fiery reds and burning oranges, with branches that pointed directly upwards so they looked ablaze. Skandar swore he could smell smoke as he rode Scoundrel past them. Others had leaves of yellowy gold that bent in the breeze far more easily than their neighbours', spinning shadows beneath their boughs and crackling like electricity as they touched. And still others had enormous roots that climbed out of the earth, their branches filled with wildlife that should have lived underground – worms, voles, rabbits. Skandar even spotted a mole poking its head out of an opening in one of the trunks.

Blade and Scoundrel were very quiet; Skandar thought they understood what this place was. 'They're elemental, aren't they? Like the Eyrie walls?' he asked Flo.

Flo nodded. 'When a unicorn dies it's buried here.'

'Under its elemental tree?' Skandar guessed, but Flo shook her head.

'No, not exactly. When a unicorn is buried, the Island gives something back: a tree representing the element they wielded. Where a unicorn rests, a tree grows.' She smiled. 'It's sort of nice, isn't it?'

'Are riders buried here too?'

'Of course. The tree grows over both of them.'

'I'm glad,' Skandar said, feeling relieved even though they were talking about dying. 'I wouldn't want Scoundrel to be alone. I wouldn't want to be buried anywhere else.'

'How come they've let people graffiti all over the trees? Not very respectful, is it?' Bobby said from behind them.

Mitchell sighed. 'Do you always expect the worst of everyone?'

'You're hardly one to talk. Remember what you said about Skandar and Scoundrel when you first met them. I believe your exact words were *"the unicorn's a danger; this Skandar character's a danger"*.'

Mitchell gaped at her. 'How do you even remember that?'

'I remember everything.'

'Anyway,' Flo said, trying to head the argument off, 'it's tradition, Bobby. When a unicorn and rider die, it's an Island custom for their families and loved ones to carve their names into the bark of their tree once it's grown – usually on the first anniversary of their death. The idea is that the living watch over them in their final resting place.'

'What if the unicorn is killed first? Like Joby and Winter's Phantom? Or Erika and Blood-Moon's Equinox?' Skandar asked.

'Well.' Flo bit her lip. 'Riders have been known to carve their own name into the tree, along with their friends and family. That's what we're hoping has happened with Blood-Moon. It's a long shot, but we're hoping –' Flo looked over at Mitchell – 'that if Erika's still alive, she might have left a clue – a message.'

Bobby and Skandar were quiet, trying to make out the patterns cut into the bark of the trees as they passed. Skandar began to spot similarities: a trunk usually had the unicorn and rider names at the top, then their achievements and the names of loved ones underneath – all in different writing, as though they'd each individually carved their part. Skandar liked this idea – as the rider's name disappeared from the Tunnel of the Living, their loved ones recarved it in the bark of the tree.

'How are we actually going to find Blood-Moon's Equinox?' Bobby asked after they'd ridden quite a way into the graveyard.

'The trees are ordered by year of death,' Mitchell said brusquely, checking his map again. 'Blood-Moon's tree should be . . . Ah.' He stopped halfway down a row. 'This is it!'

Skandar hadn't needed Mitchell to point it out. It was the very first spirit tree he had seen in the graveyard, and its elemental allegiance was unmistakable. The branches, leaves, roots – even the trunk – were bright, gleaming white, and smooth as bone. Skandar felt a pull towards the tree – something similar to his bond with Scoundrel. He wanted to be near it. The tree felt like home.

'I've never seen a spirit tree before,' Flo said in wonder.

Skandar dismounted and Scoundrel immediately put his head down to munch the grass, his wings folded and his black horn glinting in the evening sunshine. Skandar was dimly aware of the others jumping from their unicorns' backs behind him, but he was too intent on reading the words on the trunk to wait for them.

BLOOD-MOON'S EQUINOX
– DIED IN BATTLE –
CHAOS CUP, JUNE 2006

CHAOS CUP WINNER 2005

CHAOS CUP WINNER 2004

ERIKA EVERHART
- DIED -
MIRROR CLIFFS, AUGUST 2006

CHAOS CUP WINNER 2005

CHAOS CUP WINNER 2004

Skandar threw his arms in the air. 'That's it, then! She's dead. I guess the Tunnel of the Living was wrong.'

'Skandar—'

'What are we going to do now? Another dead end. That's just great—'

'SKANDAR!' Mitchell yelled, causing birds to take off from the white tree's branches.

'WHAT?' Skandar shouted back. He didn't think he could bear the disappointment.

'Your name is on the tree.'

'What?'

'Your name is on the tree.'

'What?'

'Your. Name. Is. On. This. Spirit. Tree,' Mitchell said very slowly, pointing halfway down the bark.

Skandar kneeled, looking closer. Mitchell was right.

SKANDAR

Seeing his own name was strange enough, but his fingers shook as he traced two more names above.

BERTIE

And, then:

KENNA

'Isn't your sister called Kenna?' Flo asked gently.

Skandar nodded, not understanding. Not understanding at all. There was a tiny possibility – *tiny* – that someone on the Island might have carved his name on this tree, as what? A joke? But only his quartet knew Kenna's name, and his dad? He didn't think he'd ever said his name out loud on the Island. And most people called him Robert; only Skandar's mum had called him Bertie . . .

He reached out to steady himself against the white trunk.

Mitchell's voice sounded far away. 'None of Skandar's family could have carved their names into this tree – they're Mainlanders, right? And Skandar was born in 2009, but this says Everhart died in 2006, so *she* can't have carved Kenna and Skandar's names either. Unless Erika Everhart *didn't* throw herself off the Mirror Cliffs. In which case she's—'

'Mitchell, will you stop problem-solving for one second of your life?' Bobby snapped. 'This means more than Everhart being alive. Skandar, could this mean that Erika is in your family? Is she – is she your mum?'

'She can't be. Her name was—' Skandar hesitated. 'Unless . . .'

'Unless she . . . ?' Flo whispered.

'Did anyone see her jump off the Mirror Cliffs? Erika could have faked her death,' Bobby breathed.

'And then again on the Mainland,' Mitchell's voice was steady.

Skandar was shaking his head. 'My mum died just after I was born. But if this is her writing, if the Tunnel doesn't lie, then she . . .'

Skandar stared at Kenna's name on the trunk. And then he was grabbing the end of his mum's scarf, because he'd remembered. Remembered something that he couldn't believe he'd forgotten. The name tape Kenna had sewn into the scarf swam before his eyes. He'd never really wondered about Kenna's middle name. But there it was, clear as anything: Kenna E. Smith. E for Erika.

Their mum had hidden her name safely with Kenna – and it wasn't Rosemary after all.

The pull of the spirit tree on Skandar's chest tightened, and it was as though the volume had been turned down on the world. The birds, the wind rustling the leaves of the trees, the unicorns, all were silenced – as though holding their breath.

'She never died on the Mainland,' Skandar croaked. 'It means Erika Everhart faked her own death – twice. First on the Island, by pretending to jump from the Mirror Cliffs, and second on the

Mainland, just after I was born. It means she's not the Weaver . . . she's my mum.'

'Are you okay?' Flo asked, her hand hovering over Skandar's shoulder.

'Of course he's not!' Bobby exploded. 'He's just found out his mother is alive *and* she's an Islander. I mean, that's a lot for one evening!'

'Can you all just—' Skandar was struggling to keep it together. 'Can you just leave me here for a minute, with Scoundrel? I just need . . . a minute.'

They left. Where they went, Skandar didn't care. The tears fell, hot and fast down his cheeks. He began to shiver uncontrollably. Scoundrel's Luck rested his head on Skandar's shoulder, making little clicking sounds, and Skandar laid a hand on the unicorn's soft nose. Their fight over the spirit element was put aside, as Scoundrel sent waves of love along the bond, flooding Skandar's heart with a warmth he couldn't have found within himself.

His emotions were a hopeless jumble. He didn't know if he was happy or sad or just plain confused. He'd come to the graveyard for answers, but now all he had were more questions. Was Erika really his mum? If so, why had she abandoned him and Kenna? Why had she left the Island in the first place? Was this how Agatha had known his mum? Because she'd been a spirit wielder too? She'd been a Commodore! Had Dad known all along? Skandar shivered despite the warmth of the summer evening. Dad had always said his mum had loved the Chaos Cup – though she'd only seen the first televised one. Maybe it had been that? Maybe seeing the unicorns had made her leave Kenna, leave him.

Skandar rubbed the tears forcefully from his cheeks, and Scoundrel snorted, straightening up. He swallowed back the sobs he didn't have time for. He needed to find her; that was all that mattered. Surely she'd be happy to see him? Proud that he'd become a rider? Hope started to blossom in his chest. Who cared about the Training Trial tomorrow or becoming a nomad? Who even cared about stopping the Weaver? There were other people who could worry about that. Dad would be happy again. Maybe Kenna could come to live on the Island? *Their mum was alive.* She'd been one of the best riders the Island had ever seen – and she was like him. She was a spirit wielder. He was no longer alone, and all he cared about was finding her.

By the time Flo and Bobby returned, Skandar had decided he would go back to the spirit wielder prison. Even though Agatha had been moved, perhaps the others would know where Erika Everhart was hiding. This time he'd tell them who he was. This time he'd tell them he was her son.

Bobby cleared her throat as Falcon approached Scoundrel. 'Umm, does anyone know what's up with Mitchell? He's being weird. Well, weirder than usual.'

Mitchell was sitting in the shadow of a fire tree, with Red standing over him protectively, her red coat blending in with the leaves above them. As Skandar rode Scoundrel closer, he could see that Mitchell's dark brown eyes were rubbed raw behind his glasses, his black T-shirt was rumpled and his hair stuck up at odd angles.

'Mitchell, what is it?' Flo asked softly. She dismounted from Blade and went to kneel at his side. But Mitchell was staring, bug-eyed, at Skandar, who was looking down at his friend with a sinking feeling in his stomach.

'Tell me,' Skandar said almost angrily. He didn't have time for Mitchell to be having a crisis right now. He needed to get back to the prison – tonight.

Mitchell swallowed, stood up and began to pace in and out of the tree's shadow, his voice monotone. 'I went to look at some of the other unicorn trees in the graveyard. Somehow I ended up walking along the grove where they buried the Fallen Twenty-Four.' He pointed vaguely behind him.

'The twenty-four unicorns who were killed by the Weaver? On the same day?' Skandar had no idea where this was going, or why Mitchell was acting so strangely.

'At the Qualifiers in 2007, yes.' Mitchell was breathless. 'I knew what I was looking at because their dates of death all matched, and of course their riders weren't buried with them. But I noticed something else – something I'd never realised before.'

'What?' Skandar asked impatiently.

'All those unicorns that died in *different* Qualifiers in 2007. They all competed in the *same* Chaos Cup in 2006. It said so on their trees. Don't you see? The Chaos Cup in 2006 was the race when Blood-Moon's Equinox was killed. Every single one of the Fallen Twenty-Four saw Blood-Moon's Equinox die. *She* was the twenty-fifth unicorn from their Chaos Cup race. Erika was the twenty-fifth rider.'

Flo clearly wasn't getting this either. 'I don't—'

'Mitchell!' Bobby exploded. 'Just get to the point, before I set Falcon on you!'

'Don't you think –' Mitchell's hands were shaking – 'that it's strange that the Weaver killed every unicorn from that same Chaos Cup?'

'Perhaps it's a coincidence?' Flo ventured.

'I don't believe in coincidences,' Mitchell said, sounding a bit more like himself. 'The Weaver targeted those specific unicorns from the previous year's Cup. And left those riders to suffer the agony of losing their bonds.'

'What are you saying?' Skandar asked slowly.

'I'm saying, I don't think the Fallen Twenty-Four was a random act of violence. I'm saying –' Mitchell gulped – 'that it was revenge for the death of Blood-Moon's Equinox. That Erika Everhart wanted those riders to feel the same pain she did.'

Flo looked like she'd been zapped with the air element. 'Everyone thought Erika Everhart had died months before the Fallen Twenty-Four were killed, so . . . she would never have been a suspect!'

'Exactly,' Mitchell said grimly, running a hand through his hair. 'Even the imprisoned spirit wielders must think she's dead. That's why they suspect Simon Fairfax – he's the only free spirit wielder they're aware of.'

'But if Everhart was responsible for killing the Fallen Twenty-Four, then that means she's the—' Bobby frowned. 'Are you saying that she's definitely—'

'The Weaver,' Mitchell finished for her.

Skandar felt hot fury ignite inside him, as though a monster was rattling his ribcage with lava-filled hands. Scoundrel screeched in alarm, and Skandar dismounted. 'You've all gone mad! She can't be the Weaver – the Weaver's all creepy and weird. Erika's my mum!'

'Skar—' Flo reached for his arm, but he yanked it away from her.

'You've made all these assumptions,' Skandar spat at Mitchell, 'just to get to her being the Weaver. Maybe the Weaver wanted to get rid of the *strongest* unicorns? Maybe that's why the Fallen Twenty-Four were from the previous year's Chaos Cup? Did you think of that?'

'I'm not saying I'm definitely right,' Mitchell said hurriedly. 'But the thing is, Skandar, we have to ask ourselves why your mother faked her own death.'

'Twice,' Bobby chimed. 'Veeeery suspicious that.'

Skandar turned on Bobby. 'You've been calling the Weaver "Simon" for months. Why are you suddenly siding with Mitchell?'

Bobby held up both palms. 'Whoa, Skandar!'

'You're not thinking logically,' Mitchell murmured.

'OF COURSE I'M NOT!'

'The whole reason we came to this graveyard was to try to establish whether Erika Everhart is alive. You agreed that if she turned out to be alive, Erika was almost certainly the Weaver!'

Skandar turned furiously on Mitchell. 'When you've finished accusing my mum, I need you to get me into the prison. Maybe the spirit wielders knew her? Maybe they can help me find her? And I'm sure she'll give us a perfectly good explanation for everything.' Skandar was breathing hard and his voice echoed off the nearby trunks.

'But I don't want you to go looking for Everhart and end up

face to face with the Weaver!' Mitchell said, his voice hoarse. 'It's too dangerous. We don't know enough—'

'My mum IS NOT the Weaver!'

'Just hear me out.' Mitchell's voice was sad but firm. 'We suspected Simon Fairfax because he was a spirit wielder who was never caught. Why does Erika Everhart get special treatment?'

'We suspected Fairfax because Amber lied about him being dead! Because the spirit wielders told me to!'

'Erika Everhart lied about being dead, Skandar! Like Bobby says, it's very suspicious to fake your own death. Twice!' Tears of frustration were running down Mitchell's cheeks.

Skandar stared at him in disbelief. 'Not every spirit wielder is bad, Mitchell, remember? Or are you going to put me on your suspect list too? This is my mum we're talking about. My mum! The one I thought was dead my whole life. She's alive! And after all this time you expect me to just stand here and accept you telling me she's a mass murderer?'

'If Erika Everhart is your mother, there's a very high probability she's also the Weaver. All I'm saying is—'

Skandar lurched back towards Scoundrel. 'The Training Trial is tomorrow – we don't have time for this. Flo? Bobby? Let's go. I'm sure we can find a way into the prison tonight. Mitchell's going to stay out of it, just like he used to!'

Mitchell flinched as though Skandar had hit him, but Skandar didn't even feel guilty. All he felt was white-hot anger, his head buzzing with thoughts about how Mitchell was trying to ruin the fact that he had a mum and that she was alive after all this time.

'Skar, I'm not sure about this,' Flo said as Skandar swung his leg over Scoundrel's back. 'The prisoners don't even know Erika is alive. I don't think they'll be able to help. I just— What if Mitchell's right? Just because Erika's your mum, it doesn't necessarily mean she's *not* the Weaver as well.'

'FINE!' Skandar roared. 'Side with him. See if I care! Come on, Scoundrel!'

Skandar pressed his feet into Scoundrel's sides and it was as though the unicorn wanted to leave Mitchell and the others behind as much as his rider did.

'Skandar, wait!' the rest of his quartet called after him, but he was too angry to listen. In only a few strides Scoundrel's wings were out and they were soaring away, the colours of the elemental trees of the graveyard blurring below them. Up in the air, Skandar let out a roar of frustration and Scoundrel joined in as they flew faster and faster towards the Eyrie, racing the sunset.

Kenna would be here on the Island tomorrow to watch the Training Trial. Maybe, if Skandar went to the prison tonight – once it was properly dark – he and Kenna would be able to find Erika together after the race. He could give the scarf back to his mum and tell her he and Kenna had been keeping it safe all this time. Her *Island-made* scarf.

As Skandar touched down outside the Eyrie's entrance tree, he became aware of the whistle of another unicorn's wings in the air, then someone else's feet pounding behind him. He looked over his shoulder—

'Bobby?'

She skidded to a stop. 'If you want to go to the prison, I'll come. Not for you, you know? For the adventure,' she panted. 'But we're not going until *after* I've won the Training Trial tomorrow. That's the deal.'

'It's not her, Bobby. My mum isn't the Weaver. She's not. She's NOT! SHE'S NOT!' Skandar ripped handfuls of seaweed from the water wall in front of him and screamed the words up at the treetops of the Eyrie over and over. His voice was breaking and his heart was breaking with it – because Mitchell was his friend, but he was wrong and he was trying to ruin everything. Skandar had only just got his mum back – he wasn't going to lose her again.

Then Bobby's arms were round him, and she smelled like fresh bread and the citrus fizz of air magic. Her grip on him was tight as his body shook with sobs. It was as though all the feelings he'd kept in the box with his mum's old things had been emptied out at once. The waves of frustration, hope and fear washed over him like the sea over Margate beach, as the hurt, the love and the anger took up the space they'd always needed.

CHAPTER TWENTY

THE TRAINING TRIAL

Skandar woke groggily to the sound of riders sliding back the bolts of their stables, and unicorns screeching in welcome. A large globule of unicorn saliva hit his cheek, and Skandar became dimly aware of Scoundrel's Luck chewing on a clump of his hair – mercifully still attached to his head. He only had one trainer on; he could see the other had been torn apart by Scoundrel in the night – victorious at last.

'What are you doing down there?' Jamie's voice reached Skandar's ears.

The blacksmith slammed the stable door shut, and Skandar winced. His whole head ached from crying and lack of sleep. Had Bobby brought him to Scoundrel's stable? He couldn't even remember. And what time had that been? Then he sat bolt upright. His mum. He needed to find her.

But Jamie was in the way of the stable door, blocking it with Scoundrel's armour.

'Where do you think you're going?' he asked. 'Help me get this lot on him, will you?'

Skandar rubbed his eyes. 'I can't, Jamie. I've got somewhere I need to be.'

Jamie raised his eyebrows. 'Somewhere *other* than the Training Trial?'

The Training Trial. Skandar had completely forgotten.

'Oh. No. I guess not, then . . .' Skandar rambled.

Jamie grabbed his shoulder and shook it. 'Wake up, Skandar! It's not just your neck on the line here. If you're declared a nomad, I won't have anyone to make armour for. I don't want to be hammering dents out of pots for the rest of my days. Don't let me down. Don't let Scoundrel down. Don't let yourself down.' Jamie's face was fierce.

A new plan started forming in Skandar's mind. He would do the Training Trial. Bobby had said she wouldn't help until afterwards anyway. He would probably lose, but he would try his best because Kenna and Dad were coming to watch him, and then afterwards they could all find his mum together. He wouldn't care if he was declared a nomad, as long as they found her. He nodded at Jamie.

'That's better,' Jamie said, and threw a bucket of water over Skandar's head.

Jamie walked down to the racetrack alongside Scoundrel. The Training Trial was a shortened five-kilometre version of the Chaos Cup and Skandar had decided to walk Scoundrel to the course rather than waste the unicorn's energy by flying. To steady his nerves Skandar leaned forward and checked that

Scoundrel's blaze was still covered and made sure his mutation was hidden by the sleeve of his blue jacket – the riders were required to wear the colours of their own allied element for the race. He tried not to look at the hundreds of Islanders who had turned out to watch. He wondered if the Mainlander families had arrived in the helicopters. Had Kenna and Dad already taken their seats in the stands? His stomach swooped. They didn't know yet. They didn't know Mum was alive.

'Here's your helmet,' Jamie said as they neared the starting bar. 'And for the record that scarf is flammable and it's not my armour that's faulty if you get fried. Tuck it out of the way at least!'

Skandar shoved it under his breastplate.

'Also, no pressure or anything, but I would *love* to show my bard parents how well I'm doing as a blacksmith so they stop making me learn songs as a back-up career, okay?'

Skandar grimaced. 'Right.'

Jamie shielded his eyes from the sun, looking up at Skandar. 'I know we don't know each other very well yet, and I'm not exactly sure what's wrong with you today, but it can wait. For the next thirty minutes of your life, whatever it is, it can wait – do you hear? You've got guts, remember? That's why I picked you! You'll be fine. I believe in my armour and I believe in you.' As Jamie jogged away, Skandar wondered what the blacksmith would say if he knew his armour was being worn by a spirit wielder.

As he approached the start of the course, Skandar felt the bond humming with Scoundrel's nervous excitement. The unicorn kept snorting sparks, his horned head high in the air as he looked around at the racetrack, the healer tents blowing in the breeze, and the large crowd gathering on either side of the ropes.

Skandar tried to relax as other Hatchlings began to push their unicorns towards the starting bar. Their instructors had talked them through the set-up a thousand times: there were no turns in this race; it was a straight line through to the arena; any combination of elements was permissible in sky battles; a fall would mean elimination; and they had to land before crossing the finish. Skandar felt butterflies every time he imagined Scoundrel swooping into that famous arena. Maybe Scoundrel would behave, and they'd finish above the bottom five? Kenna and Dad would be watching! Maybe his mum would be watching too in secret, full of pride? The thought made Skandar breathless, as though Jamie had fixed his breastplate a notch too tight.

Skandar urged Scoundrel into the group of forty-one other Hatchlings. It was a battlefield already. A mass of sparking wings and flaming manes and tails falling like fountains, all mixed far too close together, as hooves exploded and churned the earth beneath them. It had never been like this in their training sessions – not even when they'd practised racing. The unicorns knew today was different. The air reeked of sweat and magic.

Old Starlight suddenly blocked their path to the starting bar, snorting ice crystals into Scoundrel's face. Scoundrel pawed a hoof at the ground, electricity fizzing around the bottom of Skandar's leg guard.

'Sorry!' Mariam called, as Old Starlight spun round again, eyes smoking.

Out of the corner of his eye Skandar caught sight of Red Night's Delight rearing and belching flames into the sky, Mitchell clinging to her mane and gritting his teeth. *Serves him right*, Skandar thought, his anger surging again.

Finally there was an opening at the starting bar. Skandar encouraged Scoundrel to slot between Silver Blade and Queen's Price, but he kept trying to move backwards out of the line, away from the other unicorns. Skandar didn't blame him – it was chaos.

'Are you okay?' Flo shouted over to him, as thick smoke rolled off Blade's silver back.

Skandar didn't answer. She'd sided with Mitchell.

Queen's Price reared up beside Scoundrel, who tossed his head aggressively in response.

'Watch it!' Gabriel cried, turning Price sharply away from the bar to avoid Scoundrel's horn.

'Fancy seeing you here!' Bobby shouted through her helmet, as Falcon took Price's place. Falcon seemed eerily calm compared to the unicorns around her.

The unicorns' roaring and shrieking got even louder. The air was so thick with magic it was difficult to breathe. Skandar's stomach was doing backflips, his hands shaking on the reins. Scoundrel felt wild beneath him, his weight shifting from hoof to hoof, wingtips igniting with electricity, then flames and back again. Both their emotions were swirling around – fear and excitement and anger and anxiety – and Skandar wasn't sure now whose were whose. He was so close to Flo and Bobby on either side that their armoured kneecaps scraped against each other.

'Ten seconds!' an official voice called over the tannoy.

Skandar was desperately trying to remember what his race strategy had been, when the whistle sounded. There was a creak and a loud bang as the starting bar lifted. Skandar had never felt Scoundrel move so fast. He took off within three strides, wings snapping out with a jolt. Skandar held tight to his reins, and dug his fists into the unicorn's black mane.

They were flying down the course towards the first floating kilometre marker. Scoundrel was in the middle group. In the lead Flo and Blade were locked in a battle with Mabel and Seaborne Lament. Bobby and Falcon were speeding through the air not far behind. Skandar caught sight of Lawrence and Poison Chief spiralling towards the ground – Red soaring directly above them, Mitchell's hand glowing red. There was an explosion and a shriek behind Skandar – from a unicorn or rider, he wasn't sure – followed by a bright flash. Then Dusk Seeker was barging through the air and Alastair's palm glowed blue beside Scoundrel's right shoulder.

Skandar's palm glowed green, but the effort of controlling the spirit element meant his sand shield was too slow, and Alastair shot a jet of water sideways straight into Skandar's shoulder. As Scoundrel lost speed – falling behind Dusk Seeker – water frothed from Seeker's wings, and waves moved through the air, pushing Scoundrel even further back. Skandar's only choice was to push Scoundrel higher, avoiding Seeker's blast, the salty smell of water magic clogging Skandar's nostrils. Scoundrel screeched down at Seeker as the unicorn pulled ahead. He knew they'd lost precious distance and he was desperate to use the spirit element.

Skandar could feel his palm pulsing, as though Scoundrel was trying to force the element to appear there.

'NO!' Skandar shouted, and Scoundrel roared back. He reared in the air, his hooves lighting up with the white of the spirit element, and stopped flying forward completely. More unicorns passed them.

'Please, Scoundrel, don't do it! Not with all these people watching! They'll kill us!' But Skandar could feel Scoundrel's anger vibrating in the bond and around Skandar's heart. The unicorn was going to win the race, and he didn't care what his rider wanted any more.

'Well, this is going to be *super* fun!' Whirlwind Thief had twisted towards Scoundrel in mid-air. Amber looked manic – her teeth were bared, the star of her mutation buzzing with electricity on her forehead – and then a tornado soared from her palm, straight at Skandar.

Skandar tried to summon an element – any legal element – but Scoundrel blocked every single one. He tried to make Scoundrel fly downwards away from the attack, but he reared and screeched and threw his head from side to side. To avoid slipping off his back Skandar had no choice but to throw his arms round Scoundrel's flailing neck and wait for Amber's tornado to hit them.

Then, out of nowhere, he saw Red Night's Delight. Mitchell and Red had been way ahead of them, but for some reason the unicorn was now speeding back towards Scoundrel.

'Amber!' Mitchell bellowed, and she jerked round on Thief's back. She hadn't even heard Red in the air behind her.

'Are you really going to battle me, Mitchster?' she jeered, and raised a palm to attack.

But Mitchell was quicker. A jet of fire exploded from his palm and hit Thief's flank, as Red simultaneously belched fireballs, the smoky smell of the magic filling the air. Water was Amber's weakest element, and she had no time to summon a shield. Thief slowed down and dipped to escape the flames.

Amber's tornado came within a feather-length of Scoundrel's left hoof and then veered off in the opposite direction as she lost control. In a split second Mitchell switched to the earth element and threw a barrage of rocks downwards. They caught the tail end of Amber's tornado and hurtled towards Thief. Amber's eyes widened in shock; she hadn't expected her own magic to be used against her. The jagged rocks chased Whirlwind Thief all the way to the ground.

'That's for, well, everything!' Mitchell yelled down after her.

'What are you doing?' Skandar called to Mitchell. Red was flapping her wings beside Scoundrel. Sky battles raged all around them, with debris and magic flying past.

Mitchell's face was caked in ash and dirt. 'Making sure you're not declared a nomad!'

'But you were ahead!' Skandar shouted in disbelief. He knew how much Mitchell wanted to impress his dad. 'I'm going to slow you down – just go without me!'

'Not an option.' Mitchell pulled Scoundrel's reins from Skandar's grip, and over the black unicorn's horn. Scoundrel shrieked in confusion, his wings beating furiously. 'I look out for you and you look out for me, remember? Besides, Red would never forgive me if she lost Scoundrel.'

Skandar couldn't imagine what it had cost Mitchell – who always kept to the plan, who loved rules, who liked to do everything in the right order – to turn round and fly the wrong way down the racetrack.

'I've got you both,' Mitchell said, holding up Skandar's reins. 'Don't try any magic – I'll protect you. Just follow Red and fly as fast as you can!'

Red screeched urgently to her friend and Scoundrel rumbled back. Skandar didn't know what they'd communicated, but Scoundrel finally began to fly forward – fast. They dodged Zac's flying boulder, swooped round the edge of Niamh's fire blast, flew over tendrils of electricity writhing in mid-air, and pressed onwards. Red and Scoundrel roared together as they passed the final floating kilometre marker – they knew the finish was in sight.

Just as Mitchell was firing multiple balls of flame at Kobi and Ice Prince, the shadow of a unicorn blotted out the sky above their heads.

'Mitchell!' Skandar called over the beating of their unicorns' wings.

'Bit busy right now!' Mitchell yelled, as he sent one last blast at Ice Prince. Kobi's water shield shimmered, quivered and then gushed out of the sky, leaving the way clear for Red and Scoundrel to advance. 'I'd better mutate after this!' Mitchell shouted to Skandar. 'What were you say—' But Mitchell's question died as he too saw the most powerful unicorn in the world plummeting towards the arena.

New-Age Frost.

'I can't see where he's gone!' Skandar shouted in panic. The air was so full of smoke and debris that the grey unicorn had completely disappeared.

Cheers erupted as Hatchlings began to pass the finishing line.

'We've got to land!' Mitchell cried, as the arena came into view. They soared down over a sea of upturned faces, Scoundrel and Red's horns pointing towards the sand. Scoundrel grunted as his hooves made contact, metres from the finishing line. Mitchell threw Scoundrel's reins to Skandar, and both boys pushed their unicorns as hard as they could along the final stretch of track. Cheers went up from the crowd as Mitchell, then Skandar, rode under the arch. Skandar had no idea whether he'd finished in the bottom five or not. Nobody was screaming; there was no sign of panic. Had they imagined New-Age Frost?

But then Skandar saw Flo.

He vaulted off Scoundrel, discarded his helmet, and ran towards Flo crouching beyond the finishing line; she was trying to make herself heard over the cheering of the oblivious crowd. Skandar felt like he'd lived this moment before. He was back in Margate, watching the Chaos Cup, his dad saying 'Something's wrong', the smoke clearing, the darkness lifting – the sense that nothing would ever be the same again.

Time was shifting, slowing, stopping as he heard Flo's sobbing. 'The Weaver!' Tears streamed down her cheeks. 'The Weaver's taken Silver Blade!'

Skandar bent down next to her, wishing he was walking the fault lines again, wishing Flo was just pretending. But there was no mistaking the terror in her eyes. And it was so obvious now why the Eyrie had been attacked. The Weaver hadn't wanted just any unicorn – the Weaver had wanted a silver.

Bobby and Mitchell reached them – tearing off their helmets – and all four riders crouched in a huddle, their earlier arguments forgotten. Mitchell started to make a whispered plan, determined to enlist the help of the instructors, the sentinels or even his father if it had to come to that. But Skandar knew there wasn't time. The quickest way to find Blade was with the spirit element – and that meant nobody else could be involved.

Skandar mounted Scoundrel, and Flo scrambled up to perch in front of him. In his pocket his palm glowed with the full strength of the spirit element, and her bond – a dark shimmering green for the earth element – shone out from her heart like a searchlight. Amid the cheering of the crowd, exhausted unicorns were milling about the arena, healers were attending to injuries, and riders were hugging each other. So when the quartet bolted out of the riders' enclosure, nobody gave them a second glance.

They galloped round the edge of Fourpoint, afraid to fly in case they were spotted from below. Their unicorns' hooves thundered along streets, then paths and then the floor of the forest, until they reached the outermost edge of the Wilderness. Skandar's arms were tightly wound round Flo's waist, her chainmail cold against his mutation as Scoundrel thundered onwards. They didn't talk about what it would mean for the Weaver to bond to a silver unicorn. They didn't need to.

Concentrating on following Flo's bond, Skandar barely registered how different the Wilderness was. Where Fourpoint and the Eyrie were lush and healthy, the Wilderness was barren and desolate. Clusters of leafless trees punctured a plain scorched with elemental magic. The ground was cracked and dusty with barely a blade of grass to be seen. It reminded Skandar of pictures he'd seen of the extinction of the dinosaurs – maybe some of the wild unicorns were just as old.

'How much further?' Bobby's voice sounded choked. At first Skandar thought she was just shivering. The wind was bitterly cold and not even the feathers on Bobby's arms could keep it out. But then Skandar glanced sideways at her. She was doubled over on Falcon's back, one hand on her chest, her throat rattling as she tried to suck in air.

Skandar grabbed one of Falcon's reins to slow her down.

'Why are we stopping?' Flo demanded.

'What's going on?' Mitchell called, Red snorting as he pulled her up.

Skandar ignored them and turned Scoundrel so he was wing to wing with Falcon. 'Breathe, Bobby,' he urged her. 'Breathe through it. Focus on Falcon. Focus on the bond.'

Bobby's wheezing echoed in the silence of the Wilderness. Falcon turned her grey head and gazed steadily at her rider, making low rumbling sounds of comfort.

'We need you, Bobby. You can do this,' Skandar encouraged her. And every word was true. If they were going to stand any chance of getting Silver Blade back, they needed to fight together.

'What's wrong? Is she—'

Skandar shook his head at Flo. Mitchell, for once, was quiet. Bobby's breathing changed to a whistle and finally she was able to straighten up. Her fringe was plastered to her face with sweat as she sucked in long, steadying breaths.

'Are you okay?' Skandar checked. 'Can you carry on?'

Bobby nodded a little shakily. 'Wild unicorns couldn't stop me.'

Just then a high-pitched shriek cut across the plain.

'That was Blade!' Flo cried out. 'Come on!'

Scoundrel, Falcon and Red seemed to recognise Blade's cry too, and began to call back.

Blade's shrieks were coming from a small hill up ahead. There was no grass on it, just dry soil and dust, but a cluster of skeletal trees crowned its top. And Flo's bond was shining right into it.

'Skandar?' Mitchell asked. 'Is that the place? Now what's the plan? How are we going to—'

'Mitchell, there's no time!' Bobby snapped, her voice a little hoarse. 'We go in. We get Silver Blade. We leave. That's it. *That's* the plan!'

Skandar had to agree with Bobby, because even though he would have preferred to have some kind of plan too, he couldn't think for the life of him what it would be. Thoughts were tumbling around his head. Coming face to face with the Weaver. The Weaver with a silver attacking the Mainland – Kenna screaming, Dad running. Erika Everhart. What if it was true? He couldn't decide what he was most afraid of.

Another shriek echoed through the Wilderness.

'Come on!' Flo shouted, and as though he understood her desperation, Scoundrel galloped to the top of the hill, Red and Falcon crashing through the trees behind him.

The first thing Skandar saw was Silver Blade, the green bond shining from his chest and into Flo's. The unicorn stood out anywhere, but especially in this colourless scrub of woodland. Thick vines encircled his stomach, his neck and even his head, tying him between two trees. He looked dull and sleepy compared to his usual roaring self. Was it already too late?

Then Blade's dark eyes locked on Flo and the unicorn went berserk, roaring and screaming and pulling at his ties. Flo threw herself down from Scoundrel's back and sprinted towards her unicorn, her black-and-silver hair catching the wind. But before she could reach Blade, before she could even stretch out to touch him, the trees were suddenly alive with wild unicorns. Wild unicorns with riders.

'Flo!' Skandar, Mitchell and Bobby cried out together, as one of the strangers dismounted and grabbed their friend round the waist, dragging her away from her unicorn.

Skandar desperately tried to think of a way to help her, but his mind kept short-circuiting like it used to at school when he couldn't think of anything to say. His eyes flicked around the trees. He stroked Scoundrel's neck, trying to calm down, trying to think, but the wild unicorns were closing in, the putrid stench of their rotting flesh strong in the air.

Mitchell was scanning the faces, no doubt searching for his cousin among them. When Skandar started to do the same, he recognised one of the riders, even through the white stripe disguising his features.

'Joby! Instructor Worsham, it's me!' he called, as the decaying creatures moved to block every gap between the trees. Joby's hair was out of its ponytail, hanging long and lank around his face. The symbol from the leaflet – the cracked Hatchery door – was scrawled on the arm of his jacket. His eyes flicked towards Skandar, bright blue against the white smear of paint down his face, but there was no warmth in them.

'How could you do this?' Flo wailed as two of the riders yanked on her arms to try to silence her. 'Why would you help the Weaver take Blade when you know what it's like to lose a unicorn? How could you cause that pain to somebody else – to me?' She choked on the last word.

'I am no longer in pain. I have a unicorn now,' Joby answered coldly, completely unlike himself. 'A new bond. A more powerful partnership.' The wild unicorn he was riding snorted and green slime flew from its nostrils. As it blinked a great bloodshot eye, Skandar noticed a rib sticking out from its side, and maggots burrowing around the bloody skin.

'Please help us!' Skandar said. 'If the Weaver has a silver, none of us – Islanders, Mainlanders – *none* of us stand a chance!'

But Joby didn't seem to be listening. He was gazing adoringly down at the wild unicorn he was riding, as though it was the most precious creature in all the world. And Skandar knew with certainty that Joby was never going to help them. They were on their own.

Skandar was so busy panicking that it took him a moment to notice New-Age Frost joining the wild unicorn circle.

'Welcome, spirit wielder,' a voice rasped.

The Weaver – shrouded in black – raised one long bony finger to point directly at Skandar's heart.

CHAPTER TWENTY-ONE

THE WEAVER

'How do you know what I am?' Skandar's question came out surprisingly calm.

'Your bond . . . betrays you.' The Weaver's voice sounded brittle, like treading on dead leaves, as the words came from that unsettling face obscured by white paint from the crown of the head to the tip of the chin. 'As did my soldier from the Eyrie.' The Weaver gestured to Joby with a long arm. 'He said you'd help your friend, and I'd take both a spirit unicorn and a silver today.' There was quiet chuckling from the riders round the circle.

Skandar pulled his gaze away from the Weaver at the sound. Unable to bring himself to look at Joby again, he studied the other white-striped faces. He wondered which of them was Jamie's friend Claire; Mitchell's cousin, Alfie; the healer; the tavern owner; the shopkeeper . . .

'You are looking for those you might recognise among my soldiers? Such a shame many are so feeble. The weaving process is hard to survive. Weaving two souls is always . . . risky.' The Weaver sighed and the sound was somehow more unsettling than the voice that went with it. Like a death rattle. Was it Simon Fairfax – Amber's dad – behind the paint?

'Although I am succeeding more and more. Let me show you.' The Weaver motioned to the trees and they rustled as yet more wild unicorns joined the circle, each with a white-striped rider astride. The stench of the wild unicorns was of rotting fish, of mouldy bread, of death. Their breath gurgled as though there was water in their lungs – or blood.

'How fortuitous that you brought the rest of your quartet with you, spirit wielder. An air wielder –' Bobby growled so low she sounded like Falcon – 'and a fire wielder too. Along with Silver Blade and New-Age Frost, I've gathered a full elemental set.'

'You stay away from them, Erika!' Mitchell's voice shook but he got the words out.

Skandar wanted to shut him up. This wasn't his mum; this was—

The Weaver's long neck arched as two eyelids, caked in white paint, blinked twice at Mitchell. 'No one has called me that in a very long time.'

No, please no. Please don't let it be true.

Skandar wished more than anything that he could unhear those words, that he could go back to believing his mum was someone kind, someone he could be proud of. The scarf he was wearing – wearing to give back to her – suddenly felt like it was choking him.

The contents of the shoebox back home flashed into his mind.

How could it be that the woman Dad had loved – who'd left behind a bookmark, a hair clip, a garden-centre key ring – was also this thief, this murderer? Erika Everhart had killed twenty-four unicorns before she'd come to the Mainland, before she'd even been his mum. Skandar's whole body shook. The only thing keeping his heart from flying off in fragments was the bond – and Scoundrel's tight grip on it – as images of a loving mother's face went up like smoke off a unicorn's back, and were replaced by her, by Erika Everhart – by the Weaver.

Mitchell was speaking again. 'Give us Silver Blade and Flo, or we'll tell everyone who you are. Just let us go, and we'll leave you in peace.'

The Weaver's hoarse laughter cut through the obvious lie. 'You think I would let you go? After you *threaten* me? After you tell me you know my given name? I will weave your unicorns' souls to my own, but you four will not live to tell the tale.' The paint on the Weaver's mouth cracked as she twisted her lips into a smile.

'Just think of how many more desperate souls I can weave to wild unicorns now. So many wish to be joined with a unicorn, yet the Hatchery door remains cruelly closed to them. No soldier you see here came to me against their will. They were not *taken*; they came to me willingly. And now, with the might of a silver unicorn, my loyal army will grow far bigger than I ever dreamed.'

The Weaver's soldiers cheered along with her, and Skandar wondered – from their empty eyes and vacant expressions – whether they now had any choice but to carry on fighting for the Weaver.

'That's right, that's right,' the Weaver hissed. 'We will take down every sentinel. The Island's defences are weak at best; I've been testing them for months. The Mainland will be mine. The Island will be mine. I'll be unstoppable.'

'Please.' Skandar's word was barely above a whisper. 'This isn't who you are – it can't be.' Emotions were crashing over Skandar like wave attacks, but he was holding on to one thought, one shining beacon of hope. Erika had carved his name on Blood-Moon's tree *after* she'd left the Mainland. That had to mean something. His mum simply hadn't recognised him yet, and that was all right, that was okay, because he'd been a baby when she'd seen him last. But if he told her who he was, maybe he could convince her? Maybe he could make her see that she didn't have to be the Weaver? She could just be Erika Everhart. She could just be his mum.

Almost involuntarily, Skandar pushed Scoundrel towards New-Age Frost. Scoundrel fought against the danger, hissing and baring his teeth, snapping out his wings to make himself look as big as possible in the grey unicorn's giant shadow.

'You have to stop this,' Skandar said, his voice choking. 'Please, look at me,' he begged. 'Can't you see who I am? Don't you recognise me?'

'You are a spirit wielder, barely out of the Hatchery. And I have no need of you.'

Skandar felt the wild unicorns closing in step by step – ancient bone-splintered knees and rotting hooves pounding the hard ground.

'Joby hasn't told you my name, has he?' Skandar shot a look

at his old instructor. 'He didn't think it was important. He didn't know.'

'What does your name matter to me?' the Weaver rasped. 'In a few minutes you'll be dead and your name will be of no consequence.'

Skandar could feel tears of desperation running down his face. He let them fall. If she could just understand who he was, then surely she'd stop? If the hole in her heart was as big as the one she'd left in his, then surely it would change things.

He took a deep breath. There was a story his dad had told him on Chaos Cup day almost a year ago. A story about a promise made to a baby, sealed with the softest touch on a palm.

'It's me, Mum.' Skandar's voice shook. 'Look –' he gestured down at Scoundrel –'you promised me a unicorn – and here he is. I became a rider, just like you wanted me to.'

The Weaver blinked, the white paint on her eyelids exaggerating the movement.

Skandar could hardly speak through his tears now, but he managed seven more words. 'My name is Skandar Smith.' He unwound the black scarf from his neck, and held it out to her over Scoundrel's wing. 'And I'm—'

'My son,' Erika Everhart said, the light of recognition finally igniting in her haunted eyes.

Silence. Even the unicorns were still.

'Has it really been thirteen years? How . . . how did you . . . Ahhh.' The sound of understanding opened her mouth like a yawn. 'Ag–a–tha.' She said each syllable of the Executioner's name slowly, delightedly, like she was tasting them. 'My little sister.' Erika reached out for the black scarf in Skandar's hand, snatching it hungrily. 'I should have guessed. She gave me this scarf just before I entered the Hatchery.'

'Sister?' Skandar blinked through his silent tears. 'Agatha's your sister? The Executioner?' He remembered how Dad had seen something familiar in Agatha, almost like he'd recognised her. Agatha begging him, *Please don't kill the Weaver*.

'Your sister – my aunt – brought me to the Island?'

'Just as Agatha took me to the Mainland.' Erika's eyes had a faraway look, as she tenderly placed the scarf round her own long neck. 'After Blood-Moon . . . after the twenty-four . . . I had to hide. I had to get away. When I was at my weakest on the Mainland, I wrote to her . . . before. I asked her to ensure my children became riders. I should have known. Agatha Everhart always keeps her promises. I should have stopped her. Did Agatha bring Kenna too?' Erika looked behind Skandar, as though her daughter might be standing there.

Something about it made Skandar furious with her. Wasn't she pleased to see him? She seemed to care more about the scarf than him, more about where Kenna was than the fact that he was standing in front of her. Questions burst out of him. 'But why wouldn't you come back for us yourself? Why Agatha and not you? And what about Dad? You left us; you left me! Why? Why did you do it?' His voice broke on the last word.

'The Island was calling me. I had things I needed to do. Plans I needed to put in motion.' Erika gestured at her soldiers.

'What?' Skandar spat. 'And that was more important than me? More important than Kenna, and Dad?'

'You're a child. You don't understand these things yet. But you will.'

Skandar shook his head roughly. He was so angry now that he'd completely forgotten to be frightened of the rider on New-Age Frost's back. He'd spent his whole life missing his mum, his whole childhood wishing her back to life. And now she was here and she didn't seem to care about him at all. She didn't even seem *sorry*.

'It's your fault that Kenna isn't here,' he said, trying to get a reaction. 'Spirit wielders are barred from even trying the Hatchery door, and I bet Kenna's one like me. Because of you, she'll never hatch her destined unicorn. She'll never get to come home!'

'My son.' Erika Everhart spread her arms wide. 'You speak of *destined* unicorns. But destiny should play no part in whether a person becomes a unicorn rider. Look at my soldiers – I gave them unicorns because they *wanted* them, not because they opened a stubborn old door. And when we fly to the Mainland, I can weave your sister a bond with a wild unicorn of her choosing. Fairfax chose his new unicorn, didn't you?'

Erika nodded over to one of the wild unicorn riders. Simon Fairfax had his daughter's eyes.

'You are my blood, my kin, my son. Join me, Skandar. Together we can promise everyone a unicorn, destiny be damned.'

For a fraction of a second Skandar considered it. The shimmering idea took hold: of belonging with his mum; of giving Kenna the unicorn she so desperately wanted; of finding out finally who he was; of slotting the piece of missing jigsaw back into his heart; of weaving their family together so that it could be whole again.

'Join me,' Erika Everhart urged him. 'As my son you will be faithful to me and help me build my army. You will wield the death element by my side. We will bond Mainlanders to wild unicorns – including your sister, your father. We will become unstoppable. Our army of outcasts will do our bidding. We will rule the Eyrie, the Island, the Mainland. Yes. Together we will be stronger. I see that now.'

But Skandar saw something different. He saw the Island devastated, the Hatchery dark and empty, its great door rent in two. He saw the suffering of the wild unicorns etched across human faces – mortality and immortality weaved together to live in desolate disharmony. He saw Kenna and Dad surrounded by death and destruction. He saw himself with all the power in the world and it made him shudder. The shining image of Skandar's reunited family – all living on the Island together – shattered.

And the truth of it all unfurled for Skandar as though he'd always known it deep down. For his whole life he'd been wishing he had a mum to tell him who he was. But now that she was here asking him to make this choice, he realised that he didn't need her to tell him at all. Skandar knew exactly who he was. He was brave. He was loyal. He was kind. He didn't like hurting people. He was scared sometimes, but that made him braver. He was a spirit wielder, but he was also Skandar Smith from Margate, who loved his sister and his dad, even though sometimes loving Dad was hard. He didn't need to know if Agatha had brought him for good or for evil, because he could choose to be good. He was a good person. And he'd never join the Weaver – even if she happened to be his mum.

The Weaver urged New-Age Frost nearer to Scoundrel, and Skandar noticed how it didn't seem quite human, the way her body moved like vapour under her shroud. Her dark eyes were hungry, drinking him in. Skandar was reminded of the wild unicorn that he had seen on his very first day on the Island. The way its eyes had been so very sad, as though it was looking for something in him that it had lost.

'I'm sorry that Blood-Moon's Equinox died; I really am.' Skandar's voice was soft. 'I can't imagine the pain. But it was an accident! And you've been punishing this island for that tragedy ever since.'

'Blood-Moon's death was not an accident.'

'You're never going to replace her,' Skandar said. 'However many bonded unicorns you steal. However many wild unicorns you shackle to people desperate to be riders. However powerful you become. The truth is, Erika, you can't ever get Blood-Moon back. You can't. And your unicorn would never have wanted this life for you. She would have been so disappointed – and so am I.'

'You don't know what you're saying,' the Weaver hissed. 'You've been indoctrinated by the Eyrie, the Council, the Silver Circle. Look how quick they were to enlist my sister as the Executioner, to turn on the spirit wielders, to keep them out of the Hatchery like all the others they consider *unworthy* of a unicorn. They want the Hatchery to keep us all out – all of us without a perfect bond. My soldiers are proof that doesn't have to be the way of things.'

'Your soldiers only do as you ask.' Skandar had guessed it the moment he'd looked into Joby's face. His instructor might have wanted a unicorn more than he wanted to do the right thing, but he never would have betrayed Silver Blade to the Weaver. Not without something else going on. 'When you weave them, they're tied to you, aren't they? They want what you want. They obey you completely.'

'They're happy. They have the unicorns I promised them. And I am here to lead them, and openly wield the spirit element. Isn't that something you want too, Skandar? Freedom?'

Skandar shook his head. 'What you have isn't freedom! All you care about is power and revenge. But you've forgotten that there are more important things. I'll never join you.'

A light went out in the Weaver's eyes. The change in her was subtle and sudden – and deadly. For the first time since he'd revealed who he was to her, Skandar felt frightened of the Weaver.

'You're making a mistake,' the Weaver spat at him. 'There is nothing more important than power. Nothing! But I cannot waste time trying to make you understand. You are not yet worthy to ride at my side!'

'I will *never* ride at your side!' Skandar replied; it was half shout, half sob.

The Weaver lifted a long finger. 'Seize the unicorns! I want them alive,' she shrieked.

Chaos. The white-striped riders began to close in on Scoundrel, Falcon and Red. Bobby shouted in rage and a lightning bolt hit the tree closest to Silver Blade, which exploded, splinters flying everywhere. Mitchell threw fireballs at the Weaver and

New-Age Frost as they slipped behind a protective wall of wild unicorns. Skandar saw a flash of black and silver as Flo managed to wriggle free from the soldier holding her and vaulted on to Silver Blade's back. Her palm glowing red, she burned away the vines holding him, and the silver unicorn roared in triumph.

'We're still surrounded,' Skandar heard Bobby yell over the bellowing of the wild unicorns, as Flo rejoined Falcon, Red and Scoundrel in the centre of the trees.

'They can't attack,' Mitchell called. 'They can't risk killing us yet – not if she wants our unicorns.' But Skandar was barely listening. His palm was glowing white with the spirit element, and he was looking – really looking – at the wild unicorns and their riders. He could see cords of white joining them together, but they were different from his friends' bonds. They didn't look as seamless or as stable. They looked as though they could be unravelled.

Agatha had been right: only a spirit wielder could stop the Weaver's plan.

Though tears were still streaming down his face, somehow Skandar's mind was clear. He had to protect his friends. He had to protect his unicorn.

'Can you throw elemental magic at the wild unicorns?' Skandar shouted to his quartet. 'Don't aim to hit them. I just need a distraction. I think Scoundrel and I can do something.'

They nodded at him, then at each other, their palms lighting up with fire, air and earth magic. The elemental attacks mixed with the blasts of the wild unicorns and soon the air was thick with the stench.

'Are you ready to try this?' Skandar whispered to his unicorn, as he let his palm glow white. The smell of Skandar's own element filled his nostrils: cinnamon, leather, but also a vinegary sharpness. He reached out with the white light, carefully aiming its tendrils towards the shining cord between the nearest wild unicorn and its rider. Once the light had wrapped round the unstable bond, Skandar's fingers danced through the air as though he was playing an invisible instrument. And when the bond snagged, he moved his wrist this way and that as though he was sketching. Scoundrel was still – concentrating along with his rider – as they pulled and unravelled the false bonds. Skandar had never felt so connected to his unicorn; they'd never worked so closely together, their magic completely in harmony.

It felt right to undo the bonds – natural – and Skandar could sense that Scoundrel understood that too. He met no resistance from the woven connections, almost as though the bonds knew they should never have been made. One by one the wild unicorns quietened, collapsing to the ground. Their riders blinked in surprise, looking up as though they were waking from a long and fitful sleep.

'What's wrong with you?' screamed the Weaver, as she watched wild unicorn after wild unicorn fall around her. 'Get up!' she shouted at her soldiers. 'Get up, I order you!' Then her eyes came to rest on Skandar, who had just unravelled the final bond between Joby and his wild unicorn. Both of them fell to the ground – alive but unmoving.

'SPIRIT WIELDER!' the Weaver screeched, and galloped the full-grown might of New-Age Frost towards Scoundrel's Luck.

Skandar froze. Suddenly all he could think was that there was no way to escape this. The Weaver was coming for Scoundrel; the Weaver was going to destroy their bond; his mum was going to do this to them, the very worst thing. He was too slow; she was too fast.

But then Silver Blade reared up between Scoundrel and New-Age Frost. He pawed the air with his hooves and flaming rocks flew from them, forcing Frost backwards.

'How dare you take Silver Blade from me!' Flo looked every inch the fearless Chaos rider. The authority in her voice rang out like an Eyrie bell.

The Weaver ducked down against New-Age Frost's neck in surprise as a rock soared past her cheek.

Silver Blade's eyes blazed red and he roared fire at the sky. For the first time Skandar truly understood the power of a silver – the terrifying combination of majesty and power. Then, as Flo let out another cry of rage, her palm glowed bright green and she summoned a shield of thick glass between Frost and the rest of her quartet.

'Skar!' Flo called, her arm trembling with the effort. 'Come on! I don't know how long I can hold this, but her bond? Can you break it?'

'Get back!' Skandar yelled at her as the Weaver threw flames at the shield. 'It's not safe. What if she hits Blade?'

'Seriously, Flo, what a time to get so freakin' fearless!' Bobby shouted.

'He's a silver, remember?' Flo called back, earth magic fizzing from her palm. 'The Weaver can't kill him with spirit.'

'No!' Skandar cried. 'But she can use the other elements to kill *you*!'

CRACK. A line spread across the surface of Flo's glass shield.

'Don't want to rush you –' Mitchell's voice shook – 'but that shield isn't going to hold forever so—'

'Get on with it, Skandar!' Bobby flicked her reins at his knee.

Skandar snapped into action. He reached out with the spirit element through the cracks in Flo's shield, feeling for the bond between the Weaver and New-Age Frost. He hadn't seen it at first – it was so thin and loosely woven round another blue shimmering bond that Skandar thought it would be easy.

'Argh!' Skandar felt a painful wrench near his own heart. He couldn't see his and Scoundrel's bond, but he could feel the Weaver there, trying to part them. Scoundrel's Luck screeched in confusion and alarm.

Then Scoundrel reared, high and slow, his legs kicking out towards New-Age Frost. The black unicorn bellowed a sound that Skandar had never heard him make before – like the cry of a wild unicorn. And through Flo's fracturing shield, behind the shrouded figure of Erika Everhart, Skandar saw the wild unicorns begin to rise from the ground.

The Weaver must have sensed that something was wrong, because she looked over her shoulder. The grip of her spirit magic loosened on Skandar's bond. The wild unicorns now circled New-Age Frost like vultures, slime dripping from their mouths, their transparent horns ghostly in the half-light.

'You can't control them any more!' Skandar yelled through the shield. 'You thought they were your soldiers, but they're not.

Wild unicorns are born free – freer than any of us.'

The Weaver snarled, as the wild unicorns took a few more steps.

'You tried to outsmart them,' Skandar continued. He felt connected to the wild unicorns somehow; he understood how they'd suffered with the Weaver. 'You tried to give them riders they were never destined for. And it was never going to work. They're immortal. They die for ever while we die in a moment. They know the truth in their hearts – they never belonged to you!'

The wild unicorns bellowed as one. The Weaver's palm glowed blue to defend herself with water magic. But Skandar wasn't going to let her harm the wild unicorns any more than she already had.

'Drop the shield!' Skandar called to Flo, and the glass shattered. Skandar's palm glowed bright white and he punched it straight towards the Weaver's heart. The tunnel of light trapped her bond with New-Age Frost within a dazzling cocoon of spirit magic, and it splintered and thinned. But Skandar wasn't strong enough to break it completely.

Bobby reacted first. Her yellow air magic joined the white tunnel of spirit. Then Flo's green injection of earth magic, and the red of Mitchell's fire, collided with the other three strands, the colours twisting and joining with the white of Skandar's power. Skandar could feel the Weaver's bond loosening.

'Help!' he called to the wild unicorns, hoping beyond hope that they understood. Hoping that if they did, he and his friends would get out of this alive. Hoping that his and Scoundrel's bond could survive it. And somewhere deep down there was a desperate hope that maybe, just maybe, if he defeated the Weaver, his mum might take her place.

The earth shook and the air filled with raw magic – not the refined elemental magic of the bonded unicorns, not the unfocused blasts wild unicorns normally made, but all five elements combined in pulses of primal power, explosions of colour and smells and forms that Skandar had never seen. It was the kind of magic that'd been around for longer than any human could imagine. They bellowed as one, and their magic connected with the quartet's attack on the Weaver.

The bond between the Weaver and New-Age Frost snapped. The grey unicorn roared in anger, reared on his back legs and threw the Weaver from his back. The wild unicorns began to call to each other in their strange haunting cries, as Falcon, Red, Scoundrel and Blade joined in.

A wild unicorn approached Skandar and Scoundrel. It was the biggest of all of them, but it was also – by the look of its deeply decayed skin and skeletal frame – one of the oldest unicorns on the hill. Skandar wondered how long it had been alive; how long it had been dying. Its red sunken eyes bored into Skandar's and it made a low rumbling sound.

'Thank you,' Skandar whispered, and the wild unicorn turned and led its herd away, past the Weaver on the ground, away from their ex-riders now hiding in the trees and bushes, and down from the hill to join the rest of the wild unicorns in the Wilderness beyond.

The Weaver stirred and rolled on to her side. Her shroud

was hanging off her shoulder, the white paint on her face half gone. The black scarf lay like a dead snake nearby. She looked shrivelled and spent. Beneath it all, though, Skandar glimpsed a face that might once have looked like Kenna's.

Skandar took a tentative step towards her. Daring to hope he'd see something different in her eyes. A winner of two Chaos Cups. A Commodore. A mother. 'M-Mum?'

Several things happened at once. Shouts filled the air – calls of rescue – as the Weaver grabbed the black scarf and whistled a high sharp note. Sentinels on unicorns crashed through the trees, Aspen McGrath sitting behind one of them, her red hair flying in her face.

In all the confusion, Skandar didn't have time to react as a wild unicorn he hadn't seen before crashed into the woods, and the Weaver vaulted on to its back, a glowing thread between their hearts. Skandar tried to work out the allegiance of their bond but he couldn't seem to settle on a single colour as it stretched between them. The Weaver had been bonded to more than one unicorn – even New-Age Frost had been expendable.

'There!' Aspen shouted as she crashed through the trees. 'Go after them! That was the Weaver!'

'She's getting away!' Flo cried.

Skandar stayed silent. He was all out of words. Out of tears. The anger, the disappointment and the hurt were all gone. Now there was only sadness, as he watched the Weaver gallop away.

Some sentinels stayed to guard the Commodore while others gave chase into the Wilderness, but Skandar had a feeling they wouldn't catch the Weaver. Not this time.

'Can one of you young riders please tell—' Aspen McGrath stopped mid-sentence as New-Age Frost came trotting towards her. Aspen collapsed to the ground, clinging to one of his grey legs.

'I can't believe it. It's really you. I—' Aspen's voice shook with sobs. She turned her palm over. Rubbed it. Made a fist, then flattened her hand again. A deep frown creased her forehead. 'I don't understand. He's here, but my magic is gone. Look – I can't even summon the water element to the bond.' She wasn't really talking to Skandar, but he spoke up anyway because he thought he knew the answer.

'The Weaver was bonded to New-Age Frost. She only –' Skandar was putting it all together as he spoke – 'weaved her own bond over the top of yours, but I think it must have affected your magic.'

'But Frost isn't bonded to the Weaver any more?'

'No.' Skandar shook his head. 'I— We all –' he gestured to his friends – 'we broke their bond somehow.'

Aspen looked at each of them in turn, still frowning. 'I don't understand. I can feel the bond, but I just can't— Look.' She showed them her palm again. 'Nothing.' She sighed, touching one of her ice-mutated shoulders as though that might bring her closer to her unicorn. 'We're together, that's the most important thing. He's alive.' She sniffed. 'Even if our bond isn't.'

Skandar knew what he had to do. He couldn't leave Aspen and New-Age Frost like this. Not if he could help, and he'd known that he could as soon as Aspen had come into the clearing. Their bond was still there, heart to heart, though it looked frayed and feeble.

He had to help them, even if it meant he might lose everything.

'I think I can fix your bond,' Skandar said very quietly. He heard Mitchell's intake of breath and saw Flo's hand going to her mouth. They knew what he was doing; they knew what he was risking.

'How can you?' Aspen sounded angry now. 'What are you? A Hatchling? Of course you can't. Your story about breaking the Weaver's bond simply cannot be true. To even see the bond would have taken—'

'A spirit wielder,' Skandar finished for her, and he pushed up the sleeve of his blue jacket to reveal his mutation.

Aspen recoiled, moving closer to New-Age Frost. The sentinels stiffened, ready to attack. 'How? You? How did you even get into the Hatchery?'

'That's not important,' Skandar said firmly. 'We're here, and we can help you. That's all that matters.'

'Why would you risk this? Why would you help me?' Aspen asked, disbelieving.

'Yeah, why?' Bobby muttered under her breath.

'Because I'm not the Weaver –' Skandar smiled sadly at Aspen – 'and that's been your mistake with the spirit wielders all along. You think we're all like the Weaver, but we're not. I want to help you because it's the right thing to do. Because you and New-Age Frost belong together.'

'I'm assuming you'll want something in return,' Aspen said shrewdly, moving towards Scoundrel and crossing her arms.

Skandar hesitated. He hadn't realised he'd be able to bargain for something *he* wanted.

'Well,' he said slowly, thinking hard, 'first, I want you to free all the spirit wielders.'

'I can't—'

'You can. You can because we now know who the Weaver is.'

Aspen frowned. 'Who?'

'Erika Everhart.'

'She's dead.'

'She's not,' said Mitchell. 'And we can prove it.'

'The spirit unicorns are dead, thanks to the Silver Circle and the Executioner they blackmailed,' Skandar said, the disgust clear in his voice, 'but give the riders their freedom. It's the least you can do. Although you'll need to arrest Simon Fairfax – he's over there. I bet he's been helping the Weaver for years.' Skandar pointed to Amber's dad, who was still unconscious on the ground.

'I won't be able to free the Executioner,' Aspen warned. 'The Silver Circle will never agree to it. There's too much history there. And her spirit unicorn is still alive.'

Skandar paused, then nodded. He wasn't sure what to feel about Agatha just yet, but he wasn't prepared to risk the freedom of all the other spirit wielders for her.

'What else?' Aspen asked, the frown on her forehead deepening.

'Start letting spirit wielders into the Hatchery.'

'Absolutely not.'

Skandar had expected as much, but he'd thought it was worth a try. He tried something else. 'Let me train as a spirit wielder, and let everyone know it. If I finish my training, and no harm has come to anyone, let the spirit wielders try the Hatchery door again. Bring spirit back to the Eyrie.'

Aspen sighed. 'I can agree to that in theory, but it's almost the end of my time as Commodore. How do you expect me to make other people agree?'

'Write it into Island law. You've still got time. The Chaos Cup isn't until next week. And, you never know, you might win again.'

Skandar saw Aspen gulp. He knew how unpopular this would make her. But he didn't care. He wanted to train in the spirit element.

'We're agreed, then? The spirit wielders go free and I'm allowed to train openly in the spirit element, as well as the other four.'

Aspen nodded grudgingly. 'Only if you manage to fix our bond. If you can't, the deal's off.'

The Commodore climbed on to New-Age Frost's back and Skandar summoned the spirit element to his palm as easily as breathing. He turned his attention to the link between the human and unicorn souls – frayed, damaged but fundamentally intact. Skandar's bright spirit magic danced along the dull blue bond, reviving and repairing it from end to end. The white light grew brighter and brighter until the whole of the Weaver's hill shone with it. Perhaps it might even have been visible from the Eyrie, like a star born to brighten the colour-drained Wilderness.

Tears flooded down Aspen McGrath's face, as once again their bond shone bright blue and the light of the water element filled her palm. Skandar imagined how she must feel – as though she were back in the Hatchery again, the bond newly forged around her heart.

Unlike the Weaver, Skandar had needed no tricks. He hadn't needed to weave the souls to repair the bond.

Two souls destined for each other can never truly be parted.

CHAPTER TWENTY-TWO

HOME

Skandar, Bobby, Flo and Mitchell declined Aspen's offer of a sentinel escort back to the Eyrie. Instead, they took off from the tree-covered hill and flew Scoundrel, Falcon, Blade and Red over the cracked earth of the Wilderness, relieved to leave it behind as the ground beneath them became lush and green once again.

They landed in Fourpoint to delay their return to the Eyrie a little longer. After everything, Skandar was desperate to see Dad and Kenna, but it was nice – just for a few minutes – not to talk about what had happened, and what had *almost* happened, in the Weaver's woods. They all knew that before long they'd have some explaining to do once Aspen had – as she put it – worked out how to spin the spirit wielder news.

As they reached the deserted arena, the only evidence of the Training Trial was a collection of hoof prints in the sand and the blackboard of results written up in chalk. Skandar hadn't even thought about whether he'd been declared a nomad or not. It hadn't seemed so important before when it was mixed in with his mum being alive, Silver Blade being taken, and stopping the Weaver.

But now he didn't want to look at the board at all. He didn't want to be declared a nomad or have his pin smashed to pieces, and most of all he didn't want to leave his quartet. He looked at their faces, as they squinted up at the board from their unicorns' backs in the late-afternoon sun. Flo had her eyes half open as though she didn't want to look at the board either. Bobby had a smile tugging at the corner of her mouth. Mitchell's eyes were moving from side to side as though he was committing every name and position to memory.

Skandar felt a swell of love for them, which was immediately overtaken by fear – the two racing for first place in his chest. If he had to leave the Eyrie, it wouldn't be the same. They were the first – the only – friends he'd ever had, and they'd carry on their lives without him. They'd learn how to summon weapons next year, they'd talk about their dens together, compare saddles, they'd laugh at Red exploding her farts at awkward moments and continue to refuse Bobby's emergency sandwiches, trading theories about where she got her bread.

Some days would be hard and they'd lose their sky battles, and some days they'd celebrate and throw their arms round Falcon or Red or Blade. They'd probably forget all about the lonely spirit wielder who hadn't even made it through Hatchling year, the one who'd caused them all that trouble. Skandar felt a pulse of concern come from Scoundrel – feelings between them flowed so much more easily now; it was almost as though they could talk to each other through the bond.

But it didn't help. Not this time. Skandar stared down at Scoundrel's mane, refusing to look up. He didn't feel ready for this. Not after everything else. The events on the hill played out in the back of his mind. The Weaver riding right for him. Erika Everhart trying to wrench his bond away. His mum's scarf on the ground. He couldn't take any more.

'It's okay, Skar. You can look. It's okay.'

And Skandar trusted Flo. So he looked.

Roberta Bruna and Falcon's Wrath were at the very, very top. Florence Shekoni and Silver Blade were fifth – they must have crossed the line just before the Weaver swooped down! Mitchell Henderson and Red Night's Delight were in twelfth. And Skandar Smith and Scoundrel's Luck were safely in thirteenth place. Relief exploded through Skandar, and tears wet his cheeks for the second time that afternoon.

Bobby groaned. 'I *told* them to call me Bobby. Enough with the Roberta already.'

Mitchell elbowed Skandar. 'Side by side. Look!'

Skandar wiped his eyes. 'You should've come higher up than that. You practically dragged me over the line, even though I was awful to you and Flo yesterday. Thanks, by the way.' Skandar's smile was watery but wide.

Mitchell blushed slightly. 'What are friends for?'

'Well, I'm his friend, but I wasn't going to prove it by not *winning*,' Bobby scoffed.

Mitchell laughed. 'I can't believe you actually won the

Training Trial. After saying you were going to do it the whole year – you actually did.'

'You're something else, Bobby,' Flo said, laughing.

'She is that,' Mitchell muttered.

But Bobby didn't say anything. She was staring at Mitchell.

Mitchell frowned. 'What?'

'I'm assuming you know that your hair is on fire,' Bobby said offhandedly.

'Can't we just have a truce for today, Bobby?' Mitchell said weakly. 'You won the Training Trial and we just defeated the Weaver. What more do you want, honestly?'

Flo had seen it too. 'No, your hair *is* on fire! You've mutated, Mitchell!'

Mitchell's hair had been completely dark before, but now every other strand looked like it was ablaze.

'It actually looks—' Skandar started.

'Quite . . . edgy?' Bobby finished, her voice rising in disbelief.

'I look edgy?' Mitchell cried. 'Bobby Bruna thinks I look *cool*?'

'Oh, stop,' Bobby said as he pointed at her.

'You hear that, Skandar? I'm cool. I'm *edgy*. I've finally mutated and IT IS AWESOME!'

'He's never going to shut up about this, is he?' Bobby muttered to Skandar, who shook his head, grinning as Red turned her horn to face her rider to see what all the fuss was about.

'Also,' Mitchell said breathlessly, 'can I just say one thing?'

'No,' Bobby said.

Mitchell ignored her. 'Can I just say, I was actually right about Skandar from the start?'

'What do you mean?' Flo asked, patting Blade's neck. The silver unicorn and rider seemed closer than ever. The image of Flo throwing herself between her friends and the Weaver flashed into Skandar's mind – it was the absolute bravest thing he'd ever seen.

'Well, I said Skandar was very dangerous and illegal and might kill us all in our beds. And it turns out he's actually the Weaver's son, brought to the Island by the Weaver's sister!'

'Mitchell!' Flo cried. 'Are you really going for an I-told-you-so right now?'

Bobby shook her head. 'Too soon. Waaaay too soon.'

But Skandar didn't mind. Not really. He knew in the days and weeks to come that he would cry and rage and grieve for Rosemary Smith, whom he had left behind – along with a scarf – in the Wilderness. But for now, as he rode his black unicorn in the Island sunshine alongside his friends, Skandar could cope with not finding the mum he'd wanted, because he thought he might just have found himself.

An hour later, Skandar stood in front of a white marquee on one of the training areas outside the Eyrie. Scoundrel was tethered to a tree nearby, sharing the remains of a rabbit with Red, and the families of the Hatchlings were already inside, talking, laughing and clinking their glasses.

Skandar was beyond excited to see Kenna and Dad. But he was also nervous. He didn't know what to tell them about Erika Everhart. He'd never mentioned a word to Kenna about the Weaver in any of his letters, and he'd never even mentioned the spirit element, knowing that the letters might have been read by Rider Liaison Officers.

If he'd been the one to stay at home, and Kenna had come to the Island, would Skandar have wanted to know their mum had been alive all this time? Would he still have wanted to know if she'd turned out to be evil? And what about Dad?

'Thanks for waiting, spirit boy!' Bobby caught up with him just as he was trying to summon the courage to duck through the entrance.

'Sorry,' Skandar mumbled.

'Are you in a bad mood?' Bobby asked impatiently.

'Just nervous.' Skandar peered through the entrance, trying to spot Kenna's head of brown hair or his dad's face.

'About seeing your dad and sister?'

'Yep.'

'Have you decided if you're going to tell—'

'Nope.'

Bobby rolled her eyes at him and smoothed the feathers on her arms. 'Best get the whole thing over with, then.' She pushed Skandar unceremoniously into the tent.

'Congratulations, Skandar. Thirteenth place is very respectable.' Instructor O'Sullivan caught him as he took a tentative step forward. 'Especially considering you've been pretending to be a water wielder all year.' She arched a silvery-grey eyebrow.

Skandar looked around in panic. 'How do you know? Does everyone know?'

'It's not common knowledge just yet. Aspen has only told the instructors.' Instructor O'Sullivan flashed him a rare smile. 'And Dorian Manning. I'm afraid the head of the Silver Circle is on the warpath. He's deeply unhappy about you training as a spirit wielder. Some might say he's absolutely fuming. So if you do see him, make sure you're wearing this nice and prominently.'

She dropped a cold metal object into Skandar's palm, just like she had after the Walk.

The pin was made from four entwined gold circles.

'Is that—' Skandar whispered.

'A spirit wielder pin.' Instructor O'Sullivan grinned at him. 'Though you'll be an honorary water wielder as well, of course.'

'Who says?'

'Me.' And, unbelievably, she winked. 'Spirit wielders always did have courage and recklessness running side by side in their veins – and with bravery like you showed against the Weaver, there'll always be a place for you in the Well.'

Skandar's hand went to the water pin on his blue jacket.

'Perhaps you could wear both? One on each lapel? That'd really annoy Dorian,' she said, sounding gleeful as she moved away.

'Skandar! Dad! Dad, look! It's Skandar!' Kenna sprinted through the crowd, almost sending a tray of drinks flying on her way past, Skandar's dad right on her heels.

Kenna flung her arms round her brother and burst into tears. Then before Skandar knew what was happening, Dad was hugging them both to him and they were all crying. All of the year's stress – being a spirit wielder, fearing for his and Scoundrel's lives, Joby's betrayal, facing the Training Trial, battling the Weaver, finding out she was his mum – came flooding out. Not in words but in Skandar's huge wrenching sobs.

'Hey, son, hey.' Dad pulled back Skandar's head gently, so he could see his face. He wiped away the tears, something Skandar could only ever remember Kenna doing. 'No need to cry, eh? You came thirteenth! We saw the whole thing. You were incredible! The way you and that red unicorn teamed up . . .'

And his dad was off, analysing the Training Trial. For a moment it was as though they were back in their living room in Margate watching the Chaos Cup, enjoying having a dad who cared about things, even if it was only for one day of the year.

Kenna caught Skandar's eye as Dad talked, grinning at him sideways and taking his hand. When Dad had talked himself out, he announced he was going to get another drink and left Skandar and Kenna alone to talk.

'How's stuff at home? With Dad?' Skandar asked quickly, taking the opportunity.

'Well, the rider money's really helping. And Dad just got a job!'

'What?'

'I know! It pays all right and everything. We've been looking at moving out of Sunset Heights, maybe renting a little house near the seafront or something.'

'Wow,' Skandar said. 'That's—'

'Okay, so tell me everything about Scoundrel's Luck. Everything. Can I meet him? Can we visit the stables? Can you show me your magic? Can you introduce me to Nina Kazama? Can you believe she's a Mainlander and she qualified for the

Chaos Cup?! Can we—' Kenna's explosion of questions made Skandar wonder if she and Dad were as okay as she had made out, but he let it go.

As he looked around the tent, Skandar noticed the missing faces of riders who hadn't made it through the Training Trial. Four of them had been in the other training group and Skandar hadn't really known them very well, but it was strange not to see Lawrence here.

It was hard to believe that he and Poison Chief were nomads now and – just like Albert and Eagle's Dawn – would never return to the Eyrie. Skandar tried not to think about how, without Mitchell sacrificing his position in the race, he and Scoundrel could have joined them.

For the next couple of hours Skandar had the best time ever with his family. They talked and talked. Skandar met Bobby's parents, and Flo's whole family – including her twin brother, Ebb. When Skandar introduced Dad to Flo, Mitchell and Bobby, he asked them all where they'd come in the Training Trial, and kept repeating that Skandar had come thirteenth, as if they hadn't been in the race with him.

As the quartet went to fetch more cake, Mitchell sighed. 'I wish my father was as proud of me as yours. He doesn't think twelfth is very good; he came eighth in his Training Trial. Apparently members of the Henderson family are supposed to do better.' He hung his head.

'I think it's about time you ignore your dragon of a father, Mitchell,' Flo announced, reaching for another drink. 'What you went through with the Weaver makes you ten times the better rider, so he can just . . . he can just . . . he can shut up actually!'

Bobby choked on her cake and Mitchell was so surprised that he seemed a lot more cheerful after that.

Skandar was having such a good time that he forgot all about Erika Everhart, right up until he took Kenna outside to meet Scoundrel's Luck.

Scoundrel was sweeter to her than he'd ever been to any other person. The black unicorn let Kenna stroke his neck, plait strands of his mane and even run her hand over one of his wings.

'Do you want to ride him?' Skandar asked tentatively after a few minutes.

Kenna's whole face lit up. 'Can I *fly* him?'

Skandar laughed. Trust his sister to ask to do the most dangerous thing. He wasn't entirely sure whether it was allowed, but Skandar couldn't bring himself to say no to Kenna. And somehow, he knew that Scoundrel would look after her.

Scoundrel snorted sparks as Skandar heaved Kenna up on to the unicorn's back with him. She insisted on sitting in front. 'So I can pretend you're not there.'

'Charming!' Skandar said, wrapping his arms securely round his sister as Scoundrel began to move away from the tent, his wings snapping out, ready to fly.

Kenna whooped and cheered as the black unicorn's hooves left solid ground. Skandar was grinning so much his cheeks hurt as they soared high above the Eyrie's armoured trunks. He thought back to before Kenna had failed her Hatchery exam, back to when they'd dreamed of a whole life of soaring side by side on battle-hungry unicorns.

Skandar tried to explain the bond to Kenna as the wind whistled past: the way he always felt Scoundrel's presence even when they were apart; the way they were learning to communicate by listening to each other's feelings; the way they could cheer each other up when they were sad. But Kenna was too distracted to listen; she crouched low on Scoundrel's back, her hands twisted in his mane, adjusting her balance with the dips of his wings. A lump rose in Skandar's throat – she was a natural rider.

Once Scoundrel had landed, Skandar was shocked to see that Kenna had tears in her eyes as she dismounted.

'Is there any way, Skar?' she croaked. 'Is there any way there's still a unicorn in the Hatchery for me? Waiting? Maybe they got it wrong. Maybe I was supposed to try the door too. You didn't even take the Hatchery exam! I know you can't tell me much in your letters, but nobody can hear us right now. There must be secrets; there must be more.'

Skandar wanted to hug her then, to tell her everything. About their mum, about the spirit element. But wouldn't it make it worse to know the truth? There was no guarantee that Kenna had been destined for a unicorn, but surely she'd feel more cheated – like she'd missed out on a future she could never have. He didn't know if he could do that to her.

So instead he said, 'I'm sorry, Kenn. It doesn't work like that. Even if there'd been a unicorn for you, it'd be running wild by now. It's too late. It wouldn't be anything like Scoundrel. You wouldn't want to be near it.'

'I would.' Kenna allowed herself one gut-wrenching sob. 'I

wouldn't care if it was wild,' she said more quietly. 'If it was mine, I'd want it.'

'Believe me –' Skandar pulled her into a hug – 'you really wouldn't.'

The rest of the afternoon went far too quickly. In no time at all, it seemed, Skandar was hugging Dad and Kenna on the grassy top of the Mirror Cliffs so they could take a helicopter back to the Mainland. Skandar breathed his family in, and he knew this was the moment. If he was going to change his mind and tell them, this was his last chance for a year.

'I'm so proud of you, Skandar,' Dad said, pulling away. 'You keep training that Scoundrel's Luck. You might just win some day! Always said you had it in you!' He waved and disappeared into the helicopter. And Skandar knew he couldn't tell them about Erika Everhart. He couldn't turn their lives upside down. It was a secret he would have to keep to himself. For now.

'He's much better, see?' Kenna's eyes were shining with tears again. 'We're doing just fine; you don't have to worry about us.'

'I wish I could come with you,' Skandar said, still holding her hand.

Kenna shook her head sadly. 'No, you don't. You belong here, Skar. This is your home. I think you always knew that really, didn't you?'

This is your home too, he wanted to tell her. *This is* our *home.*

But he didn't. All he said was, 'I love you, Kenn.'

'I love you too, Skar.'

She dropped his hand then and ran to the helicopter steps, her brown hair blowing across her face, and then she disappeared from view, the propellers spinning faster and faster.

Skandar sprinted away across the clifftop. Debris was being thrown about by the aircraft; it was in his nose, his hair, his eyes. He couldn't really see where he was going. Then: 'Ouch!'

'Bobby?'

'Skandar?'

As the helicopters soared over them and out to sea, the dust cleared and Skandar was left staring at an empty sky with Bobby standing next to him, hand on one hip.

The way he felt must have showed on his face, because she put an arm round his shoulders. 'Ready to go?'

Skandar didn't trust his voice. So instead, he just nodded, and Bobby led the way back towards the sound of bloodthirsty unicorns.

READ ON FOR A
THRILLING FIRST LOOK AT
SKANDAR'S NEXT ADVENTURE…

SKANDAR
AND THE
PHANTOM RIDER

CHAPTER ONE

A BLOODY PICNIC

Skandar Smith watched his black unicorn, Scoundrel's Luck,
lick blood off his teeth. It was a beautiful day for a picnic. The
August sky was bluer than water magic and the sun's warmth
kept the chill of autumn firmly in the future.

'Where have all the sandwiches gone?' Mitchell Henderson

asked, his brown glasses halfway down his nose. He shuffled on his knees, searching methodically through a wicker basket.

'I ate them – obviously,' Bobby Bruna said, not bothering to open her eyes.

'They were supposed to be for everyone!' Mitchell cried. 'I specifically divided them equally between us . . .'

Bobby propped herself up on her elbow. 'I thought this was a picnic. Isn't eating sandwiches exactly what you're supposed to do?'

'Here you go, Mitchell.' Flo Shekoni crawled across the blanket they were sitting on. 'You can have one of mine – I already took them out of the bag.' Arguments were Flo's least favourite thing, so it was unsurprising that she was willing to trade a sandwich to keep the peace.

'Did Bobby make this one?' Mitchell nibbled suspiciously on the edge of the triangle Flo had given him.

Flo laughed. 'I don't know, but I'm not having it back now! Give it to Red if you don't want it.'

Skandar lay against Scoundrel's flank, the feathery tip of the unicorn's folded wing tickling his neck. It was the most relaxed Skandar had felt since he'd arrived on the Island over a year ago. And he was happy; how couldn't he be? Skandar finally belonged. He was bonded to a unicorn. He had *friends* – Bobby, Flo and Mitchell – who wanted to go on picnics with him. The four of them made a quartet, which meant they shared a treehouse in the rider training school known as the Eyrie. They had all made it through the Training Trial at the end of their first year as Hatchlings and were about to start their classes as Nestlings.

Skandar's heart beat faster remembering the day of the Training Trial, and Scoundrel rumbled deeply, trying to reassure him. After barely making it through the race, Skandar and his friends had come face to face with a deadly enemy – the Weaver – and fought to stop her wild unicorn army attacking the Mainland.

Skandar had tried not to think about the Weaver since – or the horrifying discovery that she was his *mum*. He tried not to relive her riding towards him and Scoundrel on her wild rotting unicorn. He also tried not to think about how he hadn't told his older sister, Kenna, that their mum was alive. He rummaged in his pocket to check for the letter she'd sent just before the summer solstice. He didn't take it out. He just ran his thumb along its edge – as though that could bring her closer to him, could make him feel better about what he was hiding from her.

'Can you believe training starts again in a few weeks?' Flo said nervously as she watched her unicorn, Silver Blade, drinking from the river a few metres ahead of them.

'I wish we could start tomorrow,' Bobby said. The feathers of her mutation fluttered along her arms with excitement.

'You just want to start battering people with elemental weapons,' Mitchell groaned.

Bobby grinned dangerously. 'Of *course* I do. It's jousting! As Mainlanders say, I'm going to have more fun than a flea at a funfair.'

Skandar chuckled at Bobby's made-up expression. She winked at him.

'I'd rather stay here.' Mitchell lay back and closed his eyes. 'It's simpler.'

Skandar certainly agreed with that. When he'd first arrived on the Island, Skandar had believed there were only four elements: fire, water, earth and air. But after Scoundrel had hatched, it had become clear that they were allied to an illegal fifth element – the spirit element – just like the Weaver. With a lot of help from his quartet, Skandar had managed to pretend he was a water wielder for most of his first year. The truth had come out eventually though, and now that everyone – other than Kenna and Dad – knew he was allied to the so-called *death element*, whispers followed him along every swinging bridge and up every ladder. It was going to be a long time before the Eyrie trusted a spirit wielder.

'We get saddles before we start training,' Flo pointed out.

Skandar sighed. '*You* get saddles. I'm not sure any saddler is going to choose me.'

'You keep saying that.' Flo frowned. 'But Jamie was okay with you being a spirit wielder. If your blacksmith is fine with it, why wouldn't a saddler be?'

'Jamie knows me. It's different.'

'And he's nice,' Mitchell added. 'He said my hair was cool.' The flaming strands of his hair burned brighter, as though showing off the mutation.

'Talking of the Saddle Ceremony.' Bobby was fully upright now. 'I heard a rumour that Shekoni Saddles doesn't choose a rider every year. They're so famous that they only ever present saddles to riders they're certain will make it to the Chaos Cup.' Bobby had gone misty-eyed with longing. 'Flo, you are *literally* a Shekoni. *Surely* you know something?'

Flo shook her head, the silver in her black Afro catching the sunlight. 'Dad won't tell me anything. He said it wouldn't be fair, and I think he's right.'

'Fair, shmair. You're such an earth wielder,' Bobby grumbled, as she got up to brush mud off Falcon's grey leg. The unicorn peered down at her rider to ensure she removed it all. 'What's the point of having a saddler's daughter as a friend if she won't spill any secrets?'

It wasn't just Bobby who'd been badgering Flo for saddler information over the past few weeks. And because Flo didn't like disappointing her fellow riders, she'd taken to hiding in the treehouse to avoid them. Skandar couldn't blame the Nestlings for their interest. Securing a good saddler was key to a rider's success, so everyone was keen to know whether Shekoni Saddles would be at the ceremony. Olu Shekoni was the best saddler on the Island, but he was also saddler to the new Commodore of Chaos, Nina Kazama. Skandar still couldn't believe a Mainlander like him had won the Chaos Cup or that she was Commodore now – the most important person on the whole Island.

Scoundrel stood up – knocking Skandar playfully with his wing – and went with Falcon to join Red and Blade by the river. They began to play a game that looked like *which unicorn can kill the most fish*. Skandar wasn't even sure unicorns ate fish, but Scoundrel and Red were having great fun snapping them out of the water with their sharp teeth. Scoundrel even managed to skewer one on the end of his black horn. After a few rounds, however, Falcon sneakily froze a section of the river with an elemental blast, and Red and Scoundrel both bashed their jaws on the hard ice. Blade snorted imperiously, seemingly disapproving of their foolishness, and watched the fish swimming safely beneath the glassy surface with stormy eyes.

Skandar was glad they'd chosen the water zone for the picnic. Although they had flown less than thirty-minutes from the Eyrie, the terrain was completely different. Rivers and their tributaries ran like blue veins across the flat plane, lush grass growing along their bends. On their way they'd flown over bowing willows where the zone's residents built their treehouses, and spotted the occasional fishing boat creaking under aerial bridges criss-crossing the canals below.

In the centre of the zone Mitchell had pointed out the famous floating market, where traders from all over the Island set up stalls on the water. Some customers balanced on wooden lily pads to inspect their goods, while others rowed their purchases downstream. Near river bends, water overspilled into lakes where Islanders could swim in the clear water and thirsty animals could stop to drink – when they weren't being snacked on by hungry unicorns. The zone even had a different kind of smell—

Skandar gagged.

'Did you eat one of Bobby's sandwiches?' Mitchell asked sympathetically. 'I told her nobody likes jam, cheese and Marmite as a filling, but she never listens to anyone, let alone—'

'Can you smell that?' Skandar asked urgently.

The unicorns started shrieking loudly down by the water. Scoundrel skittered backwards up the bank, flapping his black wings in alarm. Scoundrel's fear spiralled with Skandar's own along their bond. *Not here*, he thought. *Surely not here.*

Flo grasped his arm. 'Skar, what's wrong?'

There was a gust of wind. Flo's eyes widened in horror and then Skandar knew he wasn't imagining the danger. She could smell it too: the rancid smell of decomposing skin, of festering wounds, of death. And there was only one creature it could belong to.

'We need to get out of here. If the smell is that strong, it must be close!' Skandar jogged towards Scoundrel, intending to fly him away before danger arrived.

On the riverbank, the unicorn's neck was wet with sweat. He was shrieking down at something in the water, his eyes rolling from black to red to black again. Skandar looked down too. The others moved to stand beside him.

Blood roared in Skandar's ears. Distantly, he heard Flo's scream, Mitchell's curse, Bobby's gasp.

There was a wild unicorn in the water.

And it was dead.

Skandar's mind jammed. It couldn't possibly be real.

'I don't understand,' Mitchell croaked. It wasn't something he'd usually admit to.

The wild unicorn's immortal blood swirled and churned in the flowing water. The smooth rocks and nearby reeds were coated in it, flies already buzzing around a great wound in the unicorn's chest. Skandar thought the body must have been washed downstream by the current before coming, finally, to rest in this bend of the river.

'Is it definitely dead?' Flo whispered.

Mitchell crossed his arms. 'Well, I'm not going to check.'

Skandar and Bobby jumped off the low bank and waded into the water. The smell of decay was so overpowering that tears sprang to Skandar's eyes. Scoundrel squeaked worriedly above him, sounding as young as when he'd just hatched. Skandar tried to send reassurance to Scoundrel through their bond, even though every nerve in his body was on high alert: ready to sprint up the bank at any sign of movement from the wild unicorn. Bobby's mouth was a sharp line of determination as she knelt close to the chestnut unicorn's transparent horn.

She shook her head and Skandar bent down next to her, his trousers now soaked with bloody water. One of the wild unicorn's red eyes was visible on the side of its head, unseeing. Skandar stretched out a hand and gently closed the wrinkled eyelid. Something about the thick eyelashes – so like his own unicorn's – made Skandar impossibly sad. A rumble of approval came from Scoundrel on the bank.

'I think this is a young one,' Bobby murmured. 'It's not as gross as some of the other wild unicorns we saw in the Wilderness.'

'Skandar!' Mitchell's voice rang out over the gentle lapping of the river. 'We have to get you out of here! Spirit wielder? Wild unicorn? You can't be seen anywhere near this.'

Skandar blinked up at him and Red on the bank. 'Spirit wielders can't kill wild unicorns.'

'*Nothing* can kill wild unicorns. They're supposed to be immortal *and* invincible. And yet here we are.' Mitchell ran an agitated hand through his flaming hair.

'Come on, Skar. Let's go.' Flo was already scrambling on to Blade's silver back. 'I can think of a few people who'd love to blame this on you.'

Dorian Manning's face flashed into Skandar's mind. At the end of last year, the head of the Silver Circle had been completely against a spirit wielder returning to the Eyrie.

Once Skandar was safely astride Scoundrel, he took one last look at the wild unicorn's body in the river below, fear creeping up his spine. Wild unicorns didn't die. They were supposed to live for ever; they were supposed to be indestructible. But if they could be killed – if there was some way . . . What dark power had taken the life of an immortal that was supposed to live – and die – for ever?

Mum? Skandar tried to fight the most obvious answer. The idea that she had already regained enough strength to kill an immortal creature was truly horrifying. He wanted to believe she wasn't responsible, that it would take someone *more* powerful, *more* evil to commit this impossible murder.

But Skandar couldn't think of anyone worse than the Weaver.

ARE YOU DREAMING OF BECOMING A UNICORN RIDER LIKE SKANDAR AND HIS FRIENDS?

SCAN THIS QR CODE TO FIND OUT WHICH ELEMENT YOU COULD BE ALLIED TO AND MORE...